CHAMPION OF THE ALPHA

THE ALPHA KING'S BREEDER

BOOK SIXTEEN

BELLA MOONDRAGON

For Michael. Don't die again.

CONTENTS

IT'S JUST A LITTLE WAR

LEXA

The pack house in Silverhide is cast in dim, amber light that radiates from rustic candlelit chandeliers arranged in a row high above my head. Mom stands near the dormant fireplace talking in low tones to Aunt Mercy and Uncle Jacob. Even standing beside her, I can barely hear their murmured conversation over the crowd gathered along the long wooden tables that take up most of the space in the communal dining hall. Familiar faces huddle over the remains of a rather average dinner where more wine and mead was served than anything else. There's an undercurrent of tension in the room that's so palpable I can taste it–bitter, sour, something that sticks to the roof of my mouth and can't be washed away by the wine. So do the others as they lower their heads, whispering, glancing at my mother, their Luna, for direction.

I scan the crowd and meet Chessie's gaze. Her dark blonde hair falls around her heart-shaped face–curly and bright against her dark green eyes. She's seated between her mother and older sisters, but her father, one of my dad's close friends and best warriors, is outside with several of the older men standing in wait for their Alpha to return with news about Moonrise.

Most of my pack mates don't have cell phones or computers. We live in a utopia of solitude. It's the Silverhide way.

But my stomach turns as Meg and Hara move toward Chessie to whisper in her ear. Rumors are swirling already. Some people even brought their belts full of weapons to supper.

Mom was vague about what happened, but I know it was bad, whatever it was, just based on the pale color in her cheeks. It also involved Blake, which honestly doesn't surprise me, given that anytime there's drama, it tends to lead directly to him, Maeve, or both. I don't know the details. Mom could barely form words in the moments after a despondent Uncle Sydney whisked Nora to what I assume is safety.

But Luna Aviva, the five-foot-tall half-feral Queen of the Deadlands, stands straight-spined and unbothered beside me, regardless of the fact that everything might be falling apart.

I know the precarious situation the kingdom at large is in. Whispers of war have been swirling through Eastonia for months now. For several weeks this winter, travel between territories was limited, and several battalions of royal warriors were sent into Tarsian and the furthest reaches of the Roguelands looking for anything related to the Spider and his underground crime network. News trickled into the Deadlands, of course, but I'd been away from the rumors while I spent over six months training the Ghosts and Maeve's royal army in Moonrise.

I'd seen Blake, however, just moments after his falling out with Maeve. The look on his face... gods, it's impossible to describe how broken he was.

Meg discreetly motions for me to join them, but I shake my head. I give her a short nod, tilting my head toward the door leading out of the pack house in a silent promise that I'll speak to them privately once the pack at large has been briefed. Meg, with her thick, dark red hair and shimmering brown eyes–the beauty of Silverhide according to most–looks slightly annoyed as she turns back to Hara, whispering quietly enough I can't make out the words.

I straighten, smoothing the fabric of a simple, woven, baby blue sundress over my stomach, and turn to my mom instead of watching the increasingly anxious crowd.

She glances at me and my untouched dinner. "Eat something, Lex, please."

"Everyone's looking at us. You have to say something."

"I–" She swallows, gripping the back of her chair. We've been standing for what feels like an hour, locked in murmured conversation with my parents' closest friends and family–My Aunt Mercy and my mom's best friend, Freya, mostly. Their mates have been moving in and out of the pack house–bundles of nerves. Ticking time bombs, to be honest.

No one feels easy when the Alpha is gone.

When *my dad* is gone.

"Mom," I urge, looking down into her amber eyes. "Come on, what happened?"

"I know vague details. It was a mess–"

"What was?!"

The doors to the pack house boom as they fly open. A few hushed exclamations of surprise ring out but are drowned by the thunderous footfalls of the nearly seven-foot tall man stalking through the crowd, which barely has time to part. A weight lifts off my shoulders as Dad walks into view with steps so determined the entire crowd hushes. He's dressed as he was this morning when our day started out early but normal. A slightly sweat-stained T-shirt and the jeans he wears everyday out in the fields, like he didn't have a single second to change before Uncle Sydney took him away–which is exactly what happened. His dark hair is only starting to pepper with gray around the temples, and he's clean shaven, which Mom prefers, like he took her into consideration this morning above all else.

The tired, almost desperate look in his eyes fades the second Mom meets his gaze. He ignores the rest of the pack as he rounds the table and presses a swift kiss to her forehead. It's a great feat, given their height difference. Mom gives herself a moment to melt before turning back to hard, cold steel, and Dad moves to me with a quick but tender squeeze of my upper arm–something that started as a little joke when I began to join him at the gym in the village.

He turns to the pack. All eyes hold on him as he clears his throat and… announces war has come to the Deadlands.

"What do you mean there wasn't an attack? I don't understand?" Chessie sinks onto my mattress while I hastily pack my duffle bag. I fold a few looped shirts and skirts meant for shifting over my arm before stuffing them lazily in with the rest of my gear and random belongings.

"I know as much as you do."

"Oh, don't give me that! They're your cousins!"

"I know as much as what was said during supper. Mom is leading a battalion to Teshka to stand guard on the coast, which includes my regiment–as in *you*. Are you packed already? Is that why you're here bugging me?"

Chessie rolls her eyes to the ceiling. "I haven't unpacked from our time in Moonrise in hopes of running away from my mom's incessant marriage talk."

"Well, consider this your lucky break. We'll be gone for at least six weeks."

"The whole rest of the summer?" She gapes, rising as I move back to my untidy little closet. Compared to the regal townhouse and gilded palace of Moonrise, the wooden walls and matching floors greet me in a rustically warm embrace. Compared to… well, all of my cousins, I grew up about as simply as it can get. The most important aspects of my life, other than warrior training, of course, are the spring planting and the harvest.

Which, if the Goddess sees fit, we will be back for… hopefully.

"Lexa, you have to give me some insight here–"

"The truth of it will trickle through the grapevine, and by morning, everyone will know–"

"By then, we'll be passing through Endova. Please? What happened?"

I brace a hand on the doorframe, hanging my head for a moment to gather my thoughts. "Can you keep this between us? Completely?"

Chessie gasps excitedly, "Am I about to get insider knowledge from the royal family?"

I playfully glare, but my smirk falls flat. "Yes, and I don't want Meg and Hara spreading it around. You know they will."

"Hara's a safe bet when it comes to secrets, but you're right about Meg," she says with a frown. "So? What's the deal then? What really happened in Moonrise?"

"We're not entirely sure if it was an attack or something else...." I scramble with the private debriefing I received from my dad only an hour ago. "My cousin Blake–Prince Blake of Crescent Falls, is… missing."

She cocks her head to the side. "What?"

How the hell do I even begin?

"He's a mystic, and my family believes he purposely–or maybe even accidentally–used his powers to essentially blow up the royal temple in Moonrise, and now he's gone, somewhere else, somewhere they think the Spider has gone to, as well, so we are now on watch."

Chessie takes several seconds to try to absorb this information, but I can tell it's going right over her head. She is and always has been my best friend. I love her as deeply as I assume someone would love their mate. We're not sisters by blood but of the soul, and there's nothing I wouldn't do for her. But she's a bit spacey.

"Well, that sounds awfully complicated."

Now I'm the one rolling my eyes. "All that's happening now," I begin, leveling her with a look, "is leaving for Teshka to spend our summer getting tan on their shores."

"And?"

"And… I suppose being ready to be on the front lines if anyone tries to invade us."

"Your dad didn't seem happy at all about sending Luna Aviva and battalion to Teshka."

I smile to myself. My mother is the commander of an army of women. I've been training with them, have trained them, and will now stand beside them to defend the Deadlands if it comes to that. I'm the captain of my own little unit. There's three dozen young women under my direct command, and they were chosen by me specifically. They're the best of the best.

I took six of them to Moonrise with me to help train the Ghosts. By the end of that winter, those men wouldn't even look us in the eyes.

Whoever invades will be steering their boats into a hell of my own design without realizing it before it's too late.

I hope.

Uncertainty makes my stomach quiver, but Mom calls out my name from the living room.

"Are you spending the night?" I ask Chessie.

"My bag is already here, in the kitchen."

"Of course it is." I laugh before slipping out of the room.

But my smile fades instantly when I see a man standing next to my parents—a familiar one. Lips I'm… acutely familiar with.

Austin is fitted with Ghost armor—a vision in black. His tawny blond hair is gelled back, a far cry from the last time I saw him, so causal in a T-shirt, jeans, and a ball cap he had to move out of the way before he pressed his mouth to mine, and now he's standing between my parents, in my house. To say I'm shocked would be an understatement.

"Captain Austin and his warriors will be traveling with your regiment to Teshka," Dad says.

"Are your warriors prepared to leave in the morning?" Mom asks us both.

I can't form words. My gaze is glued to Austin's face. He nods, says nothing, but his eyes hold mine for several seconds longer than necessary. Long enough to make my chest feel tight and my mind swim with memories of our encounters in Moonrise, after dark, when we'd snuck out to meet up and…

"Yes," I murmur, trying to hide the blush creeping into existence across my cheeks.

Mom turns with Austin to the door leading out to the deck, but Dad stays behind. I can feel him boring holes in my profile but refuse to look in his direction until the door clicks shut behind Mom, then I ask with great effort, "Is Nora settled?"

"She's fine. A little upset, but Ella is going to keep her busy."

"And how's everyone else?" I rush out, unable to stop myself. I need the distraction from Austin. "Blake's mate and their daughter?"

Dad runs his fingers through his hair before stepping around the worktable and grabbing a bottle of whiskey from a cabinet. "You can imagine how things are in Moonrise right now. Your uncle is in… Syd is livid with Blake, but Sarah understands, or something. Marianna and Skye are going to be fine, regardless. We'll take care of them. All of us. Last I heard, Sarah is going to convince them to bunker down in Crescent Falls for a while."

I find it momentarily hard to swallow. Dad pulls down two glasses, pours two drams, and slides one in my direction. I like whiskey. I always have—even when I was too young to have it.

Silverhide might be known for its farming, but our ragers are also legendary, according to the people my age.

"Are you ready for this, Lexa?"

"Is it necessary to travel with the Ghosts? Are they our guards or something?"

He smirks, clicking our glasses together. "You're their guards, as far as I'm concerned."

"What could possibly go wrong?" I murmur, throwing back my drink, letting the burn wash away any lingering uncertainty.

REJECT ME THEN

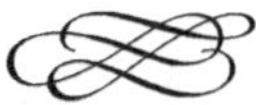

LEXA

Teshka isn't known for its pristine beaches.

The water here is gray and turbulent, the waves crashing against the shore to the songs of seagulls and the roar of the water lapping up the cliff faces. I watch the sunset over the horizon—watch it slip beneath the gray water, turning the sky a vibrant crimson that fades into streaks of violet, and as I look into the stars that slowly come into full view, I send another colorful curse down the empty mind-link to my idiot cousin Blake, who is the reason I'm stuck on the Goddess forsaken beach.

It took four days to travel here in our wolf forms. We stopped to camp every night, not a single fire lit, eating no more than a few oatcakes and washing them down with whatever water we could get our hands on. My girls made haste because that was my command. I'm not here to fuck around—not with so much at stake.

But the shoreline in Teshka, which spans nearly twenty miles before becoming so steep it's completely impassable, is just impossible. Boats can't land here. Not unless they want to be shredded to fine bits before being dragged back out to the violent water beyond. Still, I've been sitting on this beach for days now, watching the surf,

9

watching whatever idiot in Ghost armor try to catch a fish or go for a dip against the heat of the day. We've already had to rescue three of them, wasting valuable energy.

I've watched my girls get their feet and paws stitched back together after slipping over the sharp, unstable shale that marks the tide line. I've chased tarps and supplies across the barren beaches every night when the wind soars, sending rocks, ocean spray, and thick, coarse sand in its wake.

It's miserable here. Absolutely, utterly miserable.

Which is why I've been wondering why Blake was so adamant that something would happen here, and Maeve agreed.

Commander Michael of Queen Maeve's Royal Army—the Royal Guard of Moonrise—walks beside me down the beach, silent, our footsteps crunching through the shale. I peer at the stars blinking into startling focus, frowning as dark clouds roll in with the promise of a storm.

"There's no new intelligence to report from Tarsian," he says under his breath, his pale blue eyes glowing in the darkness. He's roughly an inch shorter than me and as old as my grandfather, I believe, but his reputation precedes him. The man fought in every war since the year my great-aunt Ella breached the veil into Eastonia. He stood on the battlefield in Tarsian over two decades ago, and before that, during the battle for Twin Rivers when King Kane finally fell. He's witnessed it all, which is why seeing him nervous has me especially unsettled.

"It's too quiet," I reply, and he nods his agreement.

"Are you warriors going to continue camping directly on the beach?"

"Yes. This is where we were commanded to be. I'm not going to move them off the tideline inland. That defeats the purpose of our mission."

Commander Michael hums a soft note of what I think might be praise, but it's quickly lost to the rumbling of stones being sucked back into the water as the tide rolls out.

"My forces will remain inland, then, guarding Teshka's main

village and their nearby settlements." We turn back in the direction we came, but he pauses, looking down the miles of visible beach at small warming fires cast a hazy glow over the pockets of sand where a few campsites have been stationed. "Commander Evander is in Teshka currently. I spoke to him only two hours ago."

I take a shallow breath to stop myself from asking after my mom, who's there as well, meeting with the other commanders, making plans—war plans, in the event of an invasion.

As a captain, I was not invited. As a captain, I remain with my regiment—my warriors.

"A small regiment of Ghosts is being deployed to this beach to relieve some of your warriors for a few days. Twelve total can return to Teshka. The Ghosts will take their places."

I roll my shoulders in an attempt to stamp down the sudden feeling of defensiveness roiling through my system. "Is there a reason why? Who made the command?"

"It was a joint decision between your mother—Commander Aviva," he quickly corrects, clearing his throat, "and Commander Evander. They both want their forces at their best—rested and well fed. The conditions here are harsh."

"I've already had to send five of my warriors to Teshka for healing. I can only spare another seven before our numbers fall flat."

"Send twelve back to Teshka, and you'll have twelve Ghosts at your disposal—"

"Under my command?" I turn to face him, meeting his gaze. He's a steely old man. He's seen, done, and heard enough to read between the lines I just laid out. He knows what I'm asking. He knows who I am and what I'm capable of. He knows not to fuck with me, and so do his captains and their warriors.

Still, he purses his lips, tilts his head ever so slightly to the side, and replies, "The Ghosts aren't under my command, Captain Lexa. This was not my idea. I am simply the messenger."

"Why?"

"Why me and not a lower-ranking soldier? Because they're all terrified of you. No one volunteered to pass the message along, so I offered to go. I needed the fresh air."

"That's not what I'm asking." My voice is like iron.

He steps closer, glancing down at his sandy boots. It's full dark now, and with the clouds hanging heavy overhead, I can barely make out the lines of fatigue and concern etched across the planes of his face when he says, "Queen Maeve has sensed something in her shields, as has King Ryatt. Eastonia is now at the highest level of alert. Everything has shut down–the railways, the road systems. Crescent Falls has closed their borders and deployed warriors in the event that if war erupts on our soil, it doesn't spill onto theirs. This is a very recent development."

My chest tightens. "And so we wait on the beach like sitting ducks for something to happen?"

"Yes."

"And you were sent to tell me to share this space with Ghosts?"

"They were sent to aid—"

"They will slow us down if it comes to defending the shore."

"You'll have to take that up with Commander Evander. It was his decision, but it was your mother's call to make when it came to relieving some of your regiment for a moment of rest."

I look back toward the water as another figure walks slowly into view, shrouded in shadow. I already know the cadence of his steps. His darkened outline is familiar.

"I'll make sure the Ghosts are comfortable during their stay," I reply sarcastically, and Commander Michael hears it as a dismissal.

Austin hangs back until the commander walks out of sight, his body sliding into the dim glow of the warming fires twinkling along the rocky shore.

I turn from him, picking my way over the larger rocks, walking toward the bluff overlooking the beach. Austin follows in silence for several minutes while I send a silent command through the mind-link, telling twelve of my girls to pack and go to Teshka and await my command once there. I hate it, having to pick and choose.

"This wasn't my decision, Lexa."

"Of course not," I reply hoarsely. "You weren't champing at the bit to be here or anything."

"Don't get mad at me for heeding orders–"

"I'm not–"

"What happened?"

I whirl to face him, looking down at him as he pauses on the last boulder leading to the top of the bluff. His eyes are full of stormy darkness, glowing ever so slightly, like they're full of the neon lights of Old Moonrise instead of his wolf powers. He shakes his head at me, chuckling darkly.

"What do you mean, what happened? I'm stuck sharing a beach with you and your worthless, poorly trained warriors while my own warriors are being sent back to Teshka–"

"Between us!" Austin throws his hands in the air, looking me right in the eyes.

I gape at him. I'm not sure what else to do. "What–what do you mean?"

Another low chuckle laced with frustration, maybe even disbelief, follows him as he climbs onto the bluff. "You're kidding, right?"

"Austin–"

"Did Moonrise mean nothing to you?"

My stomach twists, and a heavy sensation barrels through my chest, weighing me down. Austin closes in on me but stops only a foot away, running his fingers through his hair. He bites his lip, giving me a look intense enough to bring me to my knees if I had a lick of sense when it came to anything other than fighting.

"What are you trying to say?"

"I thought–the night before you left with your regiment–when we went to that bar, then the hotel–"

I look down at my sandals, a sharp contrast to his boots, his full Ghost garb shimmering in the darkness.

"Lexa, I *like* you."

"Oh–"

"I didn't want you to leave. I thought I made that clear."

"We didn't…. There was never a conversation–"

"Was it not good for you?"

I blink, my cheeks burning a fiery red as the memory of that night washes over me like a tsunami, rendering my senses absolutely useless. "I–it was my first time–"

"I want you, for fuck's sake. You know that. You knew that when you went back to Moonrise–"

"This is a complicated situation, Austin, please–"

"Because you're from the Deadlands? Because your father is the Alpha King?"

I meet his eyes as my heart squeezes–not from fear. Not because I don't match his feelings because I do. At least, I think I do. I never made room for any of this–for love. For the thought of being with someone. Of having a life outside of Silverhide, possibly, a life with a husband and children.

It's always felt secondary. It's always felt out of reach.

But then, I met Austin, and his pretentious gaze and cocky smiles burrowed under my skin until I couldn't ignore it. I wanted him in a way I've never wanted anyone before. I craved him.

He craved me back, and we acted on it. In secret. Behind the closed door of a shitty, rundown motel in Old Moonrise. And then we parted ways, just like that, and I felt like a new notch in his belt.

I was okay with it. I could live with it. I could get over it... eventually.

But this?

I might be prepared for my homeland to be invaded, but this?

"Is it because of your bride price?" he asks, his eyes suddenly serious. "I'll pay it."

"Austin–"

"You're my mate, Lexa," he rushes out like it's painful. "I'm almost sure of it."

My entire world stops spinning on its axis.

"We're mates. You might not feel it yet, but I can, and I have since the moment you walked into the training center and this–" he motions between us almost frantically. "This has been–the hardest thing I've ever done. Being around you. Watching you train–the most amazing thing I've ever seen–knowing you're mine and having you for just one night then watching you leave again. When Queen Maeve announced she was sending Ghosts to the Deadlands, I volunteered my regiment immediately. I had to see you again."

I resist the urge to reach for him, resist the months of longing, months of feeling like I was the only one who felt the way I feel, like there was no way this man–this warrior–this charming asshole who could get any girl he wanted–wants *me*.

I'm not a romantic. I never paid men any mind. But I was raised by a pair of mates–fated mates–parents who are desperately in love and were never afraid to show it.

I also grew up in the Deadlands. We have our customs, our beliefs. Finding my mate was never part of the equation for me. I know who I am and what my purpose is. At least, I did, until that fateful morning six months ago when I walked into the training center and saw him leaning against the wall, all blue eyes and muscles.

It had been an instant attraction, something I couldn't shake as the weeks, then months, passed. We sparred in the ring as well as in quiet corridors. I was mean to him to hide my real feelings. He ate it up. He couldn't get enough, and I fell hard.

We're both captains. That role comes with crushing responsibilities that kept us apart. Plus, he's from a pack in Crescent Falls–the son of a Beta. Our lives are thousands of miles apart.

"I know what you're thinking," he rasps, shaking his head.

"How could you possibly–"

"All the things between us? Your family and rank? That I'm from Crescent Falls and you're from here? None of that matters right now, Lexa."

"Of course it matters!"

"Do you feel the same or not?" He holds out his hands in surrender. "Reject me, if you must. Anything to put me out of my misery. I will get down on my knees, Lexa, if it's what you wish."

I stand, stunned, looking at the man who everyone said was so unattainable. Handsome, strong, and smart–he was the ultimate catch at the training center.

Yet, he has eyes for me. Me, the woman who towers over most of the men in my village. Me, the freak of nature–stronger than any man I know but my dad. Me, who came into my wolf at sixteen like my father and my grandfather, but the rest of my wolf abilities–like feeling the mate bond–are taking their sweet time to show up.

"I'm not–if you think I'm the kind of woman who'll be happy spending her day in the kitchen raising your pups–" I bite my tongue, sucking in a sharp breath.

Austin searches my eyes for several seconds. "That's not what I want from you."

"Then what do you want? Because I'm a warrior, Austin. This is my life. This is what I want for myself." I extend my hand toward the beach. "I will be Alpha of Silverhide one day. I will be *Alpha Queen* of the Deadlands. Everything else is secondary."

Austin's long, hard stare settles in my bones. He's disappointed. I can feel it.

"What do you want from me?" I damn near beg.

"I just want you–"

"And then? A pretty little wife warming your bed? Keeping your hearth fire burning?"

His jaw flexes as he grits his teeth.

"I cannot be that woman, and you know it."

"Is this really what you want? Sleeping on the ground every night? Spending your entire existence fighting?" His tone is like steel. "Is there nothing else you want for yourself?"

"No," I answer, and it's the most honest thing I've ever said, and it's… gut-wrenching. Anyone else would have fallen to their knees. Anyone else would have jumped at the opportunity being presented, at the prospect of matched feelings and… love.

Mates.

Fated… mates.

I draw my hand over my chest, physically searching for the bond I can't feel yet.

Austin nods, sucking his teeth. "So, what? You feel nothing for me?"

"That's not–that's not how I feel–"

"Then tell me–"

"I don't see how this could work. I need more time. Okay? Just–how–"

His eyes light with sudden hope.

I never stumble over my words. Never. I think before I speak. I weigh the consequences. I've always been so sure of myself. So confident. So *certain*.

Until now.

"I-I want you," I admit, hot tears of pure frustration trying to spring along my lash line, but I refuse to let it happen. "But I don't know how–"

A rush of sound barrels over the beach below us, a sharp interruption. A scream pierces the air before the fires flicker out, a stiff, unearthly breeze spreading embers across the beach like stars.

And then it's quiet.

Too fucking quiet.

SWALLOWED HOLE

LEXA

Austin brushes my shoulder as he moves in front of me, the two of us towering over the beach on our perch high above the waves. Without the fires, the beach is practically invisible, but it's the silence that's unnerving. I look out over the water with the slightest turn of my head. It's a clear, beautiful night… at least, it was. A strange storm funnels toward the shoreline, smoke-like tendrils of dark mist creeping over the sea in whirls and swirls that carry the unmistakable taste of… copper. The mist floods the beach. Strange orange-hued lightning crackles in the silent storm beyond without the warning of thunder.

Magic. It has to be.

I try to step forward, but he stops me with a hand curled around my forearm, his grip tightening in warning. Neither of us breathes. Neither of us moves. I can feel the tingle of magic between us as we send our silent commands for an explanation of the screams through the mind-link.

I tug out of his grasp and take a single step toward the edge of the bluff. A rock comes loose, pinging off the boulders below.

The second the sharp chord of another guttural scream pierces the air again, I'm moving, shifting into my wolf form before my mind has a chance to catch up with my body.

"Lexa!" Austin's voice fades as my paws meet the smooth edge of one of the wave beaten boulders below, but I'm airborne before his voice cuts out, leaping through salt and smoke scented air onto the rocky beach. Shale comes loose beneath my paws, but I don't feel the pain as it slices and breaks away. Panic ghosts through my body, settling deep in my muscles, burrowing into the very marrow of my bones—then dread. Then confusion.

Bodies move in a frustrated dance. My warriors—my girls—draw weapons in slow motion like time is standing almost perfectly still as the mist spreads over the beach, snaking over their feet, curling around their ankles.

Austin screams my name again. Another howl of fear. Another gust of copper tasting magic.

Time returns to normal, and it's violent.

I tumble into my human form, drawing the twin blades criss-crossing over my back, fastened by a halter worn by every warrior in my regiment. My blades sing as they cut through the mist, but the dark shadows tearing onto the beach curl like fog, my blades piercing... nothing. Nothing but air. It's a madhouse everywhere else. Every warrior—whether from my regiment or the Ghosts who've yet to set up their camp—hurdles into action against an unseen, but obviously aggressive, force. I watch in mingled horror and confusion as a Ghost warrior gets flung twenty feet from the shoreline, his howl of pain fading as his body spirals through the darkness blocking out the stars.

I grip my blades and sprint toward the group of women still in their human forms, weapons of choice drawn with no foe in sight.

"MEG!" I shout as smoke-like dark mist spills from the waves, tangling and twisting as it swallows the edge of the beach.

Before the mist completely shields my vision, I see Meg's fiery red hair whip around her body as she whirls in my direction. Her short blades are poised to strike, but the fear in her eyes is sharper than any knife. In a split second, she disappears, a shrill scream of what I can only describe as panic left in her wake.

The mind-link erupts in chaos with my warriors struggling to find their bearings in the darkness consuming us.

Another warrior bursts through the mist only feet away from where my feet are firmly planted, my heart racing out of rhythm. We lock eyes, and her look of pure relief sweeps through me before it gets torn away in a rip current none of us can fight.

I don't have time to even think of raising my blades toward the towering mass of onyx that cuts her down in a single swipe, her blood spraying in a sheet of hot crimson that coats me from head to toe.

My scream of horror dies in my throat. I freeze, paralyzed by fear that fills my mouth with acid when the force—the beast of air and mist—glides past me.

The warrior's head falls at my feet.

More screams of terror and pain jolt me back to reality. I take a single step forward, and a beast of shadow appears above me. Gnarled claws the color of polished obsidian careen for my face, but I dunk at the last possible second. A clicking, grinding noise follows, but I press my belly to the ground, holding my breath, silent as a fucking mouse.

"Stand still!" I scream through the mind-link. *"This is a direct order! Stand fucking still! Do not move!"* Desperate, unorganized chaos reigns through the mind-link. Screams echo all around me—male and female—as the beasts cut through every warrior stationed on the beach.

I reach through the link for my mom, gritting my teeth as the shadows dance above me, like they're hovering a few feet off the ground, waiting to strike, but they can't *see* me if I'm not moving.

"Don't move. Don't move at all. Stay where you are, and don't fucking move!" I repeat with force, but the voices in the mind-link—my entire battalion, start peeling away, blowing out like a candle.

Boots crunch over the coarse sand in a sprint. A Ghost warrior nearly steps on my head. I grab his ankle, and he falls to the ground with a sharp cry, unable to catch himself.

"Don't move!" I snarl, trembling as the air above us shifts, swirling like a void. "Don't fucking move. They–they sense movement–"

He jerks his leg from my grasp, signing his death warrant. A shadow bursts out of the mist and grabs him, dragging him away. The scent of blood is suddenly so thick I can't breathe past it, but then there's Chessie, sprinting out of the mist, her eyes wide and glowing with the promise of transformation, and I–this is my regiment. *My* warriors. *My* girls.

And they're dying. I hear it with every passing second. I can feel it in the quaking sand beneath my body. I can smell it–the fear, the pain.

And I can't do anything about it.

"Chessie!" I shout, jumping to my feet as the darkness swells behind her. Onyx arms reach for her, for us, and she stretches her arm out to me, and I–

Austin steps between us and the shadow, still in his human form but battered, his Ghost armor hanging in strips from his shoulders. Chessie launches into my arms, knocking me backward, but my eyes are locked on Austin standing like an immoveable force–a shield between me and certain death.

His certain death.

The word *no* barely leaves my lips before the mist-like claws of the creature slice through the man who just–just professed his love to me on that bluff. The man who said we were mates— he was almost certain.

He tries to turn back in my direction, but his eyes are already hollow and glassy with death when I see his face, and he twists, falling... lifeless.

I clap my hand over Chessie's mouth to block her scream of terror and let us fall onto our backs, side by side. Grief and shock slam into me, crippling me. My entire body jerks with the sudden, piercing knowledge that Austin is gone. His body lies motionless only a few feet away, his hand... outstretched.... *Oh gods. Oh, Goddess have mercy.*

"*Stay perfectly still!*" I plead into Chessie's mind, and she obeys. My voice inside her head wobbles, broken by fear and utter, unfiltered misery.

A sob tangles in my throat. My chest tightens, threatening to cave in. A warm, wet sensation begins to pool beneath us. Copper spices the air—hot, like a forge.

Austin's blood.

I close my eyes, biting my tongue to stop the scream threatening to kill us both.

Shouts ring out nearby—sharp and shrill. A sudden burst of light pushes back against the mist, and the sound that comes from the creatures will forever be embedded in my mind, seared like a brand. The clicking, gnawing groans turn to panicked screeches as the light bursts a second time, and then I see its source. A single golden arrow zooms through the night, shattering the mist to the point I can finally see the beach and what remains of the camps.

Bodies. Bodies everywhere. Pieces of bodies. Limbs, hands... heads.

Chessie trembles violently as the arrow tears back in the direction it came. New warriors storm the beach—a mix of Ghosts and Teskan warriors.

I hear Mom's war cry lift above the chaos, but she's far enough away I can't see her. A sliver of confidence creeps back into existence, and I start to sit up, but my leg brushes Austin's shredded torso and I see him and I—

Chessie launches out of my arms. I flail, trying to grab her hand to pull her back. The mist barrels back to the shore, pushed on a phantom gust of magic.

"CHESSIE!" I scream, leaping upright, reaching for her. My fingers graze her shoulder. I trip over Austin's legs. A whirling void of death opens right behind Chessie as she turns around, wild-eyed with fear, and her scream dies as the mist curls around her, squeezing her in death's embrace.

But the spray of blood doesn't come. I hit the ground, unable to right myself, my head smashing against the rocky, coarse sand and splitting on a rock. An unearthly roar comes from the water, and the waves surge like the sea is fighting back, offended by the blood tainting its water.

"Retreat," I say through the mind-link with little strength and no emotion. It's a word I've never said before.

"LEXA!" Mom's voice cuts through the haze threatening to pull me into unconsciousness. My face is wet with my blood, and my mind swims, adrenaline trying to yank me back to awareness, but I know it's fruitless. My head pounds sharply in warning that I was injured badly during that last fall. My body can take a lot. I've been sparing my entire life. I've killed people. I've been on the front lines during the small, but violent, skirmishes that took place when the Alpha Kings of Tarsian began to fall to the rebel packs. I've seen war. I've been in the thick of it.

I've never seen anything like this.

"LEXAAAA!!!" Mom's voice tinges with panic as it soars over the beach.

I get to my knees, then all fours, swaying as the corners of my vision go black. I rise, dragging one of my blades with me.

Warriors run around me, past me, heeding my command. The beach is a wash of shadows. I can't differentiate between the monsters attacking and the warriors sprinting for their lives.

"Retreat," I whisper through the mind-link. *"Retreat. Retreat–"*

Monsters of shadow lunge for the warriors. A few get snatched, drawn back with bloody, wet screams before they disappear in a tidal wave of crimson. Death is everywhere. It paints the beach, staining the sand red. The waves draw it out, scattering it, spreading the foul scent with every lapping, angry exhale coming from the sea.

I stumble, turning from the water, my mouth hanging ajar as I look up at the cliffs hanging over the beach. Warriors in their human form dart back and forth, screaming for their comrades to run, while others–Teskan warriors–send arrows flying into the mist. It won't make a difference, but the distractions the arrows cause are at least enough for the warriors scrambling off the beach to get to safety.

But I'm too far away.

I see her then, standing on the cliff, her golden bow lighting the space around her as she aims for me, aims right over the top of my head. My body tingles as magic surrounds me. It's surprisingly warm.

The monster behind me exhales long and slow, its talons clicking together as they stretch, grazing my skin.

Mom's golden arrow screams as it splits the air into pieces. I close my eyes when it pierces the dark force, shattering it. I feel the talons pull away. The monster screams its dying breath.

Mom's voice in my head begs me to move.

Chessie's laughter blocks her voice. Meg's sarcastic teasing laces through me. Austin's determined touch and the look in his eyes when he said we were mates washes me into a current I can't fight.

Dead. They're all dead.

"LEXA!" Mom's panicked scream forces my eyes open. Her golden arrow has returned to her, and she's drawing it back, but it's too late.

I feel the talons of a second beast curl around my upper arms and yank me back into the mist, swallowing me whole, and the world as I know it collapses into ash and dust.

THE CULLING

LEXA

Boots scrape over stone. Water drips down moss covered bricks with a smooth *plop, plop, plop* next to my head, where my cheek is pressed against what I can only assume is the floor. It stinks here. Like sweat, blood, and filth I refuse to describe.

I haven't moved in hours, but I've been awake. Yes, I'm aware. Yes, I can feel every ache in my body. Yes, I'm alive, but why?

The memories of the beach are hazy. I'm not sure how much time has passed or where I am. I could actually be dead, I suppose, and currently in purgatory awaiting the Goddess's final judgment. People have been moving in and out of wherever I am for the last several hours. I know that much. Facing the wall with my body curled in the fetal position, I haven't so much as glanced behind me–at the darkness, at the shadows that groan and grumble, at the sound of chains grating across the wet floor.

The *Boots*, I call them, have been coming in and out, collecting souls in silence. A key slides into a lock. A murmured command. Movement. A door closing with a sharp squeal. The scent of male sweat and grime.

But The Boots stop behind me this time. The key slides into the lock, confining me to my cell. My fingers, which have been curled into fists since I woke up, stretch, flexing. My body tingles with adrenaline, and I'm thankful for it because, otherwise, I'd dive head-first into the emotions currently threatening to render all of my training useless.

My friends are dead. I failed my regiment. I watched them get slaughtered. I watched Austin sacrifice himself to save me and Chessie, giving up his life for his mate, and I still failed Chessie. She's dead. She's dead. *She's dead.*

The memory of my mom's guttural, panicked scream burrows through my body, cutting out the sound of two sets of boots approaching where I'm curled into myself. Only a mother could make a sound like that. Only a mother could have that kind of edge to her voice, that agony.

What is she thinking now? How far has her heart caved in?

"Up," a deep, male growl resonates.

I shakily obey, but not out of fear. My legs are like lead, and my battered arms hang limp at my sides. I'm still in my leather warrior garb—a dress with loops instead of seams—meant for shifting, but my weapons are gone. Long, brutal gashes run the length of my upper arms in sets of three, but the blood has long dried, which gives me some insight into how long I was out. Hours at least. Maybe a full day or more, given the scabs forming. My healing skin crinkles and pulls when a man in dark, well-fitted leather armor clutches my forearm. I take a single step and realize the reason my limbs feel so impossibly heavy is that of thick iron manacles on my ankles and wrists, connected by even thicker chains. Not silver, but iron.

Still, I can't feel my wolf. I can't access the mind-link. I feel utterly empty of any of my lupine gifts as the guard, I presume, tugs me out of the cell toward his comrade, dressed similarly in dark leather and shockingly fine fabric. Golden thread weaves along the seams of a beautiful velvet blue overcoat covering the intricate swirling design of his leather armor. I follow the smooth, polished golden buttons of his coat up to the pointy white collar of his shirt and then his face—

I rear back, my body colliding with the second guard. He rips me to the side with a grip like iron, the pressure sinking into the horrific bruises painting my skin in shades of purple and blue.

Pointed ears. Sharp, chiseled facial features. Eyes the color of polished sapphires but too bright, too wide and large.

And behind him?

"Let me go!" I rush out, breathless with shock.

Wings. Wings sprout from his back–a pale, shimmering green in the darkness. His wings flare before tucking in tight, but the damage is done. I'm too stunned to speak again, let alone fight as his comrade drags me out of the cell and into a wet, cramped stone hallway.

Both warriors have wings and pointed ears. Both are unnaturally tall. Both are beautiful.

Fae. Fucking Faeries. The family was right. They exist. They're not just characters in the haunting folklore of Eastonia and beyond.

The air is thick as the guard–warriors–whatever the fae deign to call them–take turns pushing me, shoving me down the corridor. The chains binding my legs drag, heavy, and make it impossible to take more than a hobbling step at a time. My chest refuses to expand enough to take a full breath, but I'm trying. I don't know where I am. I don't recognize this place or these people. The smells are unfamiliar. The garbled, quick, and lifted language they speak doesn't register.

I have to get free. That's the only thought in my mind until they turn me around a corner, and blinding sunlight steals my vision completely. My eyes water as I try to raise a hand to shield my face from the light, but the chains binding my wrists weigh down my arms.

They pause, talking rapidly to each other, arguing about something. One of the guards jostles me like he's trying to make a point, and the other grunts, then says in... *the original language of the Deadlands*, a language so ancient its origins have been lost to time, "Go out there and wait for direction."

I blink, completely, utterly startled, and turn to face the man who spoke. His wings are a deep, almost amber-hued brown compared to the other faerie, but he's also different. It's hard to describe. His features are roughly beautiful, hardened in a way I find incredibly familiar. His scent is different, too. Warmer, like a crackling fire. His hands, compared to the other fae guard, are bigger, less feminine.

It's the only look I get of him as one of those hands presses against my chest and shoves me, chains and all, into the blinding sunlight.

I stumble backward, flailing blindly. My eyes sting. Bodies push and shove against me as my vision adjusts to the brightness. It's hot. Terribly so. The heat is wet, thick, and sticks to my skin as I blink rapidly, trying to see over the rippling sunlight and people—men—jostling me into what I realize is a crowd.

"Move, bitch!" a man snarls before violently pushing me out of the crowd, where I fall to my knees in the dirt.

There's a hum of noise, then applause, which nearly bursts my eardrums. My head swims, pounding with a dull ache that hasn't gone away since I hit my head on the beach. Sweat glistens along my hairline, sinking into microscopic cuts all over my body. It burns almost as much as the sun as I squint at my surroundings.

My stomach pinches, curling inward.

I'm in an arena. A massive fortress of white stone. The blinding light is the sun reflecting off the polished tiles shading an enormous crowd situated in a semicircle around the arena's base, every bench full to the brim with cheering spectators.

I whirl to look at the crowd in the arena, snapping back to reality, finally, and glare at the dozens of men shifting from side to side, scanning the area just like I am. Only a few have wings. Many are tall and built, but others hang on the outskirts of the crowd, alone, bound in chains while looking warily at the balcony situated several stories above our heads.

I look up, squinting against the sun, as another tall man dressed in rich turquoise robes steps into view on the balcony. His waist-length thick, dark brown hair lifts in a soft breeze that doesn't reach us in this pit of hell.

He raises his hands and silences the spectators.

"Lexa!"

I whirl toward Meg's voice, my heart leaping into my throat when she just barely comes into view. She's no more than ten feet away, trying to fight her way toward me through the men, also weighed down by chains. I glance at the fae male above us on the balcony before shuffling in her direction, my hands shaking as we reach for each other. I clutch her fingertips, trying to pull her between two of the men currently making no attempt to move out of her way, but at this point, it doesn't matter. None of this makes sense.

Meg is in much better shape than I am. That's the first thing I notice as I pull her toward me. It takes all of my strength, which isn't a good sign.

"How the fuck are we alive?" she hisses under her breath, raising her chains to try to touch my face. "How the fuck? What happened–"

"I have no idea. I don't know. What do you remember? How did we get here?"

She shakes her head, her eyes shining with panic. "I remember everything going black, then I woke up in a cell this morning. I can't feel my wolf at all, Lexa. I can't summon it!"

"I know. Neither can I." I look around, trying to gauge whether any of these men are shifters like us. They must be. It's so easy to tell the fae apart. But some men are just enormous. Handsome. Rugged. Like true, full-blooded shifter males from a royal line. Still, something is off about them. I scan a few of the taller, stronger looking men. Pointed ears. So many fucking pointy ears!

"Lexa," Meg says hurriedly, shaking my arms. "Chessie–"

"She got–she's–" I can't bring myself to say it. My best friend. I loved her more than anything, more than my own life. I feel my chest beginning to cave when Meg shakes her head, her grimy red hair falling over her shoulders like stained red silk.

"She's here. I can't get to her. She's on the other side of the arena."

"What?" I rise on my toes to look over the heads of the tallest men, a first for me, but I still can't see her. "You're sure?"

"I was one of the first they brought out," she says over the jostling bodies bumping into us as they turn to the balcony. "I swear I saw her. She's okay–"

A voice booms like the sky is being split–like a god is talking down at us, to the gathered spectators. I move to cover my ears on instinct, but the chains bite into my wrists, already rubbed raw. The fae male in his turquoise robes speaks in a language I can't understand, but beneath his words, as if speaking through a megaphone, his voice changes, translated in real time to that ancient language of the Deadlands.

We all learned it growing up. I'm fluent. I can read and write the symbols and speak plainly, conversationally in the old tongue. My father might be from Crescent Falls, but I also carry my mother's blood–the blood of the surviving tribes of the Deadlands–the three tribes that carried on despite the odds stacked against them over the course of three thousand years and multiple, horrible wars. Tribes who taught their people the Old Tongue from generation to generation, never letting it die.

Now, it booms as if coming from a speaker, each word clear as day.

"Welcome!" the King of the Fae says with a bright smile as he looks at his spectators. "To the Culling!"

"The Culling?" Meg whispers, glancing up at me. "Lexa, what is this? Why is he speaking in the Dead Tongue?"

"I don't know," I breathe, transfixed on his wings. Massive silver-white wings spread out behind him, tipped with a shade of blue that matches his robes. A cord of golden ivy glints in the sunlight as he turns his head, illuminating a crown. Yeah, this is the king, for sure. He has to be.

It strikes me then. The cold reality of our situation.

"We're very far away from home, Meg," I whisper and let all of my training take over.

"Over the next several hours," the king booms, "our champions for the Trials will be chosen. Only the strongest, the most cunning, will move onto the first Trial." He looks down at the crowd at the base of the arena–us–the people in chains. But his eyes hold on mine. I feel nothing but a sudden gust of determination as I stare back, unafraid. "Only one fighter will ascend to the Trials from each round of the Culling, a fight to the death," he says, and the crowd of spectators explodes in applause. "But in this round, whoever kills the three shifter bitches gets an automatic pass."

A murmur of excitement passes behind us as the men turn to look in our direction. My hackles raise, but my wolf remains absent. There's nothing there.

"Your only objectives," I tell Meg as the fae king grins wickedly down at us, "are to get to Chessie and kill everyone who gets in your way."

Meg rolls her shoulders and smirks at one of the men now glowering down at us with a hungry expression. "This is going to be fun," she muses, but her expression is murderous.

They must think we're easy pickings.

I keep my eyes on the king as he calls for the games to begin and smooths his hand through the air. The iron shackles all over the arena break apart, and a horn blows in the distance like a death knell.

Let the games begin indeed.

SURVIVAL

Lexa

There are no weapons to be had, which is my first and only observation as the horn sounds. Before the chains binding my wrists can fall to the ground like a dead weight, I grab the chain and spin, using my body weight and height to my advantage to send the chain ripping through the air. I keep my grip tight as it makes impact across the face of the first man to turn to us after the horn blares. Blood sprays, and the thick, heavy iron manacle attached to the end of the chain cuts through his face, taking teeth and bone with it. He falls to the ground. There's a single moment of silence before all hell breaks loose.

Bodies surge in my direction, faces contorted in violence, rage, and determination. Smug, male arrogance scents the air, mingling with the blood already beginning to stain the dirt beneath my bare feet, but just as I swing the chain back around to collide with two more men, the ground beneath me begins to pull apart, shaking violently.

I teeter to the side, the chain snapping back in an uneven circle, missing my intended target.

Sharp screams cut through the crowd of fighters. Dirt pours into three gaping holes, suddenly spreading at an extreme rate of speed.

Meg leaps out of the way of the gap as it widens, her eyes wide with confusion, but I shout, "FIND CHESSIE!" before pushing and shoving into an opening in the center of the arena while everyone else is watching the ground swallow itself.

I count heads. There were fifty of us to begin with, and if Meg was honest about seeing Chessie in the group, that makes forty-seven foes. Forty-seven men wanting to kill us, to kill each other. Forty-seven souls hell bent on making sure we don't survive.

Forty-seven souls I don't give a shit about.

I sprint through the crowd, swinging the chain, using the trembling ground and the distractedness of the crowd to my advantage, but it doesn't last long.

Several opponents fall into the holes. Six in total, which means there're forty-one left. A grinding sound explodes through the arena, cutting through the cheers of the spectators, and three platforms rise from the pits, streaked with blood.

A man grabs my shoulder and tries to yank me backward, but I swing, sending the chain across his back. He stumbles away, reaching for me, but I lash out at him, the iron manacles colliding with the side of his head in a killing blow.

Forty.

"LEXAAAA!" Meg bellows as she runs at a full sprint, pointing at the tallest of the platforms. It's nearly forty feet high and caught in the glare of the sun, but as I move to the side on quick feet, keeping the men currently turning in my direction in my line of sight, I see it.

A weapons cache.

Precariously resting on the tallest platform.

Other fighters notice. The air shifts as the initial confusion and shock of the floor of the arena opening subsidies, and violence creeps back in.

Grunts and shouts of pain echo toward me while the men fight each other, strategically cutting down weaker opponents with only their hands. But I'm a target. Ten men slowly edge toward me, backing me against the inside shaded curve of the arena. My eyes are on Meg until she's lost to the sun's glare, chased by at least a dozen men.

As the first of my immediate opponents steps forward, positioning himself ahead of the pack, I see her.

"Chessie," I breathe as relief sweeps through me, untangling the knots in my heart and brain.

"What'd you say, bitch?" snarls the gnarled, but absolutely massive, fae-ish male creeping toward me, the old tongue falling from his lips in shattered vowels. There has to be some kind of difference between these men and the full-blooded fae watching our deaths with glee. I can't put my finger on it yet, but I don't have time to figure it out as it stands. Not here. Not now.

My eyes snap to his as a sudden sense of purpose replaces my relief. I'm not going to die here. Chessie, currently running across the top of the first platform, ten or so feet off the ground, isn't going to die. Meg, who is leading the men on her heels on a wild goose chase around the base of the platforms trying to exhaust them, which is an incredibly smart move on her part, she's not going to die.

I won't allow it. We trained for this. They know how to put that training into action.

The fae man is almost within reach. I press my back against the wall, exhale deeply, and smile at him.

That catches him and his comrades–at least for now–off guard. He stumbles over his own feet–fine boots to go with his even finer armor, something made for a warrior, someone trained to hunt and kill–and I strike.

The chain whips from my side, striking him in the neck.

Through the neck.

I'm moving before his head slides free from his shoulders. I send the chain barreling into the three men behind him before his body crumples to the ground. The force of the chain being drawn back requires all the strength I have, but I tear through the plated armor, through flesh, until four men fall in a matter of seconds, but the fifth man grabs the chain as it bounces back to me and pulls.

I have a second to react. A single second to stumble, to reevaluate my next move. I allow him to pull me toward him while the other men rush at us, but the second he reaches for my hair, I leap, wrapping my arms around his neck while using my momentum to twist onto his back, dragging us both to the ground. His neck snaps like a twig despite his size. I roll away as he slumps, grabbing the chain, and whip it toward the men racing in my direction, eyes wild with hatred and violence.

Bodies litter the arena. The scattered fighters stumble over dead men as I hurry to the platforms, expertly picking my way through the carnage. A distance forms between us while I fall into the shadow of the first platform. It's only ten feet tall, but two men bound out from behind it, also wielding chains. I scream in determination, sending my chain flying, soaring, through the air, letting go of the one weapon I had in my arsenal.

The chain knocks them both to the ground but doesn't kill them. No, the final blow comes from Meg, who jerks her chain across their faces while they writhe on the ground until they no longer move.

Brutal. Sickening. Explicitly violent.

But we're warriors. We'll always fight for our lives. We spent our entire lives learning how.

"Where's Chessie?" Meg shouts frantically, glancing back at the chaos painting the arena red. The men giving me chase ended up fighting each other, which is the break I need to just... think.

"She's trying to get to the second platform," I pant, desperately out of breath. "We need to get up there, to the weapons cache, before anyone else does. We need to claim that third platform and use it to kill off everyone else. We'll have the advantage from that height." I grab her arm, noticing the flayed open skin. She yanks her arm back, shaking her head.

"I'm fine. Go!"

I grab her and shove her toward the platform, silently commanding her to climb. I'm tall—far taller than the average woman. It won't take more than a jump to grip the edge, but Meg needs the extra push, which I give her.

"Come on!" she shouts, frantic, as the surviving men move away from their recent kills and in our direction instead. "Lexa!"

I leap off my toes and grip the edge of the pillar, straining as I drag myself up, but just as I pull myself over the edge, Meg's grunt of surprise, then pain, sends adrenaline and fury tearing through my senses.

I sprint toward the tall, lanky man dragging her backward by the neck. She kicks out, but his grip is impossibly strong, and her eyes bulge. He's fae, but something's off about him, too. I don't give myself a chance to think about it. I can't, not when Chessie is fighting for her life on the second platform, and Meg is passing out.

I send my fist against the underside of his jaw. The crowd goes wild, their cheers filling the arena with so much force it sends trembles through my skin. He rears back, dropping Meg, but I grab him by his torn shirt and shove him to the edge of the pillar.

"S-stop!" he grunts, turning to me with his hands raised. "D-don't kill me. I sh-shouldn't be here!" The Dead Tongue is strong and heavily accented but *perfect*. Fluent. His native tongue.

My stomach dips to my bare toes. I waver, confused, and almost make a fatal mistake.

I should have pushed him.

He lunges at me, teeth bared, but I'm a step ahead of him. His body collides with mine, but I tuck my legs in tight and then extend them, using my strength to send him careening several feet into the air. He rolls to the edge of the platform, trying to save himself, but slips over the side.

"LEXA!" Chessie cries, but I step toward the edge where the man is holding on, trying to pull himself up. The drop won't kill him. Not even close.

But if he can't save himself from the fall…

"We're all slaves, like you. We're just their entertainment," he snarls, his mouth full of blood. "We're just their entertainment!"

Meg rolls onto her stomach, panting. The six men remaining in the fight are climbing up the platform. I don't have time for this.

"We're just their–"

I kick, my heel colliding with his teeth, driving his nose inward with a wet crunch. He falls back, arms splayed, and when he hits the ground, his head bounces. Hard.

Blood seeps into the ground around his face while the crowd jeers.

I turn, grab Meg's arm, and race to the far edge of the platform. "JUMP NOW!" I scream, and then we're hurling through the air. Chessie managed to clear the jump to the second platform already, some twenty feet off the ground, but with Meg's added weight, I struggle to maintain my momentum and then my grip as we collide with the side of the platform. I clutch Meg's arm, but she dangles, her entire body flush with the blood-stained wall while I somehow manage to grab the edge. Chessie grabs my arm, yanking with all of her might, but she's the smallest of the three of us. Meg finds a notch in the side of the platform and takes some of her weight off me and then begins to climb.

We've made it this far. The men now on the first platform fight against each other. The air fills with the sound of flesh meeting flesh in violent, deadly blows. Only the strongest remain—the biggest, the meanest, the ones, I realize, the crowd is screaming for and likely betting on.

"We're just their entertainment!"

I scrub the stranger's words from my mind and pull myself onto the second platform. Meg is right behind me, panting and whining as her muscles reach their breaking point, but I turn around and pull her up.

"We need to keep moving," I say, cutting off Chessie as she shatters into relieved sobs. "We need to get to the weapons cache. The rest can wait." My voice cracks as tears spill from Chessie's eyes. I just want to hug her. I want to tell her I'm sorry for not saving her. I want to promise I'll get her home.

But right now, I'm the captain. I have work to do.

"It's a twenty-foot jump; we'll never make it," Meg grunts, bruises starting to welt across her arms and chest.

"It's just another climb," Chessie says, looking at me. "We can. We have to do it."

Meg rises, and I can tell by the look in her eyes that she's on the verge of giving up.

But she's right. Chessie won't make the jump. She's barely five feet tall. The fall would be enough to kill her instantly. Meg? She might be able to jump, find her footing, and climb, but... she's exhausted, her arms flayed and bleeding heavily.

"Stay here. Do not let those men cross." I turn before they can argue and sprint the length of the platform. The crowd goes totally, unnervingly silent the second my body is airborne.

Time slows to a crawl. I have a fraction of a second to search the side of the final platform for any openings, any chips and breaks in the stone, before we collide. The impact takes my breath away, but the fingers on my left hand sink into a break in the stone, and I hang, my ribs screaming in pain.

A hush rolls through the arena before the crowd breaks out in thunderous cheers and chants. I don't look back. I grit my teeth and pull myself up, break by break, divot by divot until my arms feel like they're going to shatter, but I find the edge of the third platform by the grace of the Goddess Herself.

Meg shouts something unintelligible below, and Chessie's shout of pain is the last ounce of motivation I need to pull myself onto the final platform. It towers over the others, giving me a full view of the arena. My vision blurs, my body begging for rest, but I sway toward the weapons cache, knocking over swords and shields before my fingers lock around the smooth neck of a bow.

I whirl with the quiver, scattering arrows, weapons clattering. I pull back three arrows at once, taking a shallow breath before aiming and sending them soaring toward the four men trying to pin Meg and Chessie to the ground. Three arrows meet their mark—head shots. Three men go down as the crowd goes wild. But the quiver is empty when I reach back, finding nothing but air.

The final man—the last man standing—raises his fist, aiming for Chessie's face, who he has pinned to the ground while Meg writhes a few feet away, her face bloodied from a similar blow, but she's reaching for Chessie, her mouth moving, too far away for me to hear.

I grab a spear twice my size and grip it. I hate spears. I'm not very well trained with them, but I can't fail.

I can't fail them like I failed the rest of my regiment.

I scream at the top of my lungs out of pure, unfiltered grief and rage. The man looks up. He's fae. Maybe. Still unnaturally gorgeous. Battered wings tucked in tight along his back. His hands are stained a deep, dark crimson, and for a single, aching moment I wonder how many of the dead bodies scattered across the arena are by his doing.

I let the spear fly, aimed for his head, his face. Then I crouch, gripping the arrow closest to me, knowing I'll have a single shot if the spear doesn't meet its mark. He starts to rise, to turn away.

The crowd hushes as the spear pierces through his neck and keeps going, soaring into the shadows on the far side of the arena, where it breaks into pieces against the farthest wall.

The shock among the crowd is so palpable I can taste it.

Meg and Chessie remain on the second platform. Alive.

There's no one else.

But the game isn't over, is it? Only one person was supposed to walk away, to ascend to whatever hell we've found ourselves in.

Today, there will be three victors or none at all.

I turn to the royal balcony and aim my last arrow at the king.

Gasps ring out, but the arena continues its silent watch.

The king just smiles at me—a sick, curious kind of smile that burrows into my bones.

But it's the dark-haired man standing a few feet away from him that catches my attention. Tall and broad, he grips the railing along the balcony, his shoulders tense and arm muscles locked as he looks down at me and stares… disappointed, I think, at the outcome.

His slightly curly hair ripples around his bare shoulders in the light breeze I can finally feel at this height, and his tan skin is covered in tattoos, but he's too far away for me to see them clearly.

Yet his eyes, a pale amber gold, shine as he turns away and fades from view.

The king raises a hand and calls an end to this round of the Culling.

TO THE VICTORS GOES NOTHING

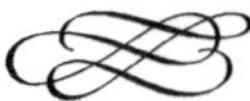

LEXA

Meg groans as I wrap a length of leather torn from my dress around her mangled upper arm. Chessie kneels nearby, tearing into her dress, dried blood crinkling off her knuckles in crimson flakes. She hands me another length of leather, but her eyes tell me the truth of the matter. Meg's in bad shape.

She closes her eyes, leaning her head against the grimy wall of the room we were thrown into several hours ago, but we're together, at least.

"She needs to eat something," Chessie whispers over the soft hum of the battle taking place above our heads. Another Culling. Sixteen so far, not including ours. The rounds take mere minutes to complete. Only five or six hours have passed, I'd guess, since our round ended.

No one has come to see us, to feed us or give us water. No medical supplies have been offered. We've been alone, trying to stop Meg from bleeding out.

I shake my head at Chessie with a sigh. "There's nothing we can do as it stands." I glance at the heavy wooden door blocking our view of what I believe is some kind of holding facility in the bowels of the arena. It's cleaner than the cell from this morning, which is a blessing. Still, Meg needs a healer as soon as possible.

We've had time to talk, though. To establish the series of events that led us here and what to do now. Meg and Chessie have both looked to me for direction, and I've done my best. I'm a warrior. A leader. I know when to fight and when to cede, and right now, we're resting, conserving what energy we have while we wait for this to play out.

Escape isn't an option. We tried that already. My nails are cracked and bloody from trying to pry open the door and knock stones from the walls. Our bodies are broken and worn. We're starving, thirsty, and covered in stinking dried blood.

Our escape will come, but not now, not when Meg is on the verge of passing out.

"Listen," Chessie says, looking up at the ceiling. The room rumbles, vibrating violently. "The platforms are lowering again. This round is over."

Seventeen rounds. Seventeen victors.

Twenty, counting us.

I rub my swollen hands over my face, scrubbing fatigue from my eyes. I've been pondering the reasoning behind keeping the three of us alive, breaking the rules the king laid out before our game began. I keep thinking of the man I killed on the platform and his damning words. He was right, I suppose. We're the entertainment.

And the crowd roared the loudest during our round. The other rounds have been quiet in comparison.

Heavy footfalls finally echo toward our holding cell. I throw a sharp look at Chessie, a silent command since none of us can communicate through the mind-link as it stands, and she quickly obeys by moving behind me, situating herself in front of Meg.

I rise from the floor, poised to strike, as the door opens, and six guards appear–all fae, all dressed finely, all carrying short blades along their belts.

They move into the room with silent determination. I shove two back as they grip my arms, but it's no use. I'm weak as it stands.

Hungry. Tired. Chessie grunts in protest as she's dragged to her feet, but the second one of the guards grabs Meg by the hair after she refuses to stand, my lips part to shout for him to let her go.

But another guard beats me to it, rattling off a sharp command in a language I don't understand. He motions wildly with his hands to the other guards, and suddenly, the grip on my arms loosens, and I watch in confusion as Meg is carefully lifted off the floor.

Chessie's green eyes shine with unease as we're led into a hallway with high ceilings and crude infrastructure. Chains and pipes stretch above our heads. The crowd noise dims, and the footsteps of the guards create the only sound—footfalls echoing into the metal rafters. A large, open space expands around us, and I turn my head toward the last inklings of sunlight stretching toward us through a wide entrance to the arena itself. People are out on the dirt—workers, I realize with a start—dragging blooded bodies into a pile.

My heart beats once, then twice, out of rhythm before returning to normal. I swallow my shock, fear, and nerves. I keep them locked up tight, tilting my chin. We're herded through one door, then another, and up several dimly lit stairwells. The narrow stone hallways lead into well-lit corridors painted in shades of beige, which transition into ornate spaces with stonework and wallpaper, similarly fashioned like the palace in Moonrise. Wealth drips from crystal sconces and scents the air with fresh linen—a far cry from the mildew and blood I've been inhaling all day.

Another string of unintelligible words fills the hallway, and the guards break formation. I startle when Chessie is led down a different hallway, jerking in her direction, but my attempt to get to her is quickly corrected. Meg is gone. I have no idea where they took her, but I'm given a sharp, determined shove as an order to keep moving, and I have no choice but to heed that command.

My heart rate skyrockets as the hallway drags on and on, but eventually I'm led through a door and into some kind of suite.

A trio of fae women in starched gray robes blink at me before turning to the guards behind me, who give them commands, I assume, in the language I can't keep up with. The grip on my arms gives way. The women move forward, replacing the guards' hands, and I'm ushered into an enormous bathroom where a tub is already running, the water casting steam toward the tiled ceiling.

My dress is peeled away by long, pale fingers. The women's voices are soft and bright as they rattle on in their native tongue, but I'm just staring at my body in the mirror, at the bruises, at the wounds that'll leave new scars. I keep staring at my reflection until they dump a bucket of hot, soapy water over my head. It burns into every gash, every scrape and scratch. Three more buckets follow until I'm deemed clean enough to be herded into the bath–which is more like a pool. I sink into the hot, soapy, heavily perfumed water, but my eyes remain on the drain in the center of the completely tiled room, watching red water swirl, gurgling into the abyss.

This must be where the victors go after the Culling. Into suites to bathe, to have blood and filth scrubbed from their skin and hair, just like me.

One woman viciously scrubs my filthy hair before combing through my tangles with her fingers. She's not gentle, but I don't flinch. I stay perfectly still, allowing another to trim my cracked nails before scrubbing them clean. The third woman stands in wait, two towels draped over her forearm. I look at her, and she meets my gaze, holding it, the corners of her mouth remaining a flat, narrow line.

I can't tell how old they are. Very young, I would guess. Likely my age. No wrinkles mark the years of their lives beside their eyes. No freckles show how many summers have passed. But they carry them-selves like experienced women–like my mother, and my many aunts, who are all in their forties.

I'm ushered out of the bath where they rub me down with towels and force me into a robe before moving back into the suite, planting me on a stool in the center of the room and beginning the long, arduous task of trying to tame my hair.

"Good fucking luck," I murmur in my native tongue, which elicits sideways glances between the women.

My stomach growls repeatedly, but no food or drink is offered. I'm lotioned, oiled, and roughly squeezed into a plain, homespun shirt and matching pants the color of dark sand. The women titter over my feet like they're debating giving me shoes and decide against it at the very moment the door to the suite opens, and four guards shuffle into the room, their leader's voice booming in that strange, musical language, and I'm off again.

The wounds on my arms and legs sting, unmended. Not even a swipe of ointment was given to aid the healing. Yet, I've been scrubbed raw and given clean clothes. My hair falls loose over my back and shoulders–shockingly clean–twisting into a wild, voluminous burst of tight waves, coils, and uneven curls–a mess of patterns I usually tame with braids or clips, but right now, I'm at my rawest.

I realize, as the hallway bleeds into a wide, ornate grand foyer in shades of white and opalescent blue, why I wasn't healed or fed or even given a moment to rest. Those things don't matter. I'm being served on a silver dish to the king like something for him to gaze upon, a shiny new trophy to add to his collection. I am a piece on a chessboard, a cog in the wheel.

My hunger doesn't matter. The likelihood my wounds will fester with disease doesn't matter.

I won my round of his sick, twisted game.

But the game isn't over.

Voices drift from a ballroom of sorts on the second floor. I'm herded inside, where several dozen men–all fae, all draped in rich robes and other finery–are mingling, but it's the group of people dressed like me–rubbed raw and exhausted like me–standing in the center of the room that snatch my attention.

Chessie and Meg are standing far apart, several men between them. Meg looks better than before but still slightly gray as I meet her eyes. The column of her throat bobs as she swallows, giving me a tight nod. Chessie doesn't look much better. Her eyes are wide and round as her gaze slips from my face to scan the room, locking on the dozens of sets of wings. Wings tucked in tight, wings relaxed. Wings, wings, wings...

I'm shoved into the line of what I realize are the victors, and I'm the last to arrive. I turn to the long table behind me where the king is standing just behind it, scanning the crowd.

But it's the blond man at his side that has a scream dying in my throat.

Hannibal Arachnis leans toward the king to whisper something in his ear. My skin prickles with gooseflesh as the detailed image painted by Maeve, Blake, and Soren comes to mind. His nearly white eyes. His unnatural height. His spidery leanness…. Yes, this is him.

The thought of Blake has me turning back to the room at large like he's suddenly going to appear. It sends a note of unease through me to think about what he'd done in Moonrise, the chaos he caused, and for what? Why?

Had he known about *this*?

I turn back to the man who brutally tortured my cousin, but his eyes scan the line of victors—twenty of us, I was right—and pass right by me without pausing. He doesn't know about the relationship I have with Blake, but things are falling into place.

These beings came to the Deadlands and stole me away to play in these games.

But where, exactly, am I?

The king raises his hands, a motion that commands silence, and silence follows. A shift floods through the crowd as fae nobles, I assume, turn to face their leader. I follow suit, glancing down the line at Meg and Chessie before facing forward, ignoring the men on either side of me.

A few males step up to the table, greeting their king with short bobs of their heads or little smiles—strange, I think. They must be friends, I believe, because of how casual this all seems. They're all young. Some show signs of the beginnings of middle age, but that's it.

The king says something to the crowd at large that's immediately repeated in the Dead Tongue by a man standing off the end of the table. He's a guard, I presume, based on his clothes.

"What a fine Culling today. An interesting Culling, I'd say, based on that fact we have *twenty* victors this year—our largest yet." The translator pauses to allow the king to continue in his native tongue, then says, "Now it is time to choose your victors. All sponsors, please, if you haven't already come to the table, do so now."

There's more shuffling in the crowd. Men gather, talking in low tones, their bodies blocking out their king as they negotiate. Plotting with each other.

Scheming over who gets whom.

After almost twenty minutes, my tired, starving body ready to give way, the men turn to us with hungry, excited eyes, but only one of them looks at me. He's not fae. I'm not sure how I didn't notice him standing at the table before, toward the far end, alone. Golden brown hair shimmers in the chandelier light, and his eyes are nearly the same color—a rich hazel. He's tall and strong, yes, but more built than the fae males around him. No wings. Large hands. A wolfish gaze that cuts into mine.

I stand a little straighter.

He's a shifter. Like me. Just a shifter.

A SPONSOR

LEXA

Sponsors step forward to claim their victors–their pets. I keep my eyes locked on the shifter at the table until Meg is suddenly shoved forward by a guard into the waiting arms of two fae males in long, emerald green robes. She thrashes, her eyes on mine, her lips pulled back in a snarl, but she's dragged out of sight, swallowed by the crowd. I step out of line, my body angled toward hers, but a low whistle stops me, and I turn to the shifter. He shakes his head at me in a very discrete motion–a silent demand to *stop*.

For whatever reason, I do.

But Chessie is next. Another fae male steps forward but leans down, speaking low in the Dead Tongue. I catch a single sentence. "It's all right. Let's get you mended, shall we?" The kindness in his pale blue eyes has my stomach flip-flopping out of sheer confusion, especially after he turns his head slightly to the shifter, who gives him another discreet motion of his head–a quick nod, a blink. *Like this was planned.*

"And who will claim the feral shifter bitch? She's the leader of the little trio," the king's translator says to the room. It quiets in an instant.

I look around. There's only a few victors left without sponsors, whatever that means. I'm one of them.

The shifter steps around the table and bows low to the king, who smirks, rolls his eyes to Hannibal, and back to the wingless wolf now straightening before him. But the king speaks in the Dead Tongue this time—fluent, like he couldn't be bothered with the language before now. "*Chasten*. I was wondering why you were here. Where is your Alpha King? I expected him to stay for refreshments after the final round of the Culling, but apparently, our wines and bites aren't good enough for him."

"He's indisposed at the moment," Chasten, I guess, says under his breath. I notice he doesn't look the king in the eyes.

"Doing what?" The king laughs cruelly.

Chasten licks his lips, hanging his head to hide the emotion I can see plainly, the grief written all over his face. "He's giving his condolences to the families who lost men in the Culling today, Your Highness, and arranging their funeral pyres. I came to claim his victor in his stead."

"Let me guess, he wants the she-wolf?" The king's eyes slide to mine. I stare at him. I don't even fucking blink.

Chasten nods, his spine rigid. "He has chosen her, yes."

"And he'll train her directly, I assume?"

"Yes, that is what he told me."

"Well," the king drawls, smiling as he meets the eyes of the fae nobility now tittering what I can only describe as excitement. "These Trials just became far more interesting, didn't they? Fine, take her."

Chasten bows once more before turning on his heels and stalking toward me, his hands tucked behind his back.

He stops short of me, however, as the king booms, "Tell your precious Alpha King I expect to see him tomorrow morning. The sponsors must meet to discuss the first game of the Trials, and I'd like his opinion on a few things."

Chasten's nostrils flare, but he doesn't turn around. His eyes meet mine and flick to the side, another silent command, and this time it definitely means *move*.

He grips my elbow. The crowd of fae parts to allow us to snake through the ballroom.

"Do not say a word yet," he says in a low warning growl the moment my lips part. I snap my mouth shut, letting him guide me out of the ballroom and back through the interlocking corridors leading to the foyer.

But we don't turn to the immaculate grand entrance. No, Chasten leads me back in the direction I came with Chessie and Meg. When the base of the arena comes into view again, now shrouded in darkness and starlight, I rip my arm out of his grasp and dig in my heels.

"I am not going back into a cell." I snarl and then shove him so hard he staggers backward several feet, huffing a pained breath. I whirl in a circle, looking for an exit, but notice he's stuffed his hands in his pockets, his shoulders relaxing. I expect him to lunge to get me back under control.

If anything, he looks relieved.

"You will not find your friends in this maze, I assure you. That's what you're thinking, right? Find them, escape this prison, and go back to the Highwoods."

"Highwoods?" The word feels funny on my tongue. "I don't know–"

"You are stuck here," he grinds out but shrugs one shoulder so casually I blink, thinking I'm not seeing him clearly. "The easiest thing to do to get out of the Trials is to just... die."

"Who are you?"

"I'm Chasten."

"I don't care about your fucking name," I seethe, my lips drawn back to showcase my very normal teeth. Gods, I miss my wolf. I miss those elongated canine teeth so badly it hurts. "Where am I?"

"What do you mean?"

"Where the fuck am I?" I swipe a hand toward the gloomy arena, at the dark splotches no doubt stained with blood.

He looks me up and down with a sigh. "They didn't even bother to heal you, did they? Those fucking bastards. Fuckin' fae pieces of shit–" His words garble together–new sounds, new words I don't know in the Dead Tongue, which is obviously his native language. My mind reels as I try to place myself in the world, in the current time. Did I travel backward? Is this the Deadlands, but centuries, if not millennia, ago?

"Who is your queen?"

"What?"

"Your Firestone Queen? What is her name?"

He blinks at me, tilting his head in confusion. "Are you all right?"

Panic floods my system like a tsunami, shattering every other sense of survival in its path. I press my hands to my temples to stop the pounding headache threatening to split my skull into pieces. My arms ache–burning with deep gashes that will take days, if not weeks, to fully heal. I'm starving. I can't think like this, but I have to figure this out.

"Come on," Chasten urges, cautiously taking my arm. "You're safe with me, okay? These fuckin' pricks won't do anything to you now that you're under our Alpha's protection. Okay? Listen, most of the guards are halflings anyway–"

"Where am I?" I rasp, tears brimming along my lower lashes. "Where am I!"

Chasten scans my face with sudden distaste. He chews his lower lip for a moment and then reaches out to... massage my head? I whip out of his touch and shove him again, not as hard as the first time, but honestly, I've lost all of my strength at this point. "Don't fucking touch me!"

"Did you hit your head?"

"No!"

"I was just checking for any injuries," he grumbles under his breath, but then he turns toward the sound of footsteps heading in our direction. He clicks his tongue. "We gotta go, okay? I'm sure someone back at the pack can answer any questions you have, but we need to get back."

"Back where?"

The footsteps come closer, carrying voices with each passing step. Chasten takes my arm and leads me into the shadows, through several narrow hallways lined with dirt and stone, but eventually, the corridor opens up again, and the night sky bleeds down on us—warm but comfortable. Dryer than the heat of the day I'd spent in the arena.

My eyes adjust to the darkness as a great, towering wall comes into view. Guards linger outside a massive set of doors—taller than anything I've ever witnessed. The top of the wall must be at least six stories high.

A feeling of dread settles in the pit of my stomach as Chasten approaches a guard—a guard with wings. They speak for a moment before the guard nods and turns, snapping his fingers at his comrades. I hug myself against a sudden chill sweeping through the air, waiting for the massive doors to swing open, but a much smaller door spills light across the ancient stone tiles beneath my feet instead.

A normal wooden door, a wicket, has been carved into the towering monstrosity I realize wasn't built to keep something out.

But to keep something in.

I take a single breath as we step through the doorway and smell… wood smoke. The door shuts behind us with a horrible clang of metal being moved back into a place, a lock, but a new world expands ahead of me, the lights and sounds of a small city replacing the quiet stillness of the arena and palace above.

Buildings stretch four stories tall in some places, precariously built with what looks like any materials that could be found. Narrow streets are made of raw earth, rusted metal, brick, and chipped stone. Light pours from open windows—firelight, candlelight—and the city itself hums with something other than electricity, something ancient. Something that comes from deep underground, like the world radiates a sense of life into this shanty-town.

Magic. The same magic that runs through the creeks and rivers that feed the farmlands and prairies back home.

My heart hangs in my throat as I move through the walled city beside Chasten, unable to bring myself to even make a sound.

"They didn't give you shoes?"

I blink, shocked back to reality. "N-no."

Another grumbled curse—something colorful, I imagine, based on the sour look on his face. He hates the fae; that's clear. The enemy of my enemy is my friend, or however the fuck the saying goes.

"What is this place?" I follow the wall–the curve, the incredible height of it.

"We call it the Glade. The fae have another word for it, but it doesn't matter to us here." His voice is low and soft but edged with disgust.

The road suddenly dips down, revealing a gradual decline into a pit of sorts. I gasp, unable to stop myself, as the rest of the Glade, confined within the wall, spreads out before me in a wash of twisting metal, wood and earthen structures. It's a massive city of wolves. Shifters. But there's poverty in this place. A desperation I can taste scents the air, mingling with the wood smoke. On the far side of the city, another set of towering doors looms in the shadows, but I can't see beyond it. Chasten continues to lead me, and I turn to look over my shoulder and see the top-most levels of the castle peaking over the wall.

I can't focus. My mind is a blur of noise and color. Chasten turns, leading me down an alley, where a courtyard opens, lit by oil lanterns. Laundry hangs static on lines stretched between the buildings facing the courtyard. Candles flicker in windows three or four stories above my head.

"In here," Chasten says, motioning to one of the tall buildings, and I follow him inside.

The smell of bread and salt hits me like a freight train, and suddenly, food is all I can think about.

"Oh, thank the Goddess!" a soft female voice shrieks. A tight hallway counts as a foyer with a shabby wooden staircase to one side, but it's sparkling clean here, even if the plaster walls are cracked, and the wood floors are gray with age and use.

A young woman tears around the corner. Light brown hair and big gray eyes fill my vision. She skids to a stop, her hand pressed against the pale cream apron covering the front of her homespun dress. She cradles the swell of an early pregnancy, just beginning to show.

Her eyes travel the length of my body from my bare toes to my face, and she cranes her neck toward the end.

She rears back, stepping into the shadows.

Chasten, however, steps between us, extending a hand to the stranger. "Lis, this is–" He pauses and then turns to me. "What is your name?"

"Lexa," I whisper, my mind locked on the smell of food coming from around the corner. Nothing else matters. I can't think of anything else right now, let alone the fact that I was thrown into an arena, forced to fight for my life, and no one even knew my name.

"This is Lexa. She's–she's Kaleb's victor."

The woman, Lis, glances between me and Chasten, wary and uncomfortable.

"Felicity," Chasten says, turning back to me, "is my wife."

I'm looking over the top of Felicity's head at the darkened hallway leading toward wherever the food is.

"Kaleb isn't here."

"I know," Chasten replies. "I doubt we'll see him until much later tonight."

"I made dinner."

"Please?" The word falls from my lips before I can stop it. I sound so desperate. I am desperate. Starving.

Felicity blinks up at me, but her steely expression softens. She smiles, but it's guarded. "There's enough to share. Come on. You must be hungry." Her eyes lock on my battered body, my unmended wounds. "We'll fix those up, too."

I don't realize at first that Chasten is gone, that he's left, walking back out into the night, but as Felicity offers me a stool at a worn wooden table in a warm, cozy room with a wood stove and several shelves–mostly empty save for a few jars of herbs–a name dances through my head. A name that sounds familiar in a strange way.

Kaleb.

But then a bowl of thin soup is placed in front of me, and any rational thought leaves my mind.

KING OF SLAVES

Kaleb

"We're out of wood for the pyres," Otto, an elder wolf, says as he smooths a withered hand down the length of a log. It's leaning precariously against the others—against stacks upon stacks of logs given to the Glade last week in anticipation for the dead. It's not enough.

It's never enough.

I turn to look at the funeral pyres, at the rows of log structures that will soon house five or six men to a pyre. Fathers. Brothers. Sons. They should each have their own. The fae know what they're doing by purposefully giving us less than we need. They always do.

"I'll find more."

Otto gives me a grim smile before turning back to the pyre that will soon be a beacon of light to guide his son, two of his nephews, and his eldest grandson home to the Goddess. He's not the only man wandering through the darkness tonight, adjusting logs and bringing handfuls of wood taken from tables and chairs—anything they can find.

It's a quiet night. Mothers wail silently into pillows. Wives tuck children in tight, drying tears in utter silence. I tried to prepare them the best I could. I tried to make it sound like dying this way was some kind of honor for the pack, but the reality of it is that they had no choice.

"Word is our victor is now in the Glade," Otto says under his breath, his voice obstructed by hammers pounding in the distance.

"She is," I murmur, tucking my hands in my pockets as the cool night air finally cuts through the thick heat. I let it fan over my body, enjoying it while it lasts. Tomorrow night, when the pyres are lit, it will be stifling. The heat will be felt in the highest reaches of the Glade, even the guards that walk along the peak of the wall that traps us inside a hell of the fae's design will sweat.

Otto goes back to his work. I already know he'll be up all night. He'll be joined by his family at some point—by the men who weren't rounded up like cattle and forced to fight to their deaths for sport.

I move through the darkness, stopping to murmur more condolences, to lend a helping hand where I can, until I reach the empty courtyard where my house, the house my great-grandfather begin building when the shifters were finally rounded up and enslaved here, rises into the stars—four stories tall and narrow, like the rest.

Chasten meets me at the center of the courtyard, his face obstructed by shadow. He looks beaten, but I expected that. He spent the evening in the palace standing as my second. He's several inches shorter than me, but our familial ties are clear—the rich curl in our hair, the amber-hazel eyes. The broad shoulders, the taller than average height.

But we're different. His father and my father were brothers. We shared a grandfather. Great-grandparents, so on, and so forth. His mother, however, was a shifter.

Mine was not.

"She's inside eating… again. She's on her fourth bowl of soup and third loaf of bread. Lis keeps feeding her. I don't think she realizes she can say no."

"I'll deal with it." My tone is guarded but uninterested. I don't have the energy for anything else after watching each round of the Culling, each round that claimed the lives of hundreds of men—shifter and fae alike. Halflings, too. So many halflings. That's what they were bred for, after all.

I run my fingers through my hair before tying it back away from my face. I'm filthy, coated in dried sweat and ash—likely blood, too—from going to claim the bodies of the fallen from the Glade.

"Where is she from, exactly? Her accent is strange," he asks.

"I'm not sure."

Chasten shifts his weight from foot to foot. "She's really fucking tall, too."

"I'm aware."

I can feel his gaze boring into my profile. He's waiting for an explanation; I know that much. Why would I choose a female shifter over the halflings and fae who have a better chance of surviving past the first trial?

"She's—"

"She has a shot," I tell him, turning to hold his gaze, "of surviving, and that's enough for now."

"Silas chose one of the other females," he says quietly, a whisper through his teeth. "I'm assuming that was your doing."

"The blonde one?"

He nods, and I feel a knot of tension untangle somewhere in my chest. Yes, the tiny blonde shifter who'd fought tooth and nail against aggressors three times her size. I'd watched her with interest but especially watched the way her comrades treated her, particularly *Lexa*. I know their names. The king boasted about them, excited for their downfall but especially about the idea of throwing a few women into the mix. He didn't say where they were from, but they're definitely not from the Glade. They're likely from one of the free packs that roam in hiding beyond the reach of Pantharas.

Lexa was a force in the arena. Smooth, calculated movements, full trust in her body. Chessie, the smallest, is a skilled fighter, but her stature is going to be a disadvantage. She's cunning from what I've seen, however, and that's an important trait to the fae. The other one wasn't of interest to me. I sensed a beat of distrust between Lexa, the obvious leader, and the red-haired woman during their round of the Culling. I took that to heart when making my decision.

"Silas owes me," I explain, turning back toward the house.

"You're really not going to explain any of this? She's staying with us, right? How are we supposed to feed her?"

"As a victor, she gets a daily ration–the same as the men in the Trials. It'll be enough for her and then some. Don't worry about that aspect."

I take a single step toward the door, but Chasten says, "*He* wants to see you in the morning. The king. The trainers are meeting at the palace to discuss the first game."

I close my eyes for a few seconds before answering, "Thank you, Chasten. Lexa's training starts tomorrow, and I need you, Colin, and Avery to help her in my absence."

"What are we supposed to do with her?"

"Prepare her for what's coming." I meet his eyes, holding. "Throw everything you have at her, and see how she reacts. No mercy. No softness. She might be a woman, but based on what I witnessed during her Culling, she is–" I can't find the word. There's nothing in the world that can describe the moment she turned her arrow on the king, her eyes wide and unafraid. "She's going to be a problem. Keep her in check. I don't care if she gets injured. Hurt her, if you must."

Chasten swallows hard but nods before turning back to the night, his shadow stretching through the moonlight until he disappears from view. I hear Felicity's soft footsteps a floor above, followed by her voice as she speaks in low tones to Lexa, I assume. I wait until I hear a door shut somewhere above my head, and Felicity appears on the stairs, her owl-like eyes shining in the darkness as she tucks her leather healing satchel under arm, throwing me an impatient look.

"There's a single bowl of soup left, if you're hungry, which I know you are. It's just cabbage. We have nothing else."

"There will be another hunt soon, I assure you." I pull my weapons' belt through the loops and hang it on a hook near the door. She looks behind me and walks down the last steps. "Chasten has gone to help with the pyres–"

"How many dead?" she interrupts with heartbreaking quiet.

I step deeper into the house, walking past her to the kitchen, where there is indeed a single scoop of thin broth left and no bread. "Four hundred from the Glade."

"That's–that's everyone that was taken–" She bites back her words, looking down at her worn shoes.

"You were told–"

"I know what I was told," she says tearfully. "It's not right, Kaleb. What's happening–it isn't right."

"You are old enough to remember the last Trials that took place. Your own father and brother–"

She turns from me and moves out of sight, but her footsteps on the stairs are sharp and determined. I scrub my hand over my face, forgoing the idea of a meal, and follow her into the darkness, but instead of stopping on the second floor, I climb to my room. I shower–cold. I dress in whatever's clean and leave again, but my feet halt on the first floor landing, refusing to move.

I can smell the healing salves. The air's scented with alcohol. Felicity is tending to Lexa's wounds. I'm sure Lexa will wake to fresh clothes and a few bites of food, which is more than she was offered in the depths of the arena–in the holding cells I know so well.

Felicity's feelings aren't misplaced. Death hangs from every doorway and window in the Glade and has for decades. I'm responsible for everyone here. Ten years ago, at the age of twenty, I became Alpha King, finishing the work my father, his brothers, and their own father began decades ago, when the enslaved packs united out of the sheer need to survive against the odds stacked against us.

I can keep them fed. It's never much, but it's enough so that our children and mothers won't starve. I can ensure the young are educated, that the traditions of our ancestors thrive in an environment where we are the lesser crowd, the pets, the disposable help and the warriors who have no choices.

Just like the men the fae rounded to compete in the Culling, even though the victors have been picked out for weeks now.

Every victor but Lexa and the other girls.

They weren't supposed to survive.

Neither was I.

I leave the house, moving back through the city under a cloak of darkness now waning to the first inklings of morning. The air shifts, already warming significantly. People leave homes carrying canvas bags, some wearing their required uniforms for their work within the palace or the fine homes of the regal, high-ranking fae who live in the city beyond.

The sun will shine on Pantharas, the capital of the fae kingdom, like it always does.

But the moon shines for us, even if we can't feel Her gifts anymore.

I walk to the far gate, the doorway that opens to the forests and plains beyond the Glade, a place some within the walled-off city have never seen. Avery, a shifter male who leads the small group of enforcers under my commander here in the Glade, looks up from a list of what I know are names—names of the dead. Names of the warriors he trained over the years. Names of our friends, our family.

His icy blue eyes hold mine in greeting.

"I need you to choose five men and prepare them for a hunt. I'm going to try to get the king to open the gate and drop his wards tomorrow night, during the funerals. They need to be the best, the most skilled."

He nods. "And the victor? Is she settled?"

Word travels fast here.

"You'll meet her tomorrow. Chasten will be training her in the sparring ring in my stead. I'll join them once I've met with the king."

Avery runs his tongue along his lower lip and then tilts his head to where the palace towers peak over the wall. "Any news?"

"I was only able to speak to Silas briefly during the Cullings, and we were not alone, so no." An undercurrent of unease runs between us. Words left unsaid. Silent understanding.

The seeds of rebellion were planted long ago, when our people were torn from their homelands and forced into servitude by the fae.

Now, some of the fae are turning on their own kind—and turning to us for help.

Lexa has no idea what she's walked into, but it's not like she ever had a choice.

"Where is she from?" Avery asks.

They don't trust her. She's not from here. She's not like us. She doesn't understand what she's now fighting for because it's so much more than her life.

"I'll find out."

"A man came to the palace gate earlier looking for you. No one recognized him, but he's some kind of fae, I believe."

I'm turning from him but edge back in his direction. "Who?"

"He didn't give his name to the guards on our side. He spoke through the door, actually. No one saw him."

"What did he want?"

"He was asking for you. He needed to speak to the Alpha King. It was during the final rounds of the Culling. The guards told him you weren't here, and he said he'd come to you when *it's time*. I don't know what that means."

Neither do I. "If he returns, find me."

THE WEIGHT OF BEING QUEEN

Maeve

Rose bushes cast in golden streaks fan out on either side of the illustrious walkway. My heels click against the smooth, alabaster tiles sparkling in the final moments of the sunset illuminating the castle in Crescent Falls in shades of gold and magenta. It's a work of art. Guards move to the side, bowing their heads as I walk up the stairs, my heart lodged in my throat, my mouth dry from lack of use.

I haven't had much to say these past few days. I haven't been able to find the words I need to convey my utter despair–especially to my family.

A butler opens the door and ushers me inside. It's all very formal, like I'm an honored guest, a diplomat, rather than a family member who's been to this castle dozens of times over the course of my life, but I'm stuck in autopilot as my footfalls echo, stretching down dimly lit, but modern, hallways that weave throughout the backside of the castle, where the more formal sitting rooms bleed into rooms full of family pictures and knickknacks, and the air still smells like... Great-Grandma Isla.

What would she say if she were still here?

"Maeve!" Maddy exclaims, turning from a bookshelf curving over a massive, but dormant, fireplace. Her deep, stormy blue eyes widen as she gasps a breath. She wasn't expecting to see me. I didn't call ahead to let anyone know I'd be here, but I had to come. I just had to.

She hurries to me while I hesitate in the doorway, grabbing my cold, clammy hands in hers, her fingers smooth and warm to the touch.

I can barely look in her eyes.

"I didn't know you were coming–"

"I'm sorry." I swallow past the knot tangled painfully in my throat, finally glancing into those wells of deep blue–blue like Sydney's eyes, the father of Blake, now missing indefinitely. Blue like Ryan's eyes, whose daughter is also missing. Both are Maddy's grandchildren. No one will mention the words "presumed dead," at least not within our family circles, but the news is all over it.

All over me.

Maddy caresses my cheek, but I can't even bring myself to give into her warmth and cry like I want to.

"You're freezing."

I sniffle, gently pulling out of her touch. "It's been a while since I've been in Crescent Falls. It's cold here."

"Barely," she whispers, giving me a playfully subdued look before releasing me. "What are you doing here? We had dinner two hours ago, but I can call for a plate–"

I cut her off with a quick shake of my head. "No, please. I'm fine. I came to speak to Marianna. Is she here?"

I already know she is. Within a day of the news that a battle took place on the southern shores of the Deadlands, Marianna, Skye, and Leona were whisked away by Sarah and Sydney, all still reeling over Blake's disappearance. It's been a full week. A full week without news of Lexa or Blake.

"She's upstairs." Maddy smiles softly as she sinks into an armchair. "She's been playing her violin every night in the orrery. I think it brings her comfort, and I have to say, I enjoy the music." She taps her manicured fingers on the armrest before continuing, "We actually have a full house as it stands. Isaac and I came here from Maatua as soon as we heard Sarah had returned with them. We're staying for a while, as it stands. We're closer to everyone in Crescent Falls and Eastonia here. Cosette and Artyom decided to take up one of the guest rooms on the third floor for the time being. Cosette home-schooled Blake, you know, for all those years. She'll be good for Skye, I think, given the circumstances."

The circumstances being that I had to completely shut down Moonrise. Not just Moonrise, but all of Eastonia is under lock and key with no inkling of if or when I'll be able to release my iron-clad shields. Skye's new school won't be starting this fall as planned. Marianna won't be raising her violin bow and leading a symphony through the first concert of the season as first chair. Life is at a standstill.

"That's wise." I don't sit. I'm not sure my legs will bend even if I willed them to. "I just came from the Deadlands."

Maddy looks at the empty fireplace, at the blackened, soot coated bricks. She swallows hard, her gaze falling to her fists in her lap. "How–how are they?"

"Aviva wasn't there. Ryan had just returned to Silverhide after trying to get her off the beach–" I force the words out as Maddy rises, sensing the pain in my voice. "This is my fault. I sent them there–"

"Aviva is the commanding officer of the faction of your army," Maddy says as she cautiously approaches me again. "She knew the risks."

"None of us knew the risks. We don't know the enemy. It was my order that she sent a regiment to the beach. She sent her best, which included her daughter, and they're gone. All of them. Along with a quarter of my father's forces."

She clutches my wrists. "We trust you."

"Do not say that to me," I whisper, my eyes watering. "Please."

She smooths a rogue lock of hair out of my eyes. "It must be an immense burden on your shoulders, Maeve. We see it. All of us do. Lexa and Blake will be found."

I roll my eyes to the ceiling and blink the tears away, letting some of the anger I've been beating down the past two weeks slip free, unchained. "Blake better be with her. Wherever he went, whatever he started… he better be with her, or I swear to the gods–"

"Maeve?" Marianna's surprised exhale forces me to turn to the doorway.

She's dressed in black–a black sweater, black slacks, her hair pulled back in a tight, neat bun that makes her look… harder. More burdened than I've ever seen her. Her dark blue eyes scan mine before she steps deeper into the room, her violin case resting against her thigh.

"Hey," I manage, but her lower lip trembles. She's waiting for news. She thinks I'm here to tell her Blake has been found, that we know exactly where he is, but I have nothing.

With my mom in Veiled Valley keeping Brie sane while Logan evacuates his pack from Emberfyll and Soren drumming up an army in the Roguelands as the new Alpha King, with my grandpa Ryatt by his side as added muscle if necessary, I've been alone. Just me and Fallon, who better be sleeping right now, likely tucked against Jane's arm while Patton plays the guitar or whatever the hell he does to calm my baby in a way no one else can. I won't be gone long. I promised Fallon I wouldn't be.

But I had to see Marianna to remind myself that Blake still has a human side.

His mark is a smooth, clean crescent moon on her neck.

"Can we talk?" I ask, and Marianna quickly nods, setting her violin case against the doorway. Maddy squeezes my arm and takes her leave, murmuring something about having a tea tray sent to us, but Marianna and I just stare at each other, trying to find common ground in the fault lines between us.

"Is Skye using the spheres?" I ask, my voice cool, monotone. More empty than I anticipated.

"All the time," Marianna says quietly. She walks to the window, glancing at the sunset spreading shadows over the private parking area and garage before turning to face me, her arms crossed under her chest. "She's... Sarah has a hold on her powers, keeping them tightly wound, whatever that means. Skye can't scry for Blake as it stands, but she's been trying."

"Sarah hasn't found him through scrying, either. She told me as much."

"That's correct." Marianna swallows hard, her cheeks a little gray, her eyes lackluster. "I'm not going to stand here and pretend to understand the nitty-gritty details about powers, shields, and veils, but I know this much. I know wherever he is, he's alive. I know he had something planned down to the most minute detail because that's how he operates. And I know he'll come back." Her eyes meet mine almost in challenge. "He'll come back because he left a sphere with what I'm sure is the future waiting for us if he's successful. That was his why. It was why he left us. It was why he left me. But he made you vow to not allow him to come home."

I wave a hand to cut her off. "If he comes home, and he's... not himself."

"But how well do we even know him?" Her eyes shine with unshed tears. "Even me?"

"Don't talk like that."

"And now, his cousin is gone, and the dead are adding up. Did he have a hand in what happened in the Deadlands, Maeve?"

Something heavy and bitter twists in my gut. She's right. Right about her own mate. Blake spent his entire life shielding himself, who he truly was, from us. Marianna was the only person to ever see another side to him–a soft side, a side capable of love–and if she's questioning his motives...

"Lexa is alive. Her parents can feel it," I tell her. "I'm confident that wherever she is, wherever she's been taken and for whatever purpose, he's there, too. He'll fix this. I hate to say it, but I believe this attack– Lexa being taken–it was something he saw. Something he knew would happen but couldn't, or wouldn't, change."

"Do you trust him?" she asks. It's such a complicated question.

"I do. Do you?"

"I know he wouldn't hurt me or Skye. That's all I have to hold on to."

"Don't blame him for this, Marianna. This is far larger than us, far larger than me."

My phone buzzes in my purse. It's likely another commander or diplomat for the many Alpha Kings champing at the bit to get me alone, to get an explanation, a plan. I ignore it for now.

Maddy returns with a tea tray, carrying it in herself, and immediately senses the tension between Marianna and me. She sighs heavily, saying, "I think everyone needs to take a walk and get some fresh air."

Marianna scrubs her cheeks like tears are trickling there, but her eyes are dry as she turns from the window and hurries out of the room.

Maddy sets the tea tray down with a soft clunk, her eyes downcast on the delicate teacups and kettle. Chamomile scents the air around us, dragging me back down to reality and reminding me of who I am.

"I can't fix this until I know where they are," I tell her, using her as a sounding board. "The family is looking at me for direction, and I have no solid answers. All I can do is keep our forces active, our borders tightly secured, and wait."

"And so, we'll wait," she says, but I frown.

"It doesn't feel like enough. You likely heard the conversation I just had with Marianna. She's doubting her trust in Blake."

"She's grieving," she corrects. "Everything is always upside down when grief is involved. The family knows what to do. We've been through this before–worse, actually. You were too young to remember the war in Tarsian, but I said goodbye to everyone–to my mate. To your mother, to the mates of my sons, to my daughter." Her voice turns pained at the mention of Misty, who, like Lexa, found herself trapped in a new place, surrounded by violence.

"What do you think Lexa's doing right now?" I ask, and Maddy, to my surprise, smirks–an expression I rarely see from her.

"Making whoever took her regret it would be my guess."

"What do you think Blake is doing? These are your grandchildren. You'd know better than anyone on my side of the family."

"Blake is doing what he's always done best," she says with a heavy, but somewhat proud, sigh. "Manipulating everyone around him to bend to his will."

CHILD'S PLAY

Lexa

I'm woken up by Lis in the late hours of morning. She barely says a word to me–tiptoes around me, in fact, keeping a wide distance between us as she shows me the bathroom located on the second floor, just down the hall from my room, and leaves a set of clothes and a small plate with bread, fresh butter, and a glass of milk on the table beneath the window in my room.

My body feels leaden when I run a shower. There's not much to be had in terms of hot water, but honestly, the cool spray feels nice given this place has little in the way of air conditioning, either. My mind is locked in a haze I have a hard time breaking free of, but after my shower, I change into the clothing Lis laid out for me. Men's clothing, at least the pants. I tighten them with a belt. The shirt, however, is probably one of hers, given that it barely covers my belly button. After I eat, I tame my hair into a tight bun and start to move downstairs in search of anyone who can tell me where to find my friends, but I look up at the stairwell that snakes four stories, and I feel a sudden desire to snoop.

I've never been one to just allow the world to keep turning regardless of the situation. I'm a planner. A leader. A defender. An eldest daughter and older sister. I want everything to be in order, and I hate–*I hate*–being out of control.

Not knowing where I am makes my skin crawl. Not knowing where Chessie is... gods, it's wrecking me. I wouldn't have been able to sleep last night had Lis not offered me tonics to help put me under, which I accepted, but I know from now on I need to be at the top of my physical abilities.

I climb the stairs to the quiet, empty third floor. The house is larger than it looks–like it was built for multiple families or perhaps multiple generations. There's a second kitchen on this floor, seldom used or so it appears, and four good-sized bedrooms–all of which are empty, save for a few dusty tables, some random boxes of fabric, and... weapons.

I smooth my hand over a short blade I doubt anyone has touched in many years before sliding it into the pocket of the male trousers I've been given.

I move on, my feet sending a dusty echo as I climb the stairs to the fourth floor, but then Lis speaks somewhere behind me. "You can't go up there. Those are Kaleb's rooms."

I pause, my hand gripping the railing. Everything in this place is well built but very old, like this particular building was constructed centuries ago, but it's well maintained, even though it's built of scraps of metal and wood–whatever could be found.

"I was–I needed to look around."

"You need to know that you're safe?" Lis blinks up at me, and her voice wavers, cracking. That single split syllable is a silent question, I realize. She wants to know if she's safe, too, with me in her home. She's the lady of this house, I think. There are no other children around, so this baby will be her first. She's young, possibly my age or younger, and beautiful, but thin. Her wrists look incredibly delicate as she stands below me, gripping a woven basket full of laundry I imagine she just picked off the line in the courtyard.

"I'm not going to hurt you." I walk back down the stairs. "I have no reason to."

"I won't hurt you either."

I stare at her for a moment, at the hard as nails expression that flashes behind her eyes. She's not as frail as she looks, is she?

"I was coming up to tell you that Chasten will be here any minute now to escort you to the sparring ring. You'll be training there every day until the Trials begin next week, I believe. I don't know much about the details of the games."

"How do I get out of the walls around this place?"

The silence that settles between us is deafening. She considers my question, scanning my face for inconsistencies, ulterior motives. "You can't. It's heavily guarded. We are not allowed to leave. I've never been outside the walls."

"What?"

"I was born in the Glade and will die in the Glade."

"I don't—there are no trees here." I'm not sure why that's the sentence that leaves my lips first.

She gives me a simple one-shoulder shrug. "I'm not sure where you're from or what you expected, but we are not free people here. We work for the fae. We live for the fae, and we die for the fae."

I narrow my eyes. "Why?"

She shifts her basket to her other hip, taking a deep breath. The angelic, doll-like features fade in an instant, revealing the look of a woman who takes no shit and demands obedience.

I fight the smile tugging at the corners of my mouth.

Lis and I will get along just fine.

As long as I follow her rules.

"We don't have a choice. The men—four hundred men, to be exact—from our pack who died yesterday didn't have a choice. You don't have a choice but to compete in the games. This is your reality, Lexa." I reach the foot of the stairs, and she steps toward me. I tower over her, casting her in my shadow, but her expression only tightens with conviction as she tilts her chin and grinds out, "You will obey Kaleb's word. That's the main rule of this house. Kaleb is our Alpha. He's the Alpha King of the Glade, and for some reason, he chose you to be our victor, our competitor in the games."

"I haven't met your Alpha King."

"He was forced to watch the Cullings. He was there." Her voice quivers, and I feel like she wants to say more, but the image of that random man standing a few feet away from the king when I'd raised my arrow comes hurtling back to the forefront of my mind, and I pause.

"You will do your own laundry and mending. I expect you'll keep your room clean, and I also expect quiet. If you're going to fight or be aggressive, take it to the sparring ring. I serve supper every night, but if you want a spot at my table, you will contribute to the house chores, to the mending that needs to be done and the repairs–"

"I'm willing to do that," I cut in.

She purses her lips, sniffling indignantly. She scans my profile, then my body, noticing the calluses on my hands and fingers. I take the moment to look at her as she shifts the weight of the basket again, switching hands, her child-sized, delicate fingers catching the hazy sunlight drifting through the window at our backs.

But it's the tattoo on her ring finger that jolts me back into my body with a start. I step toward her before I can stop myself, my eyes narrowed and honed on the symbol–a circle with two lines just off center.

Her lips part to shout at me to back away, I'm sure, just as Chasten calls from downstairs.

I meet her eyes. "Is that your wedding tattoo?" I ask, and she narrows her eyes at me.

"Where did you say you were from?"

"I didn't," I reply and tear myself from her side, hurrying down the stairs while my mind works overtime.

All married couples in Endova and Teshka get those tattoos. My parents have them, matching sets, and every couple gets a different symbol decided upon by our priestesses.

The tattoos, the Dead Tongue being spoken… am I somehow still in the Deadlands? I find that hard to believe as I wordlessly join Chasten in the foyer, following him through the city in the unforgiving sunlight and heat that sticks to my skin. Here, it's far hotter than any summer I've experienced back home. I keep my head down as people come out of their homes to look at me. Children pause in the dirt, their eyes scanning mine—my face, my body. Silence coats the city as I, their victor, am led to the sparring ring.

I pass a group of women hanging laundry and notice the intricately woven patterns of their clothing—work that can only be done on a loom. Patterns I recognize. Sacred patterns we learned as children. Patterns that echo the stories often told around warming fires and the Harvest Festival.

My head feels suddenly heavy, the headache from yesterday coming back at an alarming rate, but Chasten halts in front of a set of metal doors and pulls them open. It's another walled off area—a pit. A pit full of bored looking men who lean along the cracked stone walls with their arms crossed, their skin tanned from the unrelenting sun.

"Let's get going. We're already hours late," Chasten barks, his voice heavy with frustration, but I'm looking at the weapon belts slung around their waists.

Chasten points to a tall man with short black hair and blue eyes—ice blue, like a glacier. "This is Colin, and that one is Avery. They're twins, if you haven't noticed. Uh, that's one's Rufus—" He points to a man with short brown hair currently sharpening the end of a spear on the far side of the pit, crouched under the shade of a makeshift metal roof covering half of the ring. "Then Colt, Gage, Samson—"

His voice trails off as he makes hasty introductions. I don't smile. I don't offer any type of greeting other than a cold look, but my mind is still reeling with unanswered questions.

"…hand-to-hand first. He just needs to know where her weaknesses are…"

I snap my attention back to Chasten.

"All right, then. Colin, you're up first."

I look at Colin as he kicks off the wall, cracking his knuckles. *Okay, so this is what we're doing.* A little roughhousing. Nothing special. Nothing that's going to help me get out of this place and find Meg and Chessie, which is my only desire.

Colin is tall, built, with large hands and lean, long legs, which I can work with. His center of balance is situated in his hips, which is normal for someone his size. He smirks at his twin brother, who remains along the wall, shifting his weight with a brow raised.

Colin doesn't even have a moment to raise a fist. I whirl, twisting my body in a sharp circle, and kick, my heel colliding with the underside of his jaw. His teeth clack together so violently the sound echoes through the ring, and he falls backward with a sharp exhale, his eyes rolling back in his head.

Every man in the ring straightens to attention in what I can only describe as utter shock, and while this is a training session, I suppose, they don't know me. They don't know my history. They don't know I train men like them. Warriors. Warriors who are only as strong and as capable as they are because *I made them that way.*

It's chaos for a few minutes, but that's all it takes for me to bring every single man to the ground without so much as breaking a nail. The loose sandals Lis gave me this morning are now resting on the far side of the ring, flung off in the carnage. Avery rolls away, holding his face, his nose bleeding profusely. Rufus, the largest of the bunch, crawls on his hands and knees, spitting blood. Colin is knocked out. Who else was there? Oh, the man cradling his balls on the verge of tears is… well, his name doesn't matter.

I rise from a crouch and turn my attention to Chasten, the last man standing, who looks bewildered as he takes several steps away from me with his hands raised.

"Are you fucking joking?" I snarl, rising to my full height. "Is this what you consider training? I was in that arena with *fae.*" I point to his friends—all clearly shifters—and the mess I made so easily. "I got lucky I didn't die during the Culling. I got lucky that whatever binding powers the fae king possessed made it impossible for a fae male to use his wings, or whatever magical gifts they have. Even if I had my wolf, it wouldn't have been a fair fight."

Chasten gapes at me.

"This is child's play," I grind out, pointing to Colin in particular, who I think might have been their best fighter in the bunch had he had a chance to prove it. "Bring me a fae male, or stop wasting my time. I have shit to do–"

"And what would that be?" booms a new voice.

Shivers curl up my spine like wisps of cold smoke as I slowly turn to face the gargantuan man who just walked through the doorway into the sparring ring.

"Fuck," Chasten hisses under his breath before scrubbing a hand down his face, but I lock eyes with the stranger—the man from the balcony. His dark brown hair, just a shade or two darker than mine, is pulled back away from his face in a messy bun at the nap of his neck. His broad, heavily muscled arms bulge through his shirt as he drops several dummy weapons—swords of wood—on the ground at his feet.

He's handsome. Gorgeous. The kind of man who would make my blood heat in an instant in any other situation than this.

His golden-hazel eyes scan the men still crawling away from me, but his expression is flat. Then, he turns his gaze to me.

"You want a fae to play with, wolf? *Are you sure?*"

I notice his pointed ears the very moment he draws back his fist.

DON'T SAY THAT WORD

LEXA

I duck under his punch and twirl around him, sending my fist into his side. My knuckles meet rock-hard flesh and bounce back. He doesn't so much as grunt in pain. He whirls, catching me by the arm in a grip like iron and yanks me toward him before I can find my bearings.

It takes an instant. My life flashes before my eyes as he flips me into the air and slams me down on my back so hard the air rushes from my lungs, my body tingling with shock.

He straddles me, pressing his forearm against my chest like a dead weight. I break past the pain and darkening vision and snatch his shirt with my free hand, my other twisted painfully behind my back. I catch the fabric. It tears over his shoulder, but his other hand grips my wrist and flattens my arm to the ground above my head, my muscles strained to their tearing point.

Mere seconds have passed. That's all it took. Seconds for a man to finally beat me in a fight.

I gasp for breath but smile around the taste of blood. "Fucking prick!"

"Did your mother teach you to talk like that?" His voice is deep, thickly accented, a rolling kind of sound that flutters through my brain like a drumbeat–sensual. But his eyes are hard as steel as he looks down at me, drinking me in, taking in the little details he couldn't see from the balcony, I suspect.

"Come, take the knife out of her pocket, Chasten," he orders, and his man scurries over to us, fishing for the blade I hid there, and snatches it away.

"We don't steal in the Glade," the man says through gritted teeth.

I spit blood at him. He grins.

"You're a wild thing." He turns to look down at my legs, which he has pinned to the ground, his left lower leg angled to bend over my knees. "Not little, by any means. How much do you weigh?"

I try to spit again, but he presses down on my chest until my heart slows.

"Calm down," he commands, but I just grin, my teeth covered in blood.

"I fear," I rasp around the tightness in my chest, "We have to marry. You just paid my bride price."

He narrows his eyes, but all around us the men shift from foot to foot uncomfortably, those standing now gazing down at the show with similar expressions of... confusion.

Chasten's muttered, *"Bride price? Who is her father? Is he here in the Glade?"* sends my mind into a sudden tailspin.

I relax against my will, and Kaleb–because this man can only be the Alpha King everyone keeps mentioning–notices. He eases up on the pressure for several seconds at a time until he finally rises, shoving me once for emphasis, and steps over me.

I roll to my side and cough blood while trying to fill my lungs.

"No more hand-to-hand. She's too advanced for that," he says to the group of battered men along the wall. "When sparring with her, shield yourselves, perhaps? Did no one think to wear their armor this morning?"

"It's a hundred fucking degrees," one of the men whispers under his breath, and Kaleb's head snaps in his direction.

Colin gasps as he comes back to his body, his hand flying to his mouth, where a thick, black bruise is spreading all along his jaw. He's checking to make sure he has all his teeth, I think.

I pant desperately, filling my lungs, and curl onto my hands and knees before wobbling to my feet.

I'm covered in dirt. Dry and red, it stains my clothes. Kaleb, however, continues to walk from man to man, inspecting, scanning, looking them in the eyes until they turn away from his gaze.

Yeah, this fucking bastard is definitely an Alpha. The born kind. I'm sure he was a real fucking problem as a kid, too. Just like me.

I bet he was a biter.

I bet he still is.

He turns his back to face Chasten, and the air leaves my lungs again.

His shirt is flayed open, the fabric falling down his back in a perfect V, highlighting tattoos and... two long, vertical scars on either side of his spine. They're flat and silver against his tan skin, healed like they've been there for a very long time.

He had wings once.

That's the only logical explanation.

He turns back to me with a glower so intense I feel the need to back up several steps, but I force my body to remain where it is.

"Where did you learn to fight? Who was your trainer?"

I tuck my chin in, looking down my nose at him as he stalks in my direction, but the closer he gets, the more I have to look up. He's taller than my dad, which is a feat. It's damn near impossible, I think, because my dad is by far the tallest person in my family of giants. But this man is tall, like the fae. His pointed ears, his rugged, but unnatural, beauty....

I raise my hands as my memories pour over Kieran, my cousin Brie's son. I think of her mate, Logan, and my stomach curls until it knots.

"Where," he asks again, his voice low and commanding, "did you learn to fight?"

"I heard you the first time."

"Then answer," he demands, arching a dark, straight brow. "Where are you from?"

I tilt my chin toward the sky to continue looking him in the eyes as he closes the distance between us. Through my peripheral vision, I see the men I just beat into a pulp saunter off, babying sprained limbs.

"My mother," I say as he postures before me, crossing his muscled arms over his chest. Sweat gleams on his skin, and I feel oddly lightheaded.

"And her pack?"

"My father's pack is Silverhide and my mother is Endovan–"

He snatches my arm and pulls me closer, leaning down to ask in a rough whisper, "What did you just say?" against my temple.

His scent is warm and rich–spiced with everything male. Everything all-consuming and heated. My body lurches, refusing to back away enough, though my heart tangles over the sudden memory of Austin. I tug away, but he pulls me back, tightening his grip.

"My mother is from Endova, in the Deadlands–"

"Never," he breathes, his breath hot against my skin, "say that word again." He suddenly shoves me back as my mind pours over his chosen tone. A dire warning is laced through each word, but his face is shockingly neutral as he turns from me to say to Avery, "I've secured the hunt. Your men will have dusk to dawn before they're forced out of their wolf forms. Make sure they make use of it."

Avery nods and takes those words as a dismissal warning. The other men leave as well, filing out of the sparring ring, but a group of young boys–children, by all means–are gathered at the doorway, pushing and shoving to get a better look at their Alpha.

And me.

Chasten hangs back, unsure whether to follow.

Kaleb turns back to me, looking down at me with so much contempt I can taste it. It's bitter on my tongue. He sizes me up again–looking me up and down–and from this distance I can see the green and gray flakes around his irises–just specks, like scattered gemstones against a blanket of gold.

He glances at the children present but doesn't dismiss them.

"Why is En–"

"No," he says sternly.

I clamp my lips shut for a single second before asking, "Why do you speak the Dead Tongue?"

He looks at me, stares at me in a way that makes me feel like he can see… everything.

"I don't know what you're talking about. Sword." He snaps his fingers, and Chasten tosses him an actual sword–something thin but sharp. I glance at the dummy swords still resting on the ground several feet away, but he shakes his head. "You're past that."

"I won't need a sword once my wolf powers return."

"They won't." He lunges back several feet and swings the sword.

I duck at the last possible second, gasping. "HEY!"

"Fae prefer swordplay. It's more regal to them. More sophisticated." He points the tip at my chest before skillfully swinging it to rest at his side.

"I don't know how to use a sword," I counter.

"Nor a spear, I noticed, after that sloppy show in the Culling."

"I killed that man!"

"Barely. Had you not taken a breath–"

"How close were you watching?–"

"I'm going to make sure everything is moving along for the funerals tonight," Chasten practically shouts. He won't look Kaleb in the eyes as he scurries out of the ring, shooing the little boys out of his way.

It doesn't matter. Kaleb's eyes are locked on mine until Chasten closes the metal doors and locks us in together, then he swings again, jabbing. I jump back.

"Are you trying to kill me?"

He tosses the sword, his eyes suddenly wild as he glances at the door. "Where are you from? Don't fuck with me. Who trained you for this? Who entered you into the Culling? Your master?"

I shake my head. "I–I told you where I'm from. I wasn't trained for this. I'm a captain in Queen Maeve's royal army–"

"Where are you from?"

"I'm from the Deadlands, for fuck's sake! I was taken off the shore of Teshka–"

He raises a hand to silence me. "I will not stand for folklore. You are under my protection now, in my pack, in my city. The odds are already stacked against us, but I took a chance on you rather than letting them throw you to the demons in the king's court–"

"Where are my friends?" I rasp over his outburst. My back hits the wall. I edge to the side, toward the bow I saw hanging when I first came here.

He follows my movements along the wall as my senses scream danger. This man–he's a killer. Someone who lives and breathes violence.

But there's something soft, almost confused, in his eyes as I rip the bow from the wall, scattering arrows from the quiver like I had during the Culling. Before he can blink, I load an arrow, pointing the tip directly at his heart. A kill shot.

"You can't be from Endova," he says, but he doesn't move. He doesn't so much as look down at the arrow pointed at his chest.

"I am. I don't know what else to say. I don't know why that's so hard to believe. Where am I exactly? Your man, Chasten, wouldn't tell me."

He stares at me, barely breathing.

"Where am I? Why have I been taken? I know you know. You were on the balcony with the king. You knew my name–"

"Your friends," he rasps, eyes narrowing, "At least the blonde one. She's safe."

"I don't believe you."

"Then believe this. You are not safe at all. These games are forced, rigged. You will be fighting for your life the entire time against a victor that's already been chosen as the champion."

"I don't plan on staying."

"You cannot escape this place," he says so quietly I nearly miss it. "I don't believe you're from the homeland. I think you hit your head. I think you're delusional. A liar, and I have a pack to protect. I'll take you out of the games myself if I must."

I tremble from holding my arrow primed for so long. "I am the daughter of Alpha King Ryan and Luna Aviva of the Deadlands, granddaughter of the Patriarch Jerrod of Endova. Cousin of the Queen Maeve of the Firestones of Eastonia. I am not afraid of you. I am not afraid of the fae. I will go home. I will save my warriors, and I will leave fire in my wake!"

He stares silently, his eyes like polished gems but darkening with every passing second.

"Where am I?" I repeat, my tone leaving no room for argument. "Am I in Emberfyll? Somewhere nearby?"

He closes his eyes and winces at the mention of Emberfyll. "Put down your bow."

"No. Tell me where I am. Explain all of this."

He takes a step forward, and I fire. He catches the arrow like it's nothing, like he's had thousands of arrows aimed at his heart. He tosses it to the ground and catches me before I can turn for more.

SECRETS OF THE GLADE

My heart skips a beat, then another, as Kaleb releases his grip on my arm. His dark, wavy hair is tied back, but rogue strands fall around his chiseled face. Everything about Kaleb is masculine. His height–several inches taller than me–tall enough that he has to look down at me–catches me off guard, as well as the way he moves with a predators grace–light on his feet but with determination in every step, muscles flexed, the fabric of his torn shirt rippling down his middle.

I think he's about to cage me against the rough metal wall of the sparring ring, but he steps past me, reaching for a long, wooden spear, and fists it, turning gracefully with the weapon in his hand, like it's his toy of choice.

"You're going to learn to use these."

"Why?"

"Because you won't just be fighting men in the Trials." He whips the spear around and pins the point in the dirt with practiced grace, leaning his weight against it. "You'll be up against much worse than men."

"There's nothing worse than men," I counter, and he inspects me for a moment before giving me a smirk that ignites that heat I want to scrub from my body. It tingles, mixing with the guilt currently cutting through me like a dull blade, but I'm at its mercy. Austin died less than two days ago, I think, unless I was out for a while after being taken.

I thought he was attractive, yes. Of course I did, but he felt it far stronger than I did. I don't want to think that, but...

This strange, overwhelming feeling only grows as Kaleb postures a few feet away. Sweat glints on his golden skin, highlighting a network of webbed, interlocking scars. I bristle as my gaze slowly moves up and down his body–what I can see, at least, beyond his clothing.

My mouth goes dry when he slowly takes off his shirt, his eyes locked on mine, crumbling it before tossing it against the wall. He's massive. A god in the form of a man, really. He's not lean by any means but sculpted in a way that shows me exactly how strong he is. He could break me into pieces with his hands. He could toss me over the sparring ring wall. He could smother me. He could–

"You're in Pantharas, the capital of the fae kingdom, and over the next six weeks, you'll compete in the Trials," he says, his voice low and monotone. "Wherever you came from doesn't matter. Whether anyone is coming to your aid doesn't matter. You survived the Culling, and now you're a victor, and I chose to sponsor you because you might actually make it out of this alive if you take it seriously."

I chew the inside of my cheek, taking in his words. He continues, "If you win the Trials, if you somehow make it to the end and become the last person standing, you'll be granted whatever your heart desires by the king. Riches. Gold. A castle overlooking the lake where the fae promenade." He smirks, disgust in his eyes. "Whatever you want."

"I want to go home."

"Then win."

He tosses the spear. I catch it by reflex, but it feels unnatural in my hands. Lanky and light, I fumble with where to put my hands, and he just watches me, taking notes, I think, based on the look on his face as he watches the way my fingers move over the smooth, worn wood.

"You use a bow primarily?"

"No," I rush out, trying to stab the sharp end of the spear into the ground like he did, but it's a lot more difficult than he made it look. "Twin blades, preferably."

"Why?"

"Why not? Everyone has their favorite choice of weapon. My mother loves a bow; my father loves his fists," I say with a shrug. "Or his teeth or claws. I like my blades."

He glances at the wall where the weapons rest, scanning his inventory. Crude weapons, I realize upon further inspection. The metal doesn't glint in the hot sunlight. Everything is dull, meant for practice, and very old.

All I want to do is run. I want to shift and take off, faster than the speed of light, tearing through everyone in my way, but I can't feel my wolf at all. My senses feel as dull as the weapons hanging on rusted hooks.

I slowly turn back to Kaleb, who's still eyeing me closely, like he's waiting for me to suddenly strike.

"I believe I was given Wolfsbane," I tell him, finally just tossing the spear to the ground and closing my arms over my chest. "I can't remember a Goddess-damned thing. I don't know how I got here. I don't know how long I've been here, but I can't feel my wolf anymore. I can't feel anything but–"

"Hunger?"

I catch his gaze. He nods, stepping to the side to get out of the glare of the sun as it inches above the wall of the sparring ring, casting even more unrelenting heat directly onto us.

"You won't be able to access your ability to shift at all unless the fae deem it appropriate."

"What?"

"You can't shift in the Glade. There might be a trial where the king lifts his shields and allows you to shift, but until that moment, you're stuck in this current form."

I let my arms fall to my sides. "He's magically preventing wolves from shifting?"

He nods. "It's always been like this."

"Why? What's going on here? The wall–the Culling–the–" I point at him with a sudden realization that rocks me to my core. The pointed ears, the strength, the height and beauty... "You're fae too, but not completely."

"We're called halflings," he says dryly, like this isn't a surprise at all. "My father was a shifter, and my mother was not."

"You're harder to kill."

"I am impossible to kill," he corrects, and playful gleam lights in his golden-hazel eyes for a split second before they darken again. "But yes, halflings are very strong. We're bred that way on purpose. Shifter strength, agility, and aggressiveness with a side of fae intelligence, at least they believe. There's a small army of men like me, some women, too, but generally, we're used for other purposes."

My mouth goes painfully dry. "That's terrible."

He holds my gaze. "It is."

"And these people?" I point to the door, where life simply moves on around us. "They're stuck here, unable to shift? Unable to hunt?"

"Yeah."

"Why haven't you put an end to it? You're their Alpha King."

It strikes a nerve. His jaw twitches, and he finally breaks from the stare that's been pulling me apart, piece by piece. "You're not here for a history lesson. Pick up the spear and get–"

The door opens again quite suddenly, and Chasten reappears, this time with an elderly man, and Kaleb immediately stiffens. The old man looks at me and gives me a kind, grandfatherly smile that instantly shatters my heart. I think of my dad, then my grandpa, Isaac, and feel suddenly so utterly far from home that my knees go weak. Bile rises in my throat–fear, something I rarely feel. Something wholly new to me.

I only notice Kaleb staring at me with his eyes narrowed in what might be concern when Chasten says, drawing back his attention, "You're being summoned to the gate."

Kaleb cuts him off with a wave of the hand. "It's the extra wood for the pyres. Otto, go down and tell the men putting the pyres together to meet me at the main gate to start moving logs down into the pit." He glances at me before saying to Chasten, "Take her home. We'll continue this tomorrow after the men return from the hunt."

I'M NOT SURE HOW TO PASS THE TIME. MY MIND WANDERS AND REELS over how to get out of this situation, how to save Meg and Chessie, and my family back home, while I pace the snug, wood-lined bedroom Lis set me up in. It's sparsely furnished and stifling in the heat of the day—early afternoon, from what I can tell. I haven't eaten since breakfast, but I think that might be common around the Glade. No one looks well fed other than Kaleb and men like him—halflings. I wonder if their fae heritage has something to do with their size despite the nutritional odds stacked against them.

I only leave the room when I hear female voices through the floorboards. For a moment, I'm sure I hear Meg and race downstairs, panting as I skid to a stop in front of the two unfamiliar women now cowering and owl-eyed behind Lis, who frowns up at me, a large basket of fabric at her feet.

"Sorry," I murmur, and turn toward the stairs, but she stops me with a light touch on the arm.

"Don't be. And you two, don't be rude," she chides the two young women still looking at me in awe. "This is Lexa, and she's not as scary as she looks."

Uh, thanks?

"Elise and Miriam were just stopping by to pick up a part for their loom. I had some extra fabric to give them, but they're being awfully picky," she continues with a hint of annoyance, and the young women, both mousy blondes with bright green eyes—maybe sisters, possibly twins—whip around and move to the door so swiftly they stumble over each other on their way out, slamming the door behind them, and leaving the fabric behind.

Lis sighs heavily, shaking her head.

"I didn't mean to interrupt."

"You didn't. You saved me, honestly. They're beautiful girls but pea-brained, just like their mother."

I clamp my lips together at the insult, especially from someone as innocent looking as Lis. She's not innocent, I realize for maybe the second or third time. Lis is kind of mean. I like that about her. She reminds me of Maeve.

Lis is the queen of this house, just like Maeve is the Queen of Eastonia. I'm sure they'd get along.

She pats the swell of her belly as she looks at the door with another long, dramatic sigh, but my eyes are on the basket of fabric at her feet.

"Um, are you really not going to use that?"

"This? It's just scrap. I was thinking of making rags–"

"Can I have it?"

"Why?" The accusation in her tone is sharp, but I get it. She doesn't trust me. Yet. She'll come around.

"I can sew. I need to make a new dress for the Trials. Mine got ruined."

"You want to wear a dress during the Trials? Kaleb already has someone making you a set of armor. I'm actually supposed to be taking your measurements. I could do that now."

"No need. And I don't need armor. I just need some fabric, some leather cord, and a needle and thread."

She looks me up and down in an appraising fashion that makes me wonder if she believes someone like me is able to sit still long enough to stitch fabric together.

"What? You don't think a giantess like me can handle a needle and thread?"

"I'm just surprised. That's all." She motions to the basket. "It's yours. Take it. I'll give you some needles, but I'm going to count them in case you think you can slip one under your pillow and kill us all in your sleep."

She tilts her head down a very narrow hallway with a door at the very end, which opens to a storage room, but in the corner there's a loom, a tapestry half woven but covered in dust, like it hasn't been touched in many years.

I watch her from the doorway as she gathers the supplies I need, but my eyes dart to the loom again. It's the same as they all are–the same design, the same outcome.

I learned to weave from my aunt Freya. She's the best at it. An artist. All the girls my age did when we were young. It was part of our schooling. Some traditions didn't die even with my modern father at the helm of our pack.

"It belonged to Kaleb's sister, Alice," she says, noticing my stare.

"Belonged?" The word cracks, splitting. I clear my throat.

"Alice died a few years ago in childbirth." She rises, placing a small sewing box in my hand. "Ten years ago now, actually. I can't believe it's been that long."

"How?" Something aches deep in my chest. I can't put my finger on it, can't find where the pain comes from. It's like the grief lingering there doesn't belong to me.

Lis takes a moment to reply. I'm about to apologize for prying when she says under her breath, "Female shifters cannot have fae babies." Her eyes meet mine. She must see the question in my eyes because she continues so softly I almost miss it, "The wings, you know. They get stuck. Halflings always come from fae mothers. Alice was not fae."

I have a sudden image of the twin scars along Kaleb's back before I shove it away.

WORD FROM A FRIEND

Kaleb

The night sky melts into shades of orange and red as the first pyres are lit. Small crowds gather to throw flowers, coins, and other personal tokens into the crackling flames and smoke, which paint the sky a deep, rolling black, swallowing the stars.

I stand in the shadow of the space between two buildings, my arms crossed, my skin already prickling with the heat fanning off the funeral fires. The flames will burn all night. It'll take a massive amount of energy to burn through four-hundred bodies, but by morning, only ashes and flickering embers will remain, and the souls of those we lost to the fae and their twisted games will have been released into the world that waits for all mortals.

I'm not sure I'm going there, to be honest. I'll meet every fae king, their lords, and their warriors who allow this to happen at the gates of hell, and that's a promise.

A smooth, graceful shadow melds with mine as robes carrying the perfumed scent of roses and camphor swish to a stop beside me.

Silas sighs heavily, the deep blue hood of his cloak obstructing half of his face. A sharp nose and perfectly chiseled, almost feminine features give away his nature. He's fae. Fully fae.

He's also my brother.

A *half-brother*, at least, older than me by fifty years or so, but he looks to be only about twenty-five, which is when these bastards stop aging at a normal, mortal rate. He's young for a fairy, all things considered, yet holds a prime position within the king's court. Our mother was to thank for that.

"My men have just delivered a funeral feast to the pack house, courtesy of his Highness," Silas drawls as he adjusts the flaps of his cloak, his pale white fingers catching the firelight. "I doubled it. It should be enough food to last a week or so for the whole pack, and there's more on the way."

"You didn't have to do that."

"Of course I did. You're all starving."

"Well, that's what your king wants, isn't it? Keep us weak and hungry? We're more amiable that way."

Silas rolls his lower lip between his teeth as he gazes at the pyres, at the people now kneeling or standing just in front of the flames. "I tried to stop the king from pulling so many from the Glade, and you know that."

I flex then relax my shoulders, rolling my neck to try to ease the tension there that won't ever go away. "What do you want me to say, Silas? Do you want me to thank you? Look at these people—these women—and tell me how I should feel about four-hundred fathers, brothers, and sons being ripped from their homes to fight to the death."

Silas stands in silence for several long, aching moments before replying, "I will make this right. You know the plans in place."

I turn into the darkness, walking several paces between the buildings. "It's too late for that. The games have already begun. There's no stopping them now. No one can stop them, even your precious resistance."

Silas hurries after me, bowing his head to keep his face hidden from the shifters weaving through the streets toward the pyres along the far wall. Not that he needs to. It's not uncommon for fae lords or guards to be seen in the Glade. It's also common knowledge that Silas and I shared a mother. Halflings aren't uncommon at all.

Silas eyes another halfling as the large, lumbering man steps between us on his way to the pyres.

"Another one of our brothers?" I joke, and Silas throws me a cutting glare.

"That's not funny."

"I find it funny," I remark with a soft growl as I close in on the tangle of four-story shanties where my home rests, "that most halflings from the Glade weren't chosen for the Culling to begin with. It's what we are bred for. They all came from the fae cities."

"The king made the call, not me."

"Obviously," I reply, turning to face him. "What do you want, Silas? Did you only come to tell me you've delivered food to my starving people? Are you here to pay your respects or to rub this in my face?"

Silas eyes me coolly before replying, "I thought your victor would like to know that her friend, Chessie, is safe and settling in."

The thought of Lexa—which I've spent the entire day trying to scrub from my mind—ignites the questions that took root during her sparring session this morning and the uneasy feeling I've carried all day.

"I'd like to see Lexa myself," Silas adds, trying to step around me to access my front door. I stop him with a hand on his chest.

"No, I'll tell her anything you'd like to convey."

"Do you not trust me anymore?"

"Seeing as we're sponsors of competing victors," I begin, dropping my hand to my side, "I can't allow you to speak with her. I can't risk you trying to sway the outcome."

Silas searches my eyes. "The outcome has already been decided."

"Then all you're doing by relaying the fact you're not starving, torturing, or assaulting her friend is leading her to believe they all have a chance of getting out of this alive. They're lambs being fattened for slaughter, and you know that."

He steps into me. "The outcome of your Trial was also decided weeks before your round of the Culling, Kaleb. Now, tell me again that your victor doesn't have a chance of repeating history?"

"And yours?"

Silas leans away, his face shadowed by a flash of grief, of the cold, hard truth. "You believed that Lexa has a special connection to Chessie, which is why you asked that I sponsor her and keep her close, and I believe you're correct. They're friends. They're deeply bonded. If you can keep Lexa alive, I can keep Chessie alive for as long as possible. I'll find a way to ensure they're placed in the same rounds of the upcoming games together. We can draw out the games that way and give my people more time to act. You already agreed to this plan during the Culling. You *agreed.*"

I should ask him if Chessie has given him any idea where she's from, but I refrain.

After a beat of silence, he says, "Chessie wants Lexa to know that she's okay, and she's comfortable and entertained. She has all the books she could ever want, and she finds the maids and servants in my house friendly and warm. She also told me she enjoys my company, as well, and she wanted Lexa to know that. She's worried Lexa is going… what did she say? *Nuts* with worry. I assume that's a bad thing."

"Don't get attached, Silas."

He smirks—an expression I see in the mirror often enough. It's the only thing between us that's even close to familial. "I'll start having my men move the food into the storeroom at the pack house."

"I'll make sure you're not fucking us over on the supplies."

"I'll see you soon, then." He leaves without another word, blending into the shadows. Colin's three younger sisters step out of one of the houses lining the courtyard and quickly dip out of sight when they see me, their bodies angled toward the street as they move toward the pyres to say their respects and cast their prayers in Colin's stead, seeing as he's hunting tonight with Avery and a few other men.

I turn toward my house and exhale deeply before moving into the darkness and closing the door behind me.

It's quiet in the house. Lis and Chasten are down at the pyres with the rest of the pack. Lexa, however, is not.

I climb the stairs to the second floor and turn into the snug hallway housing her room. I don't knock. The door isn't locked. It's my house, after all.

Lexa rises from bed and curls her hands into fists, prepared to defend herself as I step into the room and close the door behind me by leaning against it. Fabric is scattered all over the room, and the beginnings of what I believe is a dress of some kind rests on the quilt covering her bedspread.

I haven't spoken to her since this morning after I practically dragged her by her hair around the sparring ring. All of my men will have new scars and chipped teeth thanks to her, but I can't readily admit it's a bad thing. She's stronger than any man I've ever trained. She's quick on her feet and oblivious to pain.

But it's clear she didn't know what it felt like to be bested, to be beaten, until today.

I catch the flicker of uncertainty in her eyes when I cross my arms over my chest and level her with a patronizing look.

"Get out," she sneers.

"Gladly. But I come bearing news of your friend Chessie. I thought you might like to know that I spoke to her sponsor."

She immediately drops her fists to her side, her deep, dark blue eyes widening. Yeah, Silas was correct when he mentioned that these two women are deeply bonded. Not sisters, though. They look nothing alike.

"And?"

"She's safe and well looked after."

"I don't believe you."

"She mentioned how you were probably going nuts with worry?"

She blinks then looks down to hide the smallest, most relieved smile touching her lips. I feel a jolt of... maybe guilt, when she looks back into my eyes. She's beautiful; I'll give her that. Hot-headed and overconfident, however, which are two traits I tend to beat out of any warrior who wants to train with my men. Overconfidence kills.

Brash, rushed decisions are a death sentence. She's going to need to learn that if she has any shot of keeping her head attached to her neck.

"Where is she exactly?"

"She's been sponsored by a fae nobleman named Silas. I know him well. He treats her fairly. More than that, I believe, knowing him."

She searches my face, but I keep my expression and feelings on the matter skillfully guarded. But there is something I need to discuss with her that's been weighing heavily on my mind all day—something I need to clear up before I end up in a duel with her father.

"You mentioned your bride price. Paying it was never my intention. Who is your father, and what pack does he hail from? I can get a message beyond the wall to clear this up—"

"Well, hopefully your messenger has a fucking boat," she says with so much vitriol I can taste it.

I arch a brow, scanning her face for inconsistencies.

"I already told you where I'm from and who my father is. I wasn't lying. I wouldn't make shit up unless it helped me get out of this fucked up situation."

"You can't be from Endova because Endova doesn't exist anymore. It's folklore."

"Well, so are the missing tribes of the Deadlands," she says pointedly. "There used to be dozens, according to the stories of my people in Endova. So is this where they went? Or have I been thrust through time and living in the days of hell and famine in the aftermath of the fall of the Firestone queens?"

"Then Eastonia still exists?"

"Of course it does," she says quietly, but her eyes turn dark with sudden rage. "And I hope… I pray they don't come for me because they'll be wasting their time."

I hold her gaze, noticing the flecks of silver around her irises—the strange way they shift and deepen, like blinking stars.

"Why would they be wasting their time?"

"There will be nothing left of this place when I'm done."

"Many men have said the same." I smooth my hands down my

thighs. "If you're done licking your wounds, I need help in the pack house."

"I have no interest–"

"If you want to eat, you will pull your weight," I cut in.

She stiffens but looks away from me, her gaze settling on the door at my back. "Training begins tomorrow–just you and me."

"Training for what? Another massacre like the Culling?"

"No," I breathe, knots tangling in my chest as I look at her–really look at her. She's so young. Somewhere in her early twenties. So confident. So impressionable. Beautiful and fierce, though. The kind of woman I might have allowed myself to pursue if I felt I had any kind of future to give to a family.

But not here. Never here.

"The first Trial is a week from now. The Beast Trial."

"Beasts?"

I nod. "You'll be allowed to shift during this Trial. I confirmed it."

"What do you mean by beast?"

"Think of the worst possible thing you could see in your night-mares," I tell her, turning toward the door, "and double it. Triple it. Come on, we have people to feed."

BROTHER OF MINE

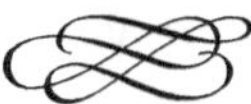

LEXA

The pack house of the Glade is remarkably similar to the ones in Silverhide and Endova. It's a single wide, airy room with multiple entrances to the outside world but no windows. Long tables stretch in its center, but smaller tables and wobbly stools meant for moving around are scattered throughout the space. There's a kitchen in the back–crude, however, with not much more than a few work tables and a wood-fired stove for cooking. But it's the storeroom off the kitchen that takes my breath away, and not for the reason it should have.

It's nearly empty. Bags of flour, oats, and rice are depleted to near critical levels–barely enough to feed a single family. Dried, smoked meat hangs from hooks on the ceiling, scrapped down to the bone. I step out of the way as another set of fae–servants, I believe–step past me carrying bags of what smells like grain. They keep stacking and stacking but barely make a dent in what's needed, and some of the ice guarding my heart melts at the sight of a barrel full of apples being wheeled in.

But I turn when Kaleb speaks in quiet tones to another fae man in more regal clothing–dark blue robes with golden thread laced throughout and crystal buttons on his lapel. Kaleb rolls his neck before looking down at the ledger in the man's hands, but then another group of fae walk into the storeroom, and I freeze, my stomach leaping into my throat.

My gasp is, unfortunately, audible. Kaleb's eyes lift to my face, but I'm staring at the two men–I think–wheeling another barrel of something past the entrance of the storeroom and into the kitchen proper.

"It's milk," the regal fae man says to Kaleb with a soft shrug. "For butter–"

"Come here," Kaleb says sternly, his words directed at me.

I'm frozen in place as the two strange beings walk past the entrance of the storeroom again and back out of sight.

"Lexa, come here," Kaleb repeats in a tone that would have cut through me like a knife had I not been fighting for my life not to faint or scream.

I move toward the entrance of the storeroom–where I've been tasked with cleaning the shelves in preparation for new supplies. I scrunch the rag in my fist until water starts to bead against my skin as I step through the doorway and glance through the door leading out of the kitchen and into a smoke scented night, where several fae are unloading barrels and bags, organizing them before bringing them inside.

The dark blond fae male smiles softly down at me when I edge toward Kaleb's side. He looks familiar, and I realize with a start that this is the man who sponsored Chessie–the one with the kind voice and even kinder words when she'd been chosen and taken. Silas.

Kaleb glances at the man before looking down at me with a rough sigh. "Are you going to manage, or do you need a moment to catch your breath?"

I break my gaze with the blond fae sponsor–wealthy, from what I can tell–and glance toward the door again. "What are they?"

"Are you going to introduce me formally or should I–"

"This is Silas," Kaleb says shortly but gives the man a nudge, forcing him back a step, putting a foot of distance between our group.

Silas rolls his eyes—blue, like the ocean—at Kaleb. "Why are you always like this? It's not like I bite." He gives me another boyish smile, his eyes gleaming with mischief. "Unless you like that, of course."

Kaleb shoves Silas hard, and the man stumbles back, his wings suddenly flaring from his back in a simmer of velvet blue the same color as his eyes.

I rear back, another involuntary gasp ripping through my teeth as my back hits the doorframe of the storeroom, and every fae servant currently organizing food on the cart outside turns to us, squinting through the glare of the light pouring through the kitchen door, illuminating the darkness beyond.

Silas's wings ripple as he tucks them back along his back and frowns at Kaleb. "That was unnecessary."

"Leave," Kaleb growls, but Silas looks at me instead, sizing me up, drinking me in.

"Did he tell you I'm Chessie's sponsor? She's fine, I assure you. A little wound up and confused, but I gather all three of you are feeling that way. You more than the rest, given that you're stuck with him." He jabs a thumb in Kaleb's direction. "He's not all bad, you know. Just a little grumpy. He doesn't eat enough, I'm afraid."

Another low, wolfish growl leaves Kaleb's throat, but I stare at Silas and Kaleb for several seconds, furrowing my brow as sudden glaring similarities glimmer to the surface. Their mouths are the same—the same expressions twitch at the corners of their lips. The high, chiseled cheekbones and strong, expressive brows…

I glance at Kaleb, who looks into my eyes like he's desperately trying to tell me something, but then, the two men come back into the kitchen, ignoring us as they move to the storeroom.

I can't ignore them, though. One has scaly gray skin that shines with an oily sheen. His eyes are far too large for his face and totally black, but a honeycomb of muted color lies within, like a fly. Spindly wings a quarter of the size of Silas's flicker as he helps his companion carry in two more heavy bags of grain. The other is similar, with strange, almost webbed skin in a color I've never seen outside of a forest before. Both have grayish skin, but this second... thing is larger than the first, and he only has one wing. Just one.

Neither of the men–the beings–look at me, but when I turn back to Silas and Kaleb, who are wearing similar expressions, but Silas is the first to crack.

"You didn't tell her?"

Kaleb widens his stance, crossing his arms over his broad chest. The men wait for the servants to leave again, but the second Silas reaches for me to turn me back to the conversation, Kaleb acts.

He shoves Silas back again and grabs my wrist, tugging me through the kitchen and into the pack house proper, which is empty save for us. The doors to the city are open, however, and it's silent. A red-orange glow lights the night sky. My stomach twists at the scent of smoke filling the air.

Kaleb finally lets me go and turns to me and Silas, his eyes flicking to the fae man before glowering down at me like I'm nothing more than a splinter in his heel, and I glower back. Silas looks between us with a smirk before leaning his thigh against one of the tables.

"They're dozens of kinds of fae," Silas explains, pausing to allow Kaleb to cut in, but he continues after a moment, "High fae, like me. The pretty ones." He tosses me a charming smile and then continues, "and the others. Water fae are especially prevalent here in Pantharas–"

"Because your kings enslaved them," Kaleb cuts in, and Silas frowns.

"Yes, well, it doesn't negate the fact that the selkies and undines make up a large population here. Not in the Glade, but regardless. She needs to get used to seeing them." He turns to direct his words at me. "Anything that doesn't look like us," he explains, pointing to me and Kaleb, then to himself, "are called lesser fae."

"Why lesser?"

"Because...well..." Silas stumbles over his thoughts.

Kaleb shakes his head as he braces his hands flat on the table. "Because anyone not full-blooded high fae is considered lesser, less important, and disposable."

"Are—are shifters considered fae?"

Kaleb and Silas pause then look at each other. An identical laugh escapes them, and it catches me off guard. More so, seeing Kaleb laugh. It's entirely unnerving in a way I didn't expect. He's incredibly, overwhelmingly handsome when he smiles, even if it's at my expense.

I scowl to hide my blush.

"No, you're not fae," Silas answers.

"But he is," I say, my tone more accusatory than I intended.

Kaleb looks at me through his dark, thick lashes. I feel another jolt of awareness—of the fact he's looking right at me. Another pang of guilt and confusion works through my body like a heated blade when Austin's memory curls through my subconscious.

It hadn't... hurt in the way I expected when he died. Not like it would have hurt if we'd actually been mates.

Which only makes me feel worse.

"She's tired, Silas. We'll continue this conversation at some other time."

"Well, it is the middle of the night," Silas says with marked annoyance.

"You didn't have to stay while your men unloaded their goods."

"You haven't even thanked me for it, you know."

"I don't need to."

"Well, I'll consider those words next time I feel like being generous."

Kaleb smirks at Silas, and Silas smirks back, and then I see it. I realize it.

"You're brothers."

Both men slowly turn to look at me like they've forgotten I'm here. Silas purses his lips, glancing at Kaleb and deciding, for once, to allow Kaleb to speak first.

"We share a mother," Kaleb says, and Silas just nods like this isn't a damning revelation.

I think of Alice, a woman I've never met, while trying to meld the lines of relation between what sounds like a complicated family. I turn to Silas, speechless, hoping he's going to give me some insight, but he just backs away from the table, his body angled to leave the pack house all together. "I'm the older, wiser, and more handsome one, but yes. Unfortunately, we share some blood."

Kaleb shakes his head, but I can tell he's feeling lighter. That steely, hateful expression he's been wearing since the moment we met only this morning fades into… just him. Who he is.

Someone calls out for him in the kitchen, and he leaves without so much as casting a glance back in my direction, which makes me believe he trusts Silas to be alone with me, even if I find it impossible to trust either of them.

"Chessie told me about the battle," Silas says quietly. "On the beach, where your regiment was stationed."

"I'm not going to divulge any details."

"She also mentioned you're secretive."

I purse my lips. He smiles as if in confirmation.

"She is fine, you know. She's comfortable."

"She's not meant to be in games like this."

"I am aware."

"Then why choose her as your champion, or victor, whatever you call it? Chessie is a trained warrior, yes, but she's… she's always been softer than the rest of us. She won't win."

"She'll be with you."

"Kaleb doesn't think I have a shot either. He made it clear I can't even escape this place."

He's quiet for a moment. He looks around the shabby pack house with a soft sigh. "Kaleb was adamant I take Chessie, so I did. He chose you, and you can't take that lightly. I chose Chessie to keep her safe and out of the hands of the other sponsors. He chose you because he is the best trainer in our lands. You can, and will, win these games."

"And then what? I get whatever I want? What good is that to me if I can never return home?"

"There are other powers at play."

I glance at the kitchen, but Kaleb is out of sight. "What do you mean?"

"Give Kaleb a chance. He's not as bad as he seems. He's just… he's been dealt an impossible hand."

"Alice?"

Silas pales. "Where did you hear that name?"

Kaleb walks back into the room, and Silas leans away from me, looking grave. He clears his throat, saying in passing, "I'll see you both in a few days, whenever the king calls for a training demonstration, which I believe will be soon."

"And Meg? Is she safe? Is she all right?" I call out, but Silas stops beside Kaleb, the two of them sharing a singular look that makes me believe Meg is safe but not necessarily in the best hands.

THE CHAMPION

Lexa

Days pass in a blur of pain, hunger, and little sleep. From the moment the stars begin to fade in the sky to the second the moon rises over the Glade, I'm in the sparring ring. Kaleb is always there, always watching, always discerning every movement in a cutting silence that I believe made it possible for me to dissociate my feelings, worries, and outright concern over my situation and the welfare of my friends and the task at hand.

I can't get out of this.

There is nothing I can do to change my circumstances.

"Again," Kaleb says with no emotion, his tone dry and heavy as it bounces through the ring, off every curve of rusted metal. I throw the spear. Again and again, until my shoulder aches, and I have to switch sides. I'm right handed, but he has me practicing on the left side as well, just as often, in the event I... lose my arm.

"Again," he bellows.

I send the spear tearing through the hot, sticky air. It pierces through the abdomen of the practice dummy in the center of the ring and lodges itself in the dirt. Kaleb doesn't react even though it's the best throw I've accomplished all morning.

I stagger backward into the shade, sweat pouring down my temples and dripping down my neck. My skin gleams as I wipe my brow with the back of my hand and shake my head when he motions for me to come back, to keep at it.

"I'm done. I won't do this anymore. I don't need this training, and you know it. All fucking week, you've known it. You're just trying to keep me busy and tired so I don't scale the fucking wall like I want to."

"This is what you're going to do until the Trials begin."

"It's been a week. What's the holdup?"

This is the most we've spoken all week. Kaleb isn't a chatty guy by any means, and he normally looks at me like I'm the worst thing to ever happen to him and his pack, and that he'd rather be getting his teeth pulled one by one than spending a single second in my company.

"You really think I know?"

"Well, you're the Alpha King of the Glade, aren't you? Surely–"

"I'm a slave, Lexa. My title means very little."

"Then why do you even have it?"

He's quiet for a moment, his jaw working as he grinds his teeth– annoyed with me, I think. Of course he is. There isn't a kind, amiable bone in this man's body.

I sink to the dirt, splaying out my legs as sweat drips down my neck. I still wear the clothes Lis gave me. I'm saving my new dress for the Trials. I won't waste it here, in the dirt, where it won't be stained with blood after a long, hard day's work.

I'll sweat in rags. I don't care.

Kaleb slowly walks toward me, stepping into the shade, and leans his shoulder against one of the metal posts holding up the rusted canopy meant to keep us out of the heat.

I look up at him, tired, hot, and irritated. "I guess I should be seeking Silas out whenever I have questions about my captivity."

"Silas won't be helpful either."

"He's a lot more talkative than you are," I reply, reaching up to unravel the tight braids currently making my head pound.

He rolls his lower lip between his teeth as he eyes me, but his expression is softer than before. Still, he's silent, and I can't stand it anymore.

"You know what?" I laugh bitterly, glaring at him. "I've been through real hell and then got dropped into an even deeper level of hell where I've lived for the past week. This is insane. You know that, right? The way your pack is forced to live? Gods, when my cousins find out…" I shake my head. "You've just had me in this pit, practicing moves I already know. You don't talk to me. You don't answer my questions. Lis walks on eggshells around me and acts like she can't talk openly with me when I ask her questions, so I've just been alone–"

"Because she knows you're going to die soon and isn't trying to get attached," he says bluntly, and I laugh.

"Oh please. You don't know me."

"I know enough to know you're a spoiled princess of an Alpha King. I know you're used to food in your belly and a world that bows to you instead of the other way around."

"You don't know shit about me," I repeat caustically. Memories of the shore of Teshka funnel back, and the deep, dark grief that's been fading with each passing day twists into guilt I've been trying to beat into submission. He must catch a flicker of it behind my eyes because he latches onto it.

"Overconfidence is a killer, Lexa. You think you're ready for whenever the king comes to call, but you're not. What you'll see– what you'll be forced to do in those games… it'll change you for life. Even if you win, you'll lose."

"How would you know?" I shake my head again, chuckling. "It's not like you've even stepped foot in that arena before–"

"I won."

My heart stops. I slowly look up at him, but his expression is cast in shadow, his eyes gleaming a soft gold in the pockets of sunlight dancing through the holes in the awning above his head.

I open my mouth to argue, but only a strange whine comes out– shock, I suppose, because that's all I feel as I gaze up at this… beast of a man.

"I wasn't supposed to win," he says as he crouches, his muscles flexed all over and glistening with sweat. I feel that slight ache I've been berating myself internally to ignore, but I can't help it. Goddess, a man like him back home? Every girl in Silverhide would have been going absolutely, positively feral over him and doing anything in their power to get his attention. "Just like you're not supposed to win."

"It's fixed, then? It's a rigged system?"

"Of course it is." He leans back until he's seated on the ground just a few feet away from me, his arms resting on his knees. His scarred knuckles pop as he flexes and then curls his hands. "It's for entertainment but also distraction. Silas has been talking about a rebellion brewing for so long I'm beginning to wonder if he's dreaming it up, but the king called the games, and Silas believes it's to cover some ongoing strife between the king and the rebels."

I'm not sure what to say because this man hasn't spoken plainly to me like this... ever. I've only been here a week, sure, but he's acted like I'm some parasite until this very moment. Whatever. I can keep my cool.

"What do these games have to do with a rebellion?"

"I don't know. Not yet. Silas wants me to join, but I can barely keep my own people alive as it stands. The fae could cut off our access to food immediately. Work the servants they use from the Glade to the bone. Separate families. I walk a fine line with the king as it stands, and I can't do anything to risk my people, even if in the off chance it–"

"Frees them?"

"The shifters in Pantharas will never be free, even with a different king on the throne. It was not what our kind was brought here for."

I think of the songs and folklore I grew up with, about the tribes who faded into the mists that came at the end of the war that saw the downfall of the Firestone Queens and the veil. Mist that... took me, too.

I think of Austin's dying moment again and curl into myself.

"You still don't believe I'm from Eastonia, do you?"

"I don't know what to believe about you," he answers. "It doesn't matter, to be honest. It won't change your outcome."

"What will?"

"Training," he says, and to my great surprise, he smirks.

"You know, that's how I realized you and Silas were related. That smirk right there."

"We're not as similar as I'm sure you—and he—would like to think."

"Oh, I can see it plainly now. Whatever genetics made him kind and fun skipped you entirely, though."

He flashes another soft but short smirk, like he doesn't know how to fully smile.

"I have a sister," I tell him, and I'm unsure why I feel the need to even bring up Nora given the circumstances. "She's a year younger than me. We're barely similar, but everyone can tell we're sisters. She's like Silas—funny, soft, and sweet." I taper off as her memory chokes me half to death. I wonder if I'll ever see her again. "She loves to paint, whereas even my handwriting is atrocious. She can sing so beautifully with this high, lifted voice, and I… sound like a man, I'm sure. I don't sing often. It's just been me and her for a long time."

"You don't have brothers?"

"No," I breathe, finally meeting his eyes. "Gods, no. I nearly killed my mom, and when Nora was born and almost finished the job, my parents swore they were done."

He shifts his position, leaning closer with a look of confusion crossing his features. "But your father is an Alpha King? Who is his heir if he doesn't have sons?"

I arch my brows.

He narrows his eyes.

"You?"

"Of course. I will be Alpha Queen of the Deadlands and all the tribes one day. Is that so hard to believe?" Now, I'm leaning toward him, the space between us shrinking slowly with every breath. "Because I'm a woman?"

"The right woman can rule, sure."

"What are you saying, then? That I can't?"

The door to the sparring ring squeals as it opens, revealing the shabby buildings of the Glade melting in the hot sun. Chasten walks with determined steps in our direction, but his face is etched with unease, which has Kaleb slowly rising. "What is it?"

"You're being summoned to the castle tonight." He hands Kaleb a folded piece of parchment.

Kaleb scans the contents before crumpling the paper in his hand and turns to me briefly. "Fuck. Any word at the gate from Silas?"

Chasten shakes his head, his skin paling a touch.

Kaleb runs his fingers through his hair and turns back to me. "Go to the house with Chasten. Bathe and have Lis help you dress."

"For what?" I ask, but Kaleb is already stalking out of the ring, and I realize quite suddenly that the bubble we'd been trapped in while seeking solace in the shade… that's all it was. I'm still as alone as ever.

Chasten purses his lips, but I rise and gather the water bag I've been hauling back and forth from the house for days now and hike it over my shoulder.

"What's this about? Are the Trials starting tonight?"

"I doubt it," he says, slowing his pace to allow me a moment to catch up with him as we weave through the city. "The king likes to put on a show, and that includes for the sponsors–the rivals." He stops under an awning in front of a small shop selling leather. "Listen, you need to trust Kaleb, all right? I know he's–he can be–"

"A real fucking asshole?"

"Sure," he says, nodding in confirmation but gritting his teeth. "He… he knows a lot about the games."

"Because he is a champion?"

"I didn't realize he told you."

I step closer. "He doesn't seem to like to talk about it."

"There's a good reason why."

Lis rushes around the corner of the street in a sweat, carrying a length of smooth, woven burnt orange fabric. She sees us and huffs with marked irritation, hustling to our sides and red in the face. "Chasten! She has to leave in an hour!"

"Go," he says to us, and I look over my shoulder at him while Lis worries over the dress and what to do with my hair.

The look on his face makes me wonder what happened to Kaleb in that arena and what, exactly, I'm up against.

Because it has to be more than just surviving, doesn't it?

FORK YOU

Lexa

"Stay close," Kaleb whispers sternly over the top of my head as we follow a set of fae guards through the bowels of the castle.

"It's not like I can go anywhere," I reply under my breath, trying to wrench my arm free of his iron-like grip. He hasn't let go of me since the moment Lis and I stepped out of his house and met him in the courtyard, where, unfortunately, the man had effectively stolen my breath away.

His hair is loose, falling just shoulder-length and brushed back. Instead of grubby, coarse fabrics, he's wearing a finely made suit that fits his body like a glove and makes him look like a man I'd find in Maeve's castle–royalty.

It sent a jolt through my system, to say the least, and after the slightly open moment we'd shared in the sparring ring today, I can only assume that the look on his face when he'd seen me had him feeling the exact same way.

Shock.

The thin, almost satin-like fabric of my dress ripples over my body, every curve and muscled angle on display. Two upper-thigh-high slits show off my legs in full detail, and the halter top leaves my entire back on full display. It's not a dress I'd normally wear. I doubt I'd have a reason to wear something as beautiful as this, and I'm honestly not sure how Lis managed to fashion it to fit my body when it had been just a long sheet of fabric only an hour ago, but here I am, and I don't think Kaleb is happy about it at all.

A strand of my hair, loose and falling down my back in soft, brushed out curls, is stuck between my arm and his palm, pulling with every step I take through the shadows.

"You're ripping my hair out!" I whine, but he only tightens his grip, his eyes locked on the space above my head, like he can't bring himself to even look at me.

We're led up a stairwell into the castle proper, where the wet, grim stone walls finally bleed into wallpaper and cooled air carrying the scent of food and wine.

My skin feels like ice. Kaleb is also uneasy when I glance up at him, noticing the way his eyes crease as he scans our new surroundings.

I know we've been summoned to the castle, but I have no idea why. He seems to know, however, but hasn't said a Goddess-damned thing about it.

The guards open a set of pearlescent double doors, and a small crowd spirals into view in the center of the reception hall—everything made of crystal, everything shimmering in the light of multiple chandeliers.

Faces turn to us as Kaleb leads me down a row of white marble stairs. I scan the crowd, trembling against my will, and spot Chessie and Meg.

I lurch, but Kaleb doesn't allow me to move toward them. Yet.

The king stands at the center of the crowd. Shifters and lesser fae servants weave between bodies carrying platters of drinks and little bites to eat, but the king watches my every move when Kaleb eases us off the stairs. Once we step into the crowd, his eyes turn to Kaleb's face.

Kaleb tightens his grip. His touch is warm and solid, a surprising comfort as people and beings I don't know turn to look down at me—all of me.

Then I realize why he hasn't let me go.

"Kaleb," the king drawls with a sickly sweet kind of smile. His pale eyes dance as he takes in Kaleb's hard as nails expression, chuckling to himself. "Always a pleasure to have you at my parties. You always bring such an interesting vibe to whatever event you attend." A ripple of fae-ish laughter follows. Kaleb bristles, but he bows low, and I follow his lead even though every fiber of my being screams in protest.

"And you," the king smiles, stepping closer as we rise. "What a lovely, feral thing you are. I am so looking forward to seeing you in my special games." His tone is like honey, and he smells like everything delicious, but it's too much. It's fake, like he has some kind of shield around himself, like he's a bright light, and all the men standing around him are moths drawn to a flame.

The king glances at Kaleb with a smug grin before turning back to his party. He lifts a hand, and the doors along the side of the room open to reveal a luxurious dining experience only a few yards away.

Suddenly, Kaleb's hand clutching my arm isn't a total inconvenience. My leaden legs relax to limp noodles when he turns us toward the dining hall.

A single long table stretches the length of the dining room. Food is piled high on golden platters, scenting the air with sweets, savory offerings, and spices. After a week in the Glade, the smell of food this rich and plentiful doesn't settle like it probably would have otherwise. I just imagine the empty storeroom in the Glade.

The king beckons for everyone to follow, to squeeze into seats at the table. Kaleb remains where he is, however, as the crowd funnels into the dining room—everyone dressed in their finery and jewels—everyone but Silas, who's standing beside a confused and uneasy Chessie.

Meg, however, throws her head back in a high-pitched, girlish laugh, walking with her sponsor and his companion—both fae men, both beaming down at her like she's the salt of the earth. She doesn't so much as look back at us.

I notice. Chessie notices. Even with the distance between us, we look at each other with similar expressions of skepticism.

Silas eventually moves with the dwindling crowd, but the second Kaleb and I breach the archways of the dining room, the king motions to him, lifting an insanely full goblet of wine. "Come sit at the head of the table with the rest of the sponsors and trainers, Kaleb. Let your precious treasure mingle with her competitors. This is the only time she'll get to talk to them outside of the games."

Kaleb, his hand still wrapped around my arm, doesn't budge. A prickle of knowing skitters through my chest. I can feel the rage flowing off him like a wave of pure heat, simmering where we're joined.

"Don't pretend you like me now," I grumble, trying to discreetly pull away. "You get a break from me for the evening. You've been up my ass for seven days. Don't you want some time apart?" The sugar in my voice makes him scowl and drop his hand, but I notice the way he tightens those fingers into a fist as he begrudgingly walks to the far end of the table, leagues away from the chairs meant for the competitors.

Kaleb's touch is instantly replaced by Chessie, who pulls me to a set of empty chairs and weaves her fingers between mine under the table, her breath soft and warm against my shoulder. She squeaks, "Lexa, I'm so happy to see you!"

I glare across the table at Meg, however, who's giving me a cat-like grin. "What was that all about?" I ask, and Meg arches her brows.

"What?" She pops a grape into her mouth.

I lean forward as far as I can, glancing at the burly warriors now seated on either side of us, hissing, "You know what. That laugh? Fluttering around with your sponsor–"

She leans forward, her face half obstructed by a tiered golden serving dish loaded with pastries and fruit. "I'm just playing their game, Lexa. You should, too. Your trainer looks like he hates you and is probably looking forward to seeing your guts strewn across the arena in a few days' time." She glances around in a half-hearted attempt to confirm she's not overhead, "They will give us what we want as long as we play along."

Chessie frowns beside me, but Meg leans back, turning into conversation with a tall, lean fae man seated beside her.

I don't even look at our fellow competitors, but I can feel them looking at me as they scoop food onto their plates. Soon, the noise at the table blurs every side conversation, and I'm lost in the hum of chewing, drinking, and scraping forks.

"Are you not going to eat?" Chessie asks, giving my arm a soft nudge.

I stare blankly at my plate. "I'm not hungry."

She glances down the table at where Silas and Kaleb are seated across from each other–Silas dutifully talking to the king while Kaleb watches everyone, his expression stern and icy.

"Is Silas actually treating you well?" I ask.

Chessie swallows a bite of food and nods, hiding the softest of smiles behind her napkin. "Did he tell you I was worried sick about you? Because I asked him if he would."

I lean back in my chair, meeting Kaleb's eyes from down the table. He holds my gaze for several seconds, searching my eyes, then moves onto his next victim.

"He did."

"They're brothers, you know. Him and your Alpha King. Silas told me all kinds of stories about Kaleb. He sounds like–"

"An emotionless asshole?"

"Like a hero." Chessie sighs dramatically, her big green eyes sparkling as she looks in Kaleb's direction with her chin perched on her fist. He looks at her, furrows his brow, and quickly looks away, shifting in his chair like her sudden attention is making him entirely uncomfortable.

But then he looks at me again. Only briefly. For whatever reason, I feel a little tug deep in my chest. An ounce of warmth I quickly banish.

I've spent the entire week getting beaten up by him. Over and over. He never lets me win, and I honestly admire him for that and that alone. But still, there's never any softness about it.

He scans our surroundings like he's ready to jump out of his chair if one of these men even glances in my direction.

I purse my lips and look down at my plate.

Chessie notices, of course.

"You think he's handsome too, right? Because… he's the most handsome man I've ever seen in my Goddess–forsaken life–"

"Chessie, please–"

"You can't be serious." She coos, shaking my arm. "Gods, can you imagine him walking into Silverhide? The girls would murder each other just to get him to look in their direction. I'd beg my dad to let a guy like him pay my bride price."

I run my hand down my face, peeking at my empty plate through my fingers.

"Silas is also just downright beautiful," Chessie continues with dreamy, girlish goo-goo eyes that might actually make me go insane if she doesn't stop. "Every day after training, he takes me for a walk around his grounds. He grows roses, Lexa, and when I mentioned how pretty they were, I found a vase of them in my bedroom when I went to bed that night–"

"Would you bitches shut the fuck up?" growls the man seated on my right.

I go totally rigid, my spine locked as I discreetly reach for the fork tucked beneath my napkin. "I'm sorry, did you say something?"

"I said–"

I slam my fork into the back of his hand so hard it pierces flesh, then the table beneath. Every conversation quiets as the man howls with pain, but I reach for a pastry, taking more than a moment to find the prettiest one. I can feel every set of eyes on me as I set the pastry on my plate and unfurl my napkin, letting it fall neatly onto my lap, before making a show of looking for my fork.

"Oh," I giggle, "That's where I put it." I yank the fork from the man's hand, and he gasps in pain, sweat pouring down his temples.

I look down the table, locking eyes with the king.

He stares back, this time without the sugary sweet smile he'd given me when I'd pointed an arrow at his face last week.

Kaleb, however, glances around the table one last time before loading his plate and relaxing. He looks at me only once, and the ghost of a smirk touches the left corner of his mouth before he dips his head and finally enjoys his dinner.

SCHEMING

Kaleb

Silas's manor center rests high above the sprawling, gold-washed city. In the distance, through the glare of evening lights, I can see the castle and the shadow of the wall around the Glade behind it.

I had no reason to come here tonight other than Silas insisted, and Chessie and Lexa backed him up. I have no idea where the women are as it stands, but they're safe here, even in the latest hours of the night. Lexa not being tucked at my side still makes me uneasy, however.

Silas shrugs out of his cloak and drapes it lazily over an armchair bedecked with red and white embroidery. Everything about his manor screams luxury–the born kind. Our mother was a wealthy heiress of one of the king's advisors. His father was a lord from one of the ancient high fae families with ties to the royal family in some way, shape, or form. I've ignored the details for as long as I can. Silas is as good as a prince with coffers to show for it.

"Drink?"

"Yeah," I murmur, turning from the window to face the sprawl of his private study. The walls are dark wood, freshly waxed, and the smell of cedar is thick in the air while he pours two drams of a rich, amber liquid into crystal glasses.

"You should just let her stay the night. It's late, and I'm sure they have some catching up to do."

"The first Trial is tomorrow night," I counter. "She needs rest."

Silas sips his drink before handing the second glass to me, which I accept, inspecting the liquid before taking a cautious sip. We don't have whiskey and scotch in the Glade. Just home brew, which is wildly illegal and a death sentence if it's found during the random fae raids that take place throughout the year.

The door to the study opens to reveal a servant and several fae men, who are quickly and silently ushered into the room. I throw a glare at Silas, who ignores me and greets his friends and fellow rebels in a hushed murmur.

This is what Silas does. He spends his unlimited money, lives in luxury, parading himself to the public as the poster boy of what a high-bred high fae lord should look like, and he does it well, but on the inside, in the shadows, he's helping fund a rebellion that's picking up steam.

"Alpha King," a high fae male with dark hair and glossy gray eyes says by way of greeting as he passes me on his way to the bar cart.

"Lord Everett." I don't bob my head. I don't bow or make a show of the fact that while I am the king of my people, this man still outranks me somehow.

More lords make themselves known, and hushed conversations swirl, but I begin to edge toward the door, keeping an eye on Silas as he melts into discussions that have little to do with me… yet.

I've been to his manor multiple times over the course of my life. I know all the hallways, alcoves, and hidden rooms like the back of my hand, and it's not hard to find where he's been keeping Chessie in luxury… in the suite adjoined to his own.

I'll discuss that with him later—in length.

I stop outside the gilded door, cracked just ajar, as female voices hum through the gap. Lexa laughs softly while Chessie titters about something that must have happened in their past life, before they were dragged into these games. I shouldn't be listening in, but I can't help it, not when I only came here to stand as a buffer between Lexa and the resistance meeting taking place only a story above.

"But, like, are you okay?"

"I'm fine."

Chessie's soft sigh is like music, and somewhere in the depths of the room, the mattress creaks as she moves closer, I assume, to where Lexa's seated. "Lexa, we watched Austin *die*."

Lexa is silent for several long, aching seconds before she finally relents and replies in a breathy whisper, "There was nothing I could have done to save him in that moment."

"I know, but–"

"There's nothing to say–"

"Then why are you so pale? I said his name, and it was like you've seen a ghost."

Another long, drawn out pause hangs in the air so heavily it bleeds into the darkened corridor where I'm standing, leaning my shoulder against the doorframe with my arms crossed tightly over my chest.

"I don't want to talk about Austin."

"But–"

I push open the door and find Lexa resting on the edge of Chessie's monstrous four-poster bed, still in the orange gown from the party. She looks at me blankly, her face cast in shadows–memories she'd rather not conjure fading, I assume–as I ease into the room with a single step. Chessie, however, beams at me, popping up from between a trio of tufted pillows I'm sure smell like roses and whatever other flowers Silas worries over in his garden.

"Hi!" Chessie practically shouts, which causes Lexa to close her eyes like she's searching internally for a quiet, empty space to hide within.

"I came to say we're leaving shortly. You need to rest before the Trials begin tomorrow."

Lexa opens her eyes and looks at me but doesn't say anything. Her face is washed in concern, however, when she glances at Chessie before rising, gathering the long skirt of her gown in her hand.

Her legs shine like polished gold in the muted lamplight. She's…
glorious.

I'm not the only one who has noticed.

"You have some time. I need to tell Silas we're leaving anyway. I
just wanted to warn you."

"That was nice of you," Chessie beams, her voice like sugar–soft,
and sweet. Lexa, however, doesn't break from her somewhat cold
stare as she sits back down on the edge of the bed and angles her body
toward Chessie.

I don't know who Austin is or his significance in her life, but I can
tell just based on her posture that Chessie's line of questioning wasn't
welcome. Just his name cut deep, leaving a wound.

Curiosity blooms, but I beat it down, shutting Chessie's door
before moving back through the darkness. The maids and servants in
Silas's fine house don't pay me any mind–they never have, even as a
child, when Silas would find ways to bring me out of the Glade for a
day or two to see fae healers and eat real meals–and to be educated.

That was one thing he did for me that set me apart from the other
halflings in Pantharas. To him, I wasn't just another soldier, just
another genetic mutant bred to be pliable and aggressive. I was a little
boy. I was his brother.

Which is why I entertain his asinine plots of rebellion.

"Well, well, well, how did I know you were going to have a stroke
and check on the girls the second my friends came to call? Do you
really think I associate myself with men who'd try to take advantage
of the women in my own home?"

"I have a responsibility to Lexa and that's to keep her safe and
secure outside of the games, and you know that." Men have already
started leaving the room after a single quick drink. "What was the
meaning of this anyway?"

Silas shrugs, turning toward the last man now grabbing his cloak
off a hook near the door. He gives the man a quick nod in farewell
before stepping closer to me, replying, "Just some camaraderie before
the games. Nothing too serious."

"I don't believe you."

"Don't act like you want in now, Kaleb. You're either in with both feet or not at all. I explained that."

"What you're trying to accomplish is entirely impossible."

"Well, so were your games, and yet here you are, the champion, now Alpha King of the shifters my king keeps enslaved. You're alive, Kaleb. That was the first nail in our king's coffin, and over the past ten years, he's done nothing to try to dig himself out of his current situation." He takes a sip of his drink. "You know, they *are* from Eastonia. I confirmed it. Lord Ashcroft of the Court of Elsmire, along the coast, told me everything he knew about the plot to snatch and grab shifters from what was supposed to be Emberfyll. I'm sure you know all about Emberfyll, although even our mother wasn't born yet when those halflings managed to escape to that island and set up a colony. Emberfyll is now outside of the veil. The veil is gone. Eastonia is within reach, and the king has had players from their kingdoms for years now, but they have a new Firestone Queen. The Firestone's somehow survived after that great, bloody war."

I ease into an armchair, hanging my head. "You can't know this for sure."

"What I know for sure is that everything we've been fed about your people, and our history, has been a lie. A carefully crafted, manufactured fib force fed to us since birth. Your people were taken generations ago against their will, and Chessie's people... they carry those memories, those songs and fables, just like the people in the Glade do. The king attacked Eastonia, Kaleb. Their Firestone Queen will come to call–and soon."

I close my eyes. "I can't be a part of this."

"Consider yourself a resistance member already, Kaleb, because you chose the very victor the king wants dead the most and who now is backed by everyone who'd like to see the king himself dragged through that arena. Pantharas cannot afford another holy war, and the fae lords know it. All of them are uneasy, even those still attached to the king's hip."

"There is nothing you can do to stop the king."

"Maybe not me, but I have a new connection who's... intimate with Hannibal, that fucking beast. Hannibal is the eyes and ears of the king now that he's returned, and my new friend is going to make it possible to reach the inner circles of his court. Fear not, brother. I have it all planned out."

"Of course you do." I rise, running a hand down my face to try to sweep the exhaustion from my eyes. "You'll be king, won't you? Is that part of your plan?"

"No, *it will not be me*," he chuckles, rolling his eyes. "I am too handsome, too young, and too charming to be chained to a throne for the rest of my long, long, immortal existence. I'd like to travel, I think, maybe spend some time in Silverhide, where the girls are from... where Chessie's from." Another eye roll and a charming smile lights up his face. "But, I'll help decide who gets the throne; that's for damn sure."

"You are thinking too far ahead."

"I'm thinking just far enough ahead," he concludes with a confident smile.

"We need to make it through the games. Has your victor been adequately prepared for what she'll face tomorrow?"

"She has. Just because she's tiny, like the pixie folk, and enjoys the color pink doesn't mean she can't hold her own in the arena. Trust me, she's skilled, and she'll be fighting alongside Lexa in the third round. I've already confirmed it."

"And Meg? Any word from her sponsor?"

His eyes darken. "Her sponsor is close to the king, so no. We don't run in the same circles."

"Your Lordship? Your guest has just arrived." The maid, who dipped silently into the room, disappears before I even get a look at her face.

"Ah, good. I was hoping you'd have a chance to meet him before you left–"

"I'm leaving now." I turn from the room, stepping into the darkened corridor. "We'll watch the first rounds of the Trials together. Being in the third round will give them both an idea of–" A strangling, unsteady sensation wraps itself around my mind for a split second before ceding. I blink away the sudden haze ensnarling my senses, reminding myself not to accept a drink from Silas again anytime soon. Footsteps echo toward me before a man in a black cloak appears–tall, and agile, moving through the darkness like that's all he's known.

But it's his eyes that give me pause as he acknowledges me with a short bob of his head before turning into Silas's study. Eyes the color of polished amethyst, but so bright they could easily be considered... violet.

His gaze holds mine for several seconds before Silas shuts the door, leaving me in the shadows.

THERE'S BEEN A CHANGE OF PLANS

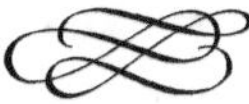

Lexa

No one wakes me up. Hot midday sunlight spills through the window, barely muffled by the curtain. It's definitely past noon when I roll myself out of bed, out of the coarse, woven sheets and onto the hard but freshly swept floor.

Something inside me shifted yesterday. Something cold and gnawing I've been struggling with since I was young. It's easy to forget that I'm still a person beyond the weapons and my skills in battle, but when I look in the rusted mirror hanging on the wall by the bed, tugging the strings that pull my shifting dress into shape, I see her. Me. Just Lexa.

Lexa, who watched her mother prime and fire that arrow that didn't make it in time. Lexa, who watched a man she cared about—maybe even a man she could have grown to love—grovel for her affection before seeing him get cut down in cold blood. Lexa, who worries about her friends more than anything else. A daughter, a sister, a friend.

A fucking princess.

I untangle the strands of my hair with my fingers before roughly braiding it. I adjust and readjust the straps and loops on my dress until it fits like a glove, every seam and stitch painstakingly in place.

It's been over a week since the Culling that determined my fate. A week of training, of trying to prove myself worthy of these games to Kaleb.

I wonder what he's thinking right now as the sun inches back toward the horizon.

Lis isn't in the kitchen when I come downstairs. I'm not hungry anyway. I doubt I'd be able to eat if I tried. My mind is locked and honed on the task at hand—staying calm. Staying collected. Keeping my head on straight, and more importantly, secured to my shoulders.

Around 3:00 in the afternoon, Kaleb arrives in silence. He glances at my dress but doesn't say a word even though he sets the pile of leather armor he had made for me on the kitchen table and turns to leave the house again. I silently follow, but we don't turn to the castle.

"Where are we going?" I ask over the quieter than usual hum in the Glade as we walk side by side into what these people call the pit—the incline down to the far gate to the outside world. Stone staircases weave between buildings and shops as I follow him deep down to a long stretch of open dirt along the wall—stained black from the funerals last week after the Culling.

Kaleb stops in front of the scorched wall, his arms crossed protectively over his chest. "Do you know why I brought you down here?"

I roll my lower lip between my teeth to try to bite back my snide comment, but it slips out anyway. "To remind me that my body could easily be added to the ash beneath our feet if I don't heed your training advice?"

"No." He purses his lips to hide a smile, but I can see it, just there, on the corner of his mouth. In another life, another time, he would have been… fun. One of those guys who took everything so seriously—competitive, assertive—maybe he would have played sports or been the Alpha of a small, rural pack like my parents. If he had freedom to be himself, that is.

We're a lot alike in that way. I've been told on multiple occasions that I'm too competitive for my own good.

"I want you," he says slowly, choosing his words like he's fanning over the weapons cache at the sparring ring, "to decide why you're fighting today, and tell it to our ancestors."

I arch a brow. "Are you finally admitting that I'm not a liar, and we share a culture?"

"I'm aware that Eastonia is real, yes, and that you're from the tribes. There's an ocean between us culturally, however, but it's not enough space to diminish the fact that you pray to the same Goddess, and our people share beliefs. So, say it. Say why you're fighting. Make it an offering to Her and everyone who came, and failed, before you."

I turn to the wall, to the coat of soot covering the thick, impenetrable iron, I believe, based on the years of decay and rust chipping away at its surface.

But then I turn to the city behind me–a city of shifters who can't access their wolves or any of the gifts that come with it.

"Can any of you feel the mate bond?"

"No. Not unless the king allows it. Every few years or so, he'll lift his magic and mate bonds snap into place but... usually, by then, people have coupled and started families. It causes issues for the pack, which is exactly why he does it that way. It keeps us in chaos." He relaxes his arms at his sides, angling his body toward mine. "I'm under the impression you lost your mate during the battle when you were taken."

I startle, turning in his direction.

He licks his lower lip, squinting into the glare of the sun. "I may have overheard you talking to Chessie about someone named Austin, and I could sense you didn't want to continue the conversation, so I stepped into the room."

I run a hand over my face. "I–I don't have a mate. At least–Austin and I–I didn't think it was that serious, but he–before he died, we'd been.... Why am I telling you any of this?"

"If you need to get something off your chest before the game today, now is the time to do it."

I huff a breath. He's not wrong about relieving myself of some of the guilt I've been carrying about Austin's death, and weeks from now, Kaleb will be history–a stranger–a hopefully fading memory while I carry on my life in Eastonia. "He told me we were mates, but I didn't feel it. I enjoyed his company, yes. I had a crush on him. I liked him. But when he said we were mates, it just tripped something in my mind. I didn't get a chance to process it as it stands because he died protecting me and Chessie." I look down at my hand, curling my fingers into a fist. "I don't know if we were mates. I'll never know now."

"That's stupid."

"What?"

He shrugs, a very casual, very male gesture that would have made my skin crawl had it not been him, for some odd reason. "How long have you been able to shift?"

"I came into my wolf early. Sixteen or seventeen."

"You'd know immediately if you'd found your mate. It wasn't him, so leave that behind. You can grieve, feel guilt over his untimely death, but don't be concerned about the fact you didn't feel a bond that wasn't there."

"Then why would he say I was his mate?" I growl, and Kaleb looks down at me like that's the dumbest question anyone has ever asked him.

"Because what you had to offer to him is far greater than anything he could have offered you. *You are magnificent.* Any man can take a single look at you and see plainly what you can add to their bloodline."

I scoff despite the sudden warmth spreading through me. Magnificent? He thinks I'm… magnificent?

He smiles a sideways, cocky grin that immediately has my hackles raised and reminds of the tidbit he added to what could have been a very nice compliment, if he actually meant it.

"You bastard!"

"Save that energy for the arena, Lexa."

A horn blares in the distance, followed by an unnerving kind of silence that creeps over my body like a million little bugs. I shiver, and he looks toward the far wall, where the palace rises, casting the Glade in its shadow.

THE INNER SANCTUM OF THE ARENA IS SICKENINGLY QUIET COMPARED to the snarling, screaming carnage taking place in the arena itself.

Kaleb crouches in front of me, tying the leather laces of my sandals tight against my calves while I watch the end of the second round over the top of his head. Blood already coats the hot, red dirt. Steam rises from crimson puddles while the two remaining victors battle to the death against a particularly vicious hellhound, I believe. It's a type of beast I've seen before. Hellhounds are rare now in Eastonia, but there's still a few that roam the Deadlands, forever tethered to their long-dead witches. I've never seen a decaying rogue in real life, however. My parents helped eradicate those undead beasts when I was a child, but here, in the arena, they're massive and gangly—gray skin falling from bones that click together with each step.

I keep my eyes wide, watching the two victors fight. Both can leave the arena once the last beast is dead. During the first round, three victors out of five advanced to whatever hell awaits us next. This round will have two now that the hellhound is falling on its side, its flesh melting into flakes of ash. I draw in a breath. Their victory is drowned out by thunderous applause.

My round is next.

Kaleb rises, using my shoulder for support. His touch is welcome, especially as he squeezes the tension from my shoulder and turns to Silas, who's hurrying in our direction.

But Silas is alone.

I blink up at him from my stool. Kaleb stiffens when Silas comes into full view, stepping into the glare of hazy sunlight pouring through the slated entrances to the bowels of the arena where we've been waiting.

"Where's Chessie?" I ask, the words falling from my tongue, which feels thick and heavy as his expression–knotted with worry–comes into startling focus. I rise, my fingers curled into fists.

Silas takes a moment to collect himself before saying, "There's been a change." The horn ending the round of the trial blares, swallowing his words. "Lexa is no longer fighting in the third round. She's in the last round of the Beast Trial. The fourth."

Kaleb turns away from us, running his fingers through his hair. Stress pours from him–I can feel it, sense his sudden, striking anxiety right in the dead center of my chest.

"But Chessie and Meg will be fighting in the third round together," Silas confirms. "Chessie's ready, Lexa. She's going to be fine."

"I know. She's a skilled hunter. A better hunter than a warrior, I admit." I close my eyes and send a brief but desperate prayer to the Goddess. "Meg will have her back. They were trained for this."

"Why aren't you with her now?" Kaleb asks.

Silas shakes his head. "The guards rounded up the victors for the third round only moments ago. That's how I found out Meg was replacing Lexa in this round."

"This should have been discussed with me." Kaleb snarls, and I bristle at his tone. Even Silas flinches.

"The king decided it."

"Of course, he did." Kaleb growls, each syllable dripping with acid.

Something's up. I can tell by the look on their faces that there's something about the fourth and final round of these games that's different from the rest.

"Did you fight in the fourth round?" I ask him.

He turns to me as the next horn blares, and the third round begins. His eyes tell me everything I need to know but that he can't say.

Yes, he did.

Yes, I'm right. There's something different about this next round.

No, there's nothing we can do to change it now.

The three of us move to the bars overlooking the arena, where several more decaying rogues race onto the dirt, kicking up dust. Two hellhounds follow, bellowing their siren songs–the almost human voices ravaged by magic and time. The victors sprint toward a weapons cache, but not fast enough for some. It's horrible. It's absolutely horrendous.

Blood sprays almost immediately, but Meg and Chessie do exactly what they were taught to do. Not by me, but by the best hunter and beast killer the Deadlands has ever seen.

My mother.

I watch them shift between their human and wolf forms effortlessly, cutting down rogue after rogue. The hellhounds move in, and they're much harder to kill, but together, working in tandem, both women make it through without a scratch.

My chest tightens with mingled thanks and unease as the final rogue takes down the last man standing–a halfling, I believe–leaving only Meg and Chessie in the ring. It's nearly over in a matter of minutes.

"Come on," I beg, gripping the iron bars preventing me from moving into the arena like my body wants me to. "Just one more. *Just one more.*"

Chessie gets the kill shot, using a blade only as long and wide as her forearm to cut through its neck. Hot black blood scatters over the arena as she turns with a bright, deliriously happy smile stretching across her face. "WE DID IT!"

Her words cut out like a staunched flame as the rogue falls onto its side.

I feel my soul leave my body, a scream ripping from my throat as Meg swings a sword, slashing Chessie across the middle.

Chessie falls to her knees, her hand outstretched to Meg, reaching for mercy, for her friend since toddlerhood.

I scream again when Meg brings the sword down one last time, and ends the round as the true last victor standing.

Alone.

PURE OF HEART

Lexa

"Look at me." Kaleb clutches my face between his hands. I can't see past him. I can't hear past the echo of Chessie's scream piercing me from all angles. My chest contorts as I try to fill my lungs with air, but it's useless. "Lexa, open your eyes."

I shake my head, blubbering as raised voices erupt all around us. Silas is screaming at the top of his lungs in the language of the fae, but I can't make out a word he's saying. It doesn't matter. I imagine Meg bringing down that sword over and over, and the way Chessie closed her eyes at the last moment before her life was torn from her body.

"NO!" I screech, but Kaleb shakes me violently, trying to drag me out of an anguish induced stupor.

He presses his forehead to mine, panting, as the lifted voices reach a peak. There's activity all around us, but he shields me from what I assume are the bodies—her body—being dragged from the arena.

"Listen to me," he breathes against my cheek. "You will go out there and take what's thrown at you because you must, not because you deserve this. You will move onto the next Trial because these games aren't worthy of you."

I shake my head. My cheek brushes against his, against his scruff. I can't even place myself in time or space. I'm floating above my body, seeing nothing but light and color. Nothing but red.

"You will move onto the next round of the Trials," he continues hoarsely, "because you'll see Meg there. You will move on because you will meet her in the ring and do what must be done. Do you understand? Tell me what you're fighting for today, Lexa."

Tears slip free from my eyes. I try to shake my head again, but he grips me, forcing me to stay still.

"Tell me what you're fighting for," he rasps against the shell of my ear.

"Chessie," I croak. "I'm fighting for Chessie."

"Then go."

He yanks me upright. Gravity hits me like a freight train. The sun is setting over the tall, curved wall of the arena, casting the space in snaking silver shadows as exterior lights flare to life, highlighting streaks of red—pathways of blood.

"Go," Kaleb repeats, and I move as guards stalk in my direction to drag me kicking and screaming into the arena. I'm sure they'd love that, wouldn't they? If I cried and begged for mercy, to see my friends face one last time before facing my own death in the fae king's twisted games?

The guards reach for me, but I shove past them, walking myself through the inner sanctum of the base of the arena, past the barred windows, past sponsors and trainers bagging up the gnarled remains of their dead.

I'm first in the arena. I stalk out before the first horn blares. Torches dance along the smooth stone railing protecting the crowd of spectators from the beasts within. Beasts like me. Beasts like me who don't fear death. Beasts who welcome violence. Beasts who know nothing else.

I stand mere inches from the weapons cache in the center of the arena. Cool night air brushes my skin, awakening my sleeping wolf. I feel those gifts stretching through my veins as the last glimmers of sunset slip below the wall and nothing but darkness remains—a cool, empty sky.

The moon is only a sliver tonight. So be it.

I won't be using my wolf anyway.

The deaths of everyone and everything in the arena would be too clean that way.

I feel rather than hear the soft chuckles and clicks of the four other victors coming up behind me. The strongest. The fittest. The most volatile. The ones the fae heckling me bid their precious gems on.

Out of my peripheral vision, I see a bandaged hand reaching for a sword in the cache–the man who I thought learned a lesson last night by means of my fork, but apparently he needs more lecturing. I have a single second to glance to the left at the entrance of the arena, looking for Kaleb, but he's gone.

The horn blares. Grates along the walls open to reveal shadows and snarls. I grip the sword the man was reaching toward and swing, screaming with effort. The sound of his now detached arm hitting the ground fades against the pounding claws and deathly snarls of the five rogues racing for me. For us.

The armless man is my bait.

I kick him into the dirt and whirl as my competitors race in every direction, grabbing whatever weapons they can grip. I toss the sword and grip twin blades, a familiar weight in my hands. The crowd above laughs and chants in their strange, musical language, but the blood rushing through my ears drowns them out.

A rogue falls with a crash that sends a sickening vibration through the arena. Four left. Another cuts through one of my competitors like a rag doll, leaving only three victors standing. I walk at a steady, determined pace down the center of the arena, smiling like a mad-woman, as a rogue sprints in my direction.

My wolf groggily begs to be released after such a long slumber.

Maybe next time.

I run toward the rogue and then fall to my knees at the last possible second, sliding painfully over bloody dirt. The rogue runs over the top of me, chirping in annoyance, but I lift my blades and slice it through its middle.

It stumbles, falling in on itself as it crumbles to the ground several yards away. I can't risk ending its immortal life humanely, not yet, not when it's calling to its undead companions who turn my way, ignoring the two other competitors completely.

Rogues are easier to kill than I thought they'd be. Stupid animals, honestly. They make it almost too simple to cut them down, even in my human form with nothing but short blades to do my dirty work. I cut through the first like butter, and then the second one falls, its severed head rolling away seconds later, ending up in the far center of the ring where the one-armed man is trying to claw his way upright to no avail.

Just like that, it's over.

The two other competitors standing cast wary, but almost grateful, glances at me as I turn to stalk to the man now crawling toward his severed arm. I can live with not being the last one standing during this round, but he's not coming with us to the next game.

A yelp echoes toward me, followed by an intense rumbling that almost brings me to my knees. A pit nearly swallows me whole. Dirt rushes toward me as the ground beneath my feet gives way. I have mere seconds to leap onto solid ground and keep running against the push and pull of the dirt floor of the arena being sucked into a wide, dark abyss before I'm overcome.

"LEXAAA!" Kaleb's voice rips over the gasping crowd. I race to the wall, plastering myself against its smooth, bloodstained surface, and look up at the spectators, where Kaleb is sprinting along the ledge, his eyes wild and shining in the torchlight.

A terrified scream breaks my focus. The armless man disappears along with the weapons cache into the pit. One of the other competitors slips, swallowed by the rushing dirt, unable to save himself.

There are only two of us now.

Me and a fully high-fae male now plastered against the wall on the other side of the arena, his wings splayed wide. I've yet to see a fae take flight, but I'd guess he doesn't have that ability here in the arena, just like my wolf was kept tethered, but now… as the scraping of chains and breathy, huffed growls echo from within the pit–I see a single creature. Just one. One really, really fucking big *thing*.

I realize the game isn't over yet.

It's only just begun.

Twin talons pierce the darkness the color of polished alabaster. I press myself against the wall, struggling to catch my breath as a second set, just as sharp and ungodly large as the first, rises from the depths.

Kaleb says my name again, softer this time, a muted plea laced through the syllables I barely catch.

The head is first. Reptilian, wide, and scaled, but with a long, narrow snout. Eyes as large as truck tires scan the arena as the... the...

"Oh, my Goddess," I whine, struggling to catch my breath as a fucking dragon lifts its body from the pit.

There are tales of these creatures in our folklore. Creatures of the elements–of fire, water, air, and earth. They were guardians of the seas and mountain ranges. Of volcanoes and the skies. They lived in a time before even the earliest gods, and yet, here one stands, and it's livid.

It roars–a deep, guttural sound that makes my eardrums sing with pain. The ground beneath me shakes violently, forcing me to bend my knees to stay upright, but the crowd above ripples with excitement and applause, loving every second of it.

I've never seen a beast like this. It's... beautiful. Long and lean, it shines in the faint moonlight–washed in dry, cracked silver-blue scales. Wings expand along its back–like a bat, but pearlescent, a kaleidoscope of blues, greens, and silvers. Like water.

A water dragon.

A water dragon bound by iron chains and forced to live within the dirt lined hellscape of the arena.

My competitor is the first to move as the dragon's body escapes the pit. He swings a sword at the dragon's long, spiked tail, drawing a deep gash along its silver skin. The dragon bellows in pain but turns to the fae man, opening its narrow jaw wide, revealing pointed teeth, sharp as uncut diamonds. Its tail lashes at my competitor, tossing him several yards into the air, and lets him fall directly onto the top of his head with an audible crunch. He twitches, and the dragon slowly, methodically, uses its tail to scoop the man into the pit–a snack for later.

I can't swallow. I stay flush against the wall as the dragon slowly looks in my direction, its chains rumbling with the moment.

"Lexa, wake up!" Kaleb screams over the crowd. "You need to move!"

I'll die this way, I suppose. It could be quick–slow and violent, whichever the dragon prefers. I can't kill this thing, though. Every fiber of my being... screams to lay down my blades. It's wrong. It's against nature to harm something this... amazing. Something trapped here, just like me.

So I do. I drop my blades. They clang to a rest at my feet.

The dragon moves as close as it can. Through slitted eyes, I see the burns on its legs from the chains–from the iron binding its magic, I think, just like silver would burn me. It's just another prisoner trapped here for their entertainment.

Its breath is hot on my skin. I close my eyes and wait.

"*You smell of trees and wheat,*" a voice whispers in my head–soft and ethereal.

I open my eyes to a view of teeth and tilt my chin until my neck strains to look at the dragon's opal-like eyes.

"I can't kill you," I whisper out loud. "I won't do it."

"*Then you'll fail the games, I fear. What will they do to you, little wolf? Bind you? Chain you? Kill you?*"

"I don't care. My friend–my friend is dead. I don't–I'd rather go with her than continue the game."

The crowd titters with excitement as the dragon changes her–I believe it's a her–position, posed to strike.

Somewhere in the distance, Kaleb has gone silent.

I look at the dragon's scales–dry and grimy. She was probably exquisite once, back when she was free and able to move through the depths, her spirit blessing the rivers and seas. I bet she *glowed.*

"Are you the last of your kind?"

"*I hope not*," she answers softly, sadly, but her position remains violent, her impressive talons digging deep into the dirt while her tail swishes.

"Can you talk to everyone or just me?"

"*Just the pure hearts.*"

Her chains dig into her legs, and the air fills with the smell of blood—her blood.

"You don't belong here," I whisper, more to myself, as I inspect her manacles. They're crudely made and massive. It would be easy to sink a blade into its mechanism and... twist....

I look back into her eyes, and into my mind, trying to connect her voice, and say, "*Can you still fly? Can you break through whatever magic is keeping you here?*"

She seems to understand because the second I crouch, my fingers brushing the hilt of my blades, her dragonish grin lights the space around us.

"Put on a show," I whisper, and move.

The crowd screams in glee as I sprint from the wall beneath the dragon's massive, barrel-like torso. She roars, whipping her lumbering body to the side as I weave between her legs. I cry out with the effort of lodging the first blade into the manacle on her left front ankle. The impact reverberates up to my shoulder, jostling me, but I twist the blade until metal snaps.

The dragon roars again, but I'm moving onto the opposite leg, weaving and sliding while she thrashes above me, doing her best to stomp me out of existence.

The crowd believes it. Every second of it.

I have one blade left.

It has to work.

I slam the blade into the lock on her right front leg. It breaks apart on impact.

"*Will you come with me, pure heart?*" she whispers into my mind.

Freedom flashes before my eyes. I imagine my parents. Nora. My grandparents. Silverhide.

But then I see Chessie's face drawn in pain and confusion, and Meg wielding the sword…

"*No,*" I whisper back. "*I have unfinished business here. Go.*"

The dragon goes completely still for a single breath, filling her lungs, her wings expanding so wide they fill the arena. Sudden chaos reshapes the crowd above as the dragon screeches and rears back, her front legs free.

Commands shouted in the fae language blur as I look up, watching the dragon's belly as she leaps off her hide legs–strong, agile, an ancient beast of a pure kind of magic. Her remaining chains snap like thin thread, and she flaps her wings, causing the spectators to run for cover as debris lifts from the arena, spraying toward the crowd.

I shield my eyes but watch as she breaks through whatever magical veil kept her imprisoned, shattering the invisible dome over the arena, and disappearing like a shadow into the starless night sky.

MY WHY

Kaleb

I rush through the chaotic swell of guards scrambling to access the arena, pushing and shoving my way through the fray. Silas shouts my name, but I ignore him as the dragon breaks free of its chains and soars into the sky, bellowing a roar that shakes the entire city.

I catch a glimpse of Lexa. She falls to her knees, and blaring bright lights fill the arena.

Guards with swords and spears race for her as the gates to the arena open, allowing them access, but I run faster, breathless, skirting around the open pit and over puddles of blood until I reach her side.

She moans, curling into herself as she succumbs to what I know is shock. Shock from the games, from the dragon, from the physical and mental agony of entertaining the crowd above, which is now being hastily dispersed.

Shock from watching her friend get executed by someone she loved and trusted.

Her cheek is ice cold against my palm.

But the guards are closing in. I scoop her into my arms and back against the wall as weapons point in our direction.

"Put her down, by order of the king!" shouts a guard in his heavy armor and mask.

"Fuck off! She won! This round is over!" I shout, clutching her to my chest as she trembles, unable to open her eyes past slits.

The guards part as the king himself stalks in my direction, followed by several sponsors and trainers, everyone arguing behind him, but most in awe of what just happened.

Silas, pale and drawn, stands toward the back of the crowd, his eyes locked on mine–grim. Empty, but curious, like there's a single sliver of life left in him.

"Enough!" the king shouts, rage lacing through the word. "Set her down, Kaleb. Allow the guards to finish the job so we can move on–"

"No," I snarl, and the king's eyes widen. "She won this round. She will move on to the next."

Several of the sponsors shift from foot to foot, nervously awaiting the king's reply, but the king scowls as he looks from me to the night sky above our heads, that scowl deepening to something murderous.

"She was supposed to kill that beast, not free it!"

"The rules of the Beast Trial state," Silas says with restraint, stepping through the crowd, "that the round is over when the last beast is *gone*. The dragon is… gone. Just in a more unorthodox way–"

"Gone doesn't necessarily mean dead," agrees one of the sponsors, but the king whips around to Silas, glaring.

Silas raises his hands in a show of surrender but adds, "The rules are ancient and are to be followed. They don't explicitly say–"

"I know what the rules say!" the king shouts, furious. He grits his teeth, panting with rage, and turns back to me and Lexa. "I will kill her myself if she pulls another stunt like that. Keep your victor on a tight leash, halfling. I will not be so merciful again." With a swish of his cloak, he stalks back across the arena, shoving a guard out of his way. His wings expand with each step, but he doesn't fly off, not yet at least.

The other sponsors linger for a few seconds before scurrying back to their victors or the bodies left behind by the game, but Silas remains.

"You need to get her out of here," Silas says shakily. "Take her back to the Glade, now."

"Are you all right?"

Silas's mouth moves, but no words come out. He looks down at his fine, polished leather shoes—stained with blood. His cloak, too, is stained crimson in the shape of the woman he carefully carried out of the arena, clutching her like a child. I'd seen it. Seen him walk off with Chessie in his arms while Lexa's round began, his warrior's golden curls cascading over the crook of his arm while he stifled sobs.

"I–I don't know how to notify her family," he says gravely. "I can't." He runs his fingers through his hair, looking entirely undone.

"I told you not to get attached."

His eyes meet mine in the bright haze of artificial fae-lights. He chuckles darkly, looking suddenly furious but keeping it contained. "You don't know the half of it, Kaleb. Go home. Do not leave the Glade unless I call for you directly."

"A lock of her hair," I say into the silence settling over the arena.

Silas stops, his back to me, and slowly turns.

"I need a lock of Chessie's hair. We'll build a pyre for her in the Glade. We'll hold a funeral."

"I cannot turn over her body to the Glade. It's against the rules as her sponsor. I'm responsible for–for that."

"A lock of her hair is all we need." I adjust Lexa's weight in my arms. I wonder how much she can hear, how aware she is currently. "That's it. She was from the tribes. We'll do it our way."

Silas nods, but his eyes are so heavy and sad that it makes my chest tighten.

He walks away, his cloak billowing out behind him in the warm, still night.

CHASTEN LEANS HIS BACK AGAINST THE WALL IN THE HALLWAY OUTSIDE Lexa's bedroom. Warm lamplight casts us both in shades of amber while Lis rises from her knees at Lexa's bedside. I feel Chasten's gaze on my cheek, but I can't draw my eyes away from the hand Lis rests on Lexa's bare shoulder.

It's hard to describe the last hour. I stood outside the gates of the Glade with Lexa in my arms while the guards–fae guards–allowed us entrance into the slice of kingdom I rule. Once inside… I was unprepared for the quiet reception that followed. My people filled their doorways, windows, and the narrow streets, some holding candles, others bowing their heads in silent solidarity. But it was the women who stepped out of their homes to bless Lexa as we passed that made me grip her harder, like I was trying to just… keep her here. Keep her safe in my arms. *Bringing her home.* Silent, gentle touches. Whispers prayers.

"We all saw the dragon," Chasten says quietly beside me, swallowing hard. "It flew right over the Glade."

"Find Colin and Avery and have them start a new pyre tomorrow morning."

Chasten turns to look at me.

"Something big. It's for one of our own."

I know word has already spread about the games, the deaths, and Lexa's triumph. My people knew three shifters, three women, had ascended past the Culling, one of them our victor. And tonight, our champion. They'll honor the wolf that didn't make it out of the arena even if I didn't make the command for a funeral.

Lis moves into the hallway on silent feet, closing the door just a crack. "She's not badly injured. A few scrapes and bruises. Her right arm is a bit swollen, but that could be anything. Morning will tell."

"Thank you, Lis," I murmur, and she bows her head as Chasten guides her down the hallway and down the stairs, where they have their own quarters just off the kitchen.

Lexa isn't asleep when I ease onto the side of her bed. She's seated and staring at the far wall, at the hazy, aged windows and the glow of the lights along the wall beyond.

I don't know why I do it, but I reach for her–this girl. This woman. This she-wolf with a body like iron and a brain as sharp as the finest of blades. A woman who cannot remain in a cage. A woman who freed a dragon today, when I'd killed one during my own games, even though every fiber of my being told me I was making the wrong choice.

Lexa stared death in the face countless times today.

She didn't need training, not like we've been doing for the past week or so. No, it's the aftermath she wasn't ready for, but I don't know how to teach her this.

"Did you kill the dragon in your games?" she asks, her face half buried in her pillow.

"I did."

"Did it talk to you?"

"No, I don't think so."

"Did you shift?"

I take a breath as she curls deeper into herself. My hand rests on the slope of her thigh, but she doesn't pull away. She seems to sink into the touch instead. "I didn't have a chance. I'm sure you felt it in the arena tonight, but being robbed of your wolf abilities for even a short period of time makes them... unstable. Unsteady. I couldn't risk it."

"What's next, then?"

"It's hard to say. The games change. Normally there are fifty years between the Trials, sometimes longer, so the games being repetitive wouldn't matter much, but this is different. It could be anything. The king will announce the next match in a few days, I assume. We'll know then."

She's silent for several seconds, and beyond the window, the lights along the wall flicker as clouds move in, promising much needed rain, I hope. It's been ages since it's rained.

"I promised her we'd make it home," she whispers, and when I turn to her, I notice tears staining the pillow.

"You'll make it home to tell her story." I squeeze her thigh. She's softer than I thought she'd be, and something alpha deep within my chest tugs at the knowledge—something warm and hard to ignore, but I try. I have to try.

"Do you think Silas loved her?"

I close my eyes at the thought of my brother. "I do."

"Like, really loved her? The way she talked about him and how kind he was to her, it felt–Chessie's always been a romantic, and I hope that maybe, somehow she got a taste of that with him, at least, before she–she–" The words fall apart into a tangled exhale, like she's trying her hardest not to sob.

"I believe he did love her. Silas is a good man. He always has been. When my sister–" I grit my teeth as Alice's memory comes sweeping into existence. It's painful to think about her, even after ten years without her presence in this house. "When my sister died, Silas took care of everything. Tried to save the baby, tried to save her. She was as comfortable as she could have been when she went to the Goddess, and he didn't have to do that for her. She was a shifter. Their only relation was me. I was also their only connection."

She peaks over the blanket, her eyes, glossy with tears, are all that's visible. "Will you tell me about her?"

I adjust my position on the bed, leaning over her, resting my elbow between the curve of her belly and thighs. It's dark in the room, with only the light shining from the top of the wall in the distance illuminating the sharp angles of her face, her cheekbones, her button nose, and her freckles that remind me of the stars.

"Alice was older than me by ten years or so. She was nearly my age now when she died, and she wasn't very nice. She was nice to me but not to others. She dominated every circle, every crowd, and she was beautiful." I pick at the frays in the woven blanket separating us. "My father was the Alpha of our pack before I combined the packs of the Glade into one after my Trials, and he was rarely home. I never knew his wife, Alice's mother, and Alice was the one who raised me after I was born and brought to the Glade. When I was nineteen, there were whispers of upcoming Trials in the fae cities. Alice knew, based on the fact I was a halfling and of age to participate, that I'd likely be chosen to compete in the Culling, and that's almost always a death sentence."

Lexa draws her legs in, brushing my arm, as her body tightens. I know this is the story she wants, even though it's the story I've yet to tell anyone out loud. Maybe it's the Goddess's will tonight. Lexa deserves a piece of me for everything she's done tonight, even if she doesn't understand the significance of her actions yet.

"Alice often worked in the house of a high fae nobleman and his family as a laundress, and she never admitted it, but I believe she offered herself to her master in an effort to keep me out of the Culling. It didn't work, and as the months passed, and the Culling grew closer, it was obvious she was with child. My father was furious, flew into a blind rage and killed several fae guards who'd ventured beyond the gates, and he was put to death for it." I lick my lips, closing my eyes as those months spiral into full color. "I became Alpha. Alice died in childbirth after suffering for almost a week in labor. No fae healers would touch her. Silas risked his life trying to save them with his connections, but they were both too far gone. They died, and the very next day, a thousand men from the Glade were rounded up for the Culling, and I was the only one who came back."

Rain patters against the window. It's a sound I haven't heard in over a year.

"What was your *why*?" she asks quietly, almost timidly.

"I wanted to kill the king for what he and his kind did to my family," I whisper, reaching to move a tight curl away from her face. "And one day, I will. But not tonight. Probably not tomorrow, either. But someday."

A LOCK OF GOLD

Lexa

The sun doesn't rise on the Glade the morning after Chessie's death. Clouds block the sunlight completely, and it pours.

I take the heavy basket covered in towels from Liz's hand as we hurry through the city, ducking under awnings to shield ourselves from the spray of the rain. It's warm. It feels rich and wet, and everywhere we look, children race through puddles, singing and dancing in the face of thunder and lightning that splits the sky into pieces.

"It hasn't rained like this here in decades," she says over the pounding rain as the pack house comes into view. "I honestly can't remember the last time it even sprinkled. It was probably your doing."

"What?" I whisper, my voice cracking from lack of use. I fell asleep last night curled over Kaleb's legs, I think. He was my last memory before the world went dark, and my grief swept me into nothingness—a numb, hollow kind of darkness. His hand lays on my hip as he told me about his sister, and... his *why*.

"You freed the dragon." Lis grins, clutching my upper right arm in solidarity, but her touch sends a sharp, bright kind of pain bouncing through me. "It's been trapped down there for so long. It blessed us with rain as a thank you. Think of all the things that can grow now! I might even see grass in my lifetime."

Her words are a shock to my system. I look at her, taking in her delicate, girlish features. She's never seen the world outside these walls. She doesn't know what grass looks like. I can't imagine.

While we wait for another blinding sheet of rain to sweep across the city, I turn my head to watch the children splashing in the puddles, their mothers standing in doorways smiling and laughing, breathing deeply the air finally, for once, not full of dust.

These people… they shouldn't live like this.

I follow Lis, weaving between buildings until we reach the pack house. I'm not sure why she wanted me to come run this errand with her, but I suppose I needed to get out of bed, eventually. My body is bruised and aching when we step out of the rain and into the warm, dry sanctuary of the pack house, where a small group of women is gathered at its center around a table.

"Any news yet?" Lis excitedly asks the group. She takes the basket from my arms and draws back the towels to reveal two loaves of bread and several tiny outfits.

"The baby came an hour ago," an older woman says with a wide smile, but her eyes show exhaustion. "Mother and baby are both well."

"Oh, thank the Goddess," Lis breathes, moving into the group. Their conversation fades, and the rain takes its place, thundering across the roof like a thousand hammers. I blink and find myself in the arena again, just like that, unable to move and forced to watch Meg grunt against the weight of the sword as she wields it a second time and slices it down on–

A large, warm presence steps behind me, fingers resting just above my hipbone. Kaleb turns me into the kitchen, a curtain flopping closed behind us, cutting me off from the news of a new life while the memories of a stolen one render me absolutely useless.

Kaleb turns to face me, silently twisting my wet hair away from my cheeks. He reaches behind his head and pulls the thin length of leather loose from his hair, tying mine back with it instead. His dark, luscious waves fall over his shoulder, curlier than usual, likely from the rain. Neither of us says a word until I finally find the nerve to ask, "Is Silas all right?"

"I saw him this morning," he replies, but his voice is tight. "He's better than I expected, but he's good at hiding these kinds of things."

"I want to thank him for being so good to her. How can I?"

"He won't accept anything. He already knows how you feel."

I close my eyes as he draws his hands over my bare shoulders, wiping rain from my bruised, aching skin. His touch stops at a particularly nasty bruise, where severe swelling wraps clean around my elbow, and sucks his teeth. "When did this one happen? When you were freeing the dragon?"

I sigh, trying to step from him so he can't see the pained look on my face when he pokes the skin. "Yes."

I meet his shrewd gaze. "This is bad, Lexa."

"I'll survive without being able to bend my elbow," I reply hoarsely as tears of agony fill my eyes. I refuse to blink them away, because once they close, I'll see that moment again, see the flash of light against a cord of metal as it meets Chessie's body, and I can't–I can't–

I yank away from him so aggressively I slam into the worktable. A pitcher of water falls to the ground with a crash, shattering.

Kaleb tries to grab me, but I painfully lift my arms, turning from him, shielding myself.

"Stop," he commands. "Lexa–"

"Leave me alone," I beg as tears–hot and acidic–drench my cheeks. I suck in a desperate breath as I fall to pieces, unable to knit myself together again. "Go–go away!"

Lis rushes into the kitchen, wide eyed and pale. "Kaleb?"

"Go away!" I cry out, but Kaleb catches me around the waist, lifting me into the air like I weigh nothing, and scoops me into his arms.

"Go find the healer and then send for Avery and Colin. I need their help," Kaleb says to Lis, dodging my attempt to rake my nails over his cheek. I scratch his neck instead, but he takes it, barely flinching.

"But Avery and Colin are helping with the pyre–"

"Go," Kaleb commands, and Lis bolts, disappearing behind the curtain while Kaleb carries me out of the kitchen through the back entrance and into the rain.

Water pelts my face. I spit, blink, trying to clear my mouth and vision from the downpour, trying to rip out of his grasp, but Kaleb is as immovable as ever. He practically kicks in the door on his way into the house and calls out for Chasten, but it's just us in the house when he pins me to the kitchen table, his forearm pressed over my chest to try to keep me still against its rough surface.

"Calm down–"

I glare at him, but he doesn't bare his teeth or scowl. His eyes are dark and heavy as he looks down at me while I crumble beneath him, trembling, unable to form a single word.

"I'm sorry," he whispers, the word painfully leaving his lips, carrying a familiar ache that cuts me to the core. "I am so sorry."

"I want to go home," I whisper, my lower lip quivering. "I want to go home!"

He leans his forehead against mine, closing his eyes. I whimper past a sob threatening to suffocate me, but his lips brush my cheekbone as he presses another whispered apology to my skin.

I relax involuntarily as his warmth radiates between us–steady and everlasting, like he's the pillar I'm leaning against, the only thing keeping me upright, and I turn my face to his, our lips only a hair's breadth apart.

"Let me go," I say against his mouth, but there's no fight in my voice.

"No," he replies just as tiredly, but his lips close over mine, and I close my eyes as… everything I thought I knew about myself, my world, and what matters collides.

I've been kissed before. This isn't my first time. I thought I knew what it should feel like–that fiery, fumbling, shallow kind of passion that's meant to scratch an itch elsewhere. It's something that's supposed to feel like instant satisfaction and then fade into nothing..

This isn't nothing.

This is… *heat*. Spine-tingling, brain-numbing warmth.

The pressure of his forearm eases as he reaches for me, caressing my face before pulling away for a single inrush of air. I feel the distance between us like a jolt of electricity, and it leaves me chilled, suddenly panicked at the emptiness left in his wake. He presses gently on my lower lip with his thumb. I open my eyes to slits at the same moment he kisses me again, harder this time, like he needs more to register this is real. Like it didn't feel real the first time, but this time?

This is… very real.

An involuntary whimpered moan leaves my lips, and they part. He sinks onto the stool beside the table and drags me down into his lap, careful of my limp, swollen elbow. His arm wraps around me, holding me steady, his hand flat on my back, fingers spread wide over my spine, his other hand gliding up my neck to tangle in my hair and tilt my head to the side, and he kisses me *again*.

I melt. I absolutely thaw in his arms. A myriad of tangled emotions begins to unravel, replaced by a bright, heavy sensation in my chest that floods through the very marrow of my bones until I am completely and utterly at the mercy of his lips, his tongue, and his teeth.

He nibbles on my lower lip, eliciting another breathy moan, and he growls in answer, on the precipice of doing something we both want.

But we'll both regret.

And we know it.

A door in the depths of the house opens, letting in the thunderous echo of the rain beyond the thick walls, and several indistinguishable footsteps hurry toward us, but he doesn't pull away. He's breathless, his body rigid with desire as he holds me to his chest, pressing one last kiss to the corner of my mouth before the tear-blurred figures of Avery, Colin, Lis, and an unfamiliar older woman come into view over his shoulder.

"I'm sorry," Kaleb whispers against my cheek, clutching me tighter than before.

"For what?"

"For this. Take her arm, and line it up with the shoulder joint–"

I screech as Avery suddenly grabs my horribly swollen and bruised right arm, twisting it painfully at an awkward angle. Kaleb clutches me tightly, preventing me from moving, while the healer and Lis stand just within my horrified line of sight, pale and owl-eyed.

Colin suddenly slams his fist against my elbow, and my vision goes black for several seconds before I careen back to the room, unable to breathe. I black out several more times from the sheer pain of it. Hands touch me, move me. Cool rags are packed around my arm. I wake up again briefly, back in Kaleb's arms, before closing my eyes to the world and burying my face in his shirt.

Someone pinches my mouth open, drops a foul tasting liquid inside, then pinches my nose and covers my mouth, forcing me to swallow. Everything gets blurry again, but Kaleb's scent remains, ever present, all-encompassing, the only thing keeping me from slipping back into my nightmares about the arena.

I'm sure hours pass while I slip in and out of lucidity. I already know I was given a healing tonic–something incredibly potent. I've taken them before. Hell, Misty has healed more than one broken or dislocated bone in my body over the years. So when I wake to complete–but finally rainless–darkness without a lick of pain, I'm only partly surprised.

I'm just somewhere I don't recognize.

I slide out of *Kaleb's* bed, my toes brushing *Kaleb's* floorboards. The door leading out of his room is ajar, light spilling from the hallway, where he's talking to someone in quiet tones–Avery, I think.

"Silas was adamant that you see him tonight. He's leaving. He said he had urgent business outside of Pantharas and won't be back until the end of the games."

"Did he mention what kind of business?"

"No, but he gave me this."

I watch the shadows drift in the ray of light creeping toward my toes.

Kaleb exhales deeply, a long, drawn-out sigh. "I'll do what I can."

"The girl's pyre is ready whenever you are. People have already begun to gather."

"Lexa will light it if that's what she chooses. She's resting as it stands."

"Is she all right?"

"She'll heal."

"I mean, with… everything?"

Silence hangs heavy for several aching seconds before Avery's footsteps descend the stairs, and the floorboards creak as Kaleb turns, opening the door to find me sitting on the side of the bed.

There's an old standing mirror in the corner of his bedroom, the frame slightly rusted, but it reflects me, then him, as he steps deeper into the room. I know I look like a mess. My hair is tied back with his length of leather, but curls fall around my face, sticking up at odd angles everywhere. I'm wearing one of his shirts, judging by the length, which fits me more like a rather scandalous nightgown, barely covering my upper thighs, but to his credit, he keeps his eyes on my face, searching, inspecting me for irreversible damage.

I won't say a Goddess-damned thing about the kiss. It was either a distraction—or it meant something to him. And if it's the latter… how can we possibly go back to despising each other?

He hesitates before extending his hand. The light from the hallway catches a pale, coiled length of hair. It's a perfect shade of gold.

WRAPPED UP TOGETHER

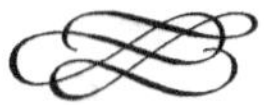

LEXA

I've been to funerals like this before but always in Endova. There haven't been many deaths in Silverhide. Our pack is young, with hardly any elders, and we've been relatively safe.

I find myself clutching Kaleb's forearm while we walk through the city under a cloak of wet, humid darkness, my mind racing over the battle on the beach. How many pyres were lit in the days that followed? Dozens? I missed them all.

Kaleb doesn't flinch away from my touch. His progress to the pit, the massive gate to the outside world, is slow, steady, letting me set the pace. My legs feel like lead despite the healing draft still working through my system. My elbow is fine now that it's set back in place, and the drafts have done their job knitting my tendons back together, but the ache in my heart remains.

A crowd has gathered along the wall. Shadowed figures of men, women, and children look up at us as we approach. I see familiar faces. Familiar curious glances. But tonight, people bow their heads in silent solidarity while I clutch Chessie's lock of hair, the only piece of her the fae king has allowed me to have.

A calf length dress borrowed from Lis—more of a nightgown, in its defense—brushes my thighs and my sandals clack against ancient stone pavers lining the ground near the wall like they're part of an old road, something built long before these walls were here. I try to think of anything else but the fact I'm now drifting toward a tall, wooden structure with a flat surface where a body should be, but isn't, because even in death, Chessie was a captive.

Kaleb fades into the background as I step forward, alone and weary. My eyes sting. Gods, I've never cried this much in my life. I've never felt so removed from my body. It's hard to describe grief this tangled.

My dad told us about Isla and Maddox—their stories, their trials and victories—but never spoke about their deaths. It was painful for him, even years later, when we were old enough to understand what it felt like to lose someone you loved so desperately that the world simply ceases to exist in the same way once they're gone.

Now I know.

I know the injustice of it.

It makes me furious but also desperately, irrationally, confused.

I thought I'd lost her once before, but I didn't have time to think about it because of my imprisoned state. This time, I've had nothing but time.

A very old woman suddenly reaches my side in the darkness. She gently clutches my wrist in her withered hand, her fingers smooth and cold on my skin. I look down into her milky eyes, and she nods to my hand, to the length of gold now warmed from my touch. This strand of curls is what we will burn tonight and give back to the Goddess so Chessie can find her way home.

A soft, ethereal hum floats through the air behind me. Women I don't know move forward, standing straight and proud behind me as I place the lock of hair as high as I can and step back. Hands touch my shoulders, my arms, as they guide me back into the fold—their fold—and when Kaleb steps forward with a torch and hands it to me, his eyes lit from within by the flames, I make a silent promise instead of speaking out loud about Chessie and her legacy.

I will be her legacy.

I will avenge the life that was stolen from her.

Meg's life is now mine to take.

And I will.

Goddess, I will.

I grip the torch and lay it on the bundles of thin sticks and straw at the pyre's base. The fire blooms epically as my heart lurches, and I let the pain of losing my best friend flow through me for the last time.

I cannot *not* cry again, though my tears are not worthy of her death. I will spill blood in her honor, and that's a vow. But my tears are not currently under my complete control.

Voices rise over the crackling fire–soft at first. It's a rhythmic hum, a lullaby, something ethereal and lovely. I close my eyes as more voices join the delicate chorus, a sob dying in my throat. My body loosens until I fold into myself, kneeling on the dirt while the flames lick upward, toward the stars.

A woman kneeling in the dirt beside me leans her head back, her face tilted up as well, and her voice rises above the rest as she sings with her entire chest, beckoning the others to follow. All around me, voices rise like the smoke funneling to the stars–voices of different depths–some pained, others hopeful.

But the song they sing is so frustratingly familiar that it brings fresh tears to my eyes even though I swear I wouldn't cry for her again, that I wouldn't let the truth of what happened become my new reality. My lips part, quivering as the lyrics awaken something primal inside of me–something damning and painful.

It's a song for a fallen warrior. A song wrapped in a mother's love and a mate's eternal grief. A song that's been sung for thousands of years in the Deadlands, often in quiet rooms where mothers rock their babies to sleep. It's sung in rooms where looms cast shadows over lonesome women waiting for their hunters to return. It's sung on nights like this–when we're forced to let go and say goodbye.

I crumble under the shared weight of anguish being loosed from lips who didn't know Chessie, yet love her. Voices of those who saw their daughters in her eyes as she fought tooth and nail to *stay*.

Guide our sister, our daughter, our warrior, home. Carry her in lengths of fur into your golden embrace, oh Goddess, so she may see the stars of your own making. Sing her Your stories. She's worthy, our young one. Take our sister, our daughter, our warrior, home. Our sister, our daughter, our warrior.

My voice radiates through the crowd in a keening cry, imperfectly harmonized, wetted by hot tears I can't fight. The fire soars, but I don't feel the heat. It's beautiful and chaotic, just like she was. Just like she's always been and forever will be. Forever young. Forever beautiful. Forever innocent.

We carry her memory. Her legacy. Our beautiful daughter of iron and claw. Open Your gates, oh Goddess, show her Your land of eternal sunlight. Let her run free in Your land of braided rivers, in Your fields of honey colored wheat. Oh Goddess, Your daughter, she comes bearing our blessings, our desperate cries. Oh, Goddess, guide her home.

My knees bite into the dirt as I lower my head, my hair falling loose around my face, sticking to tear soaked cheeks. A warm, strong hand gently clutches the back of my neck, and I'm guided sideways until my face is flush in the crook of Kaleb's shoulder. His scent cuts through the smoke, his presence slicing through the song. I turn my face into his shirt, my voice muffled by the rough fabric now soaked with my tears. I don't care. I'm beyond feeling anything but a choking sense of loss I can't make sense of, and he kneels by my side, an immoveable force of nature, the only thing keeping me from falling to pieces.

He wraps his arm around my waist and pulls me onto his lap. He rises, carrying me like an infant, turning from the pyre while standing tall, shoulders squared. I don't see how the crowd of mourners parts to allow us to pass. I don't feel the hands that stretch toward us, pressing silent blessings onto my arms, my hair, bowing their heads as he moves us toward his house. The song blooms through me, falling out of me in broken sobs and shattered syllables until I'm limp, barely able to breathe, but I *sing*. I sing until my throat aches, until my lips are raw and my chest is so tight I can't draw in a breath. Kaleb's footsteps on the stairs are silent as he carries me up, turning into his room instead of mine. He clutches me tight, carrying me like I'm weightless, just a terrified, overwhelmed, and exhausted child.

He doesn't make a sound. His chest barely moves as he takes a shallow breath.

I clutch his shirt, and he lays me down on his bed. My arms tremble as my fingers dig into the fabric. "Don't–please–don't go–" I whimper, trembling so hard my teeth clash together. "Please, just stay."

He sits on the edge of the bed, smoothing my hair away from my face while I blubber incoherently, begging him for... anything. For help, for solace, *to make it make sense.* I curl around him, sobbing into his lap. His touch smooths down my back. He leans toward me, shielding me with his body, like he's all that stands between me and the horrible, vicious world beyond.

And in a way, he is. At least for right now. At least until the pyre burns to ash, until the embers flicker for the last time. He eases further onto the mattress, dragging me with him to the center of the bed, where he tucks me against his chest, folding around me until I'm buried in him, his warmth, his touch a firm promise that he's not leaving.

And he doesn't.

Even when I open my eyes again to faint, rainy morning light trickling through the gaps in his faded curtains, he's still here, asleep, his body folded around mine, safe and warm.

Outside, rain pelts the windows again.

I lift my head from his arm before breathing deeply, taking in his heavily masculine scent. It's calming and instantly reminds me of everything that happened between us yesterday–the concern in his eyes when he'd seen the state of my arm, pressing me to the table in the kitchen downstairs, his mouth on mine...

Heat floods my body. I shudder, curling deeper against his chest, but the slightest brush of my thighs as they rub together has every nerve ending firing in rapid succession. His hand resting on my hip tightens.

He can't possibly sense this feeling trying to claw for dominance.

This want. This heat that makes it impossible to feel anything but his touch and his body this close to mine. It cuts through my grief–a needed distraction, something to numb the pain but something so strong it makes it difficult to truly feel anything else.

He shifts his position only slightly, his face buried in my hair, his breath tickling the top of my ear, and he slowly lifts his head. I close my eyes, but I know he's fully aware now that I'm awake, and we're caught, having fallen asleep together, tangled in an embrace.

The rain pattering against the window isn't loud enough to drown out my thundering heart.

He's going to ask if I'm okay, isn't he? He's going to pull away, make some gruff comment, or look at me with that hollow expression that screams disdain.

His fingertips sink into the curve of my hip. He curses under his breath, pressing a rather colorful word against my shoulder blade, and even just the touch of his mouth against my skin has a fire burning to life in my chest I can't ignore.

Neither can he.

He inhales against my skin, his teeth grazing my shoulder where the straps of my gown have fallen over my arms. My lips part in a quiet, subdued whimper of pleasure I can't bite back.

Kaleb splays his hand wide over my belly, drawing me closer to him, my back flush with his chest and my ass firmly planted against his lap where I feel his desire pressed between us.

Oh, gods. What are we doing?

A bright kind of desperation floods through me. The desire to be touched by him is overwhelming every other feeling, driving me absolutely insane. He buries his face in my hair again, taking a deep breath, like he's also trying to rein himself in, but we're already in dangerous territory.

"I know you're awake," he says hoarsely into my hair. He presses against my belly again, drawing me into him and the feeling of his cock…. Gods, every aching inch of him…. Another involuntary moan escapes my lips, and he shudders. "*Lexa.*"

His fingers inch upward toward my breasts, and I can barely

contain myself when his hand closes over one. I rub my thighs together, and that's it. That's all it takes for him to growl, to roughly roll me over onto my back so I'm beneath him.

He pins my wrists together above my head with one hand in an effortless but slow motion, his eyes locked on mine, waiting for me to flinch, to tap out.

He already knows my limits. He's seen me reach my breaking point before, many times.

No man has ever beaten me down until now.

No man, other than my dad, has seen me cry—until Kaleb.

No man has ever made my body feel like this without even touching me, and when he does touch me?

He keeps his eyes locked on mine then lowers his head to press a single, deep kiss to the hollow of my throat—testing me. Waiting for me to tell him *no*.

I don't.

TASTED

Kaleb lets go of my wrists, but I'm boneless as he draws a line down the column of my throat with his tongue. He's kneeling on the bed with my legs splayed over his thighs. His massive, warm hands smooth up my legs, bunching the fabric of my gown until it's pooled around my waist. Every movement is slow, controlled, like he's questioning how far he's willing to take this or savoring the moment.

I've done this before. Had sex. It was a fumbling, slightly drunken compilation of events. Exciting and heated—but there hadn't been... this. This slow, exploratory worship. No sucking kisses in a line down to my navel. Nothing that made my muscles weak and my toes curl like everything Kaleb is doing, like he already knows exactly how to touch me, like he's already mapped every inch of my body.

I gasp a shallow breath, my eyes hooded and heavy, when his fingers brush over my pussy—the lightest touch over my panties. I'd beg at this point. I'd get on my knees and say whatever he wants, do whatever he wants...

"Are you on contraceptive drafts?"

"No—no, I'm not."

Through my hazy, heated vision, I notice the beat of hesitation in his eyes. He bows his head, his hands braced on either side of my hips. I scooch back to sit up, but he grips my lower leg.

"What's wrong?"

"Nothing, I–it's nothing." He meets my eyes, his gaze heated, still dripping with desire. "Lie down, Lexa."

"I–" Now, I'm the one fumbling over my words. His eyes are bright, vibrant amber-hazel, shining like embers in the rainy morning light. "I've done this before. I've been with a man before."

Another quick arch of his brow. I wait for him to back off, to say something demeaning, but he smooths his hands back down my thighs, tugging my panties off, and the rush of cool air is a shock to my system.

"I don't give a fuck about that," he whispers, his voice low and simmering.

"Then why–why did you hesitate–"

"Because I could hurt you. Easily." There's a new fire in his eyes, something damning, something akin to regret, maybe even fear.

"You can't hurt me–"

"Maybe not now," he says, dipping his head to press the words against my belly. "Months from now, though."

I close my eyes as his kisses dip lower, pressed beneath my navel, my hip bones. A gentle, easy kind of pleasure ripples over my skin, but my body's tight with anticipation. I reach for him, smoothing my fingers through his thick, dark hair, but his mouth hovers just below my belly button, and his breath on my skin is nearly enough to send me over the edge of no return already.

"What do you mean?" I ask with great effort, but my voice is minuscule, barely audible.

Another kiss, this time to my inner thigh. "I can't risk getting you pregnant."

I nearly reply, nearly tell him he's thinking too far ahead, but he steals any words from my lips in an instant, his mouth closing over my sex.

The noise that follows–I've never heard it leave my mouth before. I feel my body sinking into the mattress, unable to move, unable to think past the feeling of his tongue parting my folds, his mouth hot and wanting. He shudders, gripping my thighs like he's holding on for dear life, trying to keep himself restrained, and when he growls... *gods, the vibration...*

I mouth his name as my eyelids flutter shut. My legs strain to close around him, but he pries them open again, growling with satisfaction as he draws his tongue through my folds again, slow, exploratory licks that leave me breathless.

I've never done *this* before. I've never felt *this* before. When his tongue slides in a slow, expertly executed circle over my clit, I nearly cave in on myself.

I hiss out a breath, arching my back toward him, chasing the friction he's creating, and he grabs my hips, meeting the arch, lifting my legs until they're resting over his shoulder and he doubles down on his efforts and I am... *lost* to the sensation.

One of his hands snakes over my stomach to grasp my breast, kneading, his calloused hands rough on my soft, tender flesh.

"Kaleb?" I moan, my breath coming in short, hollow rasps as the tension builds so strongly I'm unable to move, terrified to lose the feeling growing so acutely I might actually cry.

He groans against my folds, and then his other hand drops from my thigh, his fingers leaving heat in their wake.

He presses two fingers inside of me, and I bite down on a scream of pleasure that I'm sure will wake the entire city if I'm not careful. I lift off the mattress again, writhing and whimpering, and he loves it. I feel him smile against my pussy, working his fingers in and out while ravishing my clit with his tongue—sucking, nibbling, drawing me closer to the edge and expertly pulling me back just before the fireworks draw out the moment.

"I've wondered," he says against my skin before licking up my slit again in a torturously slow swipe, "what you'd taste like."

"Oh, Goddess," I whine, gasping as he presses a third finger inside of me. It's almost too much. The stretch is enough to finally shove me over the edge, and when my body jerks, pleasure washing over me like a rogue wave, Kaleb groans against the current, shuddering while my inner walls spasm around his fingers. The pleasure rocks me to my center and expands until even my fingertips feel electric. I'm unable to catch my breath when he finally rises from between my knees, his mouth closing on my inner thigh in a soft bite, like he hasn't quite had enough.

I grab his shirt and pull him back to me, our mouths meeting in a crash, teeth and tongues clashing. I find the outline of his cock–hard as steel and straining against his pants. I press the base of my hand up his length, my body trembling with the promise of him filling me, stretching me to the point of pain. I want it so badly.

But he stops me, clutching my wrist, and pulls away.

"Kaleb, I want–"

"We can't," he says against my mouth.

Confusion, and a lick of anger, mute the lingering waves of pleasure and white-hot desire still washing through my body. He rises, adjusts my gown, and steps off the bed, turning just as a door somewhere levels below us opens and closes with a crack, followed by hurrying but light footfalls on the stairs that can only belong to Lis.

I pull the sheets over my body, catching a glimpse of myself in the mirror across the room while he runs his fingers through his hair, looking down at me, but I'm looking at myself, seeing the mess he's currently smirking at. My hair is… insane–a wild mane of deep brown curls with hints of wine red curling in a halo around my face. My cheeks are flushed crimson, and my skin glows faintly with a hint of sweat as I tear my gaze from my reflection and meet his eyes.

He turns, giving me his back, and slips through the door, closing it behind him with a snap just as Liz's voice rings out, but muffled, too distorted for me to hear.

KALEB

Lis, out of breath and pink in the face, cradling the growing swell of her pregnancy, grips the banister as she pants, glowering up at me.

"You shouldn't be moving like that in your condition."

She arches a thin, dark blonde brow. "What're you up to?"

I roll my lower lip between my teeth, one hand resting on the railing, discreetly positioning my body in a way that hides what, exactly, I'd been up to, but I can taste Lexa on my tongue when I reply, "Making sure Lexa is resting."

"Uh huh," Lis says, her eyes narrowed to cat-like slits. "A messenger came to the gate for you–"

"I'm aware Silas needs to see me–"

"From the king. He's demanding your presence immediately."

Fuck. I step past her onto the stairs, commanding over my shoulder, "Keep her here in the house, preferably in my room. Make sure she's resting."

"I'm sure I won't do nearly as good of a job at that as you've been!" she cackles, and my cheeks heat, but I'm already on the second floor landing by the time her laugh fades, and the reality of what just happened sets it.

I try to shake the echoes of want from my mind as I step into the rain, which feels foreign on my skin. I don't just claim women. It's not something I allow myself. I tell myself I'm too busy, and I am, if I'm being completely honest. Sure, I've occasionally given in to my needs, my desires, but only when it's been so long that I can't remember the feeling of smooth, soft skin beneath my hands. There's too much at stake, too many risks, to make it a regular thing.

I normally don't even think about it. I've trained my mind to quickly banish those thoughts.

That training proved null the second I saw Lexa sprint around the arena, swinging that chain, and only grew in the days and weeks since then. The arrow pointed at the king. The way my men–warriors of the fiercest design–cower in her presence. The orange dress. The fork in the hand of a man three times her size–something she did without hesitation.

Freeing that dragon and breaking her arm in the process, oblivious to the pain until a day later, when she finally allowed herself to feel anything at all.

I let myself act on the desires that have been keeping me up at night, damning myself to the truth of our situation. I cannot keep her. Even if she wins these brutal games, I will lose her because she is not meant for the same cage I can't escape, and I won't allow her to stay. *I will die before she stays.*

The king is resting on his throne when I arrive in his gilded palace atop the arena and tunnels carved by slaves. Sponsors and trainers linger, uneasy, and there're so few of us now. Only seven victors remain out of the twenty that survived the Culling. The king doesn't even look at me as he announces the next Trial will be in a week's time. He also mentions a ball that will be held for the benefactors–the high lords who fund his twisted entertainment–which each of us, and our victors, are being forced to attend... tomorrow night. Only then do his eyes slide to mine, a silent warning for my victor to behave, or else.

She won't. I already know it. I eye Meg's sponsor as he grins, speaking in quiet tones to the fae male standing next to him.

Normally, I don't have free access to the capital city of Pantharas. I can't move freely here and require an escort, but today has been different. I leave the palace, prepared to take the tunnels near the arena back to the Glade, but I'm stopped by a fae guard who slips me a note before turning and walking away.

I read it quickly, absorbing Silas's handwriting, his quick, concise message, and toss the piece of paper into a sconce as I walk out of the palace and into the city center instead, the paper melting into the magic that lights the city, burning it.

Fae guards turn their backs to me instead of questioning why I, the halfling king of the slaves, is walking where I'm not allowed, and I realize how deeply Silas's influence has trickled in the last few weeks. The king has no idea about the serpent that lurks in his court, does he?

Silas's manor rises in the center of the city. The sun sinks toward the horizon again. His message initially chastised me for not coming to speak to him before he left last night, but then it bled into instructions about the upcoming ball, about the gown he had commissioned for Lexa and his opinions on what I should wear, like I'll listen.

He mentioned a guest now taking up residence at his manor in his absence and that he'll return by the finale of the Trials. I'm supposed to come… say hello, according to Silas, and not be so rude, or however he worded it.

That guest doesn't greet me when I step into the foyer and turn to the wide, airy reception room to a man seated in an armchair, books splayed across a table in front of him.

The man with violet eyes looks up, meeting my gaze.

"Who are you?" I ask, not warmly like Silas would have preferred, and he gives me the slightest lift of his lips in answer.

"You can call me the Architect."

I feel an odd, unsteady sensation grip my body as I look down at what used to be pristine, light wood floorboards now stained heavily with blood. My stomach twists as I look back at the man, asking, "What happened here?"

"A miracle."

DROWNING IN A DRESS

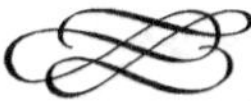

Lis clicks her tongue and fluffs the fabric of the impossibly massive ballgown that would look gorgeous on literally anyone else but me. The dress alone takes up my entire room at Kaleb's house, so I'm at the pack house instead, stripped down to my undergarments while half a dozen Glade women fuss over yards and yards of dark blue satin the same color as my eyes.

"Don't step on it!" Lis screeches, glowering at a young woman now ducking her head and scurrying to hide behind a woman I believe is her mother, based on their similar physical traits. Everyone follows Liz's commands, however, and after two grueling hours, I've been stuffed into a corset so tight I might actually pass out and then into a dress with a skirt so wide and heavy I'm not sure I can even walk in it.

"I can't breathe," I hiss, my hand pressed against my stomach.

"Good, that means it fits. See, I knew you had a waist somewhere. Plus, you have all those muscles to protect you from any internal damage." Lis waves a dismissive hand and steps back to admire her torture while the other women buzz around me like bees, sticking bronze pins in my hair to hold back the curls. A very old woman by the name of Ethel scrubs the hell out of my nails, while her... sister?

Or elderly daughter? Whoever this other woman is rubs scented oil on my arms until they shine like polished gold.

I hate this with a fiery passion, and Lis can tell because she's smirking at me, tapping her fingers against the swell of her belly. She looks too Goddess-damned comfortable in her pants, apron, and woven blouse.

"It must be nice," I sneer, and she beams at me.

"You look a woman for once," she retorts with that cackling, girlish laugh I'll forever hear in my dreams. "You're welcome."

The first thing that comes to mind when a trio of younger women bustle in with a full-length, but heavily cracked, mirror is that I cannot let Kaleb see me like this. I just can't. I feel like an uncanny version of myself, like a princess doll little girls cry over at the toy store. Like something out of a portrait of old, hanging in a gilded but dusty frame, forgotten with time.

I doubt anyone back home has worn a dress like this in centuries, but that only proves my theory that these immortal fae beasts have no taste even after living for decades, if not hundreds of years.

Silas had his hands all over this dress, and I know it. In fact, Lis confirmed it after she boasted about Kaleb's undone appearance and red-stained cheeks when he'd just left. He left me in that bed without a single word and disappeared for the rest of the day yesterday and today.

The dress arrived this morning. Lis has spent every waking hour preparing me like a feast, meticulously scrubbing me down, brushing out my hair, and pinching my cheeks until they sting to create some kind of blushed effect, and I've been trying not to kill her. If she weren't pregnant, I probably would have.

But she reminds me of Nora. Every ounce of care, every detail, is something Nora would have done. Nora has always seen something in me I've never been able to see in myself, and that's… this.

I finally allow myself to turn to the mirror, and even if I could breathe, I doubt I'd be able to fill my lungs anyway.

The women busy themselves by fluffing the poofy sleeves before securing them around my arms. I feel out of body as I stare at my reflection, at the pools of satin and taffeta, and the impossibly pinched curve of my waist. My hair is piled on top of my head, every curl accounted for, styled just so.

Maeve would scratch my eyes out for this dress. That almost makes it palatable.

"No," I tell Lis as she turns me from the mirror. "Please, take it off. Please, I'm begging you!"

"It's going to take three hours to get this thing off of you, so no."

"I'll get on my knees and beg–"

"You won't be able to get back up, Lexa. The dress weighs a hundred pounds." Another laugh splits through my whimpering. "It's just for a night. Plus… Kaleb is going to faint when he sees you." She winks, and I fail to hide the blush now heating me from the inside out.

"From hysterics. He's going to laugh at me!"

"He'd never. He doesn't laugh. Judging by how… close… the two of you are now, I would have thought you'd know that–" She yelps then bursts into another fit of laughter when I try to snatch her by the arm, but I'm drowning in the dress and can barely move like I'm used to.

But her laugh, and the colorful curse hanging off the tip of my tongue, die the second a large shadow moves into the exterior doorway of the pack house. He steps out of the light drizzle of rain still blessing the Glade, and my heart drops into my stomach.

The last word I spoke to Kaleb was his name leaving my lips in an unrestrained moan. I haven't seen him or heard his voice since the moment he slipped out of bed, stopping us from going any further while my body screamed in silence for him to come back.

I'm out of my mind. Of all the things I should be worried about, fretting about… the Trials, the death of my best friend, my shattered regiment, being this far from home…

It's the way he looks at me as he steps into the light that makes me tremble with sudden nerves.

He looks at me in what I can only describe as shock. He blinks, narrows his eyes, and turns to Lis. "Is this the dress? This is what Silas had made for her?"

Lis crosses her arms under her chest and lifts a brow. "Yes. Did you not see it before you had it sent through the gate? Weren't you... there? Out in Pantharas for the last... thirty-six hours?"

"I was busy." He glances at me, his eyes lowering to the bodice of the dress, which is so Goddess-damned tight my breasts spill over the fabric. His gaze lingers there for a moment. He doesn't even try to hide it. I feel a blush spreading like wildfire, and his gaze slowly turns back to my eyes before turning to Lis. "We won't be back until tomorrow."

Lis furrows her brow. He turns for the door, motioning to me like I'm nothing more than an obedient dog trained to follow in step. "What do you mean?" she asks.

"I'm not risking the journey back to the Glade late tonight when the king finally releases us from the ball. We'll stay at Silas's. Tell Chasten he's in charge until I get back."

She is utterly confused and uneasy, but Kaleb stalks through the door, and I have no choice but to follow. The light from the pack house fades into the dark, wet night. Clouds cover what I think might be a full moon, but I've lost track of the cycle, especially with my wolf so far from reach.

"Wait!" I huff. "Goddess, just—I can barely walk in this!"

Kaleb halts and smoothly turns on his heel to face me only a few yards from the main gate, which rises like a massive black metal vortex in the shadows, slick with rain. I'm sure my hair is already coiling and pulling out of the pins. I feel them popping off my scalp with every minute we spend in what feels like mist at this point—thick and humid. Kaleb takes my hand, tugging me over the damp dirt and gravel, biting down on what can only be construed as a smile at my expense.

The gate grates open, revealing fae guards on the other side, but I rush past Kaleb into the spiderweb of tunnels beneath the arena and palace, already accustomed to the layout, the sights and smells.

My rapid footsteps echo, but so do his. I pick up my pace, my heart in my throat, but the dress is weighing on my hipbones so violently I feel my skin blistering.

"Lexa, stop."

"No–no, I won't. If I stop walking, I'll lose my momentum, and this beast of a dress will drag me to hell where it belongs!"

"Stop–" He grabs my uninjured arm, pulling me to a stop. The mountainous skirt swings around both of our legs, swallowing his polished shoes.

I'm on the verge of tears. A kaleidoscope of emotion hits me directly in the chest as I back against the wall of one of the many winding tunnels, trying to kick him away, but the skirt only flares wider, sucking me deeper into its depths.

"What's the matter?" he asks, chuckling a bit.

"I–I can't breathe. The dress weighs a thousand pounds, and it's hurting me–"

He kneels on the soggy ground, lifting several layers of fabric, his body half submerged in the deep blue satin. He brushes my left thigh before grasping a bunch of fabric and pulling, yanking at least two layers free. I heave a breath as he slowly tears the underskirt away, lifting at least ten pounds from my hips.

But it's the proximity that has me on the verge of gasping for air. This can't be normal. This… yearning. Praying he grazes my bare skin again.

He rises, a mass of white, thick fabric balled between his hands. I hold his gaze, and he tosses it behind him into the shadows, turning to me and lifting a brow. "Better?"

"Where have you been?"

Kaleb exhales deeply as he meets my eyes in the darkness. "I'll explain everything when we're alone."

"We're alone now."

"Barely. These caverns are crawling with guards, whether you can see them or not."

I bristle, but he extends his hand.

I tuck my hand in the crook of his arm, letting my mind wander, trying not to think about our tryst yesterday. That's all it was–a distraction. A primal form of comfort I think we both needed. Nothing more.

He stopped it from going further, and that's his business, not mine.

I swallow past the lump in my throat. The stairwell we've been traveling opens to the palace, and the dimness of the tunnels explodes with color and sound.

Music soars over lifted, spirited conversation. Champagne scents the air like sugar crystals are suspended in every breath. Apparently, wide, gaudy gowns are in style because I'm not the only one wearing one, and mine is simple in comparison to the fae women floating from circle to circle–ethereal and beautiful, their wings on full display.

A wide marble staircase leads into the ballroom, but Kaleb pulls me into an alcove sheltered by thick, red velvet curtains before we descend.

"What are you doing?" I ask into his chest. We're barely an inch apart, his body stepping into mine like he's shielding me from view. I wince as he pulls the pins from my hair one by one. I reach up to stop him as my hair tumbles down my back, but he grabs my fingers and slowly lowers my arm to my side, those deep wells of hazel holding on mine.

"We should talk about what happened," he says, his voice a low, steely growl over the hum of noise coming from the ballroom.

"About what, exactly? How you kissed me to distract me from the fact you were going to force my elbow joint back in place?

"It wasn't a distraction."

"Then you wanted to kiss me?" I jab, my eyes teasing and mouth curling in a cocky smile. He can't be serious. *I can't be serious.* But his gaze is heavy, dark, and... oh, gods, I might actually be losing my mind because he looks like... he'd do it again if he had the chance. That he wants to do it again, right now.

"It won't happen again, don't worry," he says under his breath before plucking another pin from my hair. A curl bounces free, falling against my cheek. His fingertips graze my skin in a heated, damn near feverish touch. "I like it better this way," he whispers, leaving me... tangled, breathless. Then he steps away.

Pins still remain to hold my hair out of my face, but my curls bounce down to my waist with each step we take down the stairs. Faces turn in our direction, but I keep my eyes forward on the crowd at the base of the ballroom, looking at everyone and no one, gripping the fabric of the suit Kaleb likely borrowed from Silas. I distract myself with the crowd, with our situation, instead of thinking of the way his muscles flex beneath my touch. I let my mind hone my discomfort in the dress, telling myself his rigidness is because we match, which is ridiculous. He knows it. I know it.

But then I see her, standing in the crowd, her head thrown back in laughter while entertaining her sponsor and his friends. Every other tangled feeling dies in an instant.

Meg must sense my presence, the hatred and fury radiating from me, because she slowly turns her head to look at me, and... smirks.

Kaleb's fingers glide over mine. "Do not react. Save it for the Trials."

It takes all of my strength not to leap out of Kaleb's grasp and charge.

But his grip tightens like he can sense my moves before I make them.

I keep my eyes on Meg until the crowd swallows us whole.

SNAP

I keep my hand tucked in the crook of Kaleb's arm as he guides us through the crowd, ignoring the glances, the underhanded comments in a language I don't understand but know he does. Most people give us a wide berth. Many of the women hide their mouths with fans, their jewels sparking in the light of dozens of crystal chandeliers. I can't help but notice the copious amount of food going to waste on long, opulently decorated tables, not so much as a bite taken from several dishes.

My stomach curls at the thought of the kids who race into the pack house every morning to collect their family's daily rations of grains, milk, and meat. It's never enough. The people of the Glade have never had enough.

I nearly trip over my own feet when Kaleb comes to a rough stop, like he didn't expect it, and turns to a tall fae man–a trio of them, actually–the only seemingly friendly faces in the ballroom so far.

"Alpha King," says one of them–a man who looks to be in his late forties. At least, he could be, but he could also be several hundred years old by this point. The bob of his head rocks me to my center.

Kaleb returns the gesture and seems to relax a touch, and I realize with a start these men must be friends with Silas. It's the only explanation given our cold reception by the crowd at large.

"He didn't say where he was going, only that he had business to attend to outside of the city," Kaleb says while I stand at his side, discreetly scanning the crowd for locks of fiery red hair.

"He said the same to us," High Lord Everett says under his breath, nursing his drink. "I worry he might be doing something reckless in the wake of the death of his victor."

"Chessie," I say absently, and all three fae lords turn to me. I look at them, emotionless, waiting for a reprimand that doesn't come.

"Chessie," Lord Everett corrects, his silver-blue eyes softening in silent apology.

I turn back to the crowd, ignoring the conversation again, and see her once more.

Meg floats like she owns the place, and honestly, she might. She smiles at everyone, her beauty shining like a beckon while fae men stop to stare and fae women titter excitedly over her bejeweled gown.

I move on instinct, a predator stalking its prey, but I trained her. She knows. She knows I've slipped from Kaleb's side, off my leash, and I'm now sidestepping through the crowd in her wake.

She stops to talk to a group of men, her sponsor following behind like a dutiful suitor. I stand still, guests passing between us as if in slow motion while music rips through the air in a dizzying, distorted cacophony.

She looks back at me, down her nose at me, taunting me with a smile. I shake my head. All this time. All this time I knew there was something about Meg I didn't like, that I didn't trust. She was never a team player—always the most aggressive, the most violent, but only when it benefited her specifically. Her smiles were always fake, weren't they? The secrets she swore to keep were always leaked. I gave her the benefit of the doubt every time. I trusted her.

Chessie trusted her.

Chessie loved her.

I'm going to *fucking kill her.*

A booming voice cuts through the music, and I turn, looking for the source. I look up, and there on the balcony stands the king in all his splendor, beaming down at the crowd. He speaks in the fae tongue, something I ignore, and I turn back to Meg, but she's gone.

Shit.

Fury rages through me as I slowly turn back to the balcony, scanning the crowd for any sign of her. I try to spot Kaleb in the crowd as it swarms forward, everyone jostling for a better view, but I'm caught in its center.

Several people gasp, and excited applause rings out, adding to the sudden rush of chaos, and I'm squished, tripping over gowns and shoes as the fray keeps pushing toward the balcony.

I lift my chin, out of breath, as the king beams at the crowd, but then he looks to the side of the room and that smile turns villainous.

"Alpha King Kaleb of the Glade," he says in the dead tongue–the language of my people, of his enslaved people. His tone sends a shiver up my spine–so sickly sweet I can taste it for what it is–fake. Fake and menacing. I rise on my toes, trying to catch a glimpse of Kaleb, and it's not hard to do. He towers over most of the fae men despite their already unnatural height, and his eyes meet mine, a flash of relief sweeping across his face.

He'd been looking for me, too.

But then the king booms, "With tonight being a night of celebration across Pantharas in honor of our sacred games, I must also bestow a gift upon you and your people, shouldn't I? It doesn't seem fair that while we drink wine and dance that your kind must continue to grovel, especially on such a fine full moon, not that they can even see it past the rain."

Kaleb's expression tightens. His eyes darken as he glares up at the king.

The king continues, his voice dropping to something low and teasing. "I should let them feel their wolves tonight, don't you think? Alpha King? Let your people… feel the bonds I keep at bay?"

Kaleb's jaw flexes, his eyes suddenly wild with a damning kind of panic I feel in my bones. Dread. Pure dread casts his face in shadow as the king sweeps his hand through the air in a show of glimmer silver light. He told me about this, how they're allowed to feel their wolfish gifts so rarely most couples are already with children by the time they feel the mate bond, how it causes chaos and breaks families when it happens. I try to move in his direction, but my body jolts with a sudden, sharp awareness that forces me to stand completely still. It feels like all the air has been suddenly sucked from the room.

It's like being punched in the chest. The air leaves my lungs in a whoosh as my wolf awakens, groggy, confused, trying to claw back to life. I clasp my chest as another shocking, all-consuming sense funnels through my body, like ropes of gold rushing through my veins, heavy and… everywhere.

The noise in the ballroom blurs. Everyone is moving so fast, whizzing past me like I'm stuck in time, like minutes are passing as if they are mere seconds. My heart lurches, pulling me in a singular direction, and I slowly turn, my skin prickling, my senses flooding to awareness, and… there he is, standing shellshocked as the fine, delicate golden threads of our mate bond snap into place.

Across an ocean. A turbulent, furious sea. Over mountains and valleys. Behind a wall, a gate. We found each other against impossible odds.

Kaleb stares at me, his mouth slightly ajar and pupils blown so wide I can't even see the color of his irises anymore.

The ball moves on without us while we just… stare at each other.

My mate.

My mate.

I gasp for breath as reality comes crashing down around me like I've just been suspended in midair, stuck in the feeling of my wolf returning, unable to find my footing on solid ground. My corset bites into my skin, preventing my lungs from expanding like I desperately need them to. I claw at my bodice, torn between keeping a low profile and panic, while each thread snaps into place, one by one. His scent, even from this distance, hits me like a freight train. The memory of his touch on my skin makes my skin feverish, so hot I can barely stand it.

I'm dying. I have to be dying. I can't breathe.

Kaleb is suddenly at my side, yanking me through the crowd. I gasp again, drawing in a single gulp of air before he whisks me through a darkened doorway, behind a curtain, and into a hallway used by servants, who leap out of our way while he sprints, dragging me with him.

When we breach the front garden of the castle, the cool, damp night air fans over my skin. I can't even take in my surroundings. Time moves out of control, and I have no idea where we are, whether we've left the castle grounds or not, when we pass under a stone bridge into a side street cloaked in shadow, and rows and rows of pearly white estate houses come into view.

Kaleb picks me up at some point, racing through the night, his grip tight and steady while we pass under a second bridge and the woods—*trees*—rise around us, peaking over tall white stone walls.

Only when we turn into a narrow private street between two large manors does he set me down, grasping my hand, and pushing open a gate leading into a courtyard in front of a regal mansion made of alabaster and marble, all the lights dimmed, the rooms within empty.

"Where are we?" I gasp, my mouth impossibly dry.

"Silas's house," he grinds out, his tone edging on fury as he pushes through a side door, and suddenly we're wrapped in glistening dark wood and velvet.

He closes the door behind us. A hallway expands into the shadows of the quiet, seemingly empty house. He presses me against a door, his hands steadying my hips while I gape like a fish, unable to process what's happening.

He draws a knife from his belt, and I become totally, completely still.

He meets my gaze, holding, his eyes so dark they're nearly black. With a surgeon's precision, he slowly draws the tip of the blade down the center of the bodice, cutting through the thick fabric and boning like butter, all while his eyes remain on mine—wild, damn near feral with need.

His blade cuts to my bellybutton, each snag of fabric reverberating through my bones. Sweat prickles along my hairline despite the chill now seeping into my skin, every fine, downy hair on my body standing on end under his gaze.

We should talk about this. I know we're both thinking it. Mates. We're mates—fated mates.

"Is this a trick?" I whisper, and it's all I can manage. "Did the king—did he do this to us?"

"No," Kaleb replies, slowly drawing the blade away. I jerk in surprise when he grips the bodice and tears it open, my breasts bouncing free. He hisses out a hungry breath, his gaze lowering to my skin, to my peaked nipples.

"Are you going to reject me?"

His eyes meet mine in the dimmed light of the sconces behind us.

His answer is his mouth on mine in a fiery, damning kind of kiss. A kiss that seals our fate. He grips my hip as he turns the doorknob, the door opening behind me, and backs me into the shadows of a private stairwell—unlit. I have no idea where it leads, but it doesn't matter, not when he's clawing away the remains of the bodice, tearing the fabric free from my body, ignoring the laces entirely. Fuck the dress. Fuck everything. I whine in defeat when the skirt doesn't come free as easily, but he tears it from my waist, tossing it behind him into the shadows. I claw at his shirt while he shrugs out of his jacket, buttons popping and pinging against the walls, and then I'm on my back against the stairs, stone biting into my spine, but all I can feel is Kaleb, his hands on my naked skin as he roughly pulls my panties to the side with one hand while unfastening his belt with the other.

His shirt hangs off his shoulders, his muscled chest on full display, every cord of solid muscle catching the fight glow of exterior lighting bleeding to the window at the landing above us. I watch his chest rise and fall while he hesitates, his hand on his belt buckle, his other drawing a circle over my clit that makes me shiver, arching my hips to meet his touch. I'm soaked for him. So wet, I feel my desire dripping onto his hand when he parts my folds, pressing his fingers inside me.

"Please," I beg, my voice a shattered whisper. His eyes meet mine, and I see his answer there. He's going to deny me again. But why?

STAIRWAY TO HEAVEN

LEXA

Kaleb exhales sharply, shuddering, as he draws his fingers out of my pussy. They glisten, and he closes his eyes, pressing them back in slowly, tenderly, his thumb drawing a lazy, achingly slow circle over my clit.

I'm torn between the sharp ache of dizzying pleasure simmering in my belly and the defeated, almost lost look on his face, yet I still arch into the touch, whimpering his name, tears of want beginning to shimmer along my lower lashes as he draws a sharp moan from my lips.

"I can't take it," I plead, on the verge of sobbing. "Kaleb, I need you. I want you inside me. Please–I'll do anything. *Goddess, I'll do anything–*" Another sharp moan echoes against the stone walls of the stairwell when he curls his fingers inside of me. I throw my head back, my neck bent, and while I cry out, he closes his mouth against the base of my neck, his teeth grazing my skin. The fine threads of our bond shiver, sending a rush of heat fanning over my skin, settling deep in my belly.

"You're killing me," he groans, biting down as he presses his weight against my body, grinding his hips into my upper thighs. I feel his cock straining in his pants, throbbing like he's on the verge of losing control. "You'll be the death of me, Lexa."

"Why won't you? I don't understand–"

"The wings," he rasps, biting my neck again. He groans, shuddering when my inner walls clamp around his fingers. "It'll kill you. I can't take the risk. You're in heat, Lexa. Fuck!" He grips the steps above my head, hisses out a breath like he's in pain. I try to process his words, but my brain is mush, focused on one thing, and one thing only. Him. His cock. His cock inside of me, preferably.

I bite his lower lip–hard–hard enough to draw blood. He growls low in his throat in warning, and I let him go, reaching between us to stroke the heated imprint in his trousers. He doesn't stop me when I unclasp his belt. My fingers dance over the buttons keeping us apart, and he grips my wrist.

"Please," I whisper against his mouth, taking a shaking breath. A tear slips free from my lashes, sliding down my cheek. I think I'll actually die if he doesn't take me here, right now, on the stairs. My wolf can't take it, senses a rejection that pulls me to pieces. His grip on my wrist loosens. My hand glides down his length and up again, and he takes a shuddering breath, his mouth leaving mine to press kisses along my jaw, then my neck, which I arch to allow him access to that spot he's obsessed with at the conjuncture of my shoulder.

I unfasten the buttons, my heart racing out of rhythm.

He bites down on my neck as I free his cock, my fingers curling around him. He's… impossibly big. It's going to hurt. There's no way he can fit, and I think we both know that, and I…

I guide him to my entrance, the head of his cock parting my folds– wet and hot.

He braces himself on the stairs, his knees bent, as I tease him, wetting him with my desire, and he folds, begins to move.

Another low warning growl reverberates through him. I sink into the sound, into the feeling of him grabbing my hand and pinning it to the stone at my side, preventing me from touching him, from being the one to guide him home.

I turn my face against his, closing my eyes. *"Mate,"* I breathe against his ear, the word lost in a sharp, whimpered moan as he drags his cock up and down over my clit.

"You're going to be the death of me," he repeats before finally losing his mind. I've never met a man so restrained before, so in control.

I don't want that. I want him unhinged. I want him shouting my name for all the world to hear.

With all of my strength, I hook my leg around his, forcing him to the side, then onto his back, replacing my position on the stairs. I straddle him, but he stops me before I can slide down onto his cock, his hand splayed flat against my breasts, and his eyes... Goddess.

I'm out of control. This is... this is hurting him.

"Why can't we?" I whisper, shattered by the defeated, almost panicked look in his eyes. "What–what did you mean?"

"I can't get you pregnant–"

"I don't–whether we have kids or not is the furthest thing from my mind at the moment–"

His lips part, but he hesitates, and then I get it. What he told me earlier. The wings.

"You wouldn't survive the birth," he says so softly I almost miss it. "It would kill you and the baby. It would destroy you, and I won't–I can't take the risk. Not when you're in heat, and my wolf is begging me to claim you, to breed you, because that's all I want to do right now."

I balance on his thighs as he sits up, his cock still hard between us, hot like heated steel. I smooth my hand down his length, and he closes his eyes, hissing out a breath.

"I want you," he confirms with effort. "Fuck, I... have to be inside of you. I can't stop thinking about it. The taste of you, Lexa... I can't stop."

I ease down a step, then another, cold stairs biting into my knees. I've never done this before, but every fiber of my being melds to his, and I know exactly what to do when I kneel for the Alpha King of the Glade and lick up his shaft, my eyes meeting his in the dim light. He licks his lips, transfixed, in absolute awe when I close my lips around him and suck.

He arches his neck, every muscle flexed, and reaches for me, gripping the back of my head and tangling his fingers in my hair.

It's amazing. My body is on fire while I pleasure him with my tongue, sucking him down my throat until he groans my name. I brace my arms on his thighs, moaning with each involuntary thrust of his hips, taking him deeper, savoring the taste of him.

He loses himself, finally lets go of the chains keeping him bound, and it's as beautiful as it is heartbreaking.

But suddenly… something shifts. I feel it in our bond. He can't take this—this wanting. This desperation for me, to be inside of me, claiming me. I pick up the pace, moaning around his cock, whimpering as he presses against my head while he thrusts deep and pulls out, yanking my hair back to force me to let him go with a pop that echoes all around us…

And then he's dragging me into his lap, my legs splayed over his thighs.

"Fuck it," he curses and sits me fully on his cock.

I nearly scream at the feeling of him forcing me open, stretching me to my limits, but that feeling quickly subsides, replaced by a feral need to take him, to take him as mine. I straddle him, writhing my hips, my toes curling as the sharp ache bleeds into an acute, white-hot kind of pleasure that takes up every thought in my mind.

"Is this what you wanted?" he rasps, pulling me down so we're nose to nose, his lips brushing mine.

"Yes!" I cry out, riding him like we've done this before, like our bodies were meant to always move like this. Tension coils deep in my belly. I flatten my hands to his chest, moaning and gasping. His body tightens beneath mine, his jaw flexed, his fingers digging into my hips.

In a smooth, controlled motion, he flips us over, his hand splayed wide over my spine, protecting me from the bite of the rough stone beneath us. I don't care if I'll have new bruises. I don't care about anything but the feeling of him, his body rising over mine, his cock thrusting in and out at a pace that has me blubbering incoherently, overwhelmed by the heat of it.

His hands are everywhere–gripping my breasts, splaying my legs further apart. He's completely overcome by lust, greedily slamming into me and pulling out slowly, loving the way I whimper, begging him for more.

He leans down to nibble my neck, sucking a bruise so deep it'll still be there in the morning, and that's enough to send me spiraling over the edge into oblivion, and I come harder than I ever have before.

"Kaleb!" I cry out, my legs locked, the tension almost painful as warmth blooms through my center and expands in ripples of pure pleasure. My inner walls clench his cock, spasming and throbbing. He pumps into me, growling the filthiest, most depraved things I've ever heard against my skin.

He pulls out at the last possible second, his cock pressed between us, and spills himself on my stomach. His grunt of pleasure is short-lived and broken by what I only describe as frustration, like he wants to yell, curse whoever did this to him, to us.

I am most definitely in heat. That's the only explanation for the feeling of emptiness, dread, and rejection now flooding my system, erasing the echoes of pleasure still traveling through my body.

Kaleb pulls away, shrugging out of his shirt, his face cast in cold shadow. He uses the remnants of my atrocious ballgown to clean me up, and then drapes the shirt over my shoulders and scoops me off the steps.

I'm exhausted but left wanting as he carries me upstairs and into the unfamiliar, thankfully empty, house. He knows where he's going because he turns into a room that faintly smells like him, like he's been here before, slept on the massive fourposter bed he's now laying me on. I grab his hand before he pulls away completely. "Stay."

"I need to go back to the Glade for a few hours and make sure no one is killing each other while the shields are down," he says, and I can hear the vitriol in his voice, the frustration lacing through every syllable. "I'll come back. You're safe here."

"Is there no one else around?"

"No. There shouldn't be. Silas took his household staff with him, and his guest is not here tonight."

"His guest?" This conversation is trivial, meaningless. I want to draw him back to bed to… I don't know, fix this? Somehow? Try to work through the damning revelation that we're mates and the world around us is actively burning to the ground?

He turns around, giving me his back.

A cold kind of dread steals any other thought from my mind when those twin scars on either side of his spine catch the lamplight.

"You had wings," I whisper.

He lowers his head, adjusting his belt. His failure to reply is answer enough.

"What–what happened to them?" I ask, my lower lip trembling as he slowly turns to face me.

"I was a halfling born from a slave father. I wasn't allowed to keep them. They were cut off when I was born."

My chest convulses, but he edges toward the bed, reaching for me. I lean into his palm as he caresses my cheek, smoothing his thumb over my lower lip.

"We'll discuss this later."

"Will we still feel the bond in the morning?"

"I don't think so," he says with heartbreaking quiet, and then he leaves me in the dark, alone.

EXACTLY WHAT SHE WANTS

Kaleb

I'M FUCKED.

My chest aches as I put distance between me and Lexa, walking steadily through Pantharas toward the castle, resisting the urge to shift. Shift, for what would be the first time in years. My body sizzles with fragments of desire left untouched. This is a damning night, to say the absolute least.

My hair is slightly damp with sweat, tucked in soft curls around my fingers as I run my hand through it, trying to force my mind back to reality, but it's currently trapped between my mate's legs. It's the mate bond. There's no other explanation for this need to claim and consume her, bending her to my will, and she wants me to. Lexa, who has never knelt for any man, any king, knelt for me. Lexa, who could kill a man with her bare hands, begged me to fuck her, to take her as mine, and I regret not doing it then and there, leaving my mark on her skin with my cock buried deep, unburdened, not thinking of the future we won't have and the risk of a child—a beast like me—taking her into an early grave.

I had to physically tear myself from that bedroom and leave her. Every fiber of my being is screaming to go back.

The gate to the Glade doesn't open when I approach. Fae guards stand ready, armed, and refuse to move, now allowing me to pass.

"The king's veil over the Glade is lifted," one of them sneers. "You can't enter."

"I'm the king of the Glade," I snarl, but the guard's wings expand, and he steps forward, jabbing a long, curved blade in my direction.

"Sleep in the arena like the filthy fucking dog you are, halfling!"

My nostrils flare. I scan the line of guards. This was the trick, the plan, of the fae king. He had no idea that Lexa and I are mates, but he knew damn well that chaos would funnel through the Glade the second he dropped his magical veils and allowed the full moon's power to take hold of every shifter within. He didn't want me to return tonight. He wanted me separated from my people, unable to rule like I'm entitled to.

I won the Trials ten years ago. My prize was exactly what I asked for—his fucking blessing to unite the packs under one Alpha. Me.

It made us stronger. It kept us alive. Infighting died.

The king has found ways around my attempts to keep the peace in the Glade.

I shake my head at the fae men posturing in front of the gate. Howls break through the silence. It's a chilling, foreign sound after so many years without even seeing a wolf.

I turn from the gate. It's no use. Once the moon sets and morning comes, I'll be allowed back inside to deal with whatever mess awaits me.

The real issue at hand is being back in Lexa's presence.

She's exactly where I left her when I arrive back at Silas's house, curled in the bed, her eyes wide and fully awake as she lifts on an elbow to watch me. I lean on the door to close it. Her hair falls loose over her naked breasts, heavy and perfectly rounded in the slivers of moonlight now breaching the clouds, and my dick hardens at the sight of her glowing in the center of the bed.

She feels it, too, through our bond. The bond I should reject. The bond I prayed I'd never feel for anyone, but there she is, my mate, beckoning me back to bed like a siren.

Lexa doesn't say a word. Her expression is guarded, cast in darkness. She slowly leans back against the cushions, the sheets grazing her belly and thighs as they drift down her body to pool between her knees. She lets her knees fall apart, giving me a stunning view of... everything. Everything I've denied myself for as long as I can remember.

She doesn't understand why. Either that, or she doesn't care. She doesn't care in the slightest evidenced by the way her fingers trace over her breasts, her stomach, and then between her legs.

I press my back to the door, turning the lock in the off chance the Architect returns from his mission at the palace, or whatever the hell he planned to do after hours upon hours of conversation about the layout of not only the palace but the arena.

"We need to talk about this," I manage to grind out, but her fingers glisten as she strokes herself and I can't think. I can't look anywhere else.

"Come to bed."

"That's your wolf talking."

"And yours is listening, isn't he? He wants this as badly as I do."

"You aren't used to being told no, are you?"

A sly smile cuts through me, nearly bringing me to my knees. I want this. I want her. I want her more than anything I've ever desired before. I would burn the world to ash if she asked it of me. I doubt she'll need my help on that front, however. She'd burn it herself. I'd hand her the torch.

And that's why the Goddess gave her to me. She's a test of my unshakable patience. The shock I needed to break into action. Something to fucking live for.

Yet in a week, I'll be sending her back into the games to fight for her life while I'm forced to watch from the sidelines... possibly with our child in her belly if I can't... fucking... control myself.

Her lips part in a breathy, faint moan that rattles me to my core. I grip the doorknob tight enough to crack the bronze as she brings a hand up to clutch her right breast. I wet my lips, growling, "You're in heat."

"Please?" she whispers, the word hitching in her throat. She draws her knees together, chasing friction, anything she can find, and I feel everything through the bond, every flicker of pleasure, every want, and her scent... gods. It wraps around me, forcing me into action. This is my mate. Mine. Every inch of her. Her mouth. Her breasts. Her pussy.

She rises on her knees, her hair falling in that thick, messy mane of curls, and crawls to the edge of the bed.

She moves with the grace of a dancer, barefoot across the fine, shallow carpet, moonlight illuminating her long, muscular legs. She's not wearing a single scrap of clothing. The confidence in each step is my undoing. She knows exactly what she wants. She's used to taking it, bending others to her will. I'm the same. We're the same.

Before I left, I took my shirt back. I didn't even bother to button it, and now her hand is traveling down my chest, her eyes shining as they meet mine.

"Keep testing me, Lexa, and you'll find out the hard way not to fuck with an Alpha," I say through gritted teeth.

She arches a brow, her fingers slipping over my belt buckle, then lower. I grab her wrist. She tries to yank her hand back, but I spin her around, clutching her to my chest. I draw a hand down her body, nudging her legs apart with my knee, and slide my fingers through her folds.

"Oh!" she moans, arching her neck, her eyes fluttering closed.

"You're ravenous, aren't you? I didn't expect this from you." I toy with her clit, loving the way her knees go weak, how she trembles. "All of this power, this strength, and I'm your fucking weakness, aren't I? How long, Lexa, have you been wondering what it would feel like to have me dominating you? Me calling the shots? Me being the one to bend you to my will?" Now, my wolf is talking, taking over, and I let him, let those wolfish, brutal tendencies finally take control.

I'm rough with her, losing my fae side while she writhes, her skin slick with sweat, and her heat pooling in my hand, but I don't stop until she's silent, focused, her pleasure reaching its peak.

I won't let her have it yet. If she wants to play games, we'll play. I'm a champion, after all.

I pull my fingers out, and she whimpers with disappointment, but the sound is short-lived. She gasps, sucking in a startled, heated breath when I grip the back of her neck and walk her back to the bed, shoving her belly down on the mattress. I'm out of my mind.

"Is this what you really want, little wolf?" I free my cock and swipe it through her folds before I thrust in so hard and deep she tries to draw her knees together, but I pin her legs down.

LEXA

KALEB FISTS MY HAIR AND POUNDS INTO ME UNTIL I'M SCREAMING HIS name. Blind pleasure rockets through me, unending, searing and splitting me into pieces. I come immediately, tightening around his cock, and he growls, slamming into me again and again. Rough. Unhinged. Years of denying himself. Weeks of denying himself of *me*. It all comes together, converging at this moment, and when he ropes an arm around my belly and pulls us to the side with my back to his chest, his cock still buried to the hilt, I realize I might have gotten ahead of myself.

His hand snakes between my legs as pressure swells, his cock expanding, locking us together.

"Kaleb!" I cry out, but his other hand curls around my throat, forcing my head back.

"This is what you needed," he rasps against the rim of my ear before groaning deeply, the sound sending another jolt of feverish pleasure rippling through my body. "This is what your wolf wants, isn't it? To be knotted."

Pain radiates through my core, but I fight against it, focusing on the way his fingers move over my clit instead. I rock against his hips, meeting him with each aching, slow thrust until we're trapped together and he can no longer move.

"I want you to come again," he breathes, his voice heavy and heated with need. "Come for me." He nibbles my ear before dipping his head to suck my neck. I moan–deep and breathy, a sound straight from my soul.

I feel the orgasm building as his body starts to tighten. His fingers leave my clit, reaching up to roughly clasps my breast, kneading and rolling my nipple. He comes absolutely, positively undone. He shudders, groaning, *"Lexa,"* before biting down on the hollow between my neck and shoulder... hard enough to pierce the skin.

Kaleb marks me, knotting me, filling me with his seed, and I lose all sense of reality.

The orgasm that rocks through me is long and slow, blossoming in soft waves before crashing down on me like a tsunami. I'm swept away, tears of relief in my eyes when my body finally settles.

We stay locked together, his leg pressed between mine. He drags his tongue over his mark, and I shiver at the sensation that settles deep in our bond.

Mine. Mine, *mine...*

My mate.

I found my fated mate.

I close my eyes and what seems like a second later I open them to full, startling daylight. Just like he said... no wolf. Only an emptiness that feels wider than before.

Kaleb is asleep beside me, his arm a dead weight across my waist.

I reach up and gingerly prod the mark on my neck to make sure it's still there, and this wasn't all a dream.

It wasn't a dream.

Reality sinks like an anchor.

I can't leave him here. I won't. I can't leave this place without him and his people. Our people.

I'm going to win the games. I'm going to kill Meg. Then, I'm taking all of us home.

Kaleb stirs, settles against me with his legs bent behind mine, the two of us fitting together like a lock and key, and it's perfect, but those feelings from last night.... Goddess, he mentioned how chaotic things become when the fae king lifts whatever he uses to keep the mate bond at bay. I can only imagine what things are like in the Glade right now.

We should be there. I didn't even ask why he came back so quickly. I'd been deranged. Out of my fucking mind with lust, and I've never, ever, felt like that before.

Guilt washes over me, forcing me out of bed. Kaleb remains, asleep, his face totally relaxed like he hasn't slept this deeply his entire life, and that's the only knowledge that keeps me going. I rifle through an armoire and find a men's shirt and a pair of trousers that aren't going to fit, but seeing as the ballgown, and my panties, are in pieces at the bottom of a stairwell somewhere in this massive mansion of a house, this is going to half to do.

I roll the trousers, securing them with a belt. I tie my hair back with a ribbon I find in the drawer of a seldom used, slightly dusty vanity. I glance at my reflection only once and see... myself. Just Lexa. Lexa the daughter, the sister, the warrior, and now Kaleb's mate.

I decide to find some food to occupy my time in Kaleb's absence and wander down the empty hallways of Silas's house, peeking into random rooms and running my fingertips over the fine furniture, the freshly polished side tables, sculptures, and vases that bedeck every surface.

I end up downstairs, walking through the shadows that stretch through the glare of early morning, and just when I decide to turn around, to seek solace in Kaleb's warmth instead of inside my head, I turn into a sitting room off the foyer.

Silas looks up at me. I startle, grabbing the frame of the archway for support after I stumble over my feet. "What are you doing here?"

"Me? I live here. What are you doing here?"

"Kaleb said you were away on business?"

He sighs, rising from an armchair near the dormant hearth. But when his eyes meet mine in the soft, golden glow of early morning sunlight, his gaze drops to my neck, to the fresh, healing scar Kaleb left on my skin. He arches a brow.

"Well. This situation just got a whole lot more complicated for all of us, didn't it?"

WHAT DID YOU DO?

Kaleb

LEXA ISN'T IN BED, AND I HAVEN'T SLEPT THIS LONG AND THIS HARD IN A very long time. Those are the first thoughts that come to mind when I squint into the sunlight pouring through the windows on the far side of the room, alerting me that a new day has dawned and all wolfish abilities are now gone again, stripped away.

I draw my hand across the sheets, settling it against my chest instead, willing myself to move from a bed that smells like us knowing damn well what happened last night is the beginning of the end.

I find Lexa within seconds, her body casting a long shadow over the foyer as she speaks in low tones to Silas, who shouldn't be here. Both turn when I come into view, lumbering down the stairs while actively buttoning a shirt I found in the armoire in the room I've always used when I stay, which is rare.

Silas wastes no time. "A conversation needs to be had," he states, stepping past Lexa into the light of the foyer.

I hold out my hand at the base of the stairs, but Lexa whirls, her eyes wide as she glances between us.

"Lexa, there's food in the kitchen. Just take this hallway to the left, and you'll find it at the very end."

Lexa narrows her eyes at Silas, but the mention of food has her feet moving before her mind has a chance to catch up. She holds my gaze, however, for the few seconds she remains in view. I feel it still—that pull. The one thing I prayed I'd never experience. The one thing I'd now give anything to feel forever.

Silas yanks me down an opposite hallway, and I allow him to do it. A door snaps shut behind us. His study comes into view, hazy golden sunlight piercing the gaps between thick blue velvet curtains.

"Tell me you didn't mark her!" he shouts, locking the door. "Kaleb, please."

I roll my jaw before turning to him. "While you were gone on *business*," I seethe, "Your king lifted his wards on the shifters last night. I wasn't allowed to return to the Glade. That's why we're here."

"I'm not asking why you're here! Why does she have a mark on her neck? Your mark, too, right? You've got to be—"

"We're mates."

"You can't possibly be in your right mind," he shouts, his face going splotchy with fury. "Kaleb you can't just—"

"I haven't imprinted on her or taken her as mine without cause. This wasn't in my control."

"What the fuck are you trying to say?"

"She's my mate. My fated mate."

He blinks once, then twice, shaking his head like the damning truth can't find a place to settle in his mind. He turns from me, bracing his hands on the back of a settee before bowing his head in surrender. "You're sure?"

"You think I would have done it if I hadn't been able to stop myself?"

"You know what comes next, right? After the final game in the Trials? You know what her finale will be? Or have you forgotten what you were forced to do in order to win?" Vitriol and panic lace through each word. I feel it settle in my bones.

"My pack has a Luna now. When she wins, and she will win, your precious resistance can charge and take over like you're planning. You should be jumping for joy—"

"I didn't plan on *this*," he says weakly, bitterly, his eyes meeting mine. Blue, like the ocean. The color passed down by the mother we share yet I've never met.

"There's nothing I can do about it now, and you know that. If anything you've ever said about the resistance is true—if your special guest's plans work—it won't come to that point."

"We're talking about your life right now, Kaleb."

"She is my life now." The words leave my lips before my mind has a chance to process them. They came from somewhere deep, some-where foreign, but feel natural on my tongue when I double down, stepping into his immediate space. "Lexa is my mate. Whether I like it, or she likes it, or it's easy or fucking impossible…. Maybe I knew that day." The column of Silas's throat bobs as he shakes his head, lips parting to cut off me, but I raise a hand. "I knew during her round of the Culling. Watching her fight for her life. That's when I knew, but I couldn't voice, couldn't let myself believe it because you're right, Silas. I will have her until that last Trial. I have until then to find a way to stop this, but if I can't, and it comes down to the very end, you will—"

"No," he cuts in, but I push ahead.

"You will finish this. Your resistance will finish this. You will get her home—" Silas shakes his head. I grip his shirt until my knuckles turn white. "You will get her home and bring every last shifter in the Glade with you when that time comes. You will return her to Eastonia."

"I can't—"

"You will," I rasp and clasp his hand. "For me, you will."

"This was never part of our deal."

"Our deal was that I'd step in as a trainer, a sponsor, so you could move forward with your resistance. I have, and I'm asking for what's owed to me. You will protect her if I can't."

"Do you love her, Kaleb?" His grip tightens around mine.

I don't know how to answer that. Maybe in another life, another time, I could say yes. That the threads of our existence have always been wound together, and I have searched for her in every lifetime, always coming up short, and now, in the worst life of all, she's here—either to save me or be my downfall. A lesson learned. A gift for every torment.

I can't think about it now, not with so much at stake.

"Swear on my life that you'll get her back to her family and ensure my pack goes with her."

"It's impossible."

"So is your guest," I remark, and squeeze his fingers. "Yet, he's here, isn't he? Your prophet?"

His eyes narrow, but he holds his tongue.

"She will go home. I will ensure she wins."

"Even if it comes down to her life or yours?" he asks.

"What would you have done for Chessie?"

The blood drains from his face. He finally lowers his gaze to our joined hands. "You have my word."

I let go before another word is said and turn, unlocking the door and leaving it open on my way out.

"Does she know?"

I close my eyes as Silas's voice reaches me when I breach the doorframe.

The floorboards beneath him creak as he turns in my direction, but I remain fixed in place.

"Does she know how this ends? Does she know how it ended for you?"

"No, and it doesn't matter."

"You marked her, Kaleb."

"I was out of mind." I look at him over my shoulder. "You can't imagine what it feels like. Having the full brunt of what makes me a wolf hit me in an instant." I slowly turn. "I am not like most halflings. You've known that from the beginning. The king has known that from the beginning, which is why my family—my father and my sister–are dead. It was punishment. I am a shifter, Silas. Last night–if that's all I get with her, it will have been a blessing."

"And will it be a blessing for her when you–"

"I owe it to her and her family to get her home alive, and if I spill blood in order to do so, so be it. You just swore you'd protect her. You owe me this."

"You have to put her back in those games with your mark on your neck, Kaleb, for fuck's sake! You can't. You can't continue to sponsor her. You can't handle this anymore."

"You don't get to say that–"

"You're deranged if you think you can stand back and watch your mate fight for her life through two more Trials!" he shouts, his eyes wild with a sudden, unfiltered emotion I've never seen from him. It's dark, empty, and comes from a place so desperate I can taste it on my tongue. Doom. Dread. An utterly all-encompassing kind of grief.

"Was she your mate?" I ask, already knowing the answer. No. It can't be.

Silas just stares at me, unable to even speak. I fight the smirk threatening to spread across my lips. It's misplaced–this anger at him. At his kind. Not all fae are like the king. More fae struggle under the king's rule than they prosper... even the High Lords and their royal guards who're now turning in defiance.

That's why these games were called forth, isn't it? That bitter undercurrent of distrust plaguing Pantharas? A distraction from the real issues plaguing not only my people but Silas's?

"I have to return to the Glade to clean up the mess there. We'll speak again soon."

"I'm not staying in Pantharas long," he says quickly, his voice low. "I only came back because I have what my guest asked for."

"Why not just call him the Architect?"

Silas blinks, tilting his head in confusion. "Why would I do that?"

"That's what he told me to call him when I met him here, in your house, in the same room where he helped you pack Chessie's body to be returned to Eastonia because somehow he has the ability."

"Oh," Silas murmurs, turning his face out of view. A prickle of suspicion races through me while I watch him fumble with a few of the open books on his desk. "I suppose I know him by another name."

"He asked for a layout of not only the castle but the caverns beneath the arena. I gave them to him."

Silas only nods, his eyes wide but unseeing as he strokes a page in a book.

"Who is he?"

"A friend, I suppose. Someone who wants the same thing I do."

The throne. Not to sit on, but to dismantle it.

"Be wary of who you trust, Silas."

Silas takes a deep breath, and I turn, once again, to leave, but he says, "Leave her here when you go back to Glade. Just for a few hours, until you've settled things."

"Why?"

"That's what the king wants her to see–the chaos. The heart break. He wants to plant the seeds of delusion now because the next games will be the maze, Kaleb. It's confirmed. Clean up his mess first, and then come fetch your mate. I'll feed her. She'll be fine here."

"Don't drag her into this. Leave her out of this plot."

"I will, just as long as you know that this... the end of this will crush her, whether the two of you fall in love or not."

I close the door behind me, blocking out his voice.

I find Lexa in the kitchen, which is otherwise empty and sunny. She's already rifled through his cabinets but came up short of anything to eat right away. As I come into the room, she turns to me, her eyes wide with sudden hope, and it fucking kills me.

"Hey," I murmur, bracing my hands on the work table between us–modern and sleek in comparison to the kitchens in the Glade. Cold marble chills my skin.

"Hey," she replies quietly, rounding the counter in my direction, but stops short, and a gaping distance stretches between us.

I meet her eyes. Blue, like the ocean beyond the reach of Pantharas. Dark, turbulent, and dappled with stars.

"I, um," she says, then looks down at her hands, unable to finish whatever string of words she wants to say, and it doesn't matter. She shouldn't be the one trying to close the distance, the one reaching for something I think we both know is impossible.

Yet, I say, "You're my mate even if we can't feel it right now. Not feeling it means nothing to me. You're my mate, Lexa."

"Is this smart?" she asks weakly, looking up at me.

"Not in the slightest."

"Should we reject each other?" Her voice wobbles, a hint of panic hanging from her lips. It's the worst sound I've ever heard.

"I don't want to do that."

"Me neither," she says in a whisper, and that heat–that other-worldly pull–yeah, it's there, just beneath the haze of magic keeping us in chains. It's been there the entire time. "Now what?"

LEGEND HAS IT

"Now what?"

Kaleb moves in, reaching for me. I close my eyes as his fingertips graze my cheekbone, and I don't fight it when my body instinctively leans into his touch. It's short lived. His thumb grazes my cheek like he's counting the freckles before he pulls away, and then I'm alone, in a kitchen so dated yet opulent, hungry and confused.

I find a little box of cookies, and that's going to have to be enough unless Silas returned here with his entire staff, but... I think we're the only two beings in the house as it stands.

I should probably gather the gown in that stairwell, but I have no idea where the stairwell is... but I'm sure, based on the raised voices I heard moments ago, that Silas is already well aware of the situation now.

He finds me after twenty minutes. I'm still in the kitchen with my knees tucked to my chest perched on a bench beneath a wide window letting in light from his back garden. He glances at the empty box of cookies before moving toward the stove, which he lights by simply moving his hand over the grate, and pulls a kettle to rest over the flames.

He has his wings tucked in tight along his back as he moves, searching the cabinets like he, too, isn't used to being in this room, being the one making what smells like coffee, which I haven't had in ages.

"I didn't know fae drank coffee," I say absently, picking fibers from my oversized pants.

He shrugs, pulling two mugs from a cabinet. "Based on what we know about your folk, in your mystical, theoretical lands, I didn't know you even existed."

I lean my head against the window and fix him with a glare, which he smiles at, rolling his eyes back to his task.

"In all honesty, Eastonia and the lands of shifters are supposed to be a myth. That's what we're taught during our school years. You can only imagine the surprise when our king began to rumble about–about–"

"Invading?" I rest my chin on my knee, arching a brow.

"I fail to understand, even years later, why it's necessary," he replies under his breath, and then he's sitting at the table across from me, gently pushing a cup of black coffee in my direction. "I don't know where they keep the cream and sugar."

"Why'd you dismiss your staff if you knew you were coming back so quickly?" I want to ask where he went to begin with, but honestly, the last three or four days have been a complete blur.

"I wasn't under the impression I'd be back so quickly, but I found something that might be useful to a friend of mine, so I came back."

"That's all rather secretive."

He smirks, taking another sip.

"There are things you don't need to know, things Kaleb wouldn't want you directly involved in. This is, unfortunately, one of them."

"Can you at least tell me where you went?"

"Why does it matter?"

"Because I'm in a new world and trapped within walls meant to keep people like me caged. It seems like you have the freedom to come and go as you please."

He's silent for several seconds, lost in thought. "It's not as easy as that, but yeah, I suppose that's close to the truth. I had to go up north to what we call the Highwoods, but don't repeat that to anyone. Except your mate, of course. It's a kingdom outside of our king's control. Shifters and fae live there together in peace. It can be done."

My cheeks prickle with a blush I'm totally sure is his doing. Just the word mate has my body on edge. It's a strange feeling. That feral lust is gone, yes, but new feelings remain. It's hard to describe. I'm sure it would be easier if I could feel everything in full.

"Why does your king not allow shifters to… be what they are? Why take those powers from them?"

"It's a complicated answer."

"I know enough, I guess. Kaleb told me it's to keep everyone desperate."

"That's part of it. Shifters are often more powerful–in terms of raw strength–than fae. We're whimsical." He smiles with a teasing flutter of his fingers before that smile fades to a beaten kind of neutrality, like he hasn't slept in days. "Shifters rely on the moon for their gifts, but I'm sure you know that–"

"Actually, no. What do you mean?"

He takes a sip before leaning back, tilting his head as he scans my face. "You don't feel most powerful, most called to your lupine gifts, when the moon is full?"

"I mean, sure. It beckons, I suppose, but I can shift whenever I want normally. There's never anything holding me back."

That confuses him greatly, which confuses me.

"Really?"

I nod, taking an experimental sip of my coffee. It's strong as hell and bitter but trickles through my system, awakening my sleep addled brain. Whatever senses I have left begin to wake up, and I notice the shielded look behind his eyes, like he's silently begging for something. I'm not entirely sure what, so I say, "Did you think we could only shift during a full moon?"

"I... I guess so."

"That's silly. Whoever told you that knows nothing about wolves. It's voluntary, too."

"But the mate bond isn't?"

"No." I smooth a hand over the surface of the table. "It's not."

Silence swells. I resist the urge to talk about Chessie, to ask him if he's all right, to be honest. His cries of anguish had been the only thing I'd heard or seen during those moments after her death before it all went hazy, and my mind clung to survival instead.

"Magic isn't an infinite resource," he begins after a few moments of heavy silence–heavy enough I can hear the groans and clicks of the massive mansion all around us. "It's something that can wane, something that can be taken and controlled."

"It's... not," I reply slowly, meeting his eyes. "Magic is everywhere where I'm from. It literally bleeds from the ground in some places in the Deadlands. You can feel it in the woods in the Roguelands. It's in the water that flows through Crescent Falls and Eastonia, all the way to Maatua, buried under the sand of Tarsian."

Silas tilts his head, enraptured. What's going on here? In Pantharas? Are all these people trapped, unable to feel any of this?

"My family has magic," I say, practically involuntarily as a sweeping sense of unease curdles through my veins. "We're still not sure how, or why, it came about. How some of us are so different from the others. My–I'm sure Kaleb has mentioned to you what I told him about my family when I first arrived."

He shakes his head, which shocks me. "Whatever is said between you and Kaleb remains your business. He's not that type of man."

"What type of man is that?"

"You can trust him with your life." He holds my gaze intensely. "It's a rare form."

It is, even back home. My chest tightens around a fleeting warmth I've been desperate to hold onto since I woke up this morning and continue, "There're two branches of my family. My great-grandparents united what we call Crescent Falls, a northern territory on our continent. They were the Alpha King and Luna Queen for a long time, and they had two children, my grandfather, Isaac, and his sister… Queen Ella." I fold my hands around my coffee mug. "Isla was a witch." I meet his eyes, sending my silent questions into the space between us. Do they have witches here? Are we similar at all? "And Maddox had… according to our scholars… enough Firestone blood to… get the ball rolling, genetically."

Firestone bounces through the room. Silas narrows his eyes and suddenly widens them, like the word is familiar–not just something he's heard before. No, it means something to him.

I go on, "My great-aunt Ella pulled down the veil around Eastonia. Her mate, Ryatt, is what we call a Shadowsynger–"

"Oh," Silas breathes, closing his eyes. "My gods."

"What?"

A sideways, disbelieving smile touches the corner of his mouth. "Go on, please."

After a beat of hesitation, I do just that. "A wolf of shadow. He was the King of the Roguelands and waged war against the last of the Old Kings, King Kane. They united Eastonia under one crown, which now belongs to my cousin Maeve, the first full-blooded Firestone Witch to take the throne again after… but you know what I'm talking about, don't you?"

"The Great War," he says softly, opening his eyes. "It's just a legend."

"Not where I'm from."

He smirks, methodically rising, taking our coffee mugs with him. With his back to me, he says, "What do your people say about the era of the Firestone Queens?" He refreshes our mugs.

"Not a lot. There's too much we don't know. The Deadlands was a Firestone kingdom, they think. Some believe it was the first, older than Moonrise, our capital."

"I meant about the war," he corrects, pouring fresh coffee into each mug.

I chew the inside of my cheek for a moment, waiting for him to return before continuing, "We don't know enough to be sure. My mother's people–the tribes–they have their own history. But it's theorized now that... our enemies during that time were... possibly your kind."

"You'd be correct if that's what you also believe."

"Then there were fae in Eastonia?"

"Yes. Our oldest ancestors. Our heroes and villains of every story told to fae children. The fact that you exist proves they're not just myths." He slides the coffee in my direction, and I accept it without hesitation. "We were not banished from your lands. We shouldn't have been there in the first place. We invaded, tried to convince the Firestones to give us their magic. Our narrative about them is negative–they were evil, monsters of fire and seduction. But they had the shifters on their side, their beasts, so the fae took as many of the wolves as they could after a war that waged for centuries, and Eastonia faded away, never to be seen again, and our kings have wasted the magic of Pantharas, hoarding it, turning it into currency that cannot be replaced or regenerated, and you...." He brings his cup to his lips. "You have no idea what a fae king would do to have everything you have as his own."

"They want our magic?"

"All of it."

"Why?"

"Because," he says, the saddest of smiles touching his lips, "We're immortal, Lexa, but we cannot heal our own wounds. Children are rare–so much so that we are slowly dying out. We can fly, but only a few of us are granted the freedom to use any of the gifts of light and sound we should have naturally. It's all for the king, and he wants more."

I cock my head. "Does he have a name? He's always just addressed as the king."

"I'm sure he does, but I doubt he remembers it. He's... at least a thousand years old."

I pale. "So... a few decades to plan between when the veil fell and... now... means nothing to him, does it."

"No," Silas says slowly as the puzzle pieces begin to fall into place.

"He sent scouts, didn't he? To look for Eastonia again?"

"Long before the veil was destroyed. Explorers, yes. First, halflings. They found Emberfyll and revolted."

Now I'm the one closing my eyes, thinking of Logan. "They set up their own kingdom."

"Centuries ago, yes. Those with strong fae gifts put a veil around it, and we lost them. Then the king sent fae scouts, his most powerful, loyal supporters, and they disappeared for decades, until recently when... Hannibal Arachnis returned home on what he said were the wings of Firestone magic. Few believed him."

I think of the battle that took place on that distant island off the shore of Tarsian, of the Viper, and Maeve and Ryatt. "Maeve had no idea what she was doing."

"She did not know fae can harness powers from others. He likely used her power to get home, sapping her energy while his comrade died, yes."

"Your king wants to take Eastonia, doesn't he?"

"Our kind placed kings in your lands before the last dawn of the war, when the Firestones fell. It was a last effort to take control, and your Goddess trapped them inside as punishment. Now, the veil is gone, and he sees it as ripe for the taking."

"He will be sailing into hell," I warn, and Silas nods.

"We will not let it get that far," he says to me. "That's why you're here. The King of Pantharas's reign will come to an end when your games do."

"How do you know?"

"I've seen it."

I narrow my eyes. "How?"

"I made a new friend–"

"Lexa?" Kaleb's voice echoes through the house, drifting into the kitchen, and Silas looks down into his coffee, his lips pinched shut.

JUST ARIS

Aris

Maddy and Isaac's home in Maatua is shockingly cozy in comparison to the castles and palaces each side of the family calls home. Myself included, seeing as I still haunt the ancestral, gloomy castle older than the dawn of time itself in Veiled Valley. Here in Maatua, it's nothing but wide, open skies and the softest turquoise water, with sand like butter, so light it falls like snow through my fingers while I watch the tide roll in.

A dark-haired, violet eyed little girl kneels a few feet from the tide line, dutifully dusting sand from a massive clam shell Kieran gave her, while my three-year-old nephew is a few yards away, squealing against the gentle waves lapping his toes while he hunts for more shells.

I'm not sure how long I've been out here with them–Skye, Kieran, and Fallon, who's currently seated in my lap, double chins and chubby cheeks rosy as she watches the bigger kids play. An hour, maybe? Maybe more?

The private beach stretches as far as the eye can see. No one can bother us here. The reporters and paparazzi who stalk my family's every move are most definitely lying in wait at the gates to the exclusive neighborhood where Maddy and Isaac now live full time, but they can't enter.

I mean, they could. The only thing stopping them is the promise of Isaac's wrath and magic.

Imagine them getting a picture of me like this. Innocently holding a baby. While I keep tabs on my nephew and… well, I'm sure Skye will grow up calling me uncle, even though I'm technically a cousin in a removed way. Who knows at this point? There's so many of us now, and I'm watching the next generation play in the sand while the rest of the adults confer in the quiet solitude of the beach house behind us without me.

Anyway, a picture of me surrounded by children would cause a buzz for sure. No one would believe it, for one. Like Blake, who was constantly in the media, some model draped over his arm as he left whatever seedy, underground EDM club he favored at the moment, I've had my pictures blasted in every gossip rag ever printed. Unlike Blake, all of my public transgressions were real–not his doctored, mind-manipulated versions. Blake played the playboy of the family, which he was exactly what people wanted to see, taking the public eye off his own siblings and my sisters, whereas I am exactly what's presented.

I love bars. Clubs. Riotous, usually very public drunken nights. I get away with it a lot more in Crescent Falls, for sure. I'm just Aris there. Some rich, spoiled bastard. I've been called a man-whore, a prick, and the scum of the earth by pretty much every woman that's ever crossed my path, and I probably deserve it.

It's not my fucking fault I'm so Goddess-damned handsome.

But it is probably my fault I haven't felt the itch to settle down yet. I can admit to that.

In my defense, I blame my family. Wholeheartedly. This is their fault.

"Let me see that sweet angel." Brie grins as she plops down beside me on the sand, her flowy linen sundress barely hiding the growing swell of her second pregnancy. She's only a few months along but glowing as she scoops Fallon out of my arms and settles her in her lap. Fallon rubs her face against Brie's forearm, gives her an experimental gnaw, and settles, going back to watching the other kids with owl-eyed amusement.

"Where's Maeve? She back yet?"

"Is she back yet?" Brie corrects me, throwing me what I know is a glare behind her massive sunglasses reflecting the first signs of the sunset. "You're going to be Alpha of Veiled Valley one day. You should start speaking like it."

"Why do you even care? It's not like Mom and Dad are even thinking about that."

"I know for a fact Mom has other things she'd like to do with her life, and Dad has his hands overly full with the Ghosts."

I lean back, bracing my hands against the sand, and tilt my face to the last inklings of warm, tropical sunlight. "It won't happen for me anytime soon. I'm fine being just the prince, anyway. I enjoy my freedom and being the forgotten middle child. It works in my favor."

"You've been–" She lowers her voice to a whispered hiss, "slutting around for years, Aris. Do you really think no one has noticed how easily you tend to slip away and do whatever the hell you want?"

I smirk into the golden haze of the sunset now draping over the beach, casting long shadows on the sand. "I'm a Shadowsynger, Brie. Slipping into the shadows–being an actual shadow–is what I was made to do. You can't fault me for that, just like the family can't take fault in what I like to do in my free time. Blake's mess, Maeve's scandal, and your disappearance give me more freedom than I'll ever have again. I'm enjoying it while it lasts."

Skye rushes up to Brie to show her a shell Kieran just found. Kieran isn't far behind, and he beams up at Skye like she's the salt of the earth. He's surprisingly calm around her, and being calm hasn't ever been part of his nature. I've wondered, over the last two days the kids have been here, whether Skye is just his new best friend, or if the little mystic is actively controlling his devilish tendencies, trapping them in her powers before they can bloom into chaos. Either way, it's been working out just fine.

"Grandma Maddy has dinner going inside. You both should go in and eat, okay? We'll come back to the beach tomorrow. How does that sound?"

Kieran's lower lip begins to tremble as he stares at his mom, the beginnings of the word "No!" trying to form, but Skye grabs his little hand and tugs him toward the grassy tide line, toward the backyard of the house overlooking the water, where adult voices drift over the soft symphony of music coming from the kitchen.

We watch them go. Kieran doesn't fight it, but Brie sighs heavily, almost wistfully, as she says, "I'm really thankful Marianna allowed Skye to be here. I think both of them needed a break."

Admittedly, I don't know Marianna very well. I'm only a few months younger than Blake, and while we grew up close, especially as children, Brie was the only one he remained close to when he went dark. I knew Blake had a girlfriend or whatever back in the day, but I hadn't been prepared for the full truth of it. Now, we're living it, watching his daughter wrap everyone in the family around her tiny, yet powerful, fingers.

I've never had anything remotely that deep. I've never loved anyone outside of my family. I've never had anyone to fight for, someone I'd lay my own life down for.

That I'd blow up a temple and risk war for.

I don't think I'm a bad person, but… I know I'm not the greatest man, either. I can't hold a candle to what my grandfather, Ryatt, and my great uncle Isaac have done. Nor my great-grandfather, Maddox. Nor my pseudo-uncles–Ryan and Syd. Hell, my father is a hundred times the man I'm sure I'll ever be.

I know I'm overlooked. I've been through warrior training, been given a captain's position in the Ghosts, but it's not my passion, by any means. Lately, with all the shit going on in Eastonia and abroad, I've been… home. Walking through the castle—alone—while everyone else deals with what could be a war on the horizon and missing family members. I just exist at this point in time.

I'll be Alpha of Veiled Valley one day, sure, but that could be decades from now.

"What's up with you?" Brie asks. I'd honestly forgotten she was still sitting here.

"Just been thinking."

"You've just been thinking about what?" She nudges my shoulder before rising with Fallon in her arms.

"Do you think they're okay?"

Brie purses her lips as she adjusts Fallon against her shoulder, swaying and patting her back. "I don't know. I want to say yes. I want to say Lexa is holding herself up–that she trained enough for whatever's happening to her. I want to say Blake has everything handled and that they're together, that he knew this was going to happen and left to intercept her and whoever took her, but I struggle to make sense of this. Maeve is doing everything she can to find them, pushing her powers to their breaking point to reach them, but...." She takes a breath, smiling sadly down at Fallon, who is here with Soren only. Maeve is in the Deadlands with Ryan and Aviva, as well as Brie's husband and mate, Logan.

"How's Logan holding up?" I ask.

Another breath–this one sharp. "He's angry. I'm sure you understand why. We spent years trying to bring a sense of peace to Emberfyll, and now it's just... gone."

"Then you'll stay in the Deadlands?"

She shrugs, her cheeks going suddenly pink in the golden light, now fading rapidly as night yawns on the horizon, another day passing without solid answers. "I hope not. Sure, it's where Logan grew up. Aviva and Ryan are his parents, all things considered. But he wanted more for his people, and so do I. And now Lexa is missing and he–" She bites the words back. "And we're having another baby, another baby that'll be like him and Kieran, and everything we know about the fae... he's struggling with it, and rightfully so. We know nothing. That's the only clear thing right now."

"Is there anything I can do?" I ask, already knowing the answer. No, it's fine. No, Aris, just remain where you are, doing whatever it is you do to fill your time. So on, and so forth.

"No," she says with a sad smile. "We're going to be okay. That's all I want."

Brie turns toward the house as the first streaks of violet paint the sky—the same color as Blake's eyes. I grind my teeth, digging deep into my powers of shadow, questioning if I could, theoretically, find him and Lexa myself. Be the hero. The one who finally put a stop to the madness tearing the family apart.

Not tonight. Tonight, Maddy is hosting the youngest generation, making pancakes for dinner, a longstanding tradition started by my great-grandfather. Tonight, Marianna is probably playing her violin again in the orrery in Crescent Falls, where Maddy says she spends most of her time—pining. Yearning for a man who might not come back.

Tonight, Maeve is probably sitting on the shore of Teshka, cursing Blake and his schemes, and wondering how the hell she's supposed to keep Eastonia safe.

Tonight, I decide not to stay in Maatua. The world spins out of control as sand turns to dark stone and dimly lit, ancient hallways. The castle in Veiled Valley whispers its secrets as I move through the darkness, up stairwells and across balconies giving a sweeping view of the gothic foyer below.

Grandma Ella is in the library when I arrive, adding the finishing touches on a new painting. She looks up at me when I move toward one of the shelves, picking a book at random, and sit down.

"What are you doing home so soon?"

"Nothing," I reply, and it's the honest truth. "I'm doing absolutely nothing." I open the book, flipping through a few pages while the house whispers around us, sending a soft gust of air skittering around the room. I smooth a page down, but the spirit of the house, in a playful, annoying mood, sprints around me—a phantom of silent chaos. A single page rustles before falling flat, and it's a picture of a forest, lightning bugs dancing, blinking in the gaps between trees.

"What book is that?" Grandma Ella cranes her neck, then smiles, her sea-green eyes crinkling. "Oh, I remember that one. It used to be one of your favorite stories growing up."

"I don't even remember it." I smooth a finger over the fading page, the illustration slowly lightening with time.

"You loved that little fox so much," Grandma Ella smiles wistfully, her voice soft and reminiscent.

"What fox?"

"This one here. Don't you see it? Guarding that shadow?" She points to the corner of the page where there is, indeed, a little white fox, and behind it, the shadow of a... a great wolf. A strange sense drifts over me as I slowly turn the page.

THE BRIDE PRICE

Kaleb's hand rests on my lower back as the guards move from the gate to the Glade. The small door cut within the metal of the ancient gate that towers so high I have to crane my neck to look up at the top of the wall gives way, and instead of constant shuffle, thunder of hammers and whining of saws, the Glade is… silent.

I'm used to people looking at me now—stopping what they're doing to turn in my direction, to follow me with their eyes.

I'm not prepared for the bows. The bobbing of heads. The quiet, suffocating awe.

Kaleb's fingers curl into a fist at the base of my spine, but I move with him like this is just another day, another day we'll spend in the sparring ring together when things were easy between us. When none of this had happened yet.

People gather in doorways or peek through open windows. Children stop their games to watch us pass. I look everyone in the eyes, questioning the curious glances—the uncertainty. But they keep bowing. To Kaleb, of course.

Tension rises all around me, suffocating, until we reach that little courtyard, and my lungs heave, drawing in a much needed breath. Lis is hanging laundry and turns around, her eyes wide when we come into view, but she calms when she sees me.

"Goddess above! I was losing my absolute mind, Kaleb, thinking something had happened to her!" She points an accusatory finger at Kaleb before snatching my arm and tugging me toward the house, abandoning the laundry basket.

I meet Kaleb's eyes, however. They're lighter than before, especially as Lis shoves me with great effort through the doorway, where he follows, out of the glare of the sun lighting the courtyard. Kaleb's shoulders relax, and I swear on the Goddess, I see the ghost of a smile on his lips before she slams the door shut and whirls on me.

"You're filthy," she says accusatorially, turning me toward the staircase. "I'm running a bath."

"I'm not filthy! Not even close."

"You smell like a man!" She gasps in the center of the stairwell and turns to look down at me, for once, standing several steps above me. "You smell like Kaleb. Why?"

Before I can answer, her eyes dart to my neck, and widen.

"Oh, my gods of the green valleys and goddesses above!"

"I need you to chill–"

"Did he do this to you? Against your will?" Lis is wild-eyed, damn near frantic as she clasps my throat and gingerly inspects the scar– still fresh, teeth marks slightly raised. I allow her to do it because I know I don't have much of a choice. Honestly, in a perfect world, I'd bring not only Kaleb but Lis home. She'd love Silverhide and the women there–the strong, take-no-shit matriarchs who run the weaving circles and spend their days gossiping about their mates, their children, and their neighbors.

"Do you really think I'd let any man bite me unless I wanted it?" I laugh, and she draws her hand back in shock, but then I see it–a lingering panic in her eyes, and the dark circles beneath. "Oh, Lis, what happened last night? The king–" "A bath first!"

"I think maybe you need it more than me. When's the last time you slept? Have you eaten anything?"

She toys with her apron, which is stained and grimy. This isn't how I'm used to seeing her.

"Come on," I grumble, taking her by the elbow and guiding her back downstairs. The rooms she shares with Chasten are right off the kitchen–nothing fancy, by any means. A single bedroom and a large, open bathroom with a basin sink and wide clay tub. This is where she washes the laundry, where she's made me wash and mend laundry during my time as a guest in this house, where she's scrubbed me down several times when I've come back from training covered in dirt and often blood.

I run the same kind of bath she's run for me–hot, with fragrant herbs to spice the water, and her homemade soap, which doesn't really smell like anything but does its job.

I sit on the counter and inspect my nails, giving her privacy while she eases her aching body into the tub, her skin shielded by bubbles, and I only look at her when she sighs heavily, her eyes fluttering closed when the hot water, which took forever to heat, rises to her chin.

"Better?"

She opens one eye. "You go first. What happened last night?"

"Well, it's a rather long story and... I'm sure you're aware how people are marked–what kind of circumstances... lead to that..."

"I'm pregnant, Lexa. Do you think I don't know what sex is?"

"I want to know what happened here." I lean forward, resting my elbows on my knees. "Kaleb returned earlier this morning and left me with Silas. What happened? Where's Chasten?" I want to know if she felt it with him–the bond snapping into place, but I don't see a mark on her neck or the ridge of her shoulders. She sinks deeper into the water, her gaze far off and tangled as she stares at the far wall.

"I was home. I was here—alone. I felt the shift first, and... everything got very loud. Chasten's voice exploded through my head and told me to stay inside, to keep the doors and windows locked, so I did. There was howling all night long."

"Did you try to shift?"

"No!" she barks, meeting my gaze. "Of course not. I'm pregnant. I wasn't sure what would happen."

"Have you ever shifted before?"

"No," she says, her voice dropping to a whisper. "I never have. I–" She glances at me, at my neck. "You felt it? With Kaleb?"

"The mate bond?"

She nods, her cheeks glowing pink from either her question, inner thoughts, the bath, or all three.

"Yeah. We did."

She rolls her eyes to the ceiling, sinking to her chin. Her disappointment is palpable.

"Did Chasten come back before the shields were dropped again?"

She shakes her head, sniffling. "He probably spent the whole night out with his mate."

"Oh, Felicity, please," I grumble. "You know that's not true. He was out doing what Kaleb couldn't. They wouldn't allow us back into the Glade."

Tears fill her eyes, but she blinks them away. "Well, he's still not back."

"Chasten wouldn't do that to you."

She sinks under the water, blowing bubbles, and when she finally breaches the surface again, giving me a sharp look through the wet locks of her hair, I take it as a dismissal.

I go upstairs to my room. I change into clothes that actually fit, kicking the clothes I borrowed into a pile in the corner. I wind my hair into a bun. Then, I hear male voices drifting through the floorboards at my feet, not long after leaving Lis downstairs to her own devices. I move like the wind, steady on my feet, and find Kaleb and Chasten in the snug foyer. Kaleb's expression is stern like always, but his eyes turn on mine and soften, which makes my chest convulse, and memories of our night together come sprinting back to the forefront of my mind.

I push the memories aside and turn my attention to Chasten, who clears his throat, drops his gaze to his boots, and bows.

I feel my spine straighten against my will, confusion prickling through me, undoing me, but again, I push past these new, conflicting feelings and say with effort, "You need to go talk to your wife."

Kaleb blinks and then turns to Chasten, who rises and winces at my tone. I take another step, standing on the landing where I'm approximately as tall as both men, looking them both in the eyes.

"Is Lis all right?" Kaleb asks gruffly, his voice tinged with concern.

"No, actually, she's in pieces because he didn't so much as check in with her last night, and now she thinks he's found his mate."

Chasten pushes past us and disappears into the shadow hallway leading to their room. Silence cloaks the foyer before a deafening click funnels toward us, the sound of Chasten closing their bedroom door and locking it pinging through my ears. I take a breath, turning my attention to Kaleb, who grips the banister, leaning to stretch his arms and shoulders. He looks up at me over the slope of his shoulder, tilting his head to the stairs in a silent command to go. Go upstairs, and not my room.

No—his.

He closes the door behind us as I move toward his bed, taking in the little details I'd failed to notice before. Kaleb keeps his space neat. Everything is dust free, the bed made, his clothes neatly folded or hung in the closet on the far side of the room where several windows pour light drifting between the equally tall buildings on either side of us. This space is strictly his, carries only his scent.

Our scent. Like I've already branded myself on him, his space, and his sheets.

There's so much we need to say. So much we need to talk about. I can tell he's thinking the same thing as he leans against the door, his hands resting on his hips, and I sit on the edge of the bed, crossing my legs.

But the next words out of my mouth are, "Are they mates?"

"Chasten didn't catch the bond, and I'm guessing she didn't, either?"

"No, but she's never even shifted before."

"That wouldn't make a difference."

"Did he feel the mate bond with someone else?"

"No, he did not." Kaleb locks the door before moving in my direction. For a moment, I see him as he was during our time in the sparring ring–cold, calculated, a man who possibly hated me.

But when he sits beside me, keeping a comfortable distance, I see him for him.

He reaches over and takes my hand, winding our fingers together. I allow it.

"Chasten spent his entire night making sure no one died, and he was successful. We just did a round, stopped at the pack house, talked to some of the elders and everyone is all right."

"I'm not sure why you're telling me–"

"Because you're the Luna now." His grip loosens, and he rises like sitting still is impossible.

"We're not married." I have no idea why the words leave my lips, but they do, and they carry through the room. Kaleb looks down at me, his muscles flexed. He moves to his dresser, fumbling with a single book resting on its surface like he needs to do something, anything, with his hands other than touch me.

I wish we could feel the bond still. I wish it were still there, pulling us together, opening up a new line of connection that would make all of this so much easier, but…

I stroke my fingertips over the rise of my breasts, looking for those golden threads.

He notices, his eyes following the soft touch, and then he meets my gaze. "What's your bride price, really?"

A choked laugh escapes my lips. "I don't think I have one."

"You mentioned that I paid it."

"My dad," I laugh, "Is from Crescent Falls, which is modern and flashy–and the shifters there are far removed from what we are on a cellular level."

Kaleb arches a brow, but there's truly nothing I can say to paint the intricacies, the borders, and the cities of Crescent Falls and Eastonia, so I just say, "He came to the Deadlands to start fresh, to give the Silverhide pack a better shot at happiness, of getting back to their roots. They were young men mostly. My mother was a young hunter, the daughter of a patriarch of Endova. And my dad brought gifts for Endova, trying to find an ally in a land that was mostly violent to them, and he accidentally paid her bride price."

Kaleb is curious but trying to hide it. He angles his body away but asks, "What was her bride price?"

"A golden elk pelt."

Understanding ripples through him, and I know, without a shadow of a doubt... like I hadn't truly believed it before... Kaleb is from the missing tribes.

My mate is the Alpha King of the missing tribes.

"And they're happy?"

"They're in love. They're mates."

He nods but doesn't look at me when he asks, "What was your bride price, Lexa?"

I bring my knees to my chest. He turns to the bed, his steps heavy and deliberate as he closes the distance between us. He braces his hands on either side of my hips, leaning down so we're nose to nose.

This is crazy. Falling for someone, falling for him, here?

This was never my plan.

The words I said to Austin flood my mind. "I cannot be a precious little wife, making your meals, having your babies..."

I search Kaleb's eyes for anything that says that's what he wants from me.

I don't see it. I just see myself reflected in his golden-hazel irises.

"If a man can beat me in a fight, he can have my hand in marriage."

"And I've paid that a few times over."

THE MAZE

LEXA

Night falls on the Glade on the day of the second Trial, but the city is more alive than I've ever seen it. Kaleb walks steadily a few feet behind me, giving room for the pack to move out of their homes to watch me pass. It's a procession, something sacred, I realize, as we walk further from the main gate that leads into the fae city beyond and closer to the solid gate to the lands none of these people have ever been allowed to even see.

Avery has been beyond the gate for the rare hunts that take place when food is so scarce Kaleb is forced to grovel at the king's feet. It's a game to the king–dangling their wolf powers in front of them, keeping them hungry and desperate. It's all I can think about when we travel into the wide pit, where houses lean at odd angles and the stench of smoke from thousands of funeral pyres burned over the years clings to everything in sight.

But there is the gate to the outside world–to freedom I can taste it on the tip of my tongue as the wide, ancient monstrosity of metal and stone rises so high I have to crane my neck to see the top.

Just like the main gate, this one also has a smaller door. I wonder what it would be like, what it would sound like if the entire mass of the gate swung open all at once. Hundreds of people could move through it at the same time. It was be amazing.

A dream.

My gaze falls from the top of the wall to the group of women gathered at the exit. Kaleb hangs back while the women move forward, dipping their fingertips in oil that they then rub over my skin. Beads of shell and bone—meticulously carved into the cycles of the moon—are threaded through my hair. They work in silence, their fingers deft, and within minutes, I am decorated and ready to serve at the Goddess's altar.

Kaleb moves from foot to foot uneasily as he waits for the door to open. A groan of metal from the other side sounds over the thrum of chatter all around us, and Avery steps forward to move curious onlookers away from the door, Colin and Chasten quickly backing him up. Within seconds, a large, cavernous space has opened up around us, and as the door swings open, revealing a sweeping darkness, I look over my shoulder at the city behind me. The people who took me in. The people looking at their Alpha and Luna with mixed expressions of sorrow and hope.

"I will return," I say in a near whisper, breathless, as I turn my attention to Kaleb.

He licks his lips, a flash of teeth before he rolls his lower lip and shakes his head, his jaw tense with anger at our situation, at my being in the games, at being forced to send his mate back into the Trials while he can only watch.

We don't have a choice. I reminded him of that only a few nights ago. He cannot get me out of the games.

Kaleb grabs my upper arm and guides me into the darkness. It's a tunnel. Narrow and low, Kaleb has to bend sharply to even maneuver through it, and it makes my back sing with tension as well, but it quickly opens to a short flight of stone steps overgrown with moss and grass. The torchlight nearly blinds me, and over a dozen fae guards join us on the walk to the maze.

We exit the tunnel, and I keep my focus on the grass beneath my sandals and the cool night air grazing my skin, the whispering of wind through massive, old-growth trees towering over my head when we're led into a forest. The walk is short and dark, giving me no inkling of where I am, what direction we're going, and my wolf remains silent, dormant, and useless once more.

Disappointment washes through me. Selfishly, I'd wanted to feel her. Not my wolf–not for whatever advantage I might have gained from her during the next game but to feel the bond again. To have that sliver of connection with Kaleb, even if just for a few hours.

The forest floor gives way to cobblestone in an instant. I nearly trip in surprise then shield my eyes from the spray of lights pouring over us. A thick buzz of what feels and sounds like electricity explodes through my ears, but I can't taste it for what it is–magic. The thick, all-consuming kind that sticks to my tongue, tasting of copper.

I squint, raising a hand to try to block the light, but Kaleb does it for me, grasping the back of my neck and forcing me to bend my head down as he rushes us through a crowd of warriors and under the cover of some kind of building, a waiting area, which expands quite suddenly in front of us.

"I can't see a thing!" I whine, rubbing my eyes–partially blinded, I think.

Kaleb shushes me, giving me a tender squeeze on the back of the neck, then crouches to adjust the laces holding my sandals to my feet. My vision begins to clear, and I gasp, my chest convulsing, as walls of thick trees and vines rise in the near distance, a gaping, yawning entrance to the maze completely shrouded in shadows.

I can't hear the crowd. I can't see any spectators. In fact, it's… quiet. Unnervingly so.

"Where are the other competitors?" I ask. Guards move in behind us, talking quietly in the fae tongue.

"This game is a one-at-a-time competition, compared to the others. Although, you might run into another victor in there if they're lost. That happened to me."

"You did the maze?"

"It's not a common event. For some reason, the king seems to be using the same games as my Trial, so… yeah, I've done the maze." He rises, his eyes on mine, his spine lengthening, but he looks confident, almost at ease, until a scream of epic proportions echoes from the entrance of the maze, carried on a brisk gust of wind coming from within.

"What's in there?"

"The maze is going to be different for everyone," Kaleb explains, busying his hands by adjusting the armor he fitted me with earlier. It's lightweight, keeping my lower thighs and calves bare, but my chest and stomach are plated in thick scales of leather, as well as my forearms. It fits me like a glove. I wonder with unease why I need it. "This place is ancient, from before the time of the fae, according to some. There's something beneath it —an old temple or something. They say it's haunted. Whatever it is, it's meant to trick you. The maze moves, Lexa. It wants you to stay. Anything you see within isn't real. Do you understand?"

"No!" I bite out, my skin prickling as another garbled scream of pain rushes toward us.

Kaleb bites down on his lower lip and scans the fae guards behind us before clutching my hip and dragging me closer, closing the distance between us.

"Listen to me. You'll make it out. You'll know the way. I don't know how else to explain it, but once I got there, once I saw—once I knew, for a fact, what I was seeing wasn't real, that it couldn't hurt me, I was able to find my way out. This game is… not many get out. I was one of four victors left afterward. It's a type of culling, a mental one. It's meant to ensure the last victors standing aren't just there by sheer luck." His grip on my hip tightens when another gurgled shout, this time laced with terror, ripples toward us before abruptly guttering out.

Fae guards shuffle uneasily, glancing around like they're waiting for commands. The tension reaches a peak, and I feel my entire body caving inward. I'm a warrior. I've seen worse than this. Why am I petrified right now? "Look at me," Kaleb rasps. The guards shout commands back and forth. "Lexa, look into my eyes right now."

I do, and he grabs my face, forcing me to look him dead in the eyes even while the guards move in our direction.

"This is real. You and I are real. What happened between us was real. Whatever you see in there–" A guard tries to yank him away, but he shoves him back, hard, "Whatever you see, whatever you hear, know this." He tucks a rogue curl behind my ear. "I will be waiting for you on the other side. I will carry you home if I have to. I will be beside you in our bed tonight. I swear on the Goddess, Lexa, I will be there." Something in his tone shreds me to my center. Dread builds then explodes through my veins as a guard snatches my arm and roughly pulls us apart.

"Kaleb? Kaleb!"

He grunts in sudden pain when the guards push and shove him, tearing us apart. I lose sight of him, but it doesn't matter because I quickly lose sight of everything when I'm shoved backward through the entrance of the maze. Total, complete darkness swallows me whole.

Silence closes me in an eerie embrace. I whirl toward what should be the entrance of the maze, but tall hedges spread out in every direc-tion. A gentle breeze ripples through the leaves, and within seconds, my eyes adjust to what little light there is to be had–silver moonlight dappled in shadows.

I have to get out. That's my only goal. Not killing, not maiming. Just surviving this new level of hell I must escape.

I take a few steps then whip my head as the hedges rustle, and in the darkness, I can just make out the shadows carved into the bushes, entrances, exits, sharp corners that I can travel toward... whatever end.

I close my eyes for a moment, digging deep, praying silently to the Goddess to show me the way, please, for the love of everything holy, Show me the way.

With a deep breath, I tear to the left and run.

The maze groans, the hedges shifting, moving, closing in and forcing me to skid to a near stop and turn to the right, where the path is less narrow and opens to multiple options for me to take. I close my eyes, letting my senses propel me forward, and I feel the breeze rushing around me as I take a sharp corner, my sandals sending a clattering echo into what I can only describe as a vat of nothing. The magic here sucks the sound from the world, like I'm in another plane of existence. Like I'm alone–utterly, wholly, alone.

It's the one thing I'm afraid of.

A deep male scream of pain explodes through my ears. My eyes force open to see a man I recognize as a fellow victor races toward me, his face in shambles, skin flayed and one eye gouged completely. I scream. I can't help it, especially when I notice his bloody fingers and the claw marks on his cheeks. He flies past me in a fit of terror so strong it rattles through my bones, and is gone in a flash, his wings shredded and hanging limp, dragging on the ground behind him.

He didn't even notice me.

Kaleb's words ring loud and clear, pulling from my fresh memory. Don't trust anything you see here. None of it is real.

Had he been real?

The scent of his blood smells real.

Chills snake over my skin. I listen to his screams from deep in the maze.

"Lexa?"

I close my eyes. Bile rises in my throat as a familiar voice cuts me to the bone. "You're not real."

"Look at me. You owe me this. You did this to us."

I shake my head. Hot tears gather along my lashes, but Austin's voice turns pleading.

"Look at me. Look at what you've done to me! Did you ever love me, Lexa?"

NONE OF THIS IS REAL

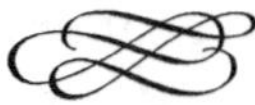

Lexa

I slowly turn to Austin's voice, opening my eyes to first my feet, then slowly look up at figures standing before me. Dozens of them. Faces I recognize. Eyes I know by heart, now milky and unseeing with death.

My body's paralyzed with fear when Austin parts the crowd. My regiment. Warriors I trained with since I was a girl.

"Did you love me as I loved you?" he asks, his voice distorted, gravely. His golden hair is stained dark with blood, and his body is… ravaged, by violence and death.

"You're not real!" I shout, my chest tightening painfully. The warriors behind him fade into the darkness, but he remains. He steps toward me, reaching for me, and I feel the touch on my cheek. I scream, stumbling away from him.

He smirks, sucking his teeth, looking me up and down, his gaze lingering on the mark on my neck, and then his gaze turns murderous. "You were mine!"

"I wasn't. Not ever. Not during the night we spent together, Austin. I would have known!"

"You fucking whore," he snarls in a tone I've never heard him use before. It's disgusting. Barbaric. Laced with so much hatred, I can taste it. It's not him.

"You're not real. This isn't you–"

"I died for you to live, not for you to fuck the first stranger that crossed your path. Your regiment died for you. Your mate will die for you, Lexa, and then you'll be alone."

"No," I whisper, trying to blink past tears. The maze groans around us, leaves fluttering in a phantom, freezing cold breeze.

"You'll be completely alone. Unloved. Unwanted. Look at me, Lexa."

"I won't." I close my eyes. "You're not real. None of this is real."

He touches me again. It's a firm–but incredibly cold–touch, like he's frozen. Like he's wet, suspended in the very sea that choked on his spilled blood that night.

"He's the enemy. You fucked the fae. You disgusting pig. You traitor. Do you think the Goddess will ever bless you? Do you think the scum you'll breed with that filth will be allowed to live?"

I scream and shove him, but my hands pierce nothing but thin air. I open my eyes in shock.

The maze whispers around me. I'm alone. Austin is gone. I'm all alone..

I whirl back and forth, my heart rate skyrocketing to the point I can hear my heart hammering in my ears. I claw my cheek where he touched me, trying to scrub the icy feeling of his dead flesh from my skin, but it's useless. A keening, otherworldly cry funnels toward me, rustling the leaves. My voice.

It's my own voice raised in the deepest kind of sorrow lifting through the maze. I slowly turn to the source, but the maze spreads out in a straight, shadowed line, beckoning me to follow the sound.

I turn in the opposite direction and run.

The hedges pass in a blur. I trip, stumble, but manage to stay on my feet. I've never felt fear like this. I try to tell myself it's manufactured. I summon Kaleb's warning, but it feels so far out of reach. Tears blur my vision. Austin's image cuts through me like a blade, and the wailing grows louder, stronger, like I'm standing outside of my body, screaming at myself, begging myself to turn around and witness the scene already branded in my brain.

Chessie's death haunts me, hunts me, as I run for my life, running from the guilt, shame, and despair of the battle on the beach, of the complicated feelings I had for Austin, for his death. I run because my life depends on it, but I've lost all sense of direction. Darkness invades my senses, rendering them useless, and now I'm at the mercy of whatever magic is here trying to bore holes in my mind, finding my deepest fears and bringing them to life.

A hedge moves, a new opening rolling into view through my tear blurred vision, and I stumble again, this time falling hard on my knees.

My mother's cry of anguish bounces through the maze. She calls out my name, over and over again, and I can't take it. I scream—wail in despair—but my body refuses to move, to get up. I cover my ears and scream again. I want it to stop. I'd do anything for it to stop. I'd cut my ears off, cut out my eyes if it meant I didn't have to see or hear any of this and just—

"Get up."

I open my eyes wide.

Blake is standing a few feet away, cloaked in black, his violet eyes misty and bright in the darkness all around him. His voice cuts through the agonized screams of my mom, Chessie, and Austin as I stare at him.

"You're—you're not real!"

"You have to get up, Lexa, please," he hisses, glancing around. He extends a hand but then thinks better of it, and his powers seem to dim before he reins them back under control.

"I can't take it," I cry out when my mom's scream echoes past me again. I press my hands against my ears until my head throbs, and then he's dragging me to my feet and shaking me so violently I feel my spine crack in several places.

"Wake up, Lexa! You have to get out of here, all right? Look at me."

I screech, trying to pull away from him, but he tugs me close and... hugs me.

A sense of relief sweeps through me, pulling me into his current. Blake's warm. He's solid. He smells exactly like I remember.

We were close as kids. I idealized him, worshipped the ground he walked on. I think I was one of the first who noticed when he started to change and pull away, and after that, Brie was the only one he let get close. It had been a loss I struggled with, especially in the years after Logan left for training and rarely came home. I felt abandoned. Those feelings shoot through me, cutting through the fear that's rendering me useless.

My hands tremble when I wrap my arms around him under his cloak and squeeze.

Into my ear, he rasps, "I'm sorry I couldn't stop this from happening to you. I knew. I knew you'd be taken, but I couldn't see why. Now, I understand, and I'm going to fix it. I need you to keep your head on your shoulders. I need you to win this, Lexa, no matter the cost."

I'm not sure if he's really here. He can't be. Nothing in this maze is supposed to be real, right? This is just a trick of my dying mind, something thrown at me like a life preserver, a last ditch effort to keep me upright.

"Hannibal is in control of this game. You need to fight it. He's throwing everything he has at you, but he doesn't know who you are yet. He's playing on the shallowest levels of your fear, that's all. You need to keep him out of your head. Block it all out, Lexa. You were trained for this. It's a mind game. You know how to play those."

I clutch him tighter.

"It's just hedges. Leaves, vines, and alders. That's all it is." He takes an unsteady breath, his chest rising and falling with the motion. "I will find you soon. You can trust Silas. He's a good man."

My fingers lock on his back at the mention of Silas's name.

"Kaleb will keep you safe. He swore."

I begin to pull away in shock, but he prevents me from moving, squeezing me tighter and keeping me from looking up into his face.

"I am so sorry for how this ends."

"What–"

"I'm going to fix it for you both. I'm going to find a way. Trust me. Please, just trust me." His voice breaks, and he begins to fade in my arms, his touch going slack. I fall in on myself as his body turns to mist, and then he's gone, and I'm left reeling.

"Blake?" I whisper, blinking. The view of his chest becomes the maze again. "Blake?!"

Silence greets me. Chills fizzle down my arms. I slowly look around. The cries and screams of everyone I love have faded, replaced by an eerie, unnatural quiet that's almost more terrifying. I reach up, dabbing my aching cheeks, and realize I've scratched myself raw.

I think of the fae man, my fellow competitor, and know how close I am to losing my mind just like he did.

What did Kaleb see here?

It was probably worse than anything I could possibly conjure.

I set out in a walk, actually thinking about my next moves instead of just sprinting. I round a corner, sure of my footing, and feel that icy cold wind nipping at my heels again but allow it to guide me for just a moment. Call it curiosity or delirium, but I don't shy away from the image in front of me–the answer to the internal question I just asked without even speaking the words out loud.

Silas closes a door, refusing to let Kaleb–ten years younger than he is now, my age, I believe–from entering the room he's guarding. Silas's shirt is deeply stained with blood as he holds Kaleb back, shaking his head, his eyes full of tears.

I know Alice is in that room without having to see her. I know the scenes playing out as I walk blindly through the maze aren't mine to recount, but I watch them, following a young Kaleb, bound in familiar chains, his glorious hair shaved to his scalp, around a corner. I keep walking, seeing his culling taking place, where he watches friends from the Glade die in front him, where he refuses to kill a single soul until the very end, when he breaks the neck of a massive fae male, his eyes set on the king.

I keep walking even when thunder booms overhead, and it begins to rain, clouds rolling in to shield what little moonlight I had to guide my path. I keep walking as Kaleb's games play out–vicious and bloody–blurred by the years he's spent trying to forget them.

Blake was right–at least, the image of him my mind created to try to bring me back from the point of no return is right. My fear is my greatest competitor here, the one thing capable of bringing me to my knees.

Kaleb's memories have somehow impacted mine. I have to use them to remind myself what he fought for and what I've been called to finish.

I will not be afraid. Not of this maze. Not of the games. Not of the king and his Trials. Not of the uncertain, ever changing future ahead of me.

I turn another corner, and the storm begins to thunder. I stop dead in my tracks. Something glows on the ground only a few feet away. My body aches with exhaustion. I'm not sure how long I've been moving, trapped here, but my legs strain when I crouch, my fingertips brushing a pale greenish-blue dragon scale.

It feels real. Heavier than I thought it would be. I look at the black sky, squinting against the cool rain calming my inflamed cheeks. Lis told me the rain that had finally come to the Glade was my doing, that I'd freed the dragon, and she'd blessed us with her gift. Water.

I clutch the scale and notice the rivulets of water rushing over the uneven cobblestone, draining… somewhere.

Draining down.

I grew up in the wilds of the Deadlands. I had miles upon miles to roam whenever I wished because I could always find my way home without fail. Follow the rivers and creeks. Let the power that runs in our braided waters guide me home, to safety.

I squeeze the scale in the palm of my hand, whispering, "Thank you."

I swear on the Goddess that I hear the dragon's answering grunt as the rain patters my shoulders with more fervor, and I move.

More screams cut through the rainy darkness, but I ignore them. Instead, I think of my parents. I think of Silverhide cloaked in snow and Solstice trees adorned with lights, the smell of cider and wood smoke. I think of the couch at home and the coffee table strewn with Nora's painting supplies. I think of an incredibly full dining room table and the lifted voices of my entire family as they gather, those rare occasions when we're all together. I think of home and find myself wrapped in Kaleb's embrace. I think of the look in his eyes when he'd turned to me in the ballroom, when our bond snapped into place.

I think of him on that balcony when I'd turned my arrow on the king, how he shook his head and turned away.

He knew then.

He felt it then, hadn't he?

My throat closes on a sob. I move faster, breaking into a run, leaping over a self-mutilated body curled on the cobblestone. More bodies. Bodies of my competitors. Meg isn't one of them. It's the only thing I notice when I turn a corner and find myself face to face with a wide, open... exit.

The arena expands before me, a gate spilling light and the sound of the spectators. The ground vibrates with their shouts and applause, but I skid to a stop, panting.

This is real. I know that without a shadow of a doubt.

But I turn back to the maze, to the darkness that claimed at least five of the remaining competitors, leaving me and two others. For now.

"Show me Chessie," I command, my voice breaking as tears fill my eyes against my will. "J-just once. Just so I can say goodbye."

Nothing happens. The rain falls, heavy and cold, washing the scent of my competitors' blood away.

"Please?" I whisper, but I'm met with a cool, gentle breeze, a soft command to just... go.

So I do.

I step into the light of the arena against gasps of shock and riotous applause, clutching the dragon scale in the palm of my hand until it breaks the skin.

WHO IS HE?

Kaleb

Silas has a private box in the arena that overlooks the grounds. I squint through the bright, unforgiving lights to the magical dome, watching rain pound the king's shields. It had been a clear, hot night before this. The rain started only minutes ago, absolutely drenching Pantharas—a flood of epic proportions. Compared to the long-awaited rain that blessed the Glade recently, this feels more like a punishment.

Silas paces, glancing at the arena, which is empty. "She should have come out by now. It's been three hours."

"She'll come," I say, my voice booming through the alabaster room. Benches in shades of pale cream take up the majority of the space. I should be down near the grates, ready to run onto the sand to get her when she arrives, but I was barred entrance to the lower levels of the arena today. The king is playing games now. Lexa shouldn't have made it past the Beast Trial, and now he blames me.

Thunder crackles, booming over the arena. Lightning flares in strips overhead, muted by the shield. I grip the railing, hanging my head.

"She should be back!" Silas curses under his breath, running his fingers through his hair. "Did you even warn her? This is the most challenging and deadly event of the Trials, Kaleb."

"Of course I warned her," I snap, teeth bared. "She'll finish."

He huffs a breath, shaking his head as he paces, unable to stand still.

A hum of excitement lifts from the crowd below us, and Silas and I both look to the far end of the arena, where a gate hangs open, the exit of the maze nothing more than a gaping shadow against a wash of polished alabaster stone.

I hold my breath for an outcome that doesn't come to fruition.

Meg rushes into the arena, soaking wet, battered, but alive. She falls to her knees, gasping for breath against a rush of applause, but my eyes lift to the king and the men enjoying the view from the royal box–including her sponsor and trainer.

"She's the one he wants to win," Silas growls, whispering a curse.

"Why?"

"Hell if I know. I do, however, know her sponsor is doing every-thing he can to win the king's favor, and Meg seems to be part of it. I have no idea what any of those men have promised her, but it's a lie. They'll cull her even if she wins the games."

I shake my head in disgust. "It's political warfare."

"Of course, it is. The king is well aware that the rebellion has taken root in Pantharas and is doing everything he can to sniff us out. He has his suspicions about me, but it doesn't matter, not now."

"What do you mean?" Another roar of applause sounds as a second competitor hurries out of the maze–a man this time. He's fully fae. I don't know his name, but I know for a fact that he was the chosen one, the one meant to win, the system rigged in his favor–until recently, it seems, now that the king is apparently leaning toward Meg being his champion.

I'm doing everything in my power to keep my head on straight as the minutes tick by, and the king doesn't call an end to the game, which means Lexa is still alive, still working through the maze.

Meg and the fae man rest in the center of the arena, but Meg rises, waving at the excited crowd, and Silas scoffs.

"Ignore her."

"You see what they've made her? She's propaganda, Kaleb. The king will use her as a talking head, showing her off like a prize to the other kings, other kingdoms who've long since freed their shifters. Look at this pretty little wolf," he sneers, his tone like acid. "See how malleable she is? How easily she bows? He'll use her in the Glade to try to turn your own people against you, using her as a promise of prosperity if they just fall in line."

"That won't happen because she won't win."

"Then, it'll be her against Lexa. You realize that? Do you think the next game will sway in Lexa's favor when it's the last game of the Trials? The king will do what needs to be done to ensure Lexa's death. You have to realize that."

"And what of your rebellion, Silas? Where do you stand now? What is the plan?"

"Now you want in?" he gripes, shaking his head. "Now that your own mate is on the chopping block–"

"What is your problem?" I shout, and he turns his back to me.

The door to the viewing room opens on a phantom wind, letting in the hum of the crowd before closing with a snap. Wet, heavy foot-steps follow in the wake of a man dressed in all black, his cloak laden with rain.

The Architect shrugs out of his cloak and drapes it over one of the benches before swiping his fingers through his wet hair, his violet eyes scanning the room and then meeting mine.

We'd spoken only briefly the last time I saw him, and I'd been uneasy about it, and rightfully so. There's something about him that doesn't sit well with me, especially his interest in Lexa. He'd asked if I'd protect her. I told him that was my duty as her sponsor and trainer, but that answer hadn't been good enough for him. He wanted me to swear.

I had.

I'd also given him all the information I knew about the palace and Hannibal, who seems to have his special interest. I'm not surprised by that, given that Hannibal is the king's seer, one of the only fae with full access to their powers without having to pay the king the magical tithe that keeps the lights on in Pantharas and the king on his eternal throne.

Silas and I watch the architect move to the railing to stand between us in silence. There's something about him that unnerves me. His face is familiar. Carved from stone I've seen before. The high cheekbones and the regal, straight nose. The shape of the eyes... I've seen them somewhere, but the color is all wrong.

The Architect turns his face to look at me. I stare, not bothering to hide it, and he sighs as he rolls his eyes back to the arena, to the open exit.

"There will be a meeting," he says to us, his voice low. "Kaleb will be called before the king. It's a distraction to get Lexa alone. She will be taken from the Glade and separated from Kaleb." I stiffen, and Silas turns, but the man continues, "Silas, you must return to the Highwoods until next week. Lexa will stay at your house starting tomorrow morning. As long as she's not in the Glade, the king's plan will not come to fruition."

"What are you talking about?"

He looks at me again, those eyes swirling with power I can feel on my skin as he inspects my expression. "The king can't charge into a High Lord's home without raising questions. He has nothing of substance on Silas to elicit such behavior. Lexa will be safe there. The king can send his guards into the Glade any time he wants without anyone doubting his motives."

"How do you know this?"

"Because I've seen it." He straightens, running his hand over his face. "And Lexa cannot be left to her own devices. I suggest one of you is with her all the time. Don't leave her with a maid or cook. She'll leave. She'll try to get back to you." He directs those last words at me, narrowing his eyes.

Then I see it. The startling resemblance.

I grab his shirt, but he seems to have been expecting this moment. He grunts but settles as I twist the fabric, pulling him onto the tips of his toes. "Who are you?"

"Kaleb!" Silas sneers. "Let him go!"

"My name is Blake," he rasps.

"Who are you?" I repeat. His violet eyes hold mine.

"Lexa is my younger cousin. Our fathers are twins. She's practically, genetically, a sister. You just noticed the resemblance, didn't you?" I let him go, shoving him back, and he stumbles before gripping the railing to right himself.

"What's going on here?" I look at Silas, arching a brow. "Did you know?" I grab Blake again, but this time he fights back, trying to shove me away. He's a match for me height-wise, but I have bulk on him, and he quickly submits when I grip his throat and whirl, backing him into a wall. "What kind of game is this? Does she know you're here?"

"No," he chokes out, but his eyes remain calm. "I showed myself to her in the maze, but she's fighting for her life as we speak. Hannibal's powers nearly subdued her."

My grip eases involuntarily.

He licks his lips before shoving me away again, and I let him.

I back toward Silas, who's wild eyed and confused. Blake coughs, struggling to swallow, bracing himself against the wall. He holds out a hand in surrender. "I came here, to Pantharas, before Lexa was taken, but I knew it would happen."

I lurch toward him, riding a wave of fury so sharp it heats my body from the inside out, but Silas grabs me and yanks me back.

Blake raises a second hand, his eyes widening when he notices the pure, unfiltered rage pouring off me. "I'm going to get her out of here–"

"Why are you here?" I shout.

"It's complicated," Blake grinds out, but then a horn blares, and the crowd goes wild below, and all three of us turn on instinct.

I rip out of Silas's hold as Lexa stumbles into the arena. Her face is covered in blood from what I can tell, and she's soaking wet, fumbling with each step as she moves into the light. The gate grinds closed behind her, closing off access to the maze. It's done. It's over.

But then she sees Meg.

"Fuck," I snarl, clutching the railing. "Don't. Lexa, don't."

Lexa straightens, her eyes narrowing on Meg, who stands several yards away.

The crowd continues to scream for the victors as the king begins to speak in the fae tongue, but Lexa ignores them all, taking several determined steps in Meg's direction.

I tear away from the railing, stalking toward the door, but guards appear the second I pull it open.

"What's the meaning of this?" I ask, whirling back to Silas, who's standing wide-eyed at the space where… Blake was just standing.

He's gone.

I look back at the arena. Guards have arrived to take the victors away. Lexa says something to Meg, but I can't hear a thing she's saying, and Meg just… smiles at her.

A sick, menacing kind of smile.

Lexa is going to fucking kill her. I can feel it like her rage is in my chest, burrowing deep.

"We're here to escort you back to the arena to fetch your victor," one of the guards says.

Silas meets my eyes. A lingering hint of shock is visible behind his big blue eyes.

"I'll see you tomorrow morning," I tell him and move. "We'll talk about this then."

It doesn't take long to reach the inner sanctum of the arena. Lexa stands surrounded by guards, her head in her hands. I shove past them, grab her arm, and weave through the crowded corridors and caverns, ignoring the sea of guards following our every step.

Blake was right. Something else is going on. There's a shift in the air as we move closer to the gate of the Glade. More guards than ever stand there. Some stare at me from beneath their lashes, giving me looks of quiet camaraderie, but the others stare in disdain, maybe even disgust.

The door within the ancient gate opens, and I usher Lexa inside without a word, scooping her up before her toes even touch the soil of the Glade, and carry her home. She doesn't fight it. Her head lulls against my chest, her cheeks scratched raw and ears covered in dried blood.

Lis and Chasten are waiting for us, but when they see her, they move back into the shadows, allowing me to quietly carry her upstairs to my bed, where I lie her down and inspect the gashes on her face... from her own nails.

"My head is killing me," she says weakly.

"Who is Blake?"

Her eyes fly open and meet mine.

WE CAN'T BE TOGETHER

LEXA

I rise on my elbows and blink up at Kaleb. My vision goes spotty for several seconds before repairing itself, but my brain feels like a leaden weight. I'm not sure I'm actually here now, in this room, bracing myself over the side of Kaleb's bed while my stomach pitches and rolls, the taste of magic heavy on my tongue. "B-Blake? Where did you hear–hear that name?" I'm going to vomit. I don't think I can help it. My body lurches, and I end up on my knees on the ground before Kaleb can steady me. I close my eyes, the room spinning for several seconds before wobbling back to normal.

He exhales sharply through gritted teeth, his hand warm and flat against my upper back. "Put your head between your knees and breathe."

"I feel like I'm on a boat."

"I've never been on a boat, but what you're feeling right now is fae magic in your body. It takes a while to dispel itself."

"I'm going to be sick–"

"Fight it," he commands, and I adjust my position on the hard floorboards and do as he says. My neck tingles with tension when I hang my head between my knees and take several deep, aching breaths. I smell like rain and the maze–a thick, woodsy, wet smell that makes that nausea return in an instant, but I think of anything but that feeling–the feeling of fear still echoing through my body like a tide, pushing and pulling every nerve.

"Am I actually here?" I ask, my cheeks heating. I know it's a stupid question, but I can't help it.

"You are."

"I saw you," I whisper, squeezing my eyes shut. "I saw you in the maze."

His hand curls into a fist along my spine before flattening again. "What did I say to you?" His voice nearly breaks with a pinch of panic.

"Nothing. I didn't–I was seeing memories from your life. Your games. Alice's death, I think. I don't know why. I–I–"

"It's because we're mates, Lexa. We're bound. The maze… whatever kind of magic lurks within, it saw that piece of me that belongs to you."

I open my eyes to look at him, to take in his features like I'm taking a picture, weaving him into memory. We've said we're not going to reject each other. That fact–that we are mates and will remain as much–is set in stone.

But the what ifs are still there, wedging a rift between us. I never thought I'd be in this position in more ways than one.

Then, my mind softens, the grip of the magic from the maze loosening, but one memory remains clear.

"Blake," I whisper, and his expression darkens. "He's my cousin. I saw him in the maze, and… You must have seen my memories, too. He's, uh, he's a… he's something else–"

"He's here."

"What do you mean?" My voice sharpens in disbelief.

"Silas's guest. Your cousin. They're one and the same."

I shakily rise to my feet, and he allows it but stays close, the ghost of a touch on my elbow while I tremble, every appendage tingling from lack of use. "There's no way—" I bite back the words, grimacing as I shake my head, which pounds like someone's taking a hammer to my temple. "You know what? There is a way for that bastard to be here. Do you know what he's done back home? What he did before spiriting here, however long and however much power that took?" I look up at Kaleb but barely see him through my anger. "He blew up a temple. Not just any temple, but the Temple of Moonrise, the capital of Eastonia. He blew it up, left it in ashes and embers, and left behind his own mate and daughter–"

"He's assisting the rebellion."

"Oh, I bet he is. He always has his hands in something!" I push past him and stumble toward Kaleb's ensuite bathroom–nothing more than wood paneling and a shower made of stone. It's the only shower in the entire house from what I gather, and right now, it's mine, even if the water is lukewarm at best. I fumble with the handle, droplets shimmering before spraying in a steady, slightly heated stream. I feel Kaleb's presence before his shadow cuts through the muted light of an oil lantern on the counter, setting the water droplets alight like liquid gold.

"I have to ask," he says, his voice low and steady. "Are you involved in whatever plan he had when he came here?"

I pause, my fingers drifting over the armor I already know I won't be able to get off by myself. "What exactly are you asking? Are you asking if I–if I lied to you about what happened on that beach? If I lied about my regiment being slaughtered–"

"No," he rasps, and he touches me. I flinch.

I regret it immediately.

Kaleb pulls back, his fingers hovering over my upper arm, then closes them into a fist. "Lexa, I have thousands of people to think about. Over a dozen small packs under my command. Alphas. Beta. Pack members. Parents and children. Silas is playing a dangerous game, and you're involved, whether I like it or not."

I keep my eyes on the water dampening the stone that encompasses one half of the room. The temperature rises, and heat blooms in wisps of steam rising from the water, now warm to the touch, while he cautiously begins to undo the straps of my armor.

"And you're involved," I reply under my breath, trying to bite back my feelings, "because your mate is involved, correct? Otherwise, you would have never allowed your brother to rope you into this... into this mess."

"I would have chosen you regardless of whether or not we ended up mates."

I close my eyes as the armor covering my shoulders and chest falls away. He sets it on the counter behind him, his touch moving to my hips, then my lower belly, where he deftly–but silently–unlatches my belt and pulls it away.

"We don't have a future together," I tell him, and it breaks my heart to hear the words out loud. "But you already know that, don't you? That's what you're trying to say, isn't it? Now that Blake is here and I have a way home?"

The armor guarding my thighs loosens to the point that it simply falls off, leaving me in thin, tight fabric shorts–something Lis called underoos, which made me laugh at the time, and a tank top of a similar material. I'm practically naked and totally, utterly exposed to Kaleb.

My heart is, too.

This is the conversation I dreaded having the most... with anyone.

"We're worlds apart," he replies in confirmation, his voice shifting as he turns from me, facing away from me like he can't take it, and I get it. I reach for the spray of the water and let the warm rush of it fan over my fingers. "I can't make promises I know I can't keep."

"Why would the Goddess do this to us? Bind us like this?"

"I don't have the answer."

"Well, Blake might." I turn, watching through the last bits of unsteamed glass in the mirror over the vanity. He braces his hands on the counter and bows his head, refusing to meet my eyes. "Do you know what he can do? He can see everything. The future. Into people's minds. He can look past the planes of our existence into what he calls the tapestry, where all of us, every menial, insignificant soul, carries a thread that creates a... masterpiece. He can see it."

Kaleb raises his head just enough to look at me, but his expression is dark, exhausted, like whatever light was within him has officially blown out. "He can manipulate it, Kaleb. That's why–"

"I don't give a fuck about your cousin," he says with effort and turns. "I care about my pack. I care about you–you surviving these Trials–"

"And then what? I survive. Sure. I can do that. You know I can win this."

Kaleb takes a shuddering breath. I edge toward him, raising my hands in surrender. "But then what? My cousin is here, which means– which means Maeve, my other cousin, is not far behind. The two of them together are going to spell disaster for everyone involved. I win, and then what, Kaleb? There's going to be war in Pantharas. The people of the Glade can't stay here. They need to get out."

"I will do what I need to do. It's not your responsibility. It's mine."

"I'm your mate. You called me your Luna!"

"And you are."

"Then why say–"

"Because you cannot stay," he cuts in, his eyes dark and heavy with conviction. "You will not stay here. Not in the Glade, not in Pantharas. You will return home to your people."

"And your people?"

"I will do what needs to be done to ensure their freedom."

He's hiding something. I can almost taste it in the air between. It's thick and bitter–a bold lie.

"And us?"

He takes a single step toward me and then stops. He's close enough to touch. Mist hangs heavy in the air between us, and the water continues to run, wasted, likely growing cold again. I let it.

"We agreed not to reject each other," he says, taking another calcu- lated step. "I think it was wise, given our circumstances as victor and trainer. It gives us an advantage."

I find it suddenly impossible to swallow. This side of him? It's different, closed off. Like he's decided to build a wall between us, and honestly, I... can't argue with his point. What in the world are we supposed to do? Fall desperately, madly in love? Talk about a home together, children, cozy nights by a fire? Because where would we do that? In what peaceful world would a situation like that exist for us?

It kills me that he's right. That being mates makes us stronger, even if we can't feel it at its full strength. But his mark on my neck burns with fresh heat with every inch he moves, closing the distance between us while my heart begins to race.

What I know is right—what must happen—battles against what I want.

And it's him.

The only man who has ever beaten me in a fight. The only man who could ever go toe to toe with me and walk away with only scratches. The only man who's been worthy, in my fucking opinion.

And I would let him go if it meant going home, wouldn't I?

Wouldn't I give him up?

Wouldn't I regret it for the rest of my miserable life?

It's just like what Austin's ghost said in the maze. I'm alone. I'll live alone, and I'll die alone. I may live honorably—a fierce warrior who fought with her entire heart for her homeland.

But that's it.

It's all I ever used to want.

Until he touches me, his thumb grazing down the column of my throat, his fingers locked on the back of my neck. He tilts his mouth over mine but doesn't kiss me even though I feel our bodies reacting at the same time, leaning in almost desperately for a single ounce of attention to the needs we both ignore. The desires we trained ourselves to forget.

A low curse flutters between us before he says against my cheek, "Tomorrow morning, you will return to Silas's house, where you will stay until the Trials end. It's safer that way."

He pulls away and is gone in a flash, leaving me reeling and trapped with my own conflicting feelings, watching the now cold water circle the drain.

I shower, scrubbing myself raw, letting the cool water numb the scratches on my cheeks. I let my mind wander over the fact that Blake is here. Whether it's fatigue or just the absurdity of my situation in general talking, it doesn't come as a surprise.

I do everything I can not to think of Kaleb and the distance he just put between us. Because he's right. It doesn't matter what we feel. There's so much at stake.

After I dry off, I curl up in a tight ball in his empty bed, watching the first light of day creep over the wall, and when I close my eyes, Silverhide expands around me.

A FATHER'S BROKEN HEART

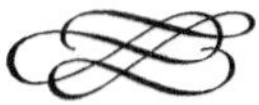

Soren

Silverhide is gorgeous in the morning. Wispy fog snakes through the trees as I stomp through wet, almost shin high grass. The little cabin on the edge of the main part of the village is tucked in the shadow of a crop of trees, their leaves morphing to a bright yellowish green as they dry. Yeah, I feel the change in the air. That first jarring cold morning of the upcoming season. Fall is on the horizon, which means Lexa and Blake have been missing for almost a month.

It's hard to believe it's only been a year since Maeve and I found each other, thrust together as some joke of the Goddess. The joke's on Her, however, because my mate is currently tucked tight in a bed we lovingly shared–naked–her scent all over my skin, just how I like it. Is She irritated that we made it through her trials, or is that what She wanted all along?

Our daughter, our precious demon of fire and wrath, blinks into the sunlit fog, gnawing on my shoulder and curling her little talons in my hair beneath the rising sun.

I'm a blessed man, I suppose. It could be worse. I could have power, like Blake. I could be the one battling some unseen force in an unfamiliar place. I could be the mate left behind.

Instead, I'm going to eat a warm breakfast before hanging out and hoping I can be useful in some way.

Ryan isn't seated when I reach the pack house, which is never that busy in the early mornings. It's mostly men in here now, grabbing a quick breakfast before heading back out to the harvest, which begins today. I came here two days ago, joining my mate after spending almost a week with Maddy, Isaac, and several other family members in Maatua–mostly children.

It was meant to be a vacation for Skye. Leona followed, as she always does, giving Marianna space to find her bearings. It's been rough. Everyone is on edge, including Ryan, who looks so beaten and dragged that he barely looks up from his coffee when I approach a mostly empty table already stacked with food.

He nods, tilts his head to offer me a seat, and continues to brace a hand against the table while sipping from his coffee. He does give Fallon a quick smile that she skeptically accepts, however.

"I see how it is," he grumbles playfully, and the smile that follows might be his first authentic one in a long time. "She's in her stranger danger phase now, huh?"

"Well, you're not a stranger. She's just grumpy. She didn't want to leave Maatua, I think."

"No one does." I sit across from him, and I notice he hasn't touched the food.

Of course, I want to ask about Lexa but refrain. It's none of my fucking business, but as a father to a daughter, I can only imagine how he's feeling. Like the world has collapsed? Like he wants to set fire to the universe and watch it burn? Probably.

"Did Skye stay behind?" he asks.

"Yeah, as far as I know, she was going to travel back to Crescent Falls on the ferry with Leona later this week if the weather holds. Leona and Maddy aren't in a rush to get back."

"Sydney mentioned Marianna is–" He cuts himself off, looking down into his coffee.

"Yeah, she's fucking miserable."

Ryan bites back a flat, knowing smile. It's not appropriate, but neither is my nonchalant attitude about all of this, I suppose.

"Thank you for talking to Logan for me while you were on the islands. I meant to find you last night after you arrived with everyone, but Maeve told me to give you a minute to adjust after the jump."

"It's not that bad once you're used to it. I was more worried about letting go of Fallon and losing her in the aether."

"Well, if she's anything like her mother, she'll be jumping on her own in a few weeks, anyway. We lost Maeve multiple times in her youth."

Now, I'm the one biting back a smile as I shovel eggs and a variety of breakfast meats onto a plate. Fallon, still far too young to eat solid food, fists a piece of bacon like her life depends on it. Ryan raises a brow but doesn't say a thing when Fallon sucks on the bacon, settling in my lap quietly.

"She looks like you," Ryan muses, leaning back.

"I know. She really does." I adjust her onto my other thigh. "I think Maeve is jealous, honestly, especially with Skye around, who is a mirror image of Marianna."

"She'll get one who looks like her. Nora is Aviva's twin but with my easygoing personality, whereas Lexa..." He tapers off, his expression suddenly cast in shadow. "She's her mother's daughter even if she looks like me and Syd. Like Blake." There's something between the words I can't decipher. A worry, I guess, that laces through each syllable.

"You think she's okay?"

"Yes, she is." He clears his throat, looking down at the worn surface of the table instead of meeting my eyes. "She's like her mother. Lexa can focus on anything but her own fear and immortality. She'll be fine." I don't like his tone. The note of... knowing. Yeah, that's it. Like he knows something about Lexa that others don't.

I don't have to pry, thankfully, because I was about to, but then he continues. "Aviva is the best warrior in our kingdom by far. She's always been that way. Just feral but calculated and meticulous. Her mind and body work in tandem, and she's always four or five steps ahead of any enemy–beast or man."

"Well, then you're probably right, especially if Lexa and Aviva are similar."

"But their hearts are as fragile as glass," he whispers, drowning the words with coffee.

Fallon coos softly, and Ryan grins at her, but it's damped by a grief I can't describe.

"Aviva won't return to Silverhide until there's news of Lexa. I had to come back. The harvest begins today and will take up every waking moment over the next three weeks. I can't miss it, even if it means leaving my mate alone to stitch herself back together. She's stubborn and headstrong–immovable. Lexa is the same. And I know she's all right. That's my only consultation. But I also know she'd throw her life at a cause even if it meant she couldn't return. She'd give her life to win whatever battle Blake is waging there; that's my guess. I think Aviva knows it, too, and it's brought back memories she'd rather not remember."

"What do you mean?"

Ryan shrugs one shoulder, sighing deeply. "Aviva was Lexa's age when we married. It was arranged, as you've probably come to understand. We didn't know each other. Her father was desperate for the marriage, and I found out way after our fate had already been sealed. Aviva buries her emotions until there's nothing left. She used hunting and sneaking off into the woods to help stomp out any residual emotion. She closed herself off, even to me, even when we bonded and realized we loved each other. It took her years–took her becoming a mother–for her to begin to open up, to say how she feels and vocalize what she really needs from me."

Fallon wiggles, spitting out the slice of bacon on my lap and reaching her grubby, oily fists toward my plate. I ignore her when she snatches a sausage and curls it in her little hand.

Ryan continues, "Lexa grew up a mirror image of her mother personality wise, and I got a glimpse of who Aviva was as a child and how her mother's death changed her. Lexa never had to go through what Aviva did. She has had more freedom to just be who she is, but I've worried about her for years. She wants to be fierce and unstoppable, and we've let her. My daughter is tough and talented. She has no dreams of settling down. But she hides her softness. She doesn't say what she really wants, but I see it sometimes, especially between her and Nora. Lexa has a soft heart. She hides it. My only prayer at night has always been that she finds a mate who sees that in her."

He plants his hands on the table with a deep sigh. "And I now know she had a fling with one of Evander's captains in the Ghost army because his parents went to Teshka to retrieve his body," he says, closing his eyes. "And she didn't say anything, but his parents knew about her, about them. Apparently, he was head over heels. Witnesses say he died protecting her. I know in my heart she didn't feel the same way about him."

I roll my lower lip between my teeth, unsure what to say.

"I'm sorry," he grumbles, running his fingers through his hair. "There's no reason to be talking about this."

"It's fine. That's kind of my sole purpose in the family as it stands. Maeve has been trauma dumping on me since the day I met her."

His dark, stormy blue eyes meet mine and hold, a glimmer of mirth shining in the morning sunlight. A spirited giggle races through the room, however, and then Kieran is launching into Ryan's arms.

Logan–tall, muscular, with dark hair and brilliant greenish-hazel eyes–follows but sits at the table instead of tackling Ryan, which is what Kieran is trying to do. Logan breathes deeply before turning to me with a slightly smug smile. I don't know him well yet. He's quiet but has a playful streak that only comes out when Brie's around–and that woman hangs the moon for him. It's obvious to everyone. He loves her.

And as of three days ago, when some of the family gathered in Maatua, he's moving his entire pack from Emberfyll to the Deadlands.

"You're right about the valley right there," he says, pointing a finger into thin air to the west. "It wouldn't take much to build a road that connects Silverhide to what I think I'll have to call New Emberfyll."

"I'm sure you can be more creative than that." Ryan smirks, but there's relief in his eyes. He raised Logan, turned a boy into a man–a warrior. An Alpha. Now, he's coming home. Ryan is relieved, even if he won't voice it.

"We have a few weeks to build. I think we can at least get some houses up and a pack house in that amount of time."

"With the harvest going on, you'll have extra sets of hands, for sure. Jerrod is already sending over at least two dozen of his men to help us out. I can spare a few of my own carpenters for you."

Brie struts into the room, cradling the swell of her stomach. Another baby–another son, according to Maeve, who apparently knows everything. I believe her. "Where's Maeve? It's almost eight o'clock!"

"Do you think Maeve willingly wakes up with the sun?" I laugh, but Brie scoops Fallon out of my arms.

"Why is she so greasy?"

"Bacon," Ryan says in a laugh, and Brie frowns, her voice lifting to chide me about how she's too young, on and on, but I'm looking at the open door to the pack house, to the wide, sweeping valley of Silverhide, and beyond.

Blake, you fucking bastard, I think, grinding my teeth. Grief over the loss of a friend sweeps through me. He's a real friend, as much as I hate to admit it, and I likely never will. Look at what he's missing. Look at what he'll miss if he truly believes he's not worthy of this life, this kingdom, and us.

WHO'S TO BLAME?

LEXA

I slept an entire day away. I couldn't bring myself to even attempt to get out of bed. It wasn't a weakness in my body–nothing sore or aching. I've always lived and loved routines. I feel my best when I know exactly what a day will bring–or at least should bring. But lately, everything has been so upside down. My spirit is shattered, and there's nothing I can do to fix it other than succumb to the fatigue that's been draining me for weeks without my wolf to help keep me balanced.

So, I laid in Kaleb's bed, surrounded by his scent, watching the sunlight play over the ceiling, watching the shadows creep in as the sun began its slow descent back toward the horizon–another day passing, another day further from home. Another day with too many questions and far too little answers.

I allowed myself to think about Chessie. I mapped her from memory, sinking so deeply into my thoughts that I could almost feel the cool bite of the creek that runs through the center of Silverhide and that slightly scratchy pink jumpsuit I used to wear almost every day, the pants rolled up to knees while Chessie and I did our chores, stomping laundry into submission and carrying baskets of wool to the weaver's cottage to be spun into yarn. I let the memories sink further, stretching wide, until my entire childhood came into startling focus. Blake was there, a constant presence, someone I thought I knew. Someone I loved. Someone I deeply cared for… idealized like a god.

I only dragged myself from bed when the sun set, and darkness swept through the room, the heat of day draining so swiftly, I shivered as I moved downstairs, where I ate a quiet, sparse dinner. The only words whispered were from Lis, the only other person in the house, who'd said, "The pantries at the pack house are empty again. Fae guards came and raided it," while swirling her spoon around her practically empty bowl of spent grain cooked in water–no salt, no sugar.

She didn't need to explain why the pack house was raided, why there is now barely any food left for anyone in the Glade. It's punishment. My punishment. Kaleb's punishment, directed by the king. Punishment for simply surviving longer than I should have.

Kaleb didn't return that night. I slept in my old room instead, finding it dim and stale. Only in the earliest, still dark hours of the morning did he come to fetch me, giving me a fresh, thick cloak made of wool and clothes that actually fit in a somewhat modern style, which was surprising, but I didn't have a chance to ask questions, and to be completely honest, I couldn't find the nerve to even say a single word to him.

He'd made things clear enough. I'd echoed his sentiments even though every fiber of my being screamed in protest. We are mates– that's all. It's not that deep.

Kaleb looks worn and withdrawn as he knocks hastily on the door in the alley behind Silas's manor. The sun hasn't even risen yet, and the streets are empty, save for a few fae guards walking in pairs under a cloak of shadow. We were met at the gate in the Glade by a trio of guards, and it became clear almost immediately that they were not wholly aligned with the king. They made a great effort to make it look like they were escorting us somewhere by force, but when we reached the long stretch of manors, their facades cast in dim, silver moonlight, they disappeared, having escorted us to what I realize is safety.

I will not be returning to the Glade.

That knowledge sweeps through me, pummeling me like a battering ram when the servants' hallways give way to the almost blinding, warm light of the formal foyer, where Silas and Blake are waiting.

Kaleb falls back, standing a foot or two behind me so I can't see his face, but my gaze is locked on my cousin.

I've been thinking about this moment since I found out he was here. Part of me yearns to slam into him, to hit him, to scratch his eyes out and demand answers, torturing him until he gives them up. But I was there the day he showed us how powerful he really is–when he extinguished Maeve's eternal flame with a single flick of his wrist. I'll never forget the look on her face.

And I'll never forget seeing Blake like this.

Something has changed. His face is the same–the same sharp lines, the same depth and shine to those strange eyes–but it's the new shadows and creases, the lines of exhaustion and hope, that are so desperately unfamiliar. His hair is longer than I've ever seen it, the same dark, wine red as mine, nearly black in the right lighting. But it's longer now, mussed, ruffled, and curling viciously at the ends, a far cry from the gelled back style I've always seen him in. He's dressed casually in color–a creamy white top, navy blue pants, his hands tucked in the back pockets.

He looks–if it's possible–bigger. Stronger. Broader in the shoulders, like he's spent these past weeks fighting, or training, for whatever he already knows is coming.

If I had seen him like this back in Moonrise, I wouldn't have recognized him at first glance.

He looks at me in the same way for several long moments, no one saying a word, but then his gaze drops to the mark on my neck, and he closes his eyes and grits his teeth.

Silas clears his throat, sensing the shift in the tension threatening to ignite between our sorry group. He holds out his hands in surrender, stepping into the center of the foyer. "All right, then. This is how this is going to go." He glances over my head at Kaleb, arching a brow that screams to dare to challenge him, but Kaleb remains silent. "I must return to the Highwoods. Lexa will stay here with Blake until the next Trial. The guards aligned with the rebellion will be at your disposal, Kaleb, in the meantime. You'll be able to move freely across the city to see her–"

"That won't be necessary," Kaleb cuts in sharply, and my heart cracks.

Silas purses his lips for a moment, lowering his gaze to his polished shoes, then says, "You're being called before the king today. I doubt anyone will be sent to the Glade to fetch you until this afternoon, but I wanted to give you ample warning. I don't know what he wants or what's planned. The king has been keeping me at arm's length lately, not allowing me within his circle, which begs the question of how much he knows about our resistance and who is feeding him information about its members. Blake will take over my efforts for now." He motions to Blake, who still hasn't opened his eyes.

Silas looks around, waiting for one of us to argue. When we don't, he continues, "I have eyes on my manor. Lexa is safe here, Kaleb."

"It's not his problem anymore," I quip, then I'm moving like the wind, my body propelling me forward through space and time before my mind can catch up. I'm upstairs and alone within seconds in a house I don't know well enough to immediately find a private place to unravel, but a snug alcove does the trick.

Male voices lift from downstairs, but I can't make out the words. Silas is arguing with Kaleb, who gives him a gruff reply before his footsteps sound, fading. There will be no goodbyes. There doesn't need to be. Kaleb was firm when he said I'd be staying here, and I am not in the position to argue.

Silas will come to show me to my room, I'm sure. A maid or someone will ensure I have everything I need, which is nothing. I brought nothing with me but the dragon scale I found in the maze and haven't let out of my sight since. It's tucked in my pocket. It's the only tangible thing I have in this world that's my own.

It's not Silas who casts a heavy shadow over the fine, shallow carpet covering this wing of the house. Blake comes to a stop in a streak of hazy sunlight, turning his head to me. Silence hangs between us like a bell waiting to be rung. He's obviously waiting for me to make the first move, to start the fight he thinks is coming his way. He knows me. Knows what I'm capable of. Our fathers are twins. We're closer than cousins in that sense. Our blood is nearly the same.

"I knew you'd be called here," he says, his voice booming toward the angled ceiling without much force at all. "I saw it. Not you specifically, but what She called the Warrior's Daughter. You are Aviva's child, and thus, I came to the conclusion that something would happen, and you'd be pulled into the mess our family has been fighting for almost four years now. That vision gave me the clarity I needed to find Hannibal and come here, to his door, without needing to use my daughter's powers to strengthen my own like I feared."

"You're welcome," I manage to grind out. I'm shocked at how calm I am, but anger still rushes through my veins, driven by my racing heart. "For making this so easy for you."

"This has not been easy–"

"Did you know that my entire regiment would die?"

He rolls his lower lip between his teeth, shaking his head.

I step out of the shadow of the alcove, anger turning to rage that I ball in my fists, keeping them locked at my sides. "Did you know Chessie would die? Did you see it?"

He holds my gaze for several seconds before replying, "I did not–"

"Did you even care to look?"

"Everyone believes I have infinite power to see the future, to follow every single fucking lifeline thrown from the stars, but that's not how this works. We have free will, Lexa. One step, one single blink, can throw a prophecy off kilter. I see outcomes, Lexa, not the moments leading up to them. I see a war so vividly I can taste the blood and smell the rot, and that's why I'm here. That's why I gave up everything, and everyone, to be here–with you–so we can stop it from happening."

"You threw me into hell!" I shout, but he doesn't flinch. Color heats his cheeks, his skin tinged darker than usual, now a soft, golden hue instead of his normally pale, icy undertones. Like he's a living being again and not a shadow of death that has been haunting our family for a decade.

"There was nothing I could do to stop this from happening. That's what you need to understand. I'm here now. I'm fulfilling my vengeance and stopping a war before it's begun. I'm here with a purpose." He looks at my mark again, taking a shallow breath before his eyes meet mine in the golden haze. "And so are you. You can believe this is my fault all you want, but do you honestly believe the Goddess would have blessed you with a mate you'd never have the opportunity to meet?"

I edge toward him, pivoting at the last second to avoid a collision, and snarl in passing, "Do you realize that Kaleb and I have no future after this? I cannot stay. He cannot leave his people."

"So you're giving up that easily?"

"I am giving up nothing," I hiss, trying to ignore the gaping hole in my chest now growing with every passing second. "I'm in this situation against my will. Kaleb and I are mates—that's certain—but we can't even feel it under the yoke of his king. We had one night, Blake. It will never be like that again. He made that clear. My prerogative is going home."

"You're not giving him enough credit for what he has to do—and be—in this regime."

"I can't get through to him, just like Marianna couldn't get through to you." If I slapped him, it would have had the same effect.

I walk away with no destination in mind, but I can't do this. I can't have this conversation now. Maybe not ever.

CALLING HIM OUT

Kaleb

The ballroom in the palace is crowded but so quiet I can hear the echo of my footsteps. I didn't bother to bathe, let alone change into something more appropriate for this occasion. My shirt is dust-stained red and wilted from a day spent in the sun, in the sparring ring, where I beat my tension into submission until I couldn't so much as lift my arms anymore.

Fae guards stomp beside me, flanking me on either side until we reach the top of the staircase leading down to the wide, ornate ballroom where a crowd of mostly men waits. The balcony overlooking the ballroom is wrapped in banners, like some kind of celebration is being held soon, the decorating in the early stages.

A celebration for the victor, the champion, of the Trials that are not yet over.

Several faces turn as I move down the stairs on my own. My boots leave red-hued dirt in their wake, a bright stain on the marble tiles—like blood. Like every step is a reminder of the blood spilled only to entertain these beings now turning to watch my approach, chandelier light illuminating the tips of their pointed ears and their glistening wings.

I was called from the Glade just like Silas said I would be, but I expected a formal one-on-one with the king, not this. That's probably coming.

I see sponsors and trainers alike situated around the crowd. Meg's trainer is here, but her sponsor is not. The only other victor still in the running–a fully fae male whose name I don't recall–is nowhere to be seen. His sponsor is here, looking pale as he glances around, careful not to look directly in my eyes when I come to a stop next to the only friendly face in the room.

High Lord Everett tucks his wings in tight to allow space for me to stand beside him and moves to the side so we're practically shoulder to shoulder. A soft hum of muffled conversation expands around the room again, and Everett says in a near whisper, "You just missed the king's announcement about the next game."

"It'll be a hunt, I'm sure."

"How did you know?"

"He's following the same schedule as the last Trial ten years ago. It was the obvious choice."

Everett looks over his shoulder like he's worried about being overheard. I scan the area, noticing the guards appearing out of the shadows of hallways branching off the ballroom, standing still in wait for their next command.

"If the announcement is over, why is everything still here?" I ask under my breath, and he knits his hands together, a motion that seems more like a nervous tick than a calculated movement.

"It isn't over, at least, I don't think so. The king left abruptly."

"Why?"

He grits his teeth and bows his head. I'm taller than him, but it's plain he has no intention of being overheard now. "There's been increasing reports of unrest north of here, in the Highwoods and the fae courts of Nyantha. Soldiers were sent to disband several rebel armies trying to push forward into capital territory. The free wolves have united, it seems, with the high fae of Nyantha, and the king is growing increasingly unstable according to reports from within his inner circle. He's furious wolves are getting the better of the soldiers he sent to guard the borders, and the fae of the north aren't doing anything to aid him. Shifters are luring fae into the Highwoods, and they're never seen again."

"Maybe they're defecting," I reply with a bored sigh. "Have you ever been to the Highwoods, Lord Everett? I've heard it's beautiful. The shifters have a king, you know."

"I am aware of King James."

"Alpha King James. He's a wolf," I correct. "The king of the only free wolves in Pantharas."

"Well, our king believes those wolves are property of the fae and is livid with the King of Nyantha for allowing them such freedoms."

"He believed that of the halflings who disappeared as well, didn't he?" I bite back what I nearly gave away–that Emberfyll isn't just a myth, that the rumors that the missing halflings perished in the turbulent sea blocking the king's access to Eastonia have been proven false by my mate. While I trust Silas, I don't necessarily trust his friends.

"Nevertheless, he's unstable. The Trials were supposed to be the distraction he needed to keep the other lesser fae kings and their flocks in line, but your victor's progress has resulted in conversations and side-picking. Guess which side the majority of the lesser fae kings and high lords are leaning now?"

I take a deep breath when a trio of guards moves from the shadows, cutting through the crowd in my direction.

Everett leans in further, whispering, "Everything is in place. We're just waiting for a spark now."

It jars me to my core, but I don't have a moment to react, to try to make sense of what he said. I know little of Silas's plans because I refused to involve myself. It's a fae issue. The rebellion has nothing to do with the shifters, the slaves, or the lesser fae kind. It's high fae lords against their king, but the undercurrent in the room shifts in real time as the guards motion for me to follow, and I look behind me and see hope in the eyes of men who should want for nothing.

Who know nothing about not having enough to eat. Who know nothing of watching women and children perish from starvation and lack of medical care. Who know nothing about the sound of the gate closing behind four-hundred-men who will never return home.

Now, they look at me like I'm their savior.

In reality, Lexa is the lamb destined for sacrifice, and I'm the one holding the knife at the altar the rebellion built.

I will not allow it.

Not her. Never her.

The hum of the ballroom fades as the hallway stretches, narrowing, twisting at odd angles. I follow the guards up short steps and winding staircases. I've had one other one-on-one meeting with the king–just one. It was shortly after I won my Trial and gave him my wish, which he was obliged to grant.

A wide, heavy wooden door opens to an even wider, round room with an altar at the center–a basin full of crystals so pure I can see the gleam of the king's turquoise robes through them when he swishes to face me, but it's the man a few feet to his left that makes a shiver run down my spine.

Hannibal rests his long, spindly white fingers on the top of a cane of pure onyx, his nearly white eyes locked on mine as the door closes me in with these beasts of wings and stolen power.

"Alpha King Kaleb," the king says in a sing-song voice that rattles my bones. "So good of you to come. I did not think you'd accept my invitation."

I'm done with games. I'm done. I can't take it anymore–watching my people die. Watching my mate get thrown into the fire over and over for their sick entertainment. Knowing that Silas and his rebellion are waiting for the moment to strike while my people are trapped in the Glade, unable to escape whatever war comes knocking at the gates most have never traveled beyond.

Knowing I have a mate, but I can't keep her. I can't as much as kiss her without damning myself to a hell of my own design. A mate I can't want without feeling the crushing desperation already taking root in my soul over the fact that I will lose her.

"I am a slave. I am not given choices."

The king arches his brows, but my gaze is still on Hannibal, the king's spy, they call him. I know the beast was born long before my time. He's some kind of spiritual advisor to the king and his court—someone close to the gods, they say. Someone who can see the prophecies written in the stars.

"Why are you here?" I ask him bluntly, emotionless.

Hannibal smiles. "It is so odd seeing something like you after being away so long. Half beast, half fae. An abomination, really. To taint such glorious blood with that of a dog feels like it should go against the gods, but look at you. Towering creature of muscle and death, aren't you? I was not here for your game, but heard a great many tales—"

I turn to the king, cutting Hannibal off. "What do you want from me?"

The king glances at Hannibal, but then looks at me. "I must have a discussion with you about the upcoming Trial and your victor. Don't think I don't know that she's been moved out of the Glade. You and your kind must think you're two steps ahead of me, don't you?"

"I don't know what you're talking about."

"Then, where is she? My guards were sent to the Glade at sunrise this morning to fetch her, to house her here with the rest of the victors. It's a little treat for them, in my opinion, especially her, having lived in mud and filth these past few weeks."

I cock my head. "She did not find that necessary."

"Or you, I suspect? Tell me, Kaleb, about this little pet of yours. Have you had a taste of her yet? Others are curious."

Hannibal smirks. My gaze locks on his. "Is there something funny about that?"

"You'll address me as lord—"

"I will address you as nothing. I have long denounced your church and gods. I am a shifter, which is made clear every day I spend keeping my kind alive in the Glade." I edge toward him but turn to face the king before closing the distance between us, adding, "The rules of the games are sacred. Everyone, every king, knows it. They're written in the blood of the fallen, who come from every background–high fae, lesser fae, and shifters. People like me." I look at Hannibal. "Separating victors from their trainers and sponsors goes against the rules, but you know that. I'm guessing I'm here because I am the only one who said no."

"And hid your victor instead!" the king booms. I look at him out of the corner of my eye, smirking.

"If you believe she's hidden, you must not be as close with your high lords as you believe you are, Your Highness."

"Ah, I see. Your brother, Silas, is involved." He reaches up to run his fingers through his silky brown hair, his ageless face making him look more like a sixteen-year-old boy than the ancient being he is, but his thick, deep voice betrays his age. "Silas is always up to something, isn't he? Little bastard."

"What a way to speak about your nephew." I smile, and the king's eyes lock on mine. "Did you not think I knew?"

"It's not a secret Silas's father is my brother."

"Was," I correct, angling my body to the door. "Murder is an unforgivable act to the fae, is it not? And to think, if Prince Urus hadn't met such a violent end, my brother could have been the one standing in this room eventually, a true heir to the throne, with real power. There are others who agree the wrong man holds all the power. I wonder if that's why you sold Urus's wife, my mother, into your twisted halfling breeding program after his death."

The king pales with sudden rage. "You will watch your tongue. Your title is a formality at best, halfling. You are no king. I could kill you where you stand."

"And do you think the Glade won't rise in retaliation?" I move in on him until he takes a step back, submitting. Hannibal notices and straightens as I viciously eye the men. "You may keep us in magical chains, bound to the dirt, unable to access our true nature, but you forget how resilient shifters are. Who won the war, Your Highness, in Eastonia?"

The king turns a violent purple, but Hannibal reaches, resting a hand on his shoulder. "You have such confidence–"

"And you," I snarl, cutting him off, "failed in a mission overseas. Miserably. You underestimated the family in power and came crawling back to your precious king to spin tales of glories that never happened, I assume. Have you not? Tell me, Hannibal, how long did you live in hiding, hunted by one god in particular? Can you feel how close he is now?"

Hannibal tilts his head, suspicion lighting behind his eyes. Recognition flares, and his hand drops from the king's shoulder.

"Lexa is mine," I tell him. "The Glade belongs to me. My mate will win the games, and then you will be answering to the Glade in blood."

"How dare you speak to me in such a way!" the king booms, his powers flickering around me so thickly I can taste them, but it's Hannibal I'm watching with curiosity. He's unsettled. A rat in a cage, suddenly desperate. "I could have you executed if I wished!"

"But you haven't because you know what will happen. I was the champion of my Trials. A hero. Blessed in the sacred order. You kill me, and everything you've built comes crashing down, doesn't it? But it's already weak to begin with. The High Lords and lesser kings who send their warriors into the Culling will finally see how you've twisted the sacred games and turned them into a purge. They see the cracks already." I bow deeply and turn for the door, my heart heavy in my chest. I move through the palace without being dismissed.

He'll throw everything he has at Lexa now, I know it.

It doesn't matter if he knows where she is. He can't touch her. High Lords have already placed their bets. She's untouchable everywhere but within the games themselves, and he knows it. He wanted me to come here so he could try to intimidate me. It didn't work.

A guard stops me in the depths of the arena on my way to the Glade. He pulls me into the shadows as another pair of guards moves into sight, passing us without so much as glancing in our direction. The guard slips a note into my hand and leaves as quietly as he came. It's from Chasten.

The Alphas have all agreed on one thing.

They're ready to fight.

They're just waiting for my lead.

I curl the note in my fist, glancing toward the shadow of the gate. It's nightfall, shadows creeping toward my toes as the sky turns a deep, brutal violet that fades into stars.

I step toward the gate, then pause, a decision weighing heavily on my heart.

I'LL DO IT MYSELF

LEXA

They're no maids in the manor. Not a single servant to tend the halls. Beyond the formal gates out front, fae guards rest against the spiraling columns that mark the entrance, the garden sheltered by a tall, marble wall that wraps around the entire building. It reminds me of the manors in Moonrise and some of the nicer townhomes. Crescent Falls, ever modern, favors the larger, family style homes, like Misty's place.

Silas doesn't have a TV. I haven't seen anyone with a phone, either. No video games. No computers. Just... books. Books Silas likes. Books about war and politics.

The sun isn't nearly as warm today. I move through the house, exploring. I slept well last night, woke refreshed, and took a long, hot shower for the first time in weeks, scrubbing my skin raw, making use of Silas's excessive collection of soaps and oils. But now I don't know what to do with my time.

I haven't seen Blake since yesterday morning. I know he went out last night because I peeked out a window and saw him speaking to the guards at the front gate before his shadowed form moved out of the haze of the lantern lights. Now, the sun is inching toward the horizon again, painting Silas's expensive, cloud-soft carpet in milky crimson light. Another day gone. Another day closer to the next game.

The final game.

I've been wandering through the house to fill my time. It's four levels, mostly open, but I still find myself turned around and slightly lost in the tighter corridors on either wing. The sun sets, and silver moonlight trickles through the windows when I find a familiar room, and the scent that hits me when I open the door stops me in my tracks.

I've been here before. This is Chessie's room. The pink, tufted pillows and satin bedspread are disheveled, totally untouched since she climbed out of bed that last day. My heart lurches as I step inside and look around at the books scattered on every surface–love stories. Books Silas wouldn't have kept in his library… but fetched for her. Vases full of wilted roses scent the air with a slight musk of decay, petals covering the corners of the room–wrinkled and graying. I don't turn the light on. I don't want to see her footprints still pressed in the pristine carpet. I don't want to see pieces of her golden hair in the comb resting on the vanity.

But the care Silas took… is here. It's everywhere. He was devoted to her comfort despite knowing she didn't have a chance. I wonder what that felt like for him, seeing that beautiful girl so full of life and goodness. I wonder what it felt like for him to see that huge smile and glimmering eyes and then to have to send her to her death.

"It broke him."

I whirl toward the voice behind me, toward the shadow darkening the doorway.

"She broke him. I didn't think it was possible. Silas has always guarded his heart. I never thought he'd fall in love." Kaleb is wearing trousers that fit him like a glove and a shirt meant for a high-ranking fae male–Silas's clothes, I think. His hair is brushed back neatly, tied at the nape of his neck, and he's clean shaven, making him look years younger than he actually is.

He moves deeper into the room, the creeping silver moonlight setting his eyes aflame in shades of amber and gold. He doesn't look at me. His expression tightens as he scans the wilted petals lying dormant on the carpet. Then, he voices what I thought the moment I stepped foot in what I know is now a shrine to her memory. "He left it as it was the morning before the Beast Trial."

My throat works, tightening around a lump threatening to strangle me. A suffocating sob dies there, trapped with nowhere to escape. "Why are you here?"

"Why do you think?"

"I need an actual answer from you, Kaleb. You're so–so incredibly, infuriatingly, stubborn and set in your ways. I get it. I really do. We're cut from the same cloth, aren't we?" I pivot to face him but feel my body recoiling when he doesn't look at me. "I've known men like you my entire life. Men from the tribes. Men who are born for leadership. Men who would die for our culture and traditions if it means keeping them alive. I didn't realize it when you first called me Luna, but it's only because, in your mind, being your mate… it's not even for show. It wasn't to give the Glade any kind of hope. It wasn't because you wanted me to be by your side. It was just how things are done, how they were done before the tribes were taken from Eastonia."

Kaleb grits his teeth, his jaw clenched.

"You never meant it. Not the way you… should have."

He closes his eyes, sighing deeply. I watch the fabric of his freshly pressed shirt slide over the taut muscles beneath. "We don't have a future together. We've established that."

"Well, what if we did? What if there was a way out of this–for everyone? The resistance–"

"I've spent the entirety of nearly two days in Blake's company," he cuts in, opening his eyes to slits as he turns his body to mine. The distance between us feels like a gaping, yawning void full of petals– too soft, too beautiful to be there. Like none of this is real. Like I'll wake up in my room back in Silverhide and this will have been a terrible dream. A nightmare.

"Oh, of course you have," I snarl, my eyes dry despite the tightness in my throat. "What has he had you do, I wonder?"

"He's right. Silas was right. The cracks in the empire are now fault lines, Lexa, waiting for a spark. The king is sitting on a wealth of stolen power. Power he's leeched over the course of centuries, forcing other fae kingdoms to bend the knee to his will, and he might have been successful, lived on to rule another five hundred or more years had his snake, Hannibal, not returned empty-handed, breaking every promise the king made to his people. That's why he held the games. That's why he risked sending demons of shadow to sweep across the beach you were destined to be on. It's a distraction to keep people satiated by blood, but it's not working."

My jaw works, teeth clenched tight. "I don't care about any of that."

He eyes me skeptically, shifting his weight from foot to foot as he inspects my tight expression. "Your cousin came here to prevent a war on your own soil and found a war already brewing within. He found Silas easily enough. Silas is the king's nephew. I'm not sure if you know that."

I didn't. I don't voice my shock. I barely feel it. I'm not sure shock is something I can feel anymore.

"Blake has power the fae feel they were robbed of long ago. He was willing to help sow the seeds of rebellion deeper than they've ever been planted before in exchange for Hannibal's head, and we are giving that to him, even if he destroys the city to do it."

"You realize what he is, right? What he can do?"

"I'm aware. What I need to know is what you can do because there's something you've been lying about, isn't there?"

My stomach coils, but I remain standing, my feet firmly planted. "You're lying to me as well."

"This isn't about me." "Don't," I rush out, turning for the door. I can't have this conversation here in a room that smells like Chessie, a room that reminds me how I failed her so badly.

The moonlit corridor beyond the bedroom opens wide, my footsteps echoing, but I don't get far before the shadows tremble, threatening to pull me in. I imagine the beasts of mist and death from the beach, the talons and jaws full of line, black teeth. I shudder, and then he's behind me, his hands gripping my upper arms.

"I have officially joined the resistance," he says under his breath. "Chasten has been tasked with gathering the men of the Glade, readying them for whatever battle comes. The end of the Trials will mark the beginning of the war."

I resist the urge to lean into his warmth, but I don't tear out of his touch. My body and mind tangle over my desire to run but also stay.

"And you'll send me home with Blake when it begins?" I ask bitterly.

"Of course—"

"Do you—do you care?" The words vibrate, feeling foreign on my tongue as even more unfamiliar, conflicted feelings ricochet through my system. I feel suddenly like I'm standing in front of Austin again on that bluff, watching in horror and confusion while he spilled his heart to me and I felt… nothing.

Now, I feel everything. Everything hurtful and desperate with no way to voice it. I turn out of his touch to face him, and that gaping void spreads again, threatening to suck me under if I don't just… say what I need to tell him.

"I care about your wellbeing," he guts out, like it's painful, like they're not the words he wants to say. Not even close.

"Then reject me because this is hurting me more than the games ever could," I cry out, motioning to the space between us, like the world is actively opening up, swallowing us whole.

"I will not reject you," he says with heartbreaking calm, which makes my vision turn blood red.

"Why not? What's stopping you? My feelings—whatever I feel is obviously s-s-stronger—" I gasp out a breath, my lungs screaming for fresh air. I want to run. I need to shift. I want to be anywhere but here. I want to be alone, not faced with the damning consequences of finding my mate and… wanting him. Kaleb stares at me, moonlight reflecting in his eyes, making them glow. "I don't do this," I rasp, motioning between us. "I don't have—have boyfriends or crushes. I've never—even Austin." My voice cracks painfully on his name. "We had fun. I wanted him for sex–that was all–and now I'm flooded by guilt over the fact that he died, and I feel nothing, but the thought of you–of you being hurt in any way kills me, Kaleb. I can't leave you behind."

"You have to."

"I won't leave."

"I will force you to."

"Why are you doing this to me?"

He steps into the void, and it disappears, replaced by carpet. A simple trick of my mind–a defense mechanism.

"You are killing me, Lexa. From the moment I saw you in chains, you've stripped away any defenses I've had. You've burned me raw," he says, his voice low and grating. "I've never had to question my future until you were in it. I never had to ache over someone until I spent weeks pacing my room above yours, wondering what you were seeing in your dreams. I cannot keep you here. I cannot leave my pack behind to suffer if it means keeping you. I cannot allow you to stay and fall into the wrong hands."

"I am capable of protecting myself–"

"You've always been so overconfident. You're going to get yourself killed."

"I would rather die than feel like this another second," I shout, but his steely expression doesn't shift. "Reject me. I'm giving you the opportunity to do it yourself, to free yourself of the burden–"

"I will not."

"WHY?"

He shakes his head. I wish I could see inside, catch a glimpse of his thoughts. I've never been one to quietly rage. Kaleb is trained in that skill.

"Fine," I choke out, my hands curled so tightly into fists I feel my nails pinching my skin. "I'll do it."

He tenses.

"I–I–" I choke back a sob as my world collapses inward. Useless. I've never trained for this. I was never prepared for this while being prepared for literally everything else.

I can't do it.

Why can't I do it?

I whirl, sprinting into the shadows, following a familiar staircase down to the second floor of the house. I trip on the carpet runner, my legs like jelly, folding like a newborn fawn. My face hits the marble tiles coating the second floor landing with a devastating crunch, and then the tears begin, rolling down my cheeks uncontrollably. I clamber to my hands and knees but jerk to awareness when an arm loops around my waist and hauls me into the air. Kaleb kicks the door to the room I slept in last night open, nearly breaking it from its hinges, and sets me down.

I lunge.

THIS IS OURS

Lexa

It only takes one smooth motion for Kaleb to catch me around the middle and take me to the ground. My back hits the soft carpet with a thud that rattles my bones, and I jerk, diving to drive a knee between us. He gathers my wrists, pinning them above my head, and thrusts his knee between my legs, pinning me.

His eyes are bright and only inches above mine while he inspects my face for damage from my fall. Pain throbs through my forehead, but it's my pride that stings in agony.

"I told you," he says low in his throat, a soft growl that laces over my skin, "your overconfidence is going to kill you. Do you think you can still see in the dark without your wolf at your disposal?"

I go totally still, my body relaxing against my will, and fold. I submit. I give up.

"What happened to us? Why does this have to be so hard? Rejecting each other? I don't want to do it, but you're making it clear that we—we'll never be able to be together. What changed in you after the maze? You're not the same man you were when I... when I went in."

He says nothing, but the column of his throat bobs before tightening, his expression pained.

"Kaleb?" I whisper, unable to take this gutting feeling any longer. "What did I do wrong?"

He loosens his grip and rises, stepping over me and into the moonlight.

"Are you going to talk to me? Have you changed your mind about how you feel–"

"I felt my entire world shift the moment I saw you."

I pull my knees to my chest, watching him turn his head ever so slightly to look down at me.

"It was like being struck over the head and waking up with fractured memories. Like just the sight of you was enough to undo everything I've ever known. When we, the sponsors, were called to make our decisions, to vie for victors, I chose you because I was selfish, not because I thought you had a chance of winning, but because I didn't want anyone else getting you. Silas took Chessie at my urging because I knew he could keep her safe when you couldn't."

My throat restricts, but I remain on the floor, cast in his shadow as he kneels a few feet away.

"I wanted you to prove me wrong. I wanted you to be weak, to be submissive, to be just another feminine face too scared to look me in the eyes. You weren't. You are everything I deserved. Spiteful. Arrogant. High-strung. Overconfident and brash with a temper to match."

My nostrils flare at the insults, but... his tone... I'm struggling to understand what he means until he continues, "You were everything I tried to kill in my myself. If I'd been more spiteful and driven, things wouldn't have gotten this far. I could have tried to free everyone in the Glade sooner and stopped waiting for the right moment to come, and then there you were, fighting me tooth and nail, looking at me like I was the king, the person keeping you in chains."

He looks down at his hands.

"After the maze, it became clear that there're other things in motion that I can't keep you out of. I've tried. I've tried to keep you at arm's length, and when I failed, when we felt the bond, and I claimed you when I knew how selfish it was of me–"

"I wanted you," I whisper, but he shakes his head.

"I knew better, Lexa. I'm stronger than that."

"When have you ever let yourself have something you want?"

"What I want doesn't matter."

"It matters to me!"

He edges closer but hesitates, bowing his head. "Lexa, this is it for us. I need you to understand that. You will go home and have a life beyond me, and I have to be okay with that, too, but it's killing me. Before your cousin made himself known during the Maze Trial, I let myself believe that things might work out in our favor, selfishly, that you and I were paired because we have a future, but we do not. You know we don't."

"But if we did," I choke out, pain radiating through my chest like I'm digging for those threads just to feel them again. I'd do anything to feel it again. "If we had a chance, Kaleb, would you come with me? Would you bring everyone from the Glade home if it weren't so Goddess damned impossible?"

"I want to say yes," he whispers, unable to meet my eyes. "I want you to know that, Lexa, that if I could say yes, I would. But I can't give you that kind of hope."

"Why not? Why is this so hard?"

"Because I love you." His voice is ragged with emotion that he refuses to show. His expression remains tight, but his eyes are set in sorrow and it absolutely turns me inside out more than his words do. "I love you. I'd walk through hell for you and maybe that's exactly what I'm doing now, and that's enough for me. I want nothing more than for it to be enough for you."

Tears slide free, trickling down my cheeks. He moves closer, tugging my arms free from my knees, pulling me to his chest.

"I will not be going with you," he says into my hair. "I can't go. But I'm here now. That's the best I can do."

I wrap my arms around his neck and drag him down, my mouth on his.

It's a soft kiss—guarded and uneasy. A tangled sob works up my throat, but I banish it, parting my lips against his in surrender, and he folds into my touch, pressing me to the carpet. I deepen the kiss, my cheeks wet with tears as I smooth my tongue against his, memorizing his taste, the feeling of him shuddering around me.

I want just a piece of him. Something to hold on to. Something that belongs to us and not the games. I guide his hand to my breast, arching my back in silent approval as he pressing kisses down my throat, his mouth clasping around the mark he left there, a mark I'll wear for the rest of my life, even if he's not in it.

I don't know how it happens, but our clothes slowly come off. He sinks into me, grinding his hips into mine in slow, heavy strokes. I purr like a cat, unhurried, letting his warmth rush through me and awakening the little strands of our bond not touched by the king's magic. Heat blossoms in my lower belly, my body tightening in anticipation of a release I hope doesn't come because I don't want this to end.

But I writhe beneath him, and he groans against my shoulder, gasping as my body submits and softens in his hands. His cock slides into me with ease—demanding—even if his hands on my body are gentle and tender.

This isn't the frenzied lust we experienced the first time.

This is ours. Our love. Our bodies are unburdened by unseen chains. The king can't take this moment from us.

He guides my hips with each slow thrust, his breath coming in quick rasps, and my body follows his, driven to the point of no return. My arms drop to my sides, my hair falling in a halo across the carpet as he rises on his knees, dragging my hips up, and drives into me with newfound fervor.

His eyes meet mine in the silver moonlight, heavy and hooded with heat. I come undone, pleasure washing through me in a gentle, throbbing wave, my inner muscles tightening then spasming around his length, and he finally lets himself go.

He lowers himself to my body, kissing my breasts before our mouths lock. He grunts, caging me in on the carpet and pouring his heat inside of me, flooding me with warmth, and I am boneless beneath him, unable to move even if I wanted to.

"I love you," I whisper, tears dampening my cheeks. He's still hard, still inside of me, and the next kiss is… damning and so heated that my toes curl, and fresh desire rockets through me.

He takes me again on the carpet, rougher this time, claiming me over and over until our bodies are spent and morning sunlight drifts through the curtains. I'm half asleep when he pulls a blanket off the bed and drapes it over us before curling his body around mine, holding me in a tight, locked embrace, like he's terrified I'll disappear if he so much as lets go.

We sleep through the morning, and I wake to a pinching sensation deep in my belly that sends a shockwave through me, rattling me enough to come to full awareness. I sit up, squinting into the sunlight, and realize with a start I'm in bed instead of on the floor– and alone.

I slide out of the sheets, gripping the fourposter as another pinch delves through my belly like a knife and quickly retreats, leaving me slightly breathless.

I haven't given any thought to my moon cycle. I haven't had it since I arrived in Pantharas, but that doesn't surprise me in the least. It's never been regular, for one. Two, I've been under an incredible amount of stress.

I hobble toward the bathroom and find, to my relief, supplies in the event I need them. Silas is, undoubtedly, a very thoughtful man.

Chessie would have loved him deeply if she were still here.

She wouldn't have left him behind; I know that much.

Chessie would have stayed.

She's a stronger woman than I'll ever be.

I shower, dress, and move through the quiet house to the kitchen. There're still no maids here, and Blake is the only body haunting the house beside me, it seems.

He confirms it, saying, "There's coffee and fresh cream. Your mate had to go tend to his pack. He'll be back to escort you to the next Trial this evening."

I freeze, my hand stretched in midair to reach for a coffee mug on one of the tall shelves above my head. "So soon?"

"Tonight. It's a hunt. You'll be able to shift." His eyes meet mine, a dimmer violet than I remember.

"We need to talk."

"We do."

I pour a cup of coffee, taking advantage of the cream and sugar he laid out. I'm unsurprised by the lack of breakfast because I've never seen Blake eat a real meal, and I doubt he's started now.

I have so many questions. Too many. I start with the most important one.

"What are you planning on doing, Blake?"

"I'm going to kill Hannibal."

"It can't be as simple as that."

"It shouldn't be, but I was pulled here by the Goddess and found myself at the beginning of a revolution. Silas has already done all the work for me. I just need to get Hannibal alone."

I turn my mug in a circle. "Are your powers affected by this place?"

"No," he says softly, nodding in confirmation that he's aware the fae and shifter alike are stripped of their powers. "I have them well under my control."

"Then how will you do it? Kill Hannibal?"

"Publicly. I will have my moment. It's already planned. I will kill him in front of his supporters as a lesson not to fuck with our family."

"And the king? You don't think he'll stop you?"

His eyes shine a little brighter. "Your mate would like his moment with the king, and he will have it."

Dread laces through me.

"What do you need me to do?" I ask in a whisper.

He smiles—coy, sly as a fox. "Does Kaleb know you have a beast form?"

THROUGH THE ARCH

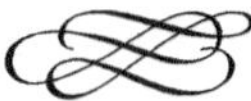

LEXA

Kaleb adjusts the loops and straps keeping my shifting dress in place, his fingers biting through the damp, rainy cold. There was a shift in the air last night, after a day spent mostly in solitude at Silas's house. I'd spent most of the day looking out of the window, watching the trees sway between manor houses and in the small parks, all of them tinged with gold—the first signs of autumn.

I missed the harvest.

Kaleb's touch is firm as he moves down my body to my sandals, checking my frame from my neck to the very tips of my toes. I'm allowed a weapon of choice tonight but only as long as I can carry it. I doubt the king knows about my use of a shifting halter, which Lis was able to craft in a matter of hours. I sent Kaleb with a sketch and measurements when he returned to the Glade without me yesterday morning.

I eye the weapons laid out on a table across the room. We're not in the city anymore. We're far outside the walls cutting off the capital from the endless woods and plains beyond. This building looks and feels like an old warehouse. It's wide and cavernous, empty save for rows and rows of massive shelving units. I can taste sea air, but I didn't get a glimpse of my surroundings before I was brought here. I believe we're near–or at–a port. Kaleb came to fetch me just before sunset and brought me to the arena, where a bag was fixed over my head, and an hour later, I was here.

Condensation drips down massive pipes directly behind Kaleb's head, falling into his hair. I inhale deeply again, trying to catch a taste of what's beyond the stale confines of the warehouse. The sea, for sure. All I can smell is salt air.

"Don't worry about the sandals," I whisper, reaching discreetly to run my fingers through his hair. My eyes dart to the guards situated on the far side of the room, their backs to a large, sliding metal door. I'm the only victor here. Meg and the other guy must be somewhere else.

"You'll be able to feel your wolf until sunrise," Kaleb says almost absently, untying the leather straps that hold my sandals in place. He weaves them back up my calves like he just needs something to do with his hands. "Or until the king calls an end to the game, whichever comes first."

He rises, and my fingers fall from his hair. Kaleb's eyes meet mine, a muted hazel-gold in the dim fluorescent light. He adjusts the loops running down the center of my dress, tightening them. When I shift, they'll pull open down my sides and belly, creating a web of thin, but generally effective, armor that I can tighten again the second I shift back to my human form. It will keep me clothed as long as I don't lose it.

"How do people watch the games when they're not in the arena?" I ask just to fill the void of silence.

Kaleb moves on to my hair, brushing the loose curls away from my shoulders, twisting the small braids back to hold my hair away from my face. "The king has eyes everywhere. There will be projections all over the city and in homes."

"Will you watch me?" I ask, meeting his eyes.

Just like the autumn shift, something has changed between us. An impasse. A quiet, gentle resolution. There's no point in fighting this anymore–what's budding between us. We'll deal with the heartbreak later. For now, we're here. Two bodies in the same place at the same time, bonded.

But his skin is still free of my mark, and I regret it. I should have marked him by now.

I will when I make it out of this game and come home to him.

I swear I will.

"I likely won't have a choice in the matter."

"If you could choose–"

"I wouldn't watch."

He doesn't need to elaborate. His eyes say everything. Watching his mate fight out in the open, in an unfamiliar wilderness, is not something he would willingly put himself through. When he grips my upper arm, I feel it in his touch as well. He's holding himself back right now, practically thrumming with the need to cut through every guard waiting for the start of the games to free me, to stop this from happening, but he can't.

They would kill us both. Slowly, I gather. A public execution if we so much as step out of line.

A horn sounds somewhere in the distance. Kaleb continues his thorough examination of me, his face set in grim determination. He's never seen me hunt. He wouldn't be this high-strung if he had. It's my favorite thing to do.

"My mother taught me how to hunt. The moment I was steady enough on my feet, I had a bow in my hand. Knife work came next. I was maybe ten when I went on my first real hunt with her, the only person in the group unable to shift. I got a deer. It was my first kill. My dad walked around with me on his shoulders that night while the pack blessed me and celebrated the moment. I feel like that moment made it clear who I'd be in the future."

Another horn blares, and the guards shuffle–not toward us, yet. It becomes clear we're being staggered–released a few minutes apart, and based on the way the sound traveled, we're being let out of these warehouses at different points of entry to whatever's beyond the steel beams and rusted pipes.

"Your parents will be proud of you when you return," he says, but his voice wavers, tightening.

I grip his forearm. "You'll meet them soon."

I don't give any stock to the grim look in his eyes. I focus on his mouth, which twitches into the curve of the only smile he can manage. It's gone before I can blink.

"Come," one of the guards bellows from the far side of the warehouse over the sudden grate of a wide, industrial door rolling up to the ceiling. The sound rakes through me, foreign compared to the hammers and rolling conversation of the Glade and the silence of the manor. Kaleb takes my arm and walks me to the weapons cache, then let's go and steps back, putting several feet of distance between us.

A fae guard replaces his position, and I realize with a start this is it. The last game has begun.

I look back at Kaleb as a sweeping, ethereal pull yanks at my subconscious before blooming into raw power that thrums through my body and settles deep in the marrow of my bones. My chest tightens to the point of pain as my wolf groggily claws to life, and the mate bond settles around my heart once more. It's not the snap I experienced last time. It's settled, a warm presence in my chest, filling a void I hadn't realized was there.

Kaleb feels it, too. He holds my gaze, his fingers curling into fists at his sides, but the second the fae guard grabs me and drags me closer to the cache, his pupils expand so rapidly his eyes go black as pitch, his body going so rigid I can see every line of muscle beneath his clothing.

"Don't," I say down the bond. "Please, be safe."

I can feel his fury through the delicate strings wrapped around my heart, but Kaleb is the most controlled person I've ever met, even for an Alpha, the most powerful wolves of all.

There's a shuffling behind me. I stare at the weapons. Kaleb grunts in pain, but footsteps cover his obvious attempts to break free. I know he's being herded out of the warehouse. I know the second I look over my shoulder again he'll be gone, and this will all be far too real.

So I choose a weapon. A spear. In his honor.

A spear I will use to get my kill, which will not be an animal or beast of the woods now visible beyond the warehouse, the first trees cloaked in fog under the spray of dim, gray light.

I will be hunting Meg.

I assume she's also hunting me.

I grip the spear. The smooth metal tip sings as I artfully swing it over my back and into the halter. It's shorter than the spears Kaleb used to train me, which will work to my advantage. It's still lighter than I'd like, but my other options are swords and short blades. I wasn't offered a bow, which was likely the king's doing.

The second the weapon is secured, more guards step forward, and I'm thrust into the sliver of moonlight dusting over the wide, gravel driveway of what is indeed a warehouse situated roughly a quarter mile from a port. The sea stretches as far as the eye can see, the water calm and glassy. I watch the horizon, noticing small islands, their lights like muted stars. Not Eastonia. Not even close. I have no idea what direction I'm facing, but it doesn't matter. Before I can even get my bearings, I'm shoved forward until I'm tucked in the trees, and a strange feeling sweeps through me when an archway appears in the woods, ancient stone coated in moss and vines creating a kind of vortex into the shadows.

I'm supposed to go through it. I feel that in my bones.

"You're meant to kill something," one of the guards says in broken Dead Tongue.

"Does it matter what it is?" I ask, doubting it's as simple as a rabbit, but he stares at me quizzically, not understanding the language.

Another horn blares nearby, and I'm shoved forward until my toes are caught in the shadow of the archway to hell, and the guards immediately step back like they're afraid to come any closer.

I look back at them, wondering if I could just kill them all instead and make a run for the port, for a boat and...

I won't leave Kaleb and his people behind. I have vengeance to enact. Meg is in these woods somewhere, and if I'm taking a life tonight, it'll be hers. One of my own.

The tragedy of it rocks me to my center. It shouldn't have come to this.

I move toward the archway and step through it. When I turn around to face the guards again, they're replaced by endless dark woods, the archway nothing but an archaic structure decaying with time. The port is gone. The lights are gone. The warehouse is nowhere to be seen.

I step back through the archway, testing it, running back in the direction I came, which gives way to just… trees. Nothing else.

I don't think finding my way out of here is part of the game.

A rustling to my left catches my attention. I nearly draw the spear then remember I have my wolf back. I shift, and it's… horrible. Pain guts me to the core as my body folds. My shifting dress, halter, and spear stay intact, but my limbs feel like they're broken in several places. It takes me several aching minutes to feel normal again, but my head throbs as I stretch my front legs, my talons digging into the soft forest ground. New scents rush at me, temporarily taking over my other senses. I wonder how long it's been since I was in my wolf form because it doesn't feel right. It feels utterly wrong, actually, like I'm weaker this way when it should be the other way around.

It's probably the king's doing.

Something large barrels out of the woods in my direction before I have a chance to catch it with sight and scent. A gaping black void funnels through the trees directly in front of me, moaning and shrieking.

I rear back, shaken to awareness, as a beast of mist appears. The same creature that killed so many on the beach in Teshka. My blood runs cold, my heart leaping in my throat and dying from fear.

I run.

A COWARD

LEXA

The forest comes alive. My wolf's body glides unsteadily over roots and rocks, the moss cool under my soft, recently unused paws. My heartbeat drives adrenaline through my veins as I barrel, often losing my balance and sliding over the unfamiliar terrain. The smells are all wrong. The creeks that run through the forest like veins drift in different directions every time I pass, making it impossible to gauge where I am and what direction I'm traveling, but I keep running. I don't know what else to do against this beast of mist still pursuing me deeper into the woods other than lie down and stay as quiet as possible, like on the beach, but I made that mistake before.

I didn't fight. I watched everyone get killed instead. It's a regret I'll carry for the rest of my life.

The beast shrieks as it gains ground, coming up behind me with its talons clinking together like dried, hollow bones. I try to ignore it, to focus on my breathing, the way my body feels as the wolf I was forced to let slumber for so long.

A freezing cold presence breathes down my back, and I know without looking over my shoulder that the beast is now above me, closing in. A bone-numbing cold talon reaches down, piercing a long gash down my back, but I dart away, yipping in pain, before it can cut through the halter. My blood scents the air, disorienting my other senses.

I feel the beast approaching again, picking up speed as I coast through the forest with no sense of direction. My eyesight blurs as blood pours down my side.

I can't fight it. Weapons don't work against them. This is all I can do.

In the hazy silver shadows, a wall of stone appears. Large boulders rest at the bottom of what I believe is a cliff, where the forest continues to stretch above me, blocking out most of the moonlight. But there's a shadow between the large stones–a break in their formation. It's either a cave, or I'm about to enter a trap.

I have no other option.

I break into a full sprint. The beast wails, its high-pitched scream echoing, bouncing from tree to tree. I race into the shadow, praying I don't hit the face of the cliff buried beneath at full speed, but that would be a quick death, all things considered.

My body splits the pure darkness and keeps… going.

I can hear my shallow breaths as I run through the darkness, the cave squeezing my body as it narrows. The beast's cries fade behind me with every step, but the narrowness of the cave quickly slows my progress. I'm forced onto my belly in the total darkness, the air growing impossibly thin, and then I shift back to human form, my wolf unable to handle the sudden lack of room and oxygen. The act of shifting widens the wound on my pain to the point my vision goes white with astonishing pain for several seconds before the world shifts back into focus.

I crawl on my belly. Sulfur hangs heavy, making my mouth numb and head hazy, but I keep moving, crawling, dragging myself as the space grows narrower and shallower until I'm nearly pressed flat.

I'm going to pass out. I don't think I can make it. I can't back up. I'm going to die here–

A blast of white light rushes toward me from the front, illuminating the snug space. I freeze.

Darkness swallows me whole again before a second blast illuminates every sharp curve and divot in the narrow cave. My body jerks, moving toward it. The blasts keep coming until the cave suddenly gives way to a more open section and the pressure on my body lightens, the air heavier and richer with much needed oxygen.

But my body just… fails. I can't get off the ground. I push up on my arms, trembling so violently my teeth clack together, threatening to chip. I think about shifting back to my wolf form, but I've scraped myself raw crawling through the tunnel that I'll shred if I do. I already know it.

How stupid could I have been?

I lower onto my elbows, slowly arching onto my knees, and rise. My head swims. I fall to my knees with a crunch, gulping air. Another blast of white light forces my eyes shut. It funnels toward me, expanding to highlight the cave where I'm resting, and I squint against it, following the light as it retreats to its source.

There's an opening.

I can get out.

I crawl, feeling my spear still resting along my spine, strapped to my now fraying halter. It must have shredded when I crawled through the cave. I still can't shift. Not only will I spread my injuries, but I'll be forced to carry the spear in my teeth, and I can't… I need my teeth free to fight if it comes to it.

The light ebbs again, starting small, like a star buzzing just beyond the narrow mouth of the cave as I approach the outside world.

But the light goes out before flaring, like someone closed their hands around the star.

It's a person. A woman. Thick, nearly white blonde hair falls down her naked body as she stands only a few yards away from the mouth of the cave. I carefully exit, gripping the mouth of the cave for support, and stare at her.

She stares back, gray eyes wide. She's young. My age or younger, possibly an older teenager. She's not part of the games, though. I've never seen her before. She's–she's…

My lips part to take a much needed breath of fresh air, and she shifts in a flash of light so bright I shield my eyes and grimace. I peek through my fingers then widen them as a white wolf appears and races away from me into the woods, which seem to go on and on with no end in sight.

Another shifter?

She shouldn't be here on the game grounds, right?

Surely, I'm not meant to… hunt her?

My throat tightens as a flash of deep red barrels out of the darkness on the white wolf's tail.

Meg in her wolf form.

Meg leaps but misses the other wolf by a hairsbreadth, and I move, my sulfur filled mind driven by impulse, by pure, undying rage. My spear rips across my back before I send it flying in Meg's direction, barely giving myself a second to line up the shot, but it doesn't matter.

This wasn't meant to be a killing blow.

The spear artfully slides across her back and hooks horizontally beneath her halter as she jets between two trees. It snags between the trees, and Meg barks with confusion, trapped, unable to free herself as the white wolf disappears into the darkness, light flooding behind her in wisps of pure, white mist.

I'll remember the girl's face because at first, I was sure it was… Great-Grandma Isla or Misty. But her eyes were wrong. She's from the same power group, however. That's clear.

There're more people like them in the world.

I can't think about it now, but Blake will want to know about this when I return, because I will return.

I stalk forward. Meg turns her wide, wolfish head, her eyes bugging when she sees me stalking up behind her. She shifts into her human form as I reach for the spear, grabbing the rough end before she sinks out of her wolf and rises on human legs in front of me , pulling the loops of her dress closed.

I have two seconds to react. A single, shattering breath. My fingers dance up the spear, and she strikes, two blades poised and lethally sharpened. I block her blades with the spear, pushing her deeper into the woods. Metal meets wood over and over. Her blades take chunks out of the spear's handle, but I move my hands like Kaleb taught me during that week when this was all we did–defense. I use the spear like a shield, and I have the upper hand. She's not facing the woods. I'm pushing her back, watching the woods fan out around us, the trees growing spindly and narrow as we reach what I know marks the end of the forest. Silver plains glisten in the moonlight beyond, a sea of rolling hills.

She hasn't noticed. She can't, because she'll shift again and run, and I'll lose her.

Her face is twisted in righteous fury as I continue to block her advances, my shoulders and spine screaming with each impact. One, two. One, two. I block each blade, halting my progress out of the woods, which she takes as her move to advance on me, and I let her.

Her right arm quivers with fatigue, and she takes a second longer to jut her blades at me, aiming for my sides, so I take my chance.

I leap back several feet, swinging the spear, knocking against the side of the face with the blunt end. Her eyes flash with confusion, and she stumbles, her exhausted arms twitching, and it's the second I need to bring her to the ground.

I hit her again on the other side of the face, knocking her sideways onto the ground. She gasps in pain as she falls, one of the blades flying in my direction in a last ditch effort to strike, but she misses, and the blade's hilt bounces off my hip bone and falls into the thick bunches of heather, forever lost.

I kick out, taking her fully to the ground, and whip the spear, pointing the tip against the hollow of her throat. She raises her second blade, but I pin her wrist to the ground with my foot until I feel bones crunch. She grits her teeth but doesn't cry out.

"I trained you better than this," I sneer.

She smiles. It's bloody.

"Looks like it's just us two now," she croaks, her teeth coated with red. I notice her hands then–bloody, torn open, like she was in a recent fight. I see the faint glimmer of almost microscope scales on her hands and arms, like glitter. The remnants of wings. My expression must give my thoughts away because she smiles again. "I took care of the last one for us."

"There is no us. Not after what you did to Chessie."

"Chessie was never going to make it. It was an act of mercy–" She gasps as I press the tip of the spear into her throat. Beads of blood trickle. Not enough to kill her. I'm not ready to let her go just yet. "You always favored her for no reason. The other girls noticed. Some thought you were lovers, did you know that? I knew better. I knew you just saw her as the weak link she was and felt doomed to protect her."

"I loved her like a sister. Like my own blood. When you killed her, you killed a part of me. You killed a part of our pack, and that's not a victimless crime."

"I did what I had to do to survive. Isn't that what you taught me?"

"Killing one of your own was never part of that."

"Do you want to know what I was offered?" she says through gritted teeth. Her smile is sickly but not forced, like she's actually enjoying this. "Immortality, Lexa. They can do that. The king offered me a life that never ends if I win and be his champion."

"You would have been a trophy he passed around," I correct. "Entertainment, Meg. That's all we are."

"But imagine," she rasps, "how powerful I could have become. I want that. You've always had everything. The popularity. The power. Austin."

Something flares deep inside my mind. I see red for a moment before my vision clears. "Austin?"

"I spent the entire winter pursuing him, but he only wanted you. You took him from me, and you didn't even want him. He was just something fun, wasn't he? Now look at you, parading around with your Alpha King. You fucking whore. Austin might never have laid down his life for yours if he knew–" I press the tip deeper, and she quiets for a moment, pushing past the pain. "You took what I wanted, so I took something you loved and killed it. I don't regret killing Chessie. She was stupid and useless. She was going to die anyway."

"Are those your last words, or would you like to say a prayer for your soul?"

I notice the blood leaking beneath her then. No wonder she isn't fighting as hard as I know she's capable of. A puncture wound that wasn't visible in her wolf form radiates blood from her side, her liver, a lethal blow. She's dying.

"Those white wolves have healing powers," she whispers, like she's reading my mind. "I was going to trap her and force her to heal me." I pull the spear from her neck, watching the blood trickle over her throat. She exhales deep, a rattling breath, and I realize as I look down at her, that she's beyond standing up.

I should leave her here. I should let her death be slow and painful. Leave her to the mercy of the beasts of mist hunting in the woods as well tonight.

There's a slice of humanity left in my heart, which is why I angle the spear over hers and say, "Our pack will believe you died a hero's death. I'll bring back a lock of your hair for your parents to do with what they will, but you will not be burned. There will not be a pyre in your honor. Your bones will settle here, far from home, your soul trapped. You do not deserve the realm of the Goddess for what you did to Chessie. You're a coward, Meg. But you already know that." I slam the spear into her heart, shattering her ribs. The light behind her eyes fades instantly, but her mouth is still stuck in that cat-like grin.

I feel her soul drifting around me with no place to land before it's carried away by the wind. The air settles. A horn blasts somewhere in the distance, and then whatever wolf senses are left within me are yanked into unseen manacles, trapping them again.

I throw down my spear and close my eyes as a brutal wind rips through the forest, letting everything go black.

BOTH OF US MUST BE DEAD

LEXA

Bright pain laces down my back with every step as I walk out of the woods and onto pearls of gravel. I'm not sure where I am, but it's not the port. A shadow rises in the near distance. My vision ebbs in and out–a wall. The Glade. I'm standing on a rise and looking down at the city, at the capital of Pantharas, and beyond.

My knees give out. Blood trails down my back. Hands grip my arms, yanking me upright. "Kaleb?" I croak, squinting against a rush of bright light threatening to blind me, but everyone around me is speaking in the fae tongue–and rapidly.

I pick out a few words but nothing substantial. Nothing that gives me any idea of what happens next.

I just won the Trials.

I won.

I did it, Kaleb. I won for us–

"I am her sponsor now. Let her go!" Silas's voice rips through the fray, and suddenly, I'm in his arms, which isn't right. He shouldn't be here. He kept having to leave, to go to the Highwoods, wherever that is.

"K–Kaleb?" I cry out. Silas scoops me into his arms, pressing me against his chest. He's arguing viciously with the fae guards surrounding us. Everyone is shouting at each other. There's a tension in the air I can taste, and then I hear the telltale sound of metal sliding from holsters, and without warning, Silas's wings flare from his back.

"Wait–" I beg, but in a split second, we're airborne, and my voice dies in my throat.

Wind rushes around me. It's almost like spiriting, but without the feeling of being pulled to pieces. My stomach drops to my toes as the air grows thin and cold, and again without warning, we're funneling to the ground. Silas's wings tuck tight around us, strengthening the rate of the fall, and I fight the darkness sweeping through my body, threatening to pull me under.

"I'm blacking out!" I warn, but my voice is lost in the rip current of the air whirling around our bodies.

His wings expand once more, velvet and dark blue taking up what's left of my vision. Why can't I see? Why can't I feel my body? I mouth Silas's name against his chest, but my teeth rattle, and my bones lurch when he hits the ground, knees bent, and a second later, he's running at a full sprint with me tightly secured in his arms.

"Secure the house!" he shouts, and dozens of footsteps thunder over what sounds like cobblestone. "Every man surrounding the manor, NOW!"

I taste smoke. I open my eyes to an orange haze. It is smoke. Something's on fire. I barely have a chance to register what's happening before the night sky bleeds into the ceiling of the servants' quarters of the manor, then the grand foyer, then–then rooms I don't remember exploring. Silas bursts through a door and shouts, "She's injured badly! Her back is flayed!"

Blake's voice rises above his. The ceiling blurs, the chandelier nothing but orbs of hazy golden light. "Lie her down on her stomach."

A soft, shallow rug meets my skin. I turn my head to the side, watching multiple sets of feet dance around me in slow motion, like time has slowed to a crawl. "Kaleb?"

"He's not here, Lexa," Silas's voice says, ragged and full of emotion I can't decipher. "Stay awake for us."

A shooting pain screams up my spine. I don't remember being this hurt, but adrenaline will do that. My mind tangles over what happened in the forest, memories overlapping out of order. I killed Meg.

I killed her.

I'm the champion.

I won.

"Fuck," Blake sneers, pulling the back of dress apart until I'm barely covered. Warm, wet liquid rushes over my skin, my sides, pooling around me. Blood. My blood.

Someone kneels near my head, their touch warm on my cheek. It's familiar. A small, delicate hand, like a child's.

"I can find something to dull the pain."

"There's no time." Blake's voice is rough, distant, like he's talking through gritted teeth from across the room, but I can feel his hands on my back. "She shifted with this injury. It tore open her back. Fuck, I can see her spine–"

I take a shattering breath as the room spins, but then the person beside me lies down, her face turned to mine. Chessie smiles softly at me, her big green eyes dancing with mingled fear and a sense of hope.

I'm dying.

I'm seeing her because I'm dying.

"I'm going to do it. I'm going to put her back together again," Blake says in a shaky voice.

"The fighting has started, Blake, we need your powers on the shields–"

"I'm not leaving her like this. She'll be fine. I'll be fine. I just need to–she has to be awake for this–"

"I'm sorry I couldn't save you. I promised I would," I say to Chessie, my eyes blurred with tears. "I'm so sorry. I love you so much–" Pain like I've never felt in my life tears me open. Someone's screaming. I realize as my mind swims with Blake's power that it's me. I'm screaming, my voice lifting to the ceiling in shrieks of agony that make the chandelier rattle. Screaming as his powers dig into my head, and suddenly, I see red. Blood red. Then it fades, and it's quiet, empty, like I'm floating in a pool on my back against a backdrop of stars, and there's no one, no sound.

I stay suspended like that for what feels like a matter of seconds, and then I sink, unable to breathe.

"They've taken the outer city. The villages beyond are under our control now, too, but the inner capital and the Glade are heavily guarded. We can't get through the king's magic. Once our men are in, they're at his mercy." Silas's voice is very far away. I reach for it, my fingers curling around soft cotton.

"Where are they keeping Kaleb?"

"The dungeons, I presume. They're asking for her. She won. She's the king's victor. He's meant to make a show of her in front of the lesser kings, to show the games still hold weight. That the rioting means nothing in the grand scheme of things. I've been told the king will make a deal if Lexa is presented to him in the arena."

"What are our options?" It's Blake's voice. He's closer. I feel his touch smoothing down my bare back, his power like little sutures against my skin, pinching.

"You have to get in front of the king, subdue him somehow. We can't access the inner city again until he's taken care of."

I open my eyes to slits. We're not in Silas's house anymore. The walls are bare plaster, old, and a window is open to fresh air. It's raining but light. Daytime. Maybe midday. I close my eyes when the light becomes too much.

"Hannibal is the one keeping the shields up around the arena. I could feel him there. We're linked somehow, likely after my torture at his hands. I took a piece of him when he took a piece of me."

"The king will do what it takes to keep Hannibal safe. He's his most trusted advisor. You'll have better luck facing the king himself."

"Look at what we've done, Silas, and tell me the king still trusts Hannibal. He did not see this coming. He still does not realize I'm here."

"What are you asking me to do?" Silas growls, and I feel the air in the room shift as a door opens outside of my blurred line of light. Soft footsteps creep into the room, but it's not enough to dissuade Silas and Blake from continuing their line of conversation.

"I need access to the orrery tower at the castle. I need Hannibal's scrying altar, his crystals. One crystal was not enough to contact Eastonia, but using the altar will be enough to get in touch with the Firestone Queen of Eastonia. Once she knows where we are, she will come. I am willing to bet my life on it."

"You would be betting your life on it!" Silas shouts. "The second you step past those shields, the king's entire army will be on your ass—"

"Shhh," Chessie whispers. "She needs to rest. You're both being so loud! I just got her back to sleep."

My eyes pop open, but I can't turn my head. I'm trapped, my spine locked.

"I'm sorry, darling," Silas murmurs.

"Can this conversation take place elsewhere, please? You're both making me nervous."

"There isn't a conversation to be had. I have to go back to the city," Blake says tartly. The bed shifts as he rises. "I'm running out of time. I have to use my powers while I still have them. I need to contact my cousin. Your resistance doesn't have the power it needs to take control of the castle, but she does."

My moan of pain alerts everyone to the fact I'm… alive, and based on the look on their faces when they rush to the side of the bed, coming in full, startling view, they're surprised.

Chessie stands between Silas and Blake, her curly blonde hair piled on the top of her head, her eyes wide and full of life. She clutches Silas's forearm and blinks down at me, looking… so alive. She's alive?

"You're—" I manage one word before pain ghosts through my back and seizes my lungs.

"Don't," Chessie rushes out, kneeling beside the bed. Silas's fingers creep over her shoulder, holding her there, like he's prepared to yank her away if I lash out. "You're okay. You just—you nearly severed your spine shifting while injured. Blake fixed it. You're going to be sore for a while, but you're okay–"

"You died. I watched you die–"

"I–I was–" She looks at Blake for help.

Blake looks at me, his violet eyes dim.

"You can heal?" Three words are enough to send my vision into a tailspin. My eyes flare with light before settling, dark spots skittering in my peripheral like bugs.

"A new talent I discovered during my… adventure here," he says lightly. I'd hit him if I were able to move. "It's not the same as what Kenna and Misty can do."

"Obviously," I rasp, looking at Chessie again. "You–you were brought back to life?"

Chessie pinches her lips closed. Silas squeezes her shoulder lovingly, his chest heaving. I look up at him and notice his eyes are downcast on Chessie before he closes them, a flash of guilt darkening the planes of his face.

"What have you done, Blake?" I murmur, pain lacing around my ribs.

"Let's give them a moment," Silas whispers to Chessie. I want to grab her as she turns from the bed and rises, following Silas out, but I'm in so much pain I can barely move.

Blake replaces her, kneeling beside the bed. He rests his head against the mattress only inches from mine. He's completely undone. Exhausted. Burned out. I can feel it in the space carved out between us.

"You knew better than to shift with an injury like that. You broke nearly every rib. You had a punctured lung and several fractured vertebrae, and your muscles were mangled nearly beyond repair. It should have killed you. The only reason you survived is because your heart continued to pump blood through your body despite being in shock the entirety of that Trial."

"I had a game to finish," I whisper, and he moves his head, his eyes angled to meet mine. "What did you do to me, Blake?"

"I call it reanimation because I'm not sure it has a name. I knitted you back together using my powers. Just imagining where things are supposed to go, where they're supposed to be. I willed it into existence. It worked."

"And you did this to Chessie?"

"For the first time. Silas had a hold on their mate bond. She was still there, a flicker of her life left, but dying, and he refused to let it go. It gave us time. It gave me time to… change her destiny. It's not natural. It's not a form of healing, Lexa, what I can do. I forced her back to life, forced her back together, and the real healing process has been slow. She's only alive because Silas is her mate–"

"That can't be possible–"

"It is. It's rare. I think fae being mated–fated mates–with a shifter is something that is so rare we're never going to find any mention of it in books or our shared histories, but they are mates, I confirmed it, and they knew before she went into her final round. She didn't tell you and regretted it immensely. She was scared to tell anyone. Silas begged me to save her, and I did. It took… everything I had at the time. He gave her his life. Gave up his immortality to keep her here. You were easier because your lifeline is like steel. You're an Alpha King's daughter. You're meant for something great, a main point in the tapestry of our universe. My powers knew that. I had to force it with Chessie, and it nearly killed me."

"I don't understand."

"Neither do I, but there's nothing we can do about it now. You need to rest. Silas is bringing in the same healer who's been taking care of Chessie. She's a shifter like us and very talented. In a few days–"

"Where's Kaleb?" My voice shatters.

Blake licks his lips, looking absolutely defeated. "He was taken to the dungeons after the start of the hunt. Several of the Alphas of the Glade under his rule were also apprehended. There's a mass execution planned in three days' time for… all of them."

"Why?"

"For aiding in the resistance. The fighting began just as the hunt did. It's happening. Their war. The war that's meant to spill onto our soil. The war I saw and the reason I'm here."

"I have to go back–" I try to push up, but my spine tingles. Blake pushes me down as gently as he can.

"This isn't your fight anymore. It's mine. I have a plan. Maeve will come. She'll come in time, I swear."

I'M GOING BACK

LEXA

An entire day passes. I count the hours, the minutes, the seconds, until time bleeds together in my head. My mind pounds like a drum, my temples splitting, and the only thing keeping me lucid is a near constant array of healing drafts being poured down my throat every hour on the hour, as if they are responsible for ensuring my heart doesn't stop beating.

In the first hour of the second day in Silas's country home in the Highwoods–a mountainous estate several hours north of the capital, I'm told–I rise from bed, gingerly testing my range of motion, feeling how taut and new my spine feels. Like the bones are made of glass.

I make it three steps before my back crumbles, forcing me onto the edge of the bed.

Bea, Silas's healer, is a stout and bossy woman, a shifter, and a beautiful one, at that. She can't be older than my age, but she's hardened, like she's seen nothing but violence, blood, and war her entire life. She doesn't take no for an answer. The woman has been torturing me, keeping me tied to the bed if I so much as flinch away from her constant, disgusting medicines and painful prodding.

But this last time, she forgot to slip my wrists back into the loops of the ropes keeping me bound belly down in the bed.

She says it's for my own good. Chessie agrees with her. Silas won't speak to me. Blake has been absent.

I'm losing my mind.

The door opens, and Chessie appears dressed in a simple white frock and cream-colored cardigan. She draws in a breath when she notices me sitting upright, but I wave her off, wiggling my toes to test the feeling in my legs before pushing myself into a standing position again.

"Lexa, please, you can't be on your feet!"

"I have to go back."

"There's nothing to go back to. Silas's resistance has the entire capital surrounded. The Alphas of the free wolves and the kings of the lesser fae are sending in their enforcements to help Silas's cause. They may get there in time to stop–"

"Where is Kaleb? Is he still in a dungeon?"

Chessie's perfectly pink cheeks drain of color, turning a sickly gray. "Lexa, please–"

"I have to go get him." It's casual. I say it like I'm simply running an errand.

Her eyes water as I take two steps and stumble, saving myself by bracing a hand against a dresser tucked against the wall to my right.

"I can't let you do it."

"I'm not asking your permission."

She steps in front of me when I try to pass her. The blood races from my brain to my lower extremities, my legs suddenly leaden and refusing to move. Frustration so hot it burns like fever drives my heart rate into a frenzy, which only makes the feeling of utter dread worse.

"Get out of my way!"

"You need to stay here." She raises her hands in surrender, but tears slip down her cheeks. "Please? Lexa, please, you have to."

"I am your captain," I remind her with a sharp bite in my voice. "You will do as I command. Move."

"You are in my house," she snarls, and I fall back, totally shocked by the tone of her voice.

My legs hit the bed, and I fold like bread dough, my body just as pliable. Chessie lingers in the doorway for several seconds, wringing her hands, before stepping forward, reaching to help me back onto my back, but she stops, pulling her hands back. "Silas and I are fated mates, Lexa."

"Blake said as much."

"I don't think you understand what I'm saying," she cuts in then clears her throat. "I am his mate, and he is mine. We knew pretty much immediately, but I wasn't sure I could trust my emotions. It felt... insane, but so did everything else we were going through. I brought it up with him. What it felt like for me. It wasn't until the king lifted his magic and allowed me to fully feel my wolf during the Beast Trial that it fully snapped into place. And then I–"

"Then Meg put a sword through your skull?"

Chessie looks down at her slippers. "I held on. I held on for–for both of you. You and Silas. I wanted to tell him I could feel it like he could now, that he could stop walking on eggshells around me and we could–" More tears roll down her cheeks in a torrent similar to the rain still pounding the windows near the bed. "I don't remember much after that. I remember feeling like I was slipping away and begging the Goddess to let me stay a moment longer. I thought She heard my prayers because I woke up a week later here, and Silas was telling me that Blake saved my life, and you were still alive, still in the games. Silas has been losing his mind over you and Kaleb." She sucks in a desperate breath. "You're his mate. That's what Silas told me. You're Kaleb's mate. I thought–I thought there was something–"

"I can't let him die in that dungeon."

Chessie blinks like she's been lost in her head, but she looks at the far wall as if there's something, or someone, there–but there's not. She's silent, her eyes glassy. She's suddenly trapped in her mind.

I freeze, unease tingling through my body. "Chessie?"

When she doesn't respond, I shakily get out of bed and sway in her direction, tripping over my own feet like I haven't totally mastered the act of walking at twenty-two years old. I reach for her, grabbing her upper arm, but she only stares forward, past me, her eyes locked on the window. . "Chessie? What's wrong?"

Her mouth moves, but no sound comes out.

"She's having a lapse," Blake says from the doorway. My hand drops from Chessie's arms.

"What?"

"I call it a lapse. I had to reanimate half of her brain. She retained most of her memories, from what we can tell, but she gets confused easily when trying to conjure them and use them to make new decisions." He steps around her to look into her eyes. "It'll pass. The lapses are growing fewer and fewer now, and they never last very long."

"Is she having a seizure?"

"No, not really. She's actively trying to build new neural pathways. She's still healing. It's difficult for her mind, so she tends to just… turn off for a moment and reboot."

"What have you done to her?"

"I saved her."

"At what cost? Is she still Chessie?"

"Yes. She is. But she had a lethal brain injury. It'll take months to fully heal from that. It's a miracle she's still herself and not locked inside the part of her mind that survived. I built her a new one, and she's filling it as we speak."

I stare at my cousin in horror and awe. "You really are a god, aren't you? You cheated death. Only a god can do that."

He says nothing for a moment, but his eyes flick to a random corner of the room. "When we return home, you cannot say a word about this to anyone."

I struggle to understand why.

"I need you to swear it."

"Why?"

"Because this skill of mine isn't natural. It goes against the Goddess. If I am a god, Lexa, I am the God of Death, sure, if we're calling it what it is, and what I've done for you and Chessie has just allowed you to live a little longer for my own gain. That's the only reason it worked. It's not healing. It's selfishness."

My stomach pitches. It takes me a moment to respond, to process what he just said. "You need to save Kaleb. You need to save him and everyone in the Glade. I don't care about the rest. I'll swear. I'll keep this secret for you."

"You're going back, regardless of what I do. I can already see it." His eyes meet mine, Chessie still standing between us, her eyes locked on the rain trickling down the window. "You'll go back and make a huge mess."

"He's my mate. I'm not going to let him die."

"He wants you to leave."

My jaw clicks shut.

"I was able to speak to him. I used my shields to get into the capital unseen, and I found him."

I shake my head.

He continues. "He made me vow to get you out of Pantharas."

"It's not your call to make."

"I will be traveling back to the capital tonight to face off with Hannibal. I'll be using his altar, the way he was able to try to spy on us from Pantharas, using my daughter's dreams as a conduit… to try to get a hold of Maeve. I'll slip into her thoughts and dreams somehow. She'll be able to find us then, and then Evander will send the entire naval force."

"I'm going with you. We're going to free Kaleb and his people."

"You are staying here."

"You cannot keep me here."

"I will put you under, lock your mind in a dark cage within your head, if you try anything."

I glare at him. "I will kill you if you try."

Chessie jerks to sudden awareness, gripping her head. She takes a step forward, glancing around the room like she's forgotten why she's here, and then turns to Blake. "Silas?"

"He's downstairs waiting for you. He made tea."

Chessie practically floats out of the room. I watch her go, wishing she'd move faster. My fingertips prickle to close around Blake's throat, but I can't do it. I can barely move as it stands.

"Fix me," I tell him with a breathy sigh. "Just do it, Blake. Use your powers to turn off the pain in my body so I can finish this."

"No."

"I won. I deserve to stand before the king and ask for my reward. The games are not over until I end it. That's how this works. I am going, whether you like it or not. I will find a way there. I will walk if I have to. I will shift and risk my life and ruin all the work you did to–"

"You're pregnant, Lexa."

I shake my head, choking on a laugh. "Shut the fuck up, Blake."

"Laugh all you want. You're risking two lives instead of one if you step a single foot outside of this house."

"You're doing whatever you can to force me to stay, but I won't. I am going back for Kaleb. You can either help me or stand back and watch me burn Pantharas to the ground, alone. It's your choice."

Blake stares at me. I stare back, unafraid, refusing to let his warnings settle. I notice it then, the flicker of power behind his eyes, so much quieter than usual.

"This place is draining you of your powers, isn't it? That's why you said you were running out of time."

"I'm using my powers to their max everyday I'm here."

"Then let's fucking finish this!"

"You are not involved."

"I am." I step toward him. The act of simply putting my toes to the ground sends a jolt of pain up my spine. I fight through it. "I'm going back for my mate. I will not leave without him and his people. I will face the king. I will go to that arena, and he will be forced to give me my reward. Those are the rules. He cannot deny me. He could not deny Kaleb when he asked to become Alpha King. He has to do it. The games are governed by magic–something ancient–not him. That magic is everywhere. I felt it in every game. The dragon. The maze. The woods. There're portals out there, Blake. He doesn't control those. Not fully. They allow him to do this as long as he follows the rules. I have to go back."

Blake takes several moments to reply. He's livid but reining his feelings in, silently going over every option.

"Tell me you wouldn't do this for Marianna and Skye," I say, and he jolts back to the present. "You'd be fine leaving them in chains?"

"Come here," he says gravely, motioning for me to close the distance between us.

I have to trust him. I have to trust I won't wake up days from now when Kaleb is already dead.

He clutches the back of my neck, his fingers digging into the hollow at the base of my skull.

"You have no idea what you're asking me to do. But I'll do it."

The world goes black, but only momentarily.

ONE ENDING AND ONE BEGINNING

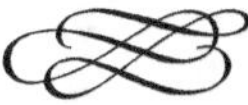

BLAKE

"Will I ever see her again?"

Lexa moves with me through the dark, our bodies falling into the shadow of manor houses that sprawl throughout the neighborhoods resting against the palace walls. The layout of this city is so similar to Moonrise that I've found it more than disorienting sometimes, like whatever ancestor of the sitting king stole the design from the Fire-stone Queens, trying to recreate the kingdom they forced to ash.

"Chessie?"

She gives a tight nod, refusing to meet my eyes. I know what she's asking—for me to look into a future that's so unstable and shifting with every second that passes. I can only give her the truth I know in my heart. "Silas loves her, but he'd let her go. When this is over, when I'm able to get you home, Chessie can decide if she's staying with him or going back to Eastonia, but Silas will not allow her to aid in the battles taking place here. I think... you agree with him on that."

Lexa nods again, but her eyes are distant, focusing on the smoke-lined horizon.

It was easy enough to get here. Lexa's healing is going better than I expected. A few extra doses of healing drafts, some herbs, and my powers blocking her pain, at least for a while, have made it possible for her to walk beside me, chin held high, a belt laden with a variety of weapons weighing down her hips.

"You can't shift," I warn after a few minutes of reflective silence, but she only narrows her eyes, squinting into the ravaged street where the riots took place two days ago. Since then, the king has cloistered himself and his loyal courtiers inside the tall, alabaster and marble wall surrounding the palace, trapping those that live closest to the palace itself and the arena in an area similar to the Glade.

And the Glade?

"It's burning." Lexa stops dead in her tracks and turns to me, hazy orange light filling her irises. "You didn't tell me."

I ignore her, checking the harness and shifting dress Chessie spent the last day mending, not that it matters now. "You cannot shift, Lexa. You'll risk ruining all the work I've done. You tore every muscle in your back and shattered your ribs. I need you to remember that. If you shift again, reopening the injury, you could die. Look at me." I grab her face, looking down at the features we share. She looks so much like Uncle Ryan, and I know, as her eyes meet mine, she's seeing my father looking back down at her. I wonder what those men are thinking right now, but I scrub the thought from my mind as quickly as it came. "Do not shift. No matter what happens. I can't save you this time. I need every ounce of energy I have to send a message to Maeve."

She shoves me back a step. "And what about Hannibal? I thought you came here to face him, to finally kill him."

"I might not need to." I look over her head at the palace, at the magical shields shimmering against the thick layer of smoke drifting toward the sky. "I think he's very old, Lexa. Extremely. I think I understand what he needed from me and what he wanted me for. He's not as powerful as he lets on. He can't do what I can."

She stares at me, her eyes narrowing in a silent command to elaborate. I lean forward, double checking her knife belt. "Don't shift. Promise me."

"No."

I grind my teeth. "You're just as stubborn as me, it seems."

"What are you going to do, Blake?"

Die. Most likely.

"Promise me something." I reach down, gripping her fingers and squeezing before she can pull out of my grasp.

"You've already made a blood oath to Maeve that she has to kill you if you come back. Don't think I don't know or understand what you're about to do, Blake. If you're going to ask me to tell Marianna you love her and that you're sorry, save your breath. I won't do it. Do it yourself when you get home. Fuck a blood oath, Blake. You're a god. You get to decide." She shoves me, giving me a glimpse of her renewed strength. It's enough to settle my stomach.

"Do not shift."

"Don't fuck up whatever you're planning to do." She snarls and stalks into the darkness in the direction of the palace, of the arena.

I have an hour tops to finish this.

The king doesn't have his shields up anymore. Fae guards are battling against the rebels–some of their comrades, even–trying to find their way through breaks in the wall. I watch Lexa approach, watch a crowd of rioters drift apart to let her pass. She's granted access without a fight because the king has been waiting for his champion for days. I don't have the luxury of simply walking through the fray. I spirit, grimacing as my powers lurch, sending me catapulting through space and time. It's fascinating, really, how different it is here compared to in Eastonia and Crescent Falls. We're blessed back home. The Goddess's gifts are rich in comparison. Here, whatever gods they worship left long ago, and the natural magic of the kingdom has nearly run dry. Even my stars are quiet, too exhausted to chat. I open my eyes and scan a dimly lit hallway somewhere deep in the palace.

Kaleb gave me a crude layout of this place. I've been able to map it myself over the weeks, slinking through the hallways dressed in guard uniforms, keeping my head and eyes down. Hannibal knows what I look like, and I know for a fact I haunt his dreams because I've been trying to dig into his head, find his power with mine, but he's impossibly shielded. Whatever power the king siphons from his loyal subjects, he gives to Hannibal. How, I have no idea, but I have a sneaking suspicion it has something to do with that vat of crystals I saw in Skye's dream.

The thought of my daughter nearly brings me to my knees.

I miss her. I miss them. I've been trying not to let their memory render me useless. I have a job to do, I keep telling myself. I will come home a better man, even if Maeve has to strip every dark part of who I am from my bones until I'm nothing but... but what I should have been for them in the beginning.

Even if it kills me.

I've given so much of myself to my family. I let the darkness eat me alive. I put so many of them in impossible situations, and now I have to end it.

I have to end the man dead set on ruining everything my family rebuilt.

Hannibal is waiting for me, his eyes locked on mine as I step into that wide, circular room from Skye's nightmares. I close the door behind me with a soft click that echoes, bouncing off every curve, and settling my body like this moment is simply a meeting back at the palace in Moonrise, a thirty-minute block in my calendar.

Hannibal's eerily young face hasn't changed a bit. His icy hair and even colder, nearly white eyes are the same, and those eyes crease as he smiles warmly, saying by way of greeting, "I thought we'd meet again."

The crystals in the vat twinkle like stars as he speaks—in rhythm with his voice, I realize. He's connected to them somehow.

He notices me looking, and that strange smile widens. "Do your kind have alchemists? They built this for the Firestone Queens so long ago. It's how we siphon and use the natural gifts of the land, you see. Faeries are tied to the seasons, the elements, and sometimes, the cosmos. Our powers are determined by those sources alone, but if we keep everything in one place, it makes certain fae more powerful than others." He taps the side of the basin with a dead kind of smile.

"Alchemists made this. Do you know of any left in Eastonia? There were so few to begin with."

"You would know, given that you spent a very long time in Eastonia."

"Not as long as you believe, and not long enough to study your people like I wanted to. I assume you came here to kill me, Blake. Before we begin, I'd like a moment to explain myself."

"I don't need an explanation."

"I think you'll find it necessary," he replies, his long, spidery fingers curling around the rim of the crystal basin, the wrinkled skin hanging off the bones the only sign of his true age. "Since you and I are so similar."

"We are not."

"Because you're a shifter," he smirks. "Filthy creatures. Smart, some, but otherwise bags of bones and blood with every brute, violent tendency our kind evolved past long, long ago. I find it odd you pledge such allegiance to that part of yourself when you have all of this to play with." He motions to my body like he can see the mystic side clearly. "But I digress. My hatred of your people comes from centuries of being on the losing side of our great war against the Goddess, I suppose."

"Were you alive for that?"

"Barely," he admits with a soft smile. "I was a child, if you can believe it. Oh, your people, your Firestones, alchemists, and mystics who aided in the war were vicious. Some fae took your side, of course, remained in Eastonia after the end and the veil fell, my parents included."

I startle but keep it contained.

"Ah, yes, I was the son of traitors, scooped up after my parents failed to return and trained to be what I am today after my gifts were discovered. I'm the only one like me left here, you know. The only one like you."

"Then the mystics are descendants of the fae?"

"No. You and I are simply chosen vessels for the prophecies of our shared universe. But you are a shifter, and I am fae, and therefore, our gifts, our visions, they contrast."

"You want a war. You want fae in control. You want the shifters as slaves. It doesn't matter what you say because you've ignored the truth. Everything you've done, everything you've told your king, has been a lie. He didn't know Lexa would win. You saw it, didn't you? Refused to believe what your own gifts were telling you?"

"A full-blooded shifter has never won the games and never will. She won't survive the final Trial."

"The final Trial has already ended. She is the champion."

Something flickers behind his eyes—his powers... waning. I squint, noticing the harsh lines visible on his skin, the way his eyes are glazed, glassy, like he's...

"You're dying, aren't you?"

Hannibal's mouth barely moves as he replies, "Your precious Fire-stone Queen is quite powerful, but it was your great-uncle's final blow that's been slowly draining me. I'd hoped, by now, that we'd be in Eastonia, that I could rebuild myself in the forges, but no. Those Shadowsyngers have always been the bane of our existence."

I narrow my eyes. This is not how I thought this would go. "You're talking about Ryatt?"

"Is that his name? Powerful beast he is." He braces his weight against the basin as the crystals flicker, dimming. "I thought it would be your queen in our way, but it's him. It will always be him."

He trembles, knees bent, and sinks against the basin. Panic rushes through my body. This isn't how it was supposed to go. I was supposed to end this. He wasn't supposed to go gracefully into death.

"What do you mean?"

"The sword of shadow," he snarls, that boyish look evaporating. "He nicked me. That's all it takes. With the right alchemist, just one... cut... is all it takes."

I lunge, grabbing him by the shoulders, and his powers tear into mine. I see visions and images of a war, of a childhood that doesn't belong to me. I try to pull my hands away, but I'm trapped in place as he bleeds his life into mine, forcing me to see it, to remember.

"That's what we wanted. One single family. We never found them," he says gravely. "Your Shadowsynger hides them well. You don't know about them, do you?"

I get a sudden, startling image of the castle in Veiled Valley, of a couple I don't know in fashions so ancient I'm sure I'm seeing memories from the Great War. A man decked completely in the armor now buried in that cave system where Ryatt found the sword of shadows as a teenager, before he even knew what he was. Aris, too, went through the ascension, taking a journey into those caves, and found the same mask I'm seeing, the same wrist armor bedecked in glowing jewels.

Their ancestors.

Another man checks the armor, his fingers bending the metal and adjusting the jewels with just a touch of his fingers.

"I wanted to be remade," Hannibal whispers. "Only an alchemist can do it. My king wanted all the power. Only an alchemist can trap it. I tried to find them in your memories the day I took you, but you didn't know, did you?"

My vision goes red—blood red—and I see Lexa in the arena, her hands bloody and eyes full of tears as she looks down at Kaleb, dead. Dead by her own hand.

"What have you done?" I gasp, shaking him. "What have you done?"

Hannibal dies in my arms, his body crumpling, turning to ash.

A roar of applause cuts through the silence that follows, coming from the direction of the arena.

BY MY OWN HAND

LEXA

No one touches me. I'm not locked in chains. The dark hallways running alongside the arena blur, smelling like rusted metal and full of smoke. The air is hotter than it should be, but when I squint through the darkness, I can just see the haze of smoke funneling from the direction of the Glade. My stomach pitches, but I have to keep my head on straight. I have to finish this, and that means an audience with the king.

He's waiting for me when I step into the bright glare of the arena.

Spectators line the curved benches overhead, but they're silent. My sandals crunch over the dirt, over old dark bloodstains. No weapons cache rises in the distance. No one else is waiting for me.

I am the champion.

There's no one else to fight.

I am here for my gift.

I stop in the dead center of the arena and look up at the balcony where the fae king waits, his teal robes lifting in a phantom breeze.

"My champion returns," he says flatly, his voice deep and cutting in the dead tongue. He doesn't bother to translate it for the fae watching. They don't matter right now.

"I am here for my reward. Nothing more."

"Is that so?" He chuckles, smoothing his hands over the railing.

"It's in the rules. I won. I am your champion, and I am due a reward of my choosing."

"And have you decided?"

"Yes."

He smiles cruelly down at me. "You're premature, I fear. There's one Trial left."

I squint up at him, unsure I heard him correctly. My confusion must show on my face because his smile widens.

"Did he not tell you, my dear?" His laugh is like acid. "I find it hard to believe, seeing as he is your trainer and not only your sponsor, with him in such an incredibly sacrificial position."

Dread hollows out my stomach. Somewhere behind me, chains clink, metal rattling as an iron, slated door rolls open. I refuse to look.

"There is one more Trial. It's meant to prove your loyalty to *me*," he says so softly I almost miss it. "But Kaleb didn't tell you that. You didn't tell you all that he had to do to win, to unite his precious people under one crown so they wouldn't continue to fight and eat each other when the food ran out!" His tone tapers into a snarl. "No, he didn't tell you what he risked being your trainer. If he'd simply sponsored you, it would have been one thing. A non-issue. But he wanted you all for himself, didn't he? Mates… they're always the downfall of your kind, aren't they? So possessive."

"What the fuck?" I whisper to myself. My skin prickles. I can't feel my wolf anymore. The second I stepped within the palace walls, it was snatched from me by the king, like usual.

"The final Trial of the games," the king grins, licking his lips, "is a fight to the death against the very person who turned you into my champion."

No.

No, no, no…

I slowly turn around.

Kaleb is several yards behind me, beaten to a near pulp, his wrists raw and bloody and held in manacles of iron so thick he can't use his brute strength to bend them away, but he's tried. His eyes meet mine in the haze, smoke lying low and rolling around our ankles. He shakes his head, saying, "Why did you come back?"

"Kill him, and you get your reward," the king shouts, and I whirl back, shaking my head.

"No! No, that wasn't part of the deal!"

"There is no deal for slaves like you. These are the rules. You aren't the champion yet, shifter. Kill him, and let me guess... you want to free everyone in the Glade? That's what you were going to ask for, wasn't it? Do you think I'm stupid, little girl?" His teeth are pointed and jagged when he smiles. I hadn't noticed before–what a monster he is. I've never been close enough to tell.

"I won't do it," I cry out, trembling. "You can't–"

Kaleb's chains suddenly drop. The sound echoes through the silence, choking me raw, and I turn, horrified as he stands there in the smoke, taking several deep breaths. "Give her twin blades," he says to the fae guard to his right, who hands him a spear and disappears into the door Kaleb just appeared out of.

"Kaleb, no."

"They'll kill us both," he says, his tone dry, but his eyes are full of regret as he looks at me. "I told them to keep you away."

"Did you think I'd let you go?" I reply hoarsely, choked by tears. "Kaleb–"

The fae guard extends the blades to me by the hilt. I refuse.

"Take your blades, Lexa," Kaleb says, his voice dropping.

I shake my head. "We can't–"

"Take them."

I realize what he's doing. It's like being kicked in the chest. It's far more painful than any injury I've ever had. "You can't do this to us."

His eyes meet mine. "You're the Luna. You're in charge when I am gone. Get everyone out of the Glade. The Alphas have a plan. Chasten has everything arranged."

"Don't do this–"

The fae guard drops the blades at my feet.

"Pick up your blades."

"I won't."

He swings the spear, and my body reacts on instinct. *Protect yourself. Remember your training.* This man is a threat. My heart and body battle as I bend backward, the spear cutting through the air only inches above me, and when I bend back, I grab the blades, tumbling toward him as he brings the spear down.

"Make it a fair fight," he says with heartbreaking quiet, and we collide.

It's the same dance from the last Trial, but I'm in Meg's position. Kaleb won't stop. He's forcing me to react, knowing my body will move, that my instincts are sound, and that I'd never just let him hurt me.

He doesn't want to hurt me. It's killing him as much as it's gutting me.

"Please," I beg, blocking another strike, but my blades sink into his spear. I yank with all my strength, trying to pull the weapon from his hands, but he's strong. He's always been so much stronger than I am.

The blades untangle from the spear, and he pulls back, whipping his weapon. My body acts before my mind has a moment to differentiate between my mate and a threat to my life, and suddenly he's still.

He gave me an opening, and I took it. I didn't–I didn't mean to–to take it.

"No!"

The word leaves my lips in a whoosh as the crowd erupts in half-hearted cheers. Kaleb drops his spear, panting in pain as he takes two steps toward me, his hand outstretched, and falls to his knees, one of my blades piercing his chest while the other is lodged in his side.

I catch him before he falls face first into the dirt.

"No, no, no, no, no!" I choke, lowering him onto the ground on his back, my hands fumbling over the blades. I pull one out of his side, and blood gushes. I press my hand to the wound, my body tingling with desperation. "Oh, Goddess, no–Kaleb? Kaleb, please!"

I try to reach for the blade sunk deep in the chest, but he grabs my wrist with the last of his strength and weakly shakes his head. "Look at me. Let me see you."

"I hate you for this." The words come out in a strangled moan. "Why did you–I can't–you lied. You didn't tell me it would come to this!"

He takes a rattling breath, and I regret my words immediately. He was my shield. The one thing keeping me sane–keeping me in the dark while I fought through an impossible situation. The one thing that was... normal and good.

And he knew it.

He tried to keep that safe for me. For us.

"I was never going to be able to escape," he says with effort, a trickle of blood wetting his lips. "But you are. You're going home, Lexa. You're taking our people with you." His hand falls from my cheek to rest on my lower belly with a soft sigh. "You're taking him home, and that's–that's enough for me to go into this–this peacefully."

"Do not die." I shake him, my voice stern and cutting–a vicious command. "You–you don't get to do this to us. We have–we have a chance. We just have to–to get through this, and we will. I promise. Kaleb? Kaleb, please, we have to go now. You have to hold on just a moment longer!"

"I love you."

"No–no, no, no, don't do this! I'm sorry. I'm so sorry, Kaleb! Don't leave me. Please? Please!" His eyes begin to shut. My heart tears into ribbons, but I can't even feel the mate bond breaking because I can't feel my wolf. I can't feel him slipping through my fingers, dying by my own hand. I scream. It's a bloody, furious, heart-wrenching scream that soars over the cheering and applause, like the spectators are watching a man–a good man–die with such... glee.

"FUCK YOU ALL!" I screech, heaving a breath between each word as I gather Kaleb in my arms, rocking back and forth. "FUCK ALL OF YOU BASTARDS!"

A sudden sharp pain floods through my body. I drop Kaleb, my arms going numb as the taste of metal–magic–fills my mouth.

"That's enough," the king shouts, suddenly only a few yards away, looking so… small and… normal as he stands in the blood-soaked dirt surrounded by his guards. He rips his magical hold, and I'm yanked forward, but I fight it, shielding Kaleb's body.

"I'm going to fucking kill you," I seethe. I pull the blade from Kaleb's heart, gripping it like my life depends on it. "I'M GOING TO FUCKING KILL YOU!"

My legs shake as I try to stand, but the king extends his hand, and a bright, golden glow erupts, striking me in the lower belly.

"I'll have none of that filth in my kingdom. You and the father were too aggressive, less malleable than I like—"

A sudden burst of dark energy steals the breath from my lungs, and then Blake is standing between me and the king, his shadow falling over Kaleb like he's the God of Death coming to collect. He lazily raises a hand, and silver light explodes all around us.

I hear a single scream. It's faint—a soft echo of what I know is death.

My vision clears. I expect to be covered in blood, but I'm whole, and teal fabric flutters in the smoky air, falling onto Kaleb's body. Golden, beautiful, fully visible threads flicker between us, Blake's powers weaving them back together.

I meet Blake's eyes as a terrible, rumbling vibration sends the dirt beneath us into a frenzy. Beyond him, the king and the guards are in tatters, dead.

The king's shields covering the arena begin to cave, and the arena itself, the ancient, bloody magic holding it together, crumbles.

The entire palace is splitting open.

"Oh, my gods," I breathe.

"Go. Lexa, GO. The Glade. NOW!" Blake shouts, his power dancing around us full of electricity.

He's bringing it all down. Every piece. Every lick of power the king stole. He's releasing it.

"Blake—"

"GO!" he screams, his eyes so bright and violet I can't see his face. The glow is intense, overwhelming. I feel the chill coming off him. He's going to deplete before he stops.

I reach for Kaleb, but Blake shouts, "I have him. GO! Get everyone out of the Glade, now!"

I gasp, his words tangling in my ears, as my wolf abruptly returns, the mate bond in tatters tearing my chest open from the inside out before settling.

I feel him.

Kaleb's still with us—with me.

"I said I have him," Blake rushes out, gasping as his powers burst again, making my hair rise from my shoulders. "GO." His voice strains with pain. "But do not shift!"

I rise, shift, and run toward the Glade, which is burning and now... falling with everyone trapped inside.

ALL FALL DOWN

LEXA

I WAS ONLY ABOUT SIXTEEN WHEN I CAME INTO MY WOLF GIFTS. IT happened overnight, jarring me out of my sleep. My dad and his brother were the same—early bloomers. But the same week I got my wolf and started training with my parents on how to use it, I found myself in a forest with my dad, my great-uncle Ryatt, and my grandfather, Isaac on a hunt that changed everything.

Dad was sulking, in the worst mood I've ever seen him in. His foul energy radiated off him, and I felt so uncertain and off kilter that I thought something was seriously wrong. He didn't want to be out there with us, with me. I didn't understand why until years later.

I'm like him. Like my grandfather, too.

I am not just a wolf.

It takes only a small spark of emotion to turn that wolf into something heinous and even more deadly.

Like a fucking fire melting the thick, otherwise impenetrable gate separating me from the Glade. Like a mate—a dead one—lying prone while my cousin sends the entire kingdom to the ground, likely killing himself in the process.

The second a fae guard turns in my direction, weapons outstretched and poised to strike, my body shifts from its sleek, wolfen form and bends into something large, dark as midnight, and terrifying.

I've only done this once before—shifted into what my family calls a beast form. It hurts like fucking hell, but I'm beyond feeling. I know I've done it now—likely maimed myself beyond repair when my spine sings in pain, and my lungs struggle to contract. Blake isn't a healer. Whatever he did was a poorly applied bandage. This could kill me—kill us, if I'm truly pregnant.

But I have to try, don't I?

The fae guard screams, but it's cut short as I barrel over the top of him, his skull crunching like a crispy leaf under my massive paw. My coarse, thick fur reflects the heat radiating from within the walled confines of the Glade as I race toward the gate, seeing the fires burning in the tallest buildings, flames licking toward the sky. It might be the middle of the day, but the thick smoke makes time a mere construct. It's nearly pitch black, only outlines of buildings visible against the glow of the flames. I pummel the ground beneath my paws and launch my body through the main gate like a battering ram.

Hot iron twists, groaning as the gate bends, splintering into pieces like the remains of an ancient building, and the Glade comes into startling view.

No one is left in the upper part of the city. It's burning bright and hot, open doors pouring flames into the street. I pray everyone made it out as I race toward the pit, where the city dips toward the lower gate, the gate to the wilderness and plains beyond—to freedom.

A sharp, rumbling groan echoes over the crackling flames, and the wall around the Glade cracks.

If the wall comes down in its entirety, it will bury everyone within. I cannot let that happen.

The first bodies come into view. I ignore my own pain, slowing my pace to ensure they're dead and no one needs help, but I'm... too late to offer that anymore. The pit comes into view, and I see the crowds, everyone clamoring for the lower gate, trying to find a way out when they know they're trapped.

I see Chasten in the fray, standing on one of the look-outs that rise above the dirt, trying to direct everyone to stay calm, to stay with their packs, looking for someone, shouting a name over and over that's lost in the fray, but then he sees me and panic shines bright behind his eyes.

"It's me. Lexa," I say into his mind. One pack. One people.

His shock is short-lived and quickly turns to terror as the wall continues to crumble, the guard stations at the top cracking and falling toward the Glade, shattering in the flames.

"Blake, if you can hear me," I shout through the mind-link while my paws pound over flickering embers and ash, *"everyone in the Glade is trapped! The lower gate is sealed! We cannot get out!"* Taking them back the way I came is not an option because of the fire.

I try to shift back into my human form, but I have far less control in this form. My body aches, my healing wounds reopened and torn. It'll kill me. I already know I'm on borrowed time when I skid to a halt where the wall has large fissures soaring through it, crumbling in vicious chunks that cave toward the towering buildings, smashing them into pieces, sending flames skittering between me and the crowd below.

"OPEN THE GATE FOR THEM!" I shriek through the mind-link, but Blake is silent. *"BLAKE!"*

"Get them! Round them up! If they try to run, kill them! That's a direct order!" Guards sound out behind me. I whirl, teeth bared, but they charge. They have to know their king is dead, right? Or has the chaos made communication impossible? Far more guards than I was expecting run past the threatening flames. Dozens of fully fae warriors charge out of the smoke, weapons raised, but through a wall of gray they see me, and the first few stumble.

Pieces of the wall continue to fall. If the guards make it past me...

The citizens of the Glade need more time. They've seen enough blood, enough killing. Enough death.

Another chunk of the wall falls nearby, sending more waves of flames licking directly above my head.

If I go to them, I'll be bringing the guards with me. If I don't move now, I'll miss my chance.

"Help! Chasten!" Liz's voice rises at my left. My heart sinks. I'm near Kaleb's house. I can just make out the courtyard through the smoke.

The guards move in, oblivious to the danger they're in as the wall continues to shatter.

"CHASTEN!"

"BLAKE, PLEASE!" I scream through the mind-link.

The smoke suddenly funnels. A shattering sound reverberates through the Glade, knocking smaller buildings to the ground like the earth beneath us is suddenly turning to liquid. The wall erupts, falling.

The guards scream and turn back.

I'll live if I follow them. I'll see my family again. I'll go home.

I whirl to the courtyard, leaping through the air as the Glade splinters all around me, tumbling into oblivion. Lis is in the doorway with a wet rag over her face, a basket of belongings in her arm. There're two small children with her that I don't recognize. She was trying to save them, wasn't she?

We collide, my beastly body covering the three of them as the wall fall, burying us.

I'M DEAD. I FEEL IT EVERYWHERE. IT'S NOT WHAT I EXPECTED IT TO FEEL like, but I'm no longer in pain. It's dark here. It's hot and smells of smoke and iron. I should have known I wasn't going to the Goddess. I killed too many people over the past weeks. I killed Meg, my friend, and even though it was in revenge, I knew it was wrong, deep down.

Kaleb. His memory wraps around my cold, dead heart. His scent is everywhere all the sudden, guiding me to whatever's next. I wish we'd had more time. I wish I'd had a chance to know him outside of the world where we found each other. I wonder what could have been, what memories we would have made.

Our child... Poor thing. I wanted to believe it was real, that there was a future with the three of us in it, but... my selfishness and his inability to bend led us here, didn't it?

Light flickers above me. I wonder if I'll see Blake here. Isn't he the God of Death? Isn't this, wherever I am, his rightful home?

The light grows until it's blinding. Everything goes dark again as muffled voices split the silence–the crumbling of rock and wood.

"I HAVE THEM! I HAVE THEM!"

The voice isn't familiar. It grates through me, however, igniting a sharp pain in my back that threatens to split my spine. Suddenly, the light is too much. The pain ebbs before exploding with heat. Searing, blistering heat. The smell of scorched meat. My skin. I'm–I'm burned–

My breath comes in a rattling whoosh as hands reach for me, and I'm lifted, naked, into the sunlight, through feet of rubble.

I blink, my vision swimming with stars as a blanket is draped over me, and I'm pressed against a warm, solid body.

Liz's voice lifts in a shuddering cry, and Chasten's form is a blur as he races toward us and disappears behind me.

Kaleb presses my cheek against his cheek. His heart is racing, pounding against his ribs. He whispers a prayer. Several prayers as he stands on top of the remains of his home, holding me. Cradling me to his chest like an infant. My hair falls over my face, scorched, inches lost and curls burnt to a crisp, but through the strands I see what's left of the Glade.

It's gone. And beyond?

Open fields. Forests.

The sea.

There's... something else. A mark in the sky–a long, silver wave like the aurora that's so common in the far north. It glimmers like starlight, stretching so far I lose it against the horizon, and it turns crimson, shifting in shape.

"Keep looking for survivors," Kaleb bellows and turns as the two children Lis was rescuing are pulled from a pit the size of my beast form.

My mind pulls me in and out of consciousness, trying to numb the pain with short and rapid fainting spells while Kaleb picks his way out of the Glade. The wall is gone, nothing left but several vertical feet of rubble. Wisps of smoke rise, the ground still sizzling, but it's wet.

He shifts my weight so carefully, but I still cry out in pain. He says something over and over, but my ears are clogged with ash. I grip his shirt, a clean shirt, smoothing my head over his heart where my blade should be, but he's... whole.

"Blake?" I whisper. I'm not sure what I mean—whether I'm asking if Blake did this, fixed him, or if he's still alive.

"Don't talk. Don't try to talk."

Another fainting spell sweeps me into darkness, and when I open my eyes again, I'm under the cover of a makeshift, canvas structure. A buzz of noise is everywhere—voices, bodies moving, sheets shifting and people crying out in pain. I curl my fingers into a fist and find Chessie's hand there. She looks up from her lap, eyes wet with tears, and takes a ragged breath before squeezing my fingers.

"Oh, Lexa–"

"Where am I?"

"We're near the port. You–it's been days. I thought you were dead. We've been looking everywhere for you and Felicity, and those kids." She sniffles, shaking her head.

"Did everyone get out?"

"Most," she says softly. "Most did. The fires were...the gates came down. Most were able to get out before the walls fell, from what I was told, but you were–not with them."

I'm dreaming. I have to be. I close my eyes, and I'm back in that arena, in chains, seeing the king of the fae for the first time. How long has it been?

"Did we miss the harvest?" I ask, and Chessie chokes on a sob, her smile weak but eyes bright with a laugh she can't manage to hold back.

"We did. We missed it by a long shot."

"Where is Kaleb?"

"He's nearby. He has a lot to do, you know, before you all leave."

"He said—he said he's not going." I close my eyes, reaching toward my chest, but my body curls in pain. I can barely move.

"He will hardly let you out of his sight, Lexa. Blake—he's very upset with what you've done to yourself, but I told him you get a pass. You did it. You won. Everyone is leaving. Blake was able to contact Maeve before his powers failed, and—they're coming for you."

"And you?" I try to process everything she's saying, but it's impossible. I look into those green eyes I grew up with. Memories of girlhood sprint by, so sweet, so innocent. But then I see her as she is now and the ocean stretching between us. "You love him, don't you?"

"He's sending Kaleb home with my bride price," she smiles. "Do you think my mom will be happy and finally get off my back about being married?"

"Is it over, Chessie? Is this real?"

"Look," she says, pointing through the opening of the tent at a clinic. Beyond the opening, the sky is streaked with crimson light, and in the distance, shadows bob on the water.

I close my eyes as another presence casts a shadow over my cot. Chessie grips my hand once before leaving, murmuring to the other person to let me rest, that the healers did what they could, but healing drafts are sparse, and I'm badly hurt.

Blake sinks onto the stool Chessie exited, his hand resting on mine like he's too tired to even grip it. He feels cold, but something is different now.

"What did you do?" I whisper.

"What the Goddess demanded of me. I pray it's enough."

His fingers twitch. I can't feel his powers. Normally, they buzz around him like he's made up of electric currents, but now?

"You gave them up, didn't you?"

I open my eyes, looking at him with effort. My back feels raw, my skin tight. Blake's eyes are still violet but... normal.

They no longer glow.

"Maeve will decide if I've sacrificed enough."

"They're here."

I turn my head toward Kaleb's voice as he enters the tent. Blake rises, leaving my bedside, and Kaleb cautiously replaces him, but instead of resting on the stool, he kneels, taking my hands in his.

"Come with me," I whisper, my throat tight.

His smile is one I haven't ever seen from him before.

But I have a lifetime to memorize the new lines, the dimples.

Don't I?

Don't we?

HE'S BACK

Marianna

THE FIRST FROST OF THE SEASON BLANKETS CRESCENT FALLS ON THE morning twelve ships come into view off the shore of Tarsian.

Josie, Misty's daughter, is weaving Skye's hair into two braids by the hearth where Maddy keeps watch, occasionally and discreetly checking the dainty watch on her wrist. I stand near the window, watching golden and red leaves tremble on the trees along the wall of the garden before they sway down to the shimmering, silver grass. The sun rises on Crescent Falls, then Eastonia, on what I know will be a historic day.

We got the news about the ships headed back in our direction a week ago. Since then, every member of the family has been debating next moves. Aviva and Ryan are readying the Deadlands for the arrival of what Maeve said would be approximately three thousand people, including hundreds of children, none of them in good shape. They need food and medicine. Kenna is there now, setting up clinics in Teshka and Endova, preparing to accept the new arrivals before they settle in tent camps being erected in the river valleys that weave throughout the tribal lands, and further north, in Silverhide.

Evander is with his mate. His forces are there to lend a helping hand, organizing what could easily be chaos, while the rest of his men are on those ships, the ones sent the second Maeve got word of Lexa's location.

Misty and Cole have gone to Serpentia–both to help heal where it's necessary and Misty to mark the occasion, taking her notes to add to her lifelong research, to close gaps in her knowledge of what happened before and after the original veil fell around Eastonia.

Ella, Ryatt, Soren, and Maeve have gone to the Roguelands first, from what I understand, to gather Soren's forces–his army of bandits and misfits–and then they will travel to Tarsian, joining Maeve's royal forces, Evander's ghosts, and whatever rebels the Alpha of Tarsian is using to guide the missing packs home.

Sarah is in Moonrise, from what I understand, doing something with Blake's mystics.

My stomach pinches, my chest caving inward just a touch, at the thought of what she's seeing when she scries.

Josie rises, tucking a lock of deep golden blonde hair behind her ear, and turns to Maddy. "Anyone want coffee?"

Maddy gives her grandchild a soft smile in confirmation that she will, in fact, accept a cup. Josie's blue eyes meet mine, but I can't bring myself to even move, let alone speak. She looks so much like her mother and has every beautiful, wistful characteristic I've seen in the portraits and pictures of Isla scattered throughout the castle. It's uncanny, honestly. She just nods, extending a hand to Skye with the silent promise of making her a cup of hot chocolate, and I watch them disappear around a corner.

Only then does Maddy rise and move to my perch near the window, checking her watch once again.

"We should have some news any minute now," she tells me. I feel her gaze scanning my profile, but my eyes are glued to the trees, to the leaves drifting on a soft, cold breeze.

I took a pregnancy this morning. I've been avoiding the truth for almost two months.

The memory of clutching either side of the porcelain sink, bowing my head as reality swept me into oblivion, still stings. It's a fresh ache that threatens to pull me to my knees every waking second. I should be thrilled. This should be the beginning of something great, a fresh start for all of us.

Yet, I stand here in the early autumn sun, unsure if Blake is on one of those boats, and if he is… if the blood oath he forced on Maeve will prevent him from coming home.

Rapid footsteps echo into the sitting room off the foyer. It's been the favorite gathering place of the family in the weeks since I came here, Blake's side of the family seeking solace. Isaac speeds into view, shrugging on a wool coat over his pale gray sweater. Maddy stiffens, turning to her mate, her stormy, dark blue eyes wide with concern.

"The first three boats just made it to port in Serpentia," Isaac rushes out.

"Are you going?"

"No, I'm meeting Sydney at the temple. He's gathered some Alphas there, and they're waiting for news of whether he needs to move his forces to the border with Eastonia." He steps into the sitting room, determination setting his features in shadow. "We'll wait for more news there. Do you want to come?"

"I'll stay here with the girls. Don't worry about us." She clutches his fingers while he presses a quick kiss to her temple before he pulls away, raising his phone to his ear, and disappears in a gust of pale, opaline mist. "All right then," she whispers to herself, taking a deep, grounding breath. "It's happening. They're home."

I feel my body moving before my mind registers the change in scenery. The private kitchen meant for the family's personal use opens up around me, soft white and pale wood finishes closing me in a familiar embrace. Skye sits at the kitchen island holding her mug of hot chocolate, her eyes hazy and distant. I'm sure she feels it in the air–the change coming. With all of her power, it's been difficult for all of us to remember she's just a kid, and her understanding of the situation comes with a childlike immaturity. She knows Blake left. She knows he was in danger, that Lexa was in danger. She knows they're coming home, but everything else?

Does she know that her father might not be the same man he was when he left, or if he is, we may never see him again?

"Here," Josie says, placing a hot cup of coffee in front of me. I whisper my thanks but can't bring myself to lift the mug to my lips. I feel like I'm drifting through space and time just waiting for the other shoe to drop, like the entire trajectory of my life could shift at any moment.

I think of the sphere he left behind, the future he painted for me. The boys–the babies I'm likely pregnant with. Skye finding her footing in a world not meant for someone like her, finding peace, finding love. Blake and me growing old together, surrounded by family in that house on that still empty plot of land in Moonrise.

Had it been a lie? A pretty goodbye with a bow on top?

"Do you want to go for a walk?" Josie asks Skye. "We can collect leaves."

"Why?" Skye asks, dipping her finger in the pile of whipped cream floating on top of her hot chocolate.

Josie shrugs, spooning rainbow sprinkles on top of the cream. "I don't know. They're just pretty right now. Maybe we can make something with them to give to Cosette. You know how much she loves your drawings..."

Their conversation fades. Skye and Josie move outside, bundled in coats as they move through the back garden, disappearing behind a row of withering rose bushes.

I can't see through space and time. I can't see the bluff where Maeve is standing overlooking the sea, her eyes scanning the boats pulling into the port, the boats waiting their turn. I know she fretted over where these people, these stolen people, would land when they finally arrived. I know she worried over how to move them to the Deadlands, where they belong, their ancestral home. She kept her knowledge of what she knew quiet, however. How she knew where they were, what had happened. I can't see inside her mind now as her powers stretch, looking for one person in particular.

I can't see the moment when she spots him on the bow of the last ship to arrive, how she moves when her powers sizzle, reaching for his in a silent question that's been plaguing her for weeks now, maybe even years.

All I can do is imagine.

Can she trust my mate with not only her life, but her kingdom? Is there a future for them both here, two gods living and thriving in peace—neighbors, cousins, and maybe… friends?

Can she allow him to live, or will the blood oath decide for them?

Is he the villain in her narrative or the hero?

A thundering of footsteps echoes through the house. I rise from my chair near the window as Maddy's voice lifts from the other side of the castle, but not in alarm. Blake's mark on my neck prickles. My heart slows to a crawl. I slowly turn to the kitchen door.

"Where is she?!"

Tears sting my eyes, but I blink them away, desperately trying to clear my blurred vision when the kitchen door opens with a whoosh, and… and there he is, dressed in a light gray T-shirt and jeans, his dark hair mussed and violet eyes wild, but not with his powers.

They're wild for me. A yearning, impossible kind of desperation, like our separation had him on his knees for weeks and—it's over. *He's home.*

I have only seconds to react, to take him in, to see the new light shining behind his eyes—life. Our life. The vision he painted into existence—before we collide.

Blake's hand clasps the back of my neck as he holds me to his chest, gasping a prayer into my hair as we fall to our knees.

Blurred figures linger in the shadows beyond the door when I peek over his shoulder. Maddy rests her hand against her heart, takes a deep breath, then moves onto the patio, where Skye is now sprinting, trying to access the house and her father.

"I'm so sorry," Blake says against my temple, the words strained and broken, shattering as he draws in a sharp breath. "Gods, Mari-anna, I am so sorry. I love you. I love–"

I wrap my arms around his neck and squeeze, burying my face in the crook of his shoulder, and I let it all go. The anger, the grief, the uncertainty. It floods through me in waves before being drawn back out to depths we'll never reach again. No, it's over. He's here. We made it out.

Skye's sob cuts through the kitchen. He reaches for her, gathering us together on the floor, pulling her between us. He presses a kiss to her forehead before gathering me back, his fingers tangling in my hair at the base of my skull, and I feel his smile against my cheek, and the tears I don't think he's ever allowed himself to shed.

They fall like little diamonds on his cheeks.

He's not the same man who left Moonrise weeks ago.

He's the man I fell in love with almost a decade ago.

He's back. He came back for us.

I take his hand and press it against the soft curve of my lower belly, pulling away long enough to look into his eyes. His eyes... they're different–softer, more shifter-like than they were before, like he gave something up to be back here with us.

He leans his forehead against mine, closing his eyes as we finally get our happy ending.

"Let's go home," he whispers. "I want to take you *home*."

BLAKE'S FINGERS GRAZE MY HIPBONES, HIS BODY CURLED AROUND MINE in the warm, familiar nest of our bed in his suite. The palace in Moonrise hasn't changed over the weeks. I haven't been back since the day Sarah whisked us away before Maeve shut the entire city down after Lexa was taken. The shattered windows were repaired, the glass vacuumed from the carpet. Even the cracks in the plaster are like new, no signs of the carnage that came the morning Blake... went away, finally allowing the voices in his head to speak their truth.

He presses a kiss to my bare shoulder blade, and I melt into the touch, closing my eyes.

We've been back for two days now. Two days of... bliss together, making up for lost time. But that ends a few hours from now.

I roll over to face him, nose to nose. He gathers me close until our bodies are flush, and I map the planes of his face with my fingertips, the sharp curve of his cheekbone, his nose.

"I'm still the same person," he whispers into the early morning darkness, the moonlight still drifting over the sheets.

"So much has changed."

He presses his lips to my knuckles, his eyes meeting mine–a cool, but calm, violet. "I want you to come with me to Veiled Valley. I want you to hear... everything. Everything that happened. I want you there."

I shake my head, tucking his hair, longer than I've ever seen it, behind his ear. I've been dying to ask several questions, but they stick to the tip of my tongue. I want to know how he's here, what happened when they broke the blood oath, how he was able to return to me like... this.

"Are your powers gone?"

His lips brush over my cheekbone. "No."

"Then... how?" I don't know how to explain it, but I can't feel his shields anymore. His powers don't dance around the room. He doesn't look overcome by voices or visions.

"You," he says, and it answers every question, every why and how. "Everything I did, everything I made happen, was because of you, for you. That's what my powers were trying to show me... that I had something to fight for, and I had to."

"That doesn't make sense," I laugh, but he steals the words with a kiss.

"It doesn't have to. It's done. We have an entire future to look forward to."

I can't help myself. "Aren't you tired of having to look into the future?"

"Not this one."

WHERE AM I?

LEXA

TIME IS A CONSTRUCT IN MY MIND WITH NO BEGINNING AND NO END. I remember being dragged onto the baking sand, my fingers slipping free from Kaleb's. I remember being carried and laid on hard metal, hazy figures hovering over me dressed in white, like angels, their masked faces haloed by blinding fluorescent light. I have a feeling there were times when I was awake, when I'd open my eyes to slits and catch Kaleb's scent all around me, my cheek pressed to his chest. I remember swaying. Constantly swaying.

"We've kept her mostly sedated," says a voice I don't recognize, and suddenly I'm being lifted again, my body little more than skin and bones as a scent I haven't encountered in ages hits me like a brute force directly to the chest.

"And her man? I was told she has a mate now. Where is he? Was he on that boat?" Logan's voice is rich and stern as he shouts the question over a barrage of overlapping voices. If there is a reply, I don't hear it. I curl my fingers in Logan's shirt, my tears of disbelief wetting the fabric. "I've got you. Don't cry, Lexa. You'll kill me,"

Logan says, his tone dropping to a breathy whisper. He tucks my face against his shirt as he sidesteps through what must be a huge crowd. "Hey! Find the man they call Kaleb! That's a direct order! Do it now!"

My bones feel impossibly hollow. Logan carries me like I'm weightless, and the sterile, metallic scent that's been rendering my senses useless suddenly lifts, and the sun shines down so viciously, so heated, that my skin prickles, and my eyes burn. Am I back in the Glade? Are the fires still burning?

"Move. MOVE!" Logan snarls, and then I'm jostling in his arms as he breaks into a sprint. Noise is everywhere. I can't make sense of it. A car horn blares somewhere in the distance. Everyone is shouting orders, voices overlapping. I focus on Logan's heartbeat instead. If he's here, Brie will be nearby, unless we're in… Emberfyll.

Oh, my gods.

Am I back in Eastonia?

I try to lift my head, but my back is completely, utterly bruised. My muscles strain from lack of use, and I slump, a dead weight in my brother's arms. He clutches me loosely, like he's worried he'll hurt me. I wonder if he can see the black and purple bruises covering most of my body, bruising I can feel with each step he takes.

The sunlight suddenly fades. A door slams, and voices lift in alarm. I gasp and then moan as Logan tries to lay me down on a cool, flat surface, my tender spine trembling on impact.

"Lexa!"

"Ryan, stop!"

My eyes open to slits. The two faces peering down at me come in fuzzy focus. Kenna leans down until we're nearly nose to nose, and I feel her hands pressing against my chest, her powers coasting over my battered skin.

"Let me see her--please--" A choking sob comes from the left. My eyes slide to the side while Kenna continues to press her powers under my skin, a prickling cold tracing over every muscle, numbing me to the bone.

Mom, Dad, and Logan stand side by side. Mom's eyes dart over my body, her mouth moving but her words so tangled by sobs they're unintelligible. I've never seen her cry before.

Dad is just staring at me, his expression shifting between rage and a heartbreaking kind of thanks. Logan has a hand on them both, like he's the only thing keeping them upright.

"She's in very poor shape," Kenna says, her voice so near I can feel her breath on my cheek. "I need healers. As many as you can find." Her powers flood over my arms and chest before moving lower, my belly going stiff and cold as they sink to my bones, and she lets out a stifled gasp. I look up at her, unable to speak, unable to move. Her silver eyes hold mine. "A baby?"

Dad jerks, his face going purple with fury. Logan must have lost his grip on Mom because she lunges forward, taking my face in her shaking hands, her cheeks wet with tears and curly red hair wild. "Lexa," she croaks. "I thought–I thought they killed you. What did they do to you? My–my–"

Kenna's powers reach my spine, and the world tilts, my vision going so blurry all the faces in the room fade to fractals of light before going black.

I wake up with a jolt that screams fresh pain down my back. It's dark. A window above the bed at my side lets in nothing but starlight as I scan an unfamiliar room with stucco walls. Misty slouches in a chair right next to bed, her hand resting on my thigh, her fingers ice cold and frosty on my bare skin.

I try to sit up and choke on a breath, like my lungs aren't used to working properly. Misty lurches out of what must have been a deep sleep because she looks utterly disoriented before her eyes meet mine.

We stare at each other for several seconds.

"I wasn't sure you'd wake up for a while." She reaches up to rub her eyes, her fingertips nearly blue in the faint light coming from a candle burning on a table top in the corner of the room. She flexes her frozen hands with a wince, but her eyes don't leave mine. "Are you feeling… anything? Any pain?"

"Yes," I whisper, my throat tightening.

Misty rises and sits on the edge of the bed, smoothing my hair away from my face. "What happened to you, Lexa?"

"I–where's Kaleb?"

Her eyes give nothing away, but her lips turn in, flattening. My heart quickens. He didn't come, did he? I imagined all of it. Everything–

"He's quite worried about you. He got in a little fight with Logan, I... they're fine–both of them. A broken eye socket and shattered fingers are nothing for my powers, but... he's downstairs explaining everything to Evander, Ryatt, and Ryan. They've been talking for hours. I came up here to sit with you to give your mom a break. I had to force her out. I hope she's resting. I don't think she's slept since you–since you left."

A myriad of emotions hit me, knocking my heart sideways. I curl into the fetal position, my hand pressed against my stomach on instinct. Misty runs her fingers through my hair in a way that makes me feel like a kid again–safe. Safe and home.

"Where are we?"

"Serpentia. You're not well enough to move yet. Kenna has her hands full with the clinics. Everyone from... where you came from... is being treated before they're allowed to move on."

It's too much. My head pounds as she continues, "Everyone is going to the Deadlands. That's the last plan I heard before I came upstairs. But you can't go anywhere until your back is better. You were... Kenna and I were just talking about how we've never seen anything like–"

"Blake healed me."

Silence swells between us. I look up at her, drinking in her shock. "What?"

"I got hurt before, and he healed me. Knitted my back together using his powers."

"He doesn't have healing gifts."

"He doesn't. It's something else." I close my eyes, wincing as memories flood my mind. Then, I remember. "Did he... did Maeve..."

"Blake is in Moonrise with Marianna and Skye. She called us

about an hour ago and said everything was fine, that he's asleep. He…
he's different, isn't he?" She strokes my leg absently. "He did something with his powers. Are they gone?"

"I don't think all the way, but he saved us. He saved Kaleb's life. He
freed everyone from–from the Glade, and he tried to save Kaleb
while I had to–" I flinch, the ghost of the memory of that knife
sinking into Kaleb's flesh sending me into a sudden tailspin. "No–no–
no! I didn't want to. He–he said I had to–"

"Oh, honey," Misty rushes out, caressing my cheek as tears flood
the pillow beneath my head. "It's over now. It's all over. You're home.
You're going to be all right."

The door opens to reveal my dad and Kaleb. They don't both fit in
the doorway, so Kaleb stays behind as Dad steps into the room,
shocked and upset that I'm awake. He speaks rapidly to Misty, but the
words tangle in my ears. I'm just looking at Kaleb, and he's returning
my gaze, exhausted.

But free.

I burst into tears.

"Give them some space, okay? I'm serious. There's so much you
could be doing right now." Misty tugs Dad's arm, forcing him out of
the room. "Ryan, for fuck's sake. Your mate is in shambles downstairs.
She hasn't slept in weeks. Lexa will be here in the morning. She's not
going to disappear."

Dad grabs Kaleb by the shirt. It's modern, likely something from
the ship that carried us home. "You're going to take care of her, okay?
I'm leaving this to you." I've rarely heard Dad talk in the old tongue. It
sounds so foreign coming from him, but his words and tone are
perfectly clear.

"I am. I gave you my word."

"I gave you mine," Dad says, but his voice sounds more threatening
than anything else.

Misty groans, muttering something under her breath about Alpha
men, and shoves Dad out of the snug space with all of her might,
slamming the door shut behind them.

The room swims for several seconds, and then Kaleb's in my arms, his face buried against my neck, and I'm dragging him to the bed that wasn't designed for two people, let alone someone his size, at all. The frame squeals in protest, but I don't care. Nothing else matters.

I choke back sobs until my tears run dry. He holds me tight, our bodies prostrate on the mattress like we haven't touched in weeks. Maybe it has been that long. I barely remember a thing.

"How did we get here? What happened?"

Kaleb gathers me close and shushes me. "You need to be resting."

"Blake? He was allowed to go home?"

He nods, swiping tears from my cheeks with his thumbs. "Lexa, everyone is fine." He presses his mouth to my forehead in a tender kiss. "You did it. You brave, idiotic, feral woman." His mouth meets mine in a kiss that would sweep me off my feet if I were standing. "I love you. I love you, Lexa. I–I didn't get a chance to say it before."

"You did," I whisper against his mouth, breathing him in.

"I should have said it long before."

We lie like that for some time. He tells me everything he remembers, which is a lot more than me, because by the time the naval forces arrived, I'd given in to my injuries, and he'd held me on that beach for hours until the first warriors breached the surf. Blake had been the last to board the boats. He'd waited until every single shifter from the Glade was accounted for, and then, he and Kaleb spent the better part of two weeks healing and preparing for whatever was to come.

I wake with the sunrise the next day. Kaleb isn't beside me when I gingerly slide my feet out of bed and hobble through what I think is a townhouse tucked near the town square in the shadow of the outer areas of the University of Tarsian's sprawling campus.

Mom takes my hand and doesn't let go while Misty examines my back, and Dad pours coffee for everyone in the room.

But I'm watching Kaleb and Logan through the sliding glass doors leading out to a desert sun soaked patio, the two Alpha Kings leaning over a map of the Deadlands.

"They're deciding who gets what," Dad says quietly, smirking at

Mom. "Like *they* get to decide. As far as I know, I'm still the Alpha King of the Deadlands."

"They'll each have a piece," Mom says lightly, but her tone is broken, like her throat is raw. "Emberfyll and the Glade will keep their Alpha Kings but only as long as they play fair."

Misty smooths her fingers along my spine, stopping at the base. "Do you want to know what you're having, Lexa? I can already tell."

Kaleb turns to look into the house over his shoulder, the softest, warmest smile touching the corners of his mouth.

"No. I think I want it to be a surprise. Is the baby all right?"

"Just fine. Perfectly healthy."

That doesn't sound right. I remember the moment the king's powers struck me in the belly, the cold feeling of it.

Kenna begins to lean away, but I jolt, reaching behind me to grip her fingers.

"I need you to look for something for me." Every eye in the room turns to stare at me, but I guide Kenna's fingers back to my spine. My throat tightens when my gaze falls on Kaleb again. He's out of earshot. I'm glad for it. "Can you tell me if the baby has wings?"

THE NEW BRIDE PRICE

Kaleb

A few weeks later...

"Has anyone seen my wife?" Logan asks as he parts a small
crowd gathered around one of the many open fires scattered across
the festival grounds. The tall, dark-haired man with eyes so similar to
mine it's almost like looking in a mirror has his son, Kieran, on his
shoulders, as he sidesteps to where Lexa is perched on my thigh while
I rest on a bale of hay. He sinks down beside us, unceremoniously
dumping his son onto the hay bales stacked behind us, and Kieran
shrieks with laughter, scrambling and begging to do it again.

I'm not used to this yet. This many people just milling about for
fun. I recognize so many of the faces, even if they weren't in the Glade
with us because we're... one people. We always have been, just separated by an ocean, by magic and invisible chains.

"I think Brie's hiding from him." Lexa smirks, jabbing a thumb in

Kieran's direction. Her hair is loose and falling down her back in spiraling curls beneath a hat of pure white rabbit fur. A rabbit I hunted myself, which is also what I used to make the gloves she's wearing. She brings a cup of hot apple cider to her lips and grins like a cat at Logan, who narrows his eyes at his… sister.

Logan and I have spent the better part of three weeks together. From the moment we arrived in the Deadlands, we've been up before the sun and long after it set building structures–a camp–on the outskirts of Silverhide, where the valley funnels into the forest again. So far, it's enough to house at least half of my people and the entirety of his pack, which only numbers one-hundred or so. I've gotten to know him and his story. He's a descendant of the halflings who escaped Pantharas centuries ago. Kieran has pointed ears, like me. Brie is pregnant again.

Lexa fought him tooth and nail to secure the next valley, just beyond the shallow peaks of Silverhide, as our own. While most of the Alphas of the Glade choose to spread out and claim land for themselves, several hundred are following me and Lexa, and up until two days ago, when everyone began to gather here, at the festival grounds, we've been clearing land and preparing for the construction that will take place next spring when the ground thaws.

This winter, everyone will be staying in camps. We'll be in Silver-hide while others have spread out as far as Teshka.

Next summer will be telling, to say the least.

Especially when the festival has been so successful for mates finding each other.

"How many couples exactly?" Logan asks with an arched brow, eyeing his sister's white and taupe dress made of thick furs and cords of leather strung with freshwater pearls. The beads rattle when Lexa moves her arms, folding them beneath her chest.

"We're one of maybe fifty couples saying marriage vows tonight."

"Fifty? That's going to take forever!"

"Well, it sucks to be you." Lexa laughs, leaning her head against mine, trying to steal my warmth. "Kaleb and I are going last."

"Oh, for fuck's sake." Logan rises with mock annoyance and

nudges Lexa under the jaw with his knuckles. "I'm going to find my wife. Keep an eye on Kieran for me."

"NO!" Lexa howls, vigorously shaking her head. "You take that little demon with you! He's been biting again, and I know for a fact he swallowed at least four of the beads off my dress."

Kieran latches onto Logan's leg, laughing with mischief while Logan drags him through the crowd, and I lose sight of them against the gentle hum of conversation and the thrall of people dressed in furs to fight the frigid air.

Winter came early. The harvest festival began the same morning the first snow fell in the Deadlands. Now, the ground is mostly just damp from the heat coming off the fires.

Lexa presses close, resting her chin on my shoulder as we watch the stars coming into view through the smoke. "I suppose we should go get our tattoos now," she says with a small sigh.

"You can't, remember? Not while you're pregnant." I rest my hand over her stomach like it's second nature. It practically is. When I finally crawl into bed in the middle of the night and curl around her, that's where I reach, tucking both of them close. I feel like, since arriving in the Deadlands, I haven't seen her much. The days have been a blur of delegation and incredibly arduous tasks related to ensuring everyone from the Glade has a bed for the winter and that the Alphas who came from the Glade are settling their packs and not fighting over territory. Eventually, everyone will spread out, putting miles between pack territories, but for now, for the next winter, at least, this will have to do.

But there are no walls keeping us trapped. No power keeping us enslaved. We're free.

My son will be born free.

And, thankfully, without wings.

"I'm going to get a temporary one. The witches can do that, you know. It's a stain. Whenever we find out what design we're getting." She huffs, and I can feel the fatigue pouring off her. It's been a long day, and tonight will be even longer.

"We don't have to do it like this, you know. I can take you back to our tent and–"

"Of course we have to," she hisses, lifting her chin to look at me.

"You're falling asleep in my arms."

"I'm just enjoying the view." Her voice is soft as she looks out over the festival grounds, the rolling, frost covered hills. Wolves dart between stalls bartering food and warm drinks; others have tapestries and clothing on display. But it's the people gathering, meeting each other for the first time, finding common ground, and maybe even distant ancestors that silences both of us for a long time.

Finally, Lexa asks, "What do you think Chessie and Silas are doing?"

"I have no idea what time it is in Pantharas as it stands, but they're together; I know that much. He's probably preparing to meet Queen Maeve and the Allied Kings in Emberfyll next month. I don't doubt she'll travel with him."

"She promised she'd visit. I hope she does. Her parents are having a difficult time with this." She swallows forcefully.

"Silas is taking care of her. He swore to you that he would. He keeps his promises."

Lexa sighs and leans her weight against me, her arms snaking around my neck. "Is Silas really immortal now?"

"I'm not sure how it works. You'll have to ask Blake."

Her smile is faint. "I have a feeling we won't be seeing Blake for a while. He deserves a break."

A CROWD OF SEVERAL THOUSAND WATCHES THE MARRIAGE CEREMONY— all fifty couples, including me and Lexa, standing side by side at the top of the hill with the full Harvest moon hanging heavy in the sky. I'm familiar with the ritual, with the words spoken in the Old Tongue. I'm still learning the language of Lexa's father and the people of the Deadlands, but the Old Tongue is mostly spoken during ceremonies.

It's surprisingly easy to understand their language, and I start etching it into my memory.

Lexa shivers in the cold. I smooth my fingers over hers, dragging her closer, hoping to give her some of my heat while a priestess goes on and on, speaking loud enough the teeming crowd below can hear.

I glance past the old crone marrying us and forty-eight others to the row of older men watching the procession with a critical eye, especially Lexa's father, Ryan, and her maternal grandfather, Jerrod, the patriarch of Endova.

Jerrod glares at me, but Ryan's face is smooth and unreadable as he keeps his eyes fixed on my face, like he's waiting for me to crack.

"Are you ever going to tell me what happened between you and my dad when you first met?"

"No," I whisper, glancing down at her before meeting Ryan's gaze again. "It's not worth repeating."

"He apparently left no witnesses to the moment because even Mom doesn't have a word to say about it."

"All you need to know," I breathe, smoothing my thumb over the tattoo on her ring finger, pressed into her skin by magic we'll trace with permanent ink next summer, once the baby arrives, "is that he came up with a new bride price, and I paid it."

"What was it?" Lexa gasps, eliciting narrow-eyed looks of annoyance from not only the couples flanking us, but the priestess, who continues her lengthy sermon without so much as skipping a beat.

"Apparently, beating you in a fight wasn't enough. I had to make a few promises."

"Like what?"

"Don't worry about it," I whisper, shushing her when the priestess clears her throat and shoots us a glare.

It hadn't been much.

I met Logan first, her adoptive brother. He'd come looking for me when Lexa was taken off the boat, and I had to physically restrain myself from following her to the first of many clinics that were erected on the shore of the city they call Serpentia. I knew she'd be fine. She wasn't in danger there, but I had the citizens of the Glade to worry about. When a nearly seven-foot tall half fae male came barreling in my direction, I... beat the fuck out of him out of sheer habit, and he returned the favor, and he ended up being Lexa's brother, so introductions were off to a rough start.

Ryan got involved, dragging us apart, and then beat us both when he learned I was Lexa's mate, and Logan hadn't deigned to even ask, and I hadn't been in the state of mind to inquire over who Logan was, either. Bloody and bruised, he dragged us back to the townhouse the family had carved out for themselves in Serpentia, but they wouldn't let me see Lexa until I explained everything.

I was healed and fed, and then told Ryan and Aviva my life's story.

Then, I asked for their daughter as my wife.

Ryan made me swear four things.

I would never change her.

I would never take her from her family.

I would let her be soft in her secret way.

And finally, I would step aside and allow her to rule as Alpha Queen of the Deadlands, a higher station than mine, when the time came.

Of course, I swore.

There was no question.

Now, her fingers are intertwined with mine as we turn from the priestess to look out over the crowd. For a moment, I find us back in the arena, and the cheers from below are suddenly fae spectators. The image fades as quickly as it came, the dry heat of the arena turning back to cold, smoke and spice scented air.

The Trials are behind us now. My son will never be called for the Culling. My pack will never know hunger again.

Thanks to my wife. My mate.

"I love you," I say, looking down to look into her eyes as the priestess announces each newly married couple, giving each a unique blessing. Finally, she gets to us.

"I love you," Lexa whispers, squeezing my fingers. "Let's go."

"Where?"

"Anywhere. Somewhere warm."

I scoop her into my arms and turn into the starlight, the glow of the full moon behind us, unshackled, unburdened, and free.

The rest can wait.

DOWN THE AISLE

Lexa

Spring

Kaleb's hand is a solid, warm presence on my lower back as we move through Aunt Sarah's rose garden. Most of the flowers are in bloom, which is the doing of her powers, or someone's powers, seeing as the air still feels crisp, and the grass is a sharp, neon green—fresh and slightly crunchy. The deep emerald green satin of my gown stretches to its limits over the swell of my belly. My skin aches and itches, and it's taking all of my strength not to scratch. I fill my lungs, letting a breath out slow. We move through the haze of spring greens surrounded by the soft scent of roses, but Kaleb's fingers curl into a fist against my lower spine, pressing just enough to relieve some of the pressure there.

"I'm going to find you somewhere to sit down," he whispers through the hum of conversation taking place all around us.

"I'm okay, really," I insist, glancing around at familiar, and not so familiar, faces. There're a lot of people here. More strangers than I've seen since the Trials. My body locks up on instinct, still fighting feelings and fear I brought home with me without meaning to.

I haven't been able to set foot in a sparring ring in months. All winter, I haven't touched a weapon or shifted since coming home.

Kaleb knows. He hasn't said anything and hasn't pushed me to get back into training. I have a good excuse–I'm heavily pregnant, due in just two months. No one has questioned me about just lying around, letting my muscles rot.

But Kaleb gets it. He has the same feelings of unrest and uncertainty that I have but is busy settling the packs from the Glade into their new homes in the Deadlands. Logan has been helping, of course. Silverhide has been bursting at the seams all winter, but now new settlements, new villages, have cropped up along the road to Endova– new towns where everyone is free to just be wolves.

No fae kings steal their powers. No chains keep them bound. No Cullings. No mass funeral pyres.

Memories sweep me into a near stupor, and when I open my eyes again, I'm nestled on a couch in a cozy, warm, dimly lit sitting room on the first floor of Sydney and Sarah's castle. Kaleb has his hand on my shoulder while he talks quietly to Logan, both of them facing a window overlooking the stunning back garden, but my eyes find Brie's.

She looks radiant in a dress of plum purple, her hair tied back and cheeks flushed pink, but it's the new baby in her arms that really steals my attention.

Griffon is almost three months old, still a deep, healthy pink. He rests in her arms, sleepily nursing. Brie gives me a sleepy smile before turning her eyes to Logan, who matches that smile with a knowing, loving grin. He's just as happy as her–and equally as exhausted.

My hands rest on the swell of my stomach, over the baby within–a boy, we think. It's just a feeling–a knowing. We're having a son.

And he's who we did this for. Who I did this for.

"Jerrod is adamant about it," Logan says, and I blink, having missed most, if not all, of the conversation taking place around me.

"If he's serious, I don't see why not. It would be at least a hundred people—mostly men."

"Exactly. It's what he needs. More hunters, more skilled laborers. There're more women than young men of a mating age in Endova, and Jerrod and his elders are hoping new pack members will even things out. The Harvest Festival last year was the most successful yet in terms of mates finding each other, and he's hoping this year will surpass that."

"The tribes are alive again," Kaleb says under his breath and squeezes my shoulder. My fingers rest over his, but I remain silent, too overcome to speak.

I feel Logan inspecting my expression. I don't want to tell him I wanted this—having him home. Watching him set up a life in the Deadlands. He wanted to find Emberfyll so badly. It was his life's mission—what he spent years searching for then building, and now it's just gone. A base of operations for summits held between the Allied Kingdoms and the new kingdoms in the making in Pantharas. New kingdoms like the one Silas is carving out of the rubble of the capital as the king he was supposed to be.

The truth is clear, however. A truth Logan sees, I think. He has to. He knows his true origins now, the history of his people—people like my mate.

We're one people. One family. Now... free.

I look at Griffon's ears, the faint point, not nearly as pronounced as Kaleb's, and feel a smile twitching at the corners of my mouth. Kaleb squeezes my shoulder again as the door to the sitting room opens, and Grandma Maddy steps inside the room, her hands full of Blake and Marianna's twins—boys, born a month ago. Callum and Caspian. Boys everywhere. Poor Fallon and Skye.

"The ceremony is about to start. Are you all ready?"

Brie nods, and Logan quickly comes to fetch Griffon. Kaleb helps me out of the cushions my body would have liked to remain within, but duty calls—this time a wedding, which is actually a rather rare occurrence for my family.

"Where're Skye and Kieran?" I ask Brie as we shuffle through the castle toward the garden, cutting through a group of guests already drinking champagne in the back sitting room overlooking a wide veranda.

"Kieran's with Grandma Ella, I believe. Well, I hope he is because that's who I left him with earlier. Oh, there's Maeve!" Brie reaches a hand over the crowd and waves to Maeve, who whirls, looking relieved to see us.

"How many people did Sarah and Sydney invite?" Maeve asks us with a frown, adjusting a wiggly one-year-old Fallon on her hip. Her daughter grips Maeve's hair like she's holding reins and beams at me, showing off three teeth and those big, sea glass eyes that shimmer from within, the promise of power very few can even fathom. She even has a little necklace now, too, just like Maeve used to wear. It was made by family friends of Ryatt, apparently, with a small moon-stone in the center glowing a pale crimson in the sunlight–the majority of her young powers trapped within. She hasn't grown out of her golden blonde curls yet and looks shockingly like her father, who is standing under the cover of a trio of mock orange trees, their pearly white flowers in full bloom. White petals dust the ground around us. We funnel into chairs, along with at least another hundred people, which I doubt know Marianna and Blake personally, but this is a royal wedding, after all, even if this ceremony is considered intimate.

Fallon stretches out of Maeve's arms with an annoyed screech, reaching for Brie, but Brie has Griffon back, and when Logan offers to take Fallon instead, she nearly bites through his hand.

"Oh, Fallon," Maeve shushes, bouncing her vigorously. "This will be quick, and then you can take a nap with your dad. How does that sound?"

Fallon turns her curious eyes to mine, then leans back to look at Kaleb, who's seated beside me, watching the crowd like we're all in danger, and he's the only thing between us and a threat. That trait hasn't left him yet. I extend a hand, and Fallon accepts my advances.

I don't have much of a lap left, but it doesn't matter. She stares up at Kaleb like she's never seen anything quite like him before, and he eventually glances down at her, too. She grins at him and giggles, clapping her hands and squirming when he gives the smallest smile I think I've ever seen. Then, she settles, her attention stolen by the music beginning to play–violin music. It's prerecorded, and I know without a shadow of a doubt, it's Marianna playing.

The crowd hushes when Skye and Kieran stumble down the aisle together. Kieran insisted he also get to throw roses. He tosses up handfuls of petals while Skye is more meticulous about it, planning her throws by color and texture, which gives the aisle a slightly uneven look, but Brie chuckles, and Logan shakes his head with a smile as their son approaches Soren, who gives them a goofy look and motions for them to sit in the front row with their representative grandparents.

"Why did we get seated in the fourth row?" Maeve grumbles, teasing, "Don't they know how important we are?"

"It's because they knew you were going to talk," Brie hisses, and Maeve rolls her eyes to her mate and smiles at him while he gives her a cat-like glare.

"What is Soren doing up there anyway?" I ask as Fallon buries her face in my chest then lifts it to giggle at Kaleb, who's watching her with interest. I'm not sure if he's ever been this close to a baby before, let alone interacted with one. He always kept the infants and kids in the Glade at arm's length. I don't blame him. There wasn't a future for them before everything happened, and now?

I wonder what he sees when he looks at Fallon. I think it's hope.

"He's marrying them," Brie says with a soft sigh. "I'm still unconvinced he's qualified."

"Technically, they're already married, so it doesn't matter," Maeve hisses, suddenly defensive. "Sarah and Maddy threw a hissy fit when they married at the temple and didn't tell anyone until we all gathered in Maatua for Solstice."

"I don't blame them," I laugh, dropping my view to a low whisper when several heads turn in our direction with glares. Blake stalks out from the right of the altar, incredibly uncomfortable. "They wanted to be married before the twins came, and Blake is not a public show of affection kind of person. He looks like he wants to crawl out of his skin right now!"

Maeve, Brie, and I turn to watch Blake pivot at the front of the aisle, his eyes narrowed to slits, just wide enough to discreetly scan the crowd before Soren leans to whisper something in his ear.

"I think it's crazy they wanted to move up the wedding. Marianna had the boys a month ago."

"She's totally fine. Cole delivered them, and Misty used her powers to heal her right up." Maeve waves a hand in dismissal. "They're in the middle of moving into the gargantuan house in Moonrise. That's why they moved it up. I wouldn't be surprised if they locked themselves in it for the rest of the summer."

"You sound like you're upset they're moving out." Brie arches a brow.

"I'm thrilled for them. Can't you tell?" Maeve tries to smile, but her left eye twitches.

Brie nudges my shoulder as Marianna finally makes her grand appearance looking... beautiful. "She'll never admit that she loves Blake and wishes he weren't leaving the palace."

Some of the tension in my chest lifts as I watch everyone turn to watch Marianna walk down the aisle. She's dressed in pale silverish violet instead of white, which is striking against her tan skin and dark hair. I'm barely listening when Soren jokes through the informal ceremony, telling the crowd all about their ill-fated love story and how Blake is damn lucky Marianna is as calm and patient as she is because she needs to be, especially being in the center of a family of mystics.

The crowd titters and laughs, but our row remains silent, all of us lost in thought. Soren says, "I know a bit about marrying into this family. You all see them as kings and queens, as powerful beings of shadow and mist... as gods and goddesses. Maybe that's true. Maybe that is what they are, but... I think of my beautiful mate, the mother of my daughter, and know that she is just a woman. Someone capable of the deepest kind of love and sometimes grief. Someone who can make fire expand from her fingertips and also has a favorite order at every restaurant in Moonrise."

Maeve blushes, but her smile isn't something she can hide.

He goes on to talk about his friendship with Blake and getting to know Skye and Marianna, and praises Marianna for her ability to be exactly what Blake needed all this time. He talks about how his relationship with Blake changed for the better when Marianna was back in the picture.

The crowd has grown silent as they listen, getting insight into a very intimate side of the royal family. The side the general public doesn't ever get to witness.

The side no one thinks about during war times, when everything's going wrong.

We're just... normal people deep down.

Kaleb's hand is firm and warm against my thigh when the ceremony ends. A chorus of applause ripples through the back garden before guests begin to funnel into the castle, to the ballroom, where the reception has been laid out. The last couple to get married here was Liam and Charlotte, and it was a party to last the ages, but they will be king and queen one day, likely far in the future. I have a feeling Sarah and Sydney will rule for a very long time.

We don't last in the ballroom long. I pull Kaleb through the castle and up the stairs, looking for a moment of quiet, and we find ourselves in the library while music from the ballroom sends a steady vibration through the floorboards.

"How was it? Your first non-tribal wedding?"

"There were no furs or tattoos. I found it slightly confusing," he jokes, pulling me close. The tattoo on his finger catches the golden light streaming down from the rafters. Two crescent moons with a spear between them.

His lips press to mine, and the world fades away.

I love when this happens.

ARIS'S STORY

Aris

The next summer...

Veiled Valley bakes under the glare of early summer sunlight. It's around noon, I think, as I stumble up the stairs to my room, fumbling with the suitcase I haven't even seen in probably five years, let alone used in that time. It's been a while since I've gone anywhere for an extended amount of time–just to be somewhere else. Normally, all I need are my ghost-issued gloves that turn into a full suit of armor and the clothes on my back. It's not like I can't just, I don't know, snap my fingers and be somewhere else whenever I want to.

I'm giving that a rest this summer. This summer, I'm just Aris. Not the Shadowsynger heir. Not the Prince of Veiled Valley. Not an Alpha in the making. Just me.

My bedroom door opens on a phantom wind, thanks to the ever lingering spirit of the house, and my room expands around me–a wash of deep blues, silver, purples, and blacks. It's a lair of masculine darkness–every Shadowsynger's' dream. A four-poster bed with a satin bedspread is impeccably made, sunlight sparkling on the silken sheets that wrinkle and crease when I toss the empty suitcase onto its surface with a sigh. My sandy, almost golden blond hair gleams in my reflection in a gilded mirror hanging on the far wall, and I smile at myself. Not too bad looking, if I do say so myself.

My phone buzzes in my pocket. I don't even glance at the name. I know who it is–Roman, my best friend from childhood and the son of the Alpha of Sapphire Ridge, a nearby pack here in Veiled Valley. I already know what he's about to ask, too. Where the hell am I? Why haven't I just spirited to the lake house we're renting for the summer before we have to return to real life and be Alphas' sons and what not.

"What's up?"

"Where are you?"

I roll my eyes to the ceiling as I move across the room, opening my dresser drawers. "Home. Packing. I told you I wasn't coming until tonight."

"That's actually going to work in my favor. I convinced Posey to join us this summer. I wanted to give her a minute to settle in before everyone gets here."

I toss random clothing into the suitcase. "I'm honestly shocked she's willing to grace us with her presence."

"She's bored and has a friend visiting from Crescent Falls for a few weeks. I don't think you've ever met Willow, but she's an extrovert and drives Posey insane, so I extended the invitation for both."

I suck my teeth, chuckling low before quipping, "Miles was complaining about the lack of women on this trip, so he'll be happy, at least."

I imagine Roman's jaw tensing through the phone. "Well, one of them is my little sister, so–"

"Are you asking my permission for Posey to join us or what?"

"I'm just letting you know in advance–a little warning."

"When have I ever needed a warning about Posey? I've known her since we were kids." I imagine the doe-eyed woman, who barely comes up to my chest, like she's standing right in front me, blushing. Posey's always blushing. Her cheeks have been stained a perfect rosy pink since the day I met her, when she was just a babbling two-year-old in pigtails.

"We planned this as a last hurrah before we all have to settle down and grow up–or whatever–and now I'm letting my little sister and her friend crash it. You were the mastermind, so I thought I'd call you. That's all. They're on their way here as I speak, so you'll see them tonight."

"I'm still planning on picking up Miles and Tate on my way. They're meeting me at the river port."

"Think you'll make it in time for dinner?"

I brace an elbow on the overfilled suitcase to close it, yanking on the zipper. "Yeah, I suppose. It's not that big of a deal. It's a full moon tonight, I figured we go out."

"Posey was going to cook for us as a thank you for letting her join–"

"Why would she think she's uninvited?"

"Beats me. I don't know. You can ask her when you get here."

I hear lifted female voices through the phone and squint into the sunlight, sliding the suitcase to the floor. "What are you up to today while you're waiting for everyone?"

"Checking out the local amusement," he says with an obvious smirk. "I'll see you tonight."

"See you." He hangs up before the phone slides from my shoulder and falls onto the bed. I kick the full suitcase out of the way before sitting down, my interest piqued, and snatch my phone, thumbing through my contacts to the name Posey.

Our last text exchange had been months ago, when I wished her a Happy Solstice, and she'd texted me a single "thumbs up."

She's not a very talkative woman.

I ignore the phantom presence now fluttering around the room, fixing everything I messed up in the few minutes I was rummaging around my room. Dresser doors close, and the bedspread smooths, but I ignore it, sending a simple, barely thought out text telling Posey the big bedroom with the jacuzzi tub on the third floor of the rental house is mine. "Don't get any funny ideas."

She doesn't text me back, of course.

I don't necessarily blame her. I've always been in her life, always bullying or teasing her, especially when we were kids. She was an easy target–sensitive, quiet, cute-as-a-fucking button with googly-eyed glasses that made her green eyes four times as big as they were when she wasn't wearing them. Coming from a household with two crazy assertive sisters who were constantly fighting for dominance, and who took pride in physically and emotionally whooping my ass, teasing Posey was a welcome relief.

But Roman and I were the only people in the Goddess-damned kingdom allowed to even so much as throw a dirty look in her direction. If a single word was whispered by someone else, or a single hair on her head was harmed... yeah, I'd be sitting in the principal's office with scraped knees and bloody knuckles beside Roman, smirking, knowing full well we'd do it all over again and damning the consequences.

And so, for the past... twenty years, give or take, Posey has been in my life. A quiet presence, someone I think about every so often, but it's been at least five years since I've seen her.

She'd be... twenty-two now, I think. She's three years younger than me.

I'm not sure why she's on my mind as I drag my suitcase down the first spiral stone staircase. I'm not sure why the fact that she didn't text me back weighs on me when I kick the suitcase in front of me down the long, narrow back hallway leading to a second, then third, staircase that will eventually lead to the foyer. The spirit of the house follows, hurrying me along, impatiently bringing sconces to life like he's begging me to just leave already.

"What do you do when the whole family is gone?" I ask out loud, making a show of slowly bending to tighten the laces of my shoes, just to aggravate him. I always think of the spirit as a him, though I suppose I don't know for sure. A soft, breathy groan rattles the foyer, including the crystal chandelier older than my great-grandfather

Westfall. The castle of at least three generations of Shadowsyngers who came before him, rests in peace, trembling like the building itself has the ability to breathe.

I realize quite suddenly that the spirit isn't alone. Footsteps echo down the branching, shadowed hallways, and a dark form comes into view before Grandpa Ryatt follows in its wake.

He pauses in the archway, a brow raised as he looks from me to the suitcase resting on the ancient stone mosaic dappled with multi-colored light flaring through the stained glass windows.

"What are you doing back? I thought you were in Maatua for another two weeks," I ask, tucking my hands in the pockets of my ridiculously casual athletic shorts.

Grandpa Ryatt has never been casual a day in his life, as far as I know. He steps into the light, dressed in all black, the tattoos that cover his neck and fingers catching the light, the ink barely faded even though he's in his eighties now. He doesn't look a day over sixty, which is hard to understand, given that he's seen and participated in every war, skirmish, and hardship since his mate, my grandma Ella, brought down the veil between Crescent Falls and Eastonia fifty years ago.

"I got a little bored. Isaac tried to force it, but I don't think I'll ever find joy in the game of golf. It doesn't feel natural to me."

I purse my lips, eyeing him while trying to gauge his mood. He's a stern, grumpy old man most of the time. I admire him, but I do like messing with him from time to time. "Probably because you're mostly a dog, if you think about it. Chasing balls instead of hitting them with a stick is much more up our alley… biologically."

His eyes–that deep, stunning polished silver I share with him–narrow, but the slightest twitch of his lips has the tension in my shoulders relaxing. He chooses to ignore my comment and asks, "And where are you off to?"

"I'm spending a few weeks on Gem Lake, within Ruby Pack territory. I rented a house for the summer. Meeting up with some friends, you know." I shrug, resisting the desire to explain myself further.

"I assume Roman will be there?"

"Of course. Who else would I be going with?"

"I know his father is hell bent on the boy settling down by next spring." He stalks deeper into the light, giving me a look that begs a silent question. Shouldn't I also be settling down?

I've given it some thought. I'm closing in on twenty-six. I have a few years of freedom left before I need to do much of anything. I'm not a Ghost, technically. I'm also not the Alpha King of Veiled Valley... yet. Mom has that covered.

"He's nearly thirty. I wouldn't consider him a boy."

"Exactly. His father thinks he should be mated by now." He gives me another skeptical look, and I fold like thin paper.

"When you were my age, you were leading a rebellion in the Roguelands and using your powers to keep the lights on in every cabin, hut, and shanty from Twin Rivers to Veiled Valley, and I'm–" I motion to my suitcase. "I'm going to get drunk on the shore of a lake all summer, probably piss off a few women while I'm at it. If you're about to tell me it's my time to settle down, actually putting an effort into finding my mate, don't bother."

Grandpa rolls his eyes before closing them and murmuring a not-so-silent prayer to the Goddess to just take him now. "Are you happy, Aris?"

"The sacrifices of your youth allowed me to live this kind of life, so yes, I guess I should be."

"I didn't sacrifice my youth. I grew up in a very different world than you have."

I want to say it's not fair. Gods, I would kill to just be... out in the middle of nowhere, fighting the demons and monsters my grandparents told us about in their horrific, but wildly entertaining, bedtime stories. I want to say I've been watching from the sidelines while these adventures happen for them, and for my sisters, who each have wild love stories to accompany even wilder adventures, and yet I... have several online dating profiles... that I use for hookups because I just can't... I haven't found her yet. Whoever she is. Whoever I'm supposed to go to the end of the world for, to die for, to beat the odds in her name. That if finding my mate doesn't nearly kill me in the end, I'm not sure I want it?

I can't say that shit out loud, though.

"If it's any consolation, I do hope you enjoy yourself," he says with the smallest of smiles. "It's been a hard year for everyone."

"A hard several years," I correct under my breath.

He strokes his chin, his eyes meeting mine under his lashes. "You should bring your mask."

"Why would I bring my Shadow mask? I'll have no use for it there."

"You're leaving it here, then?"

"In the vault, just like you made me promise all those years ago when you left me in that cave to find my purpose—or whatever."

"It's a rite of passage."

"Well, you got a sword. I got a weird mask and some bracelets. What does that say?"

My phone buzzes in my pocket. My fingers prickle, wondering if it's Posey, wondering if she sent me another thumbs up or actually said something this time… probably the former.

He eyes my phone when I slide it out of my pocket and says, "Your grandmother and I are going to Silverhide for a while. Lexa's due soon, and Ella wants to visit Brie and Griffin. You should consider making a visit while we're all there."

"And you're going to ensure Logan and Kaleb have everything handled with their respective packs, I presume?"

He catches the hint of sarcasm in my voice and frowns. "I'm going to make sure Ryan is handling the two new young Alpha Kings in his territory—his son and son-in-law, if we're being literal." He smooths his hands down his thighs and turns toward the shadows, but stops, looking at me over his shoulder. "I understand you, you know? I get it, Aris, what you feel like you're missing, but I'm telling you now that this life you have is a blessing. I know you're bored. I know you feel like you don't fit in with the warriors in the family, but you're differ-ent. You're a Shadowsynger. We're meant for this." He motions to the foyer, to the dark stone and shadows. "It's a sacred order you've been born into. But it does mean staying in the shadows, making moves in the quiet while the world burns."

"You didn't stay in the shadows."

"I didn't have a choice." He gives me another flat smile before walking away.

I pick up my suitcase and wheel it outside, where the heavy doors to the castle snap shut behind me and lock me out immediately.

Looking down at my phone, I let out a groan when I see only a single thumbs up.

Thank you for reading! Aris's story will be out soon. Don't miss anything! Sign up for my newsletter and get a free story.

The Beta and the Maid

ALSO BY BELLA MOONDRAGON

The Alpha King's Breeder series:

Bought by the Alpha: The Alpha King's Breeder Book 1

Loved by the Alpha: The Alpha King's Breeder Book 2

Lost by the Alpha: The Alpha King's Breeder Book 3

Luna of the Alpha: The Alpha King's Breeder Book 4

Legacy of the Alpha: The Alpha Kings's Breeder Book 5

Daughter of the Alpha: The Alpha King's Breeder Book 6

Descendants of the Alpha: The Alpha King's Breeder Book 7

Shadow of the Alpha: The Alpha King's Breeder Book 8

Son of the Alpha: The Alpha King's Breeder Book 9

Spare of the Alpha: The Alpha King's Breeder Book 10

Claimed by the Alpha: The Alpha King's Breeder Book 11

Atonement for the Alpha King: The Alpha King's Breeder Book 12

Rejected by the Alpha: The Alpha King's Breeder Book 13

Abducted by the Alpha: The Alpha King's Breeder Book 14

Abandoned by the Alpha: The Alpha King's Breeder Book 15

Champion of the Alpha: The Alpha King's Breeder Book 16

The Alpha King's Breeder Books 1-3

Wolf Shifter Fairy Tale Retellings series

Beauty and the Alpha Beast: A Beauty and the Beast Retelling

Sleeping Beasty : A Sleeping Beauty Retelling

Tangling With the Alpha: A Rapunzel Retelling

Slipping Away From the Alpha: A Cinderella Retelling

The Luna's Vampire Prince series:

The Culling

The Kingdom

The Conquered

Pregnant With Four Alphas' Babies

Chosen As the Breeder

Mated to Four Alphas

Threats Against the Breeder

At War for the Breeder

The Stolen Breeder

Four Alphas, Four Babies

Becoming the Luna Queen

Descendants of the Breeder

Desired by the Devil series

Whispers of the Devil

Banter of the Devil

Murmurs of the Devil

The Mafia Kings series

Indebted to the Mafia King

<u>Loved by the Mafia King</u>

Claimed by the Mafia King

Secrets of the Mafia King

Burned by the Mafia King

Kidnapped by the Mafia King

Dark Stalker Romance series

Tempted by Sin

Fated to Sin

Secret Billionaires series

Finding the Secret Billionaire by Olivia Bhelle Kildare

Falling for My Secret Billionaire by Bella Moondragon

Driven by the Secret Billionaire by ID Johnson

Wolf Shifter Alpha Kings series

Ravens and Ruins

Sundrops and Shadows

Snowflakes and Sabotage

Waves and Wickedness

The Vampire King's Feeder series

Claiming the Alpha's Daughter

Loving the Alpha's Daughter

Finding the Alpha's Daughter

Bewitching by the Alpha's Son

Writing as B. Moon

The Boy Who Died

Sign up for Bella's newsletter here.

Or get a free novella from The Alpha King's Breeder series when you sign up here:
The Beta and the Maid

Follow Bella on Facebook here.

Follow Bella on Bookbub here.